F IS FOR FAIRY
Book Six of the Alphabet Anthologies

Edited by Rhonda Parrish

Poise and Pen Publishing

EDMONTON, ALBERTA

PRAISE FOR THE ALPHABET ANTHOLOGIES

"In A is for Apocalypse, *the world ends in both fire and ice–and by asteroid, flood, virus, symphony, immortality, the hands of our vampire overlords, and crowdfunding. A stellar group of authors explores over two dozen of the bangs and whispers that might someday take us all out. Often bleak, sometimes hopeful, always thoughtful, if* A is for Apocalypse *is as prescient as it is entertaining, we're in for quite a ride."*

—AMANDA C. DAVIS, AUTHOR OF THE LAIR OF THE TWELVE PRINCESSES

"This doesn't happen very often when I read anthologies, but I enjoyed every single selection in this book.... I'd recommend B is for Broken *to anyone who loves contemporary science fiction as much as I do. There is a lot of great material to explore in this collection!"*

—ASTILBE, REVIEWER, LONG AND SHORT REVIEWS

"This collection is a massive and magnificent assortment of truly enjoyable stories. There is simply no way to read this book and not find a story you can connect with or love. This is the book to have in your travel bag. In it you are sure to find a tale to fit any mood. Each time you open it, a new adventure begins."

—ANITA ALLEN, ASSISTANT PUBLISHER/EDITOR, MYTHIC DELIRIUM BOOKS

RHONDA PARRISH ANTHOLOGIES

Available Now

A IS FOR APOCALYPSE
B IS FOR BROKEN
C IS FOR CHIMERA
D IS FOR DINOSAUR
E IS FOR EVIL
F IS FOR FAIRY

FAE
CORVIDAE
SCARECROW
SIRENS
EQUUS

MRS. CLAUS: NOT THE FAIRY TALE THEY SAY
TESSERACTS TWENTY-ONE: NEVERTHELESS
METASTASIS
NITEBLADE MAGAZINE

FIRE: DEMONS, DRAGONS AND DJINNS
EARTH: GIANTS, GOLEMS AND GARGOYLES

GRIMM, GRIT AND GASOLINE

Coming Soon

HEAR ME ROAR
SWASHBUCKLING CATS: NINE LIVES ON THE SEVEN SEAS

CONTENTS

L.S. Johnson

Her Names

They were twelve, and between them they encompassed Dawn, Dusk, Spring, Summer, Fall, Winter, Seed, Blossom, Harvest, Maiden, Mother, and Crone; that is to say, they were complete. Thus, when a thirteenth fairy emerged from the breath of sun upon earth they were to a one confused. None of them had expected another sister. They waited for some time—perhaps there would be more? For they had come in pairs and trios before, and Spring, Summer, Fall, and Winter had practically exploded out of the same minute point of light. But no one else emerged.

Finally, they looked to Dawn, who was eldest, and she looked at the new fairy and sighed. "What *are* you?" she asked plaintively.

The fairy didn't know. She was fifteen minutes old and quite astonished at existing.

"We have to call her something," Crone pointed out. (When her trio had emerged from the breath of the sun and were asked what they were, Maiden had said "beautiful," Mother had rolled her eyes, and Crone had said "wiser than you.")

The twelve fairies looked around, trying to think of what this one, singular fairy could be. Time slipped past, and they had other tasks to do, but still they could not think of a thing.

At last Dawn, who had been up for some time and wanted to nap, gestured to the nearest object. "We'll call her Apple," she declared, "until she figures out who she is."

"She looks like an Apple," Fall said to Harvest, who agreed, and as they both knew a lot about apples everyone thought the matter settled.

Between them they found a sweet little wood no one was occupying, with pine and oak and yes, even apple trees, and they suggested to the fallen branches and stones and mud that they come together into a cottage. Once the cottage was built they each gave Apple a present for her birth-day: a narrow bed; a table and chair; the secrets of fire, sleep, and flight; a jug and a wash-basin; a pot and a bowl to eat from; a dress to cover herself; and, rather inexplicably from Crone, a large, polished spindle.

"She'll find a use for it," Crone said vaguely when the others gave her curious looks, and they didn't press the matter, for Crone was indeed wiser than all of them.

The fairies placed Apple in her new home, set everything right, gave her twelve kisses, promised to visit often, and flew away.

She was, by then, one hour old.

In her wood Apple quickly learned that she could only suggest, unless specifically invited to do more. She suggested the trees into bud every spring and suggested they drop their leaves for winter. She suggested that the bluebells spread far and wide in the dappled sunlight. She suggested a clearing where the birds and animals tested strength and will, and suggested hollows and burrows for them to nest and tend their young. She made stews and soups in her pot, and collected rainwater in her jug from the notched boughs and the fattest wildflower blossoms. She flew high above her wood and skimmed through its underbrush inches from the ground. Her sisters visited, and taught her how to suggest flower from bud and fruit from flower; they taught her the language of bees and the silent gestures of ants; they taught her to spin rainwater into dew and fog into lacy frost with her spindle. They brought her curtains and seeds and coaxed flowers into bloom all around her, until everyone said that Apple's wood was the prettiest in all the land.

They still didn't know why she was, only that she was, and they often prodded her about her purpose: why was she here, what had she come to do? But the only answers Apple could give—that she was there to make her sisters tea, or make the wood bloom, or sing songs to the birds—never seemed to be enough.

Apple would wonder about this, after her sisters left. Wasn't it enough to simply be? Why did she have to have a purpose? Even if she was a thirteenth fairy who resembled a ripe, plump apple, wasn't it enough to simply care for the world around her?

But there was no one to answer her.

Apple heard the plodding hooves first, strangely slow and lumbering, not the usual brisk passage of travelers cutting through her wood. This was a single rider, barely clinging to his horse; later she would remember how his armor glistened with moisture, shimmering in the dawn like it was made of sunlight. If he had worn a helmet, it was now lost. His face was youthful and wan and damp with sweat, and when she drew close he squinted at her as if he could not quite believe what he was seeing. Not a local man, to look at her so strangely, and with such a richly ornamented tabard.

"Are you well?" she asked, but he only blinked at her. He smelled sour and his breath was worse, and she thought, *aha, this is sickness*. Her sisters had told her about sickness, such as when tree leaves emerged puckered and curled, or white mildew dusted the late blossoms.

She led the horse to her cottage and suggested it rest and graze in the clearing, and she helped the man inside and to her bed. It took much doing to divest him of the armor, but each piece seemed to reveal a new curiosity, for she had never studied a man closely before. The patterns of pores and hairs were fascinating; the way he seemed to half-sleep, muttering and drooling, was something she had only glimpsed when flying over inns and the men in their yards. *Deeply flawed* was how her sisters described men; they spoke darkly of other patterns, such as of doing and undoing, that they could not affect unless bade to. This one, however, seemed unburdened by such complications. The whole of his being seemed to exude a singular will, and his will at that moment was to sleep in her bed, twisting and coiling like a drowsy cat.

While the man slept she fried squash blossoms and the first onions, and suggested her loaf bake quickly, and gathered a jug's worth of water. When she returned he was sitting up in bed, looking around with an amused expression on his face.

"I have brought you water," she said, smiling at him. She filled her little bowl and brought it to the bed. "You are feeling better?"

He smiled back, baring lovely teeth. "I am now," he said. He had deep blue eyes like the sky and they didn't leave her face even as he drank the water down. How strange, to watch his throat work! She wanted to poke the lump in it, but thought that would be rude.

Instead she asked, "your horse is a fine animal. Are you perhaps a lord?"

"Lady," he said, "in this moment, I am merely a man." And he seized her wrist and drew her close to him. Sour sweat and breath and those bright even teeth, opening like an animal about to bite her; somewhere her bowl broke as he kissed her deeply.

(Of course he was a king. Are they not all kings, these men? Kings of domains large and small, from whom all others flow. There are no queens without kings, no brave princes or enchanted princesses, no knights to be led astray or boldly fight, no maidens to swoon and be carried off. Not even fairies, to bestow them boons of voice and body alike; to curse them, the better to make a story worth telling.)

Afterward, Apple could not remember what had happened. The time between his kiss and when he rode away, leaving her in the tousled bed, seemed to be just out of her reach—and she did not want to reach; she did not want to remember, even as she struggled to do so. What had she said, what had he done? In her mind was a darkness now, a fullness of experience shrouded and shoved to the edges of her memory.

What had he said, what had she done? Why had he come to her at all?

The memories were shrouded, but the bruises on her forearm lingered, five purpled smudges where each of his fingers had dug deep.

Nothing she could suggest made them lighten; long after the pain had faded the five marks remained, and she took to wearing shawls and sweaters when her sisters visited, for how could she explain what she could not recall?

For some time the sound of horses made her start, as frightened as the young rabbits crossing her clearing. For some time she dared not leave the wood, cringed at the thought of flitting past farms and villages and the men who lived there, their strangeness now a looming thing. All the colors around her seemed to dull and dim, until she could not quite remember what the world had looked like before him. She forgot to spin the dew and make suggestions to the bluebells; her eyes skidded over the blight-curled leaves, her ears missed the agitations of the birds and animals, how they broke their rhythms and fought wantonly.

The corners of her wood began to smell of carcasses, and she did not think on it.

Her sisters, noting the changes, kept their visits brief and their conversations carefully worded, though among themselves they wondered if her true purpose was revealing itself at last. "Not Apple but Anguish," Dusk suggested, and they bowed their heads in acknowledgment.

"Such is the weight of purpose," Summer agreed.

"Such is the weight of being a thirteenth when we were complete," Maiden added harshly.

Crone kept her counsel, watching in her mind's eye as the wood around Anguish became shrouded and dark, as surely as pulling a blanket over itself, the better to hide from the world.

Her Self, in Stories

Some weeks after he rode away Anguish began dreaming: that she was a plump brown bird, feeding in a pleasantly sunny glade, when before her rose up a magnificent serpent, its scales glistening like they were made of light and its dark blue eyes as deep and wide as the sky above, and so lost was she in admiration that she did not struggle as it coiled itself around her tight, tight.

Months after and Anguish dreamed: she was snuggled in a warm den with her sisters, their furred bodies twining and pressing, their sweet heat smelling of flowers and sunlight and the first hint of rain. Everything was cradling limbs and beating hearts and sleep and safe, until Anguish became aware of a shape at the mouth of their den, a shrouded presence moving towards them, and suddenly all that was sweet and safe became a prison: she struggled to flee but she could not awaken her sisters, who clung harder and harder, suffocating her with blind affection, oblivious to her cries.

Alone in her wood Anguish dreamed, and when she woke exhausted she worried the dark spot in her mind like a loose tooth. Terrified of what lay behind it, unable to simply let it be, at times it seemed her sole purpose in the world was to break through that darkness; at other times she ran frantic through her wood, looking for any distraction to relieve her of its presence.

Thus she stumbled upon a couple twined together at the edge of her overgrown clearing where sunlight still penetrated, providing relief from the gloom. A horse paced uneasily through the stunted grass, and for a moment Anguish felt a sharp pain in her belly, so dizzying was the sight of the animal's embroidered caparison. The same pattern, the same bright colors, more vivid than anything she had seen since that day; her eyes filled with tears, as if she had looked straight into the heart of the sun.

But the man rolling in her grass was not him. He was wrestling with a young girl who alternately giggled and squirmed, their tangled bodies crushing weeds and blossoms indiscriminately. The girl's squeaks and squeals echoed through the wood and Anguish clapped her hands over her ears, but she could not block out their sounds.

"I tell you it's true," the man gasped, wiggling on top of the girl. "You cannot leave me here, I may never return!"

"Get away with you." She slapped his arm, laughing.

"Get away with His Majesty?" At his words the girl stilled, squinting at him. "It was the king himself who told me. He came to this very wood in his youth—got separated from the lads one night after a tourney. He fell asleep here and when he awoke he was in thrall to a foul enchantress, who tried to ensnare him—" he paused, looking around with an expression of terror. "Did you hear that?"

"I didn't hear anything," the girl said, but she looked uneasy as she spoke, and seemed not to notice when the man gathered her close.

"You must protect me," he mumbled into her neck. "Only the love of a mortal will keep the enchantress at bay..."

Anguish could not watch, then; she could not think for the sudden emotion filling her. *Foul enchantress.* Around her the serpent twined until she was breathless; above her a vast shadowed shape bore down upon her wooded den. *Foul enchantress.* When she had only been a little fairy as round as an apple, without name or purpose.

Behind her the couple grunted and gasped and then it was over, as quick as an eyeblink. Perhaps this was her purpose? *What* are *you* Dawn had asked her, and here was an answer she could give. A foul enchantress. A creature to fear, a story to whisper, the better to cow and to force, the better to make people look with dread over their shoulders, even at the height of a sunny day.

Oh yes, that was a thing she could be.

To her trees she suggested they release their burdens, and watched as their sickened branches snapped and gave way, tumbling down upon the couple while the man bellowed and the girl shrieked with fright. To her hunters, her birds of prey and her sharp-clawed mammals, she suggested that here was new prey to worry and torment.

Like me, a voice said in her mind, whose voice was that? Anguish could not tell; she pressed her hands to her ears again, smothering the cries of the couple and the calls of the animals, smothering the wind and the horse's wild whinnying, smothering her own whimpering breath.

It was easier, after that first day. Easier to suggest the trees grow twisted and wild, with branches like walls and fruit rotting on their boughs. Easier to suggest her hunting animals see all as prey, locals and travelers, shepherds and sheep. Easier to play her role, smiling at the messengers and merchants, farmers and knights, all stumbling eager into the brush and her beckoning arms only to recoil in terror as her wood became their prison. Her five bruises became so livid and stark they could be seen from a great distance; she spun her tears into dresses patterned with those marks, over and over and over.

Word traveled of the evil fairy in the wood, and when it did not travel far or swift enough Anguish flew to the top of her tallest tree and screamed it into the night so that even *he*, in the depths of his far-away castle, would hear her.

Her Curse

The day of the announcement Anguish awoke to a sickening chorus of distant cheers and ringing trumpets and she nearly vomited. Even before her sisters arrived, twittering with delight, she knew: knew, and felt betrayed yet again.

A royal child. The soothsayers predicted a new moon birth; the castle midwives predicted a girl; wasn't it all the loveliest, the most glorious?

(Only Crone noticed Anguish's misery, but she did not comment on it. Perhaps she was Anguish after all; perhaps it was her lot in life, just as it was Dusk's to bring the cold of night, or Harvest's to rip the fruit from the boughs.)

When the messenger arrived, bearing gold-edged envelopes with fat red seals, each trailing a fine ribbon, Anguish's hands stayed empty, and that gave the twelve fairies pause. The moment the messenger was out of earshot Dawn gave her a severe look and asked, "What did you do?"

"What did you do?" Winter echoed. "You should be invited, no matter your purpose; you must have done something to upset him."

Anguish met each of their gazes levelly. "What does it matter?" she asked, the scorn in her voice making them flinch. "I am Anguish after all—or so you have decided."

At her words each of the fairies blushed and looked away, save for Crone. "What did *he* do?" she asked.

And for a moment Anguish felt her resolve slipping away, felt herself small and round in her dress of tears and bruises; she wanted to run to her sister, bury herself in her arms and tell her everything. But that road only led back to Apple, unwanted and without purpose and *unsafe*, and she was not that fairy anymore.

"It doesn't matter," she said.

Her twelve sisters took their leave, downcast, unable to meet her gaze; as each flew away, back to their realms of light and dark, growth and decay, each whole and content in herself, Anguish caught at Crone's arm, staying her.

"I think I know my true name," she said in a low voice. "I think I am Anger, sister."

At that Crone's mouth quirked. "For now," she replied, and before Anger could debate the matter she flitted up into the night sky, the invitation in her hand gleaming like a distant star.

Anger had no invitation, but she soon knew the details they contained: a great feast was planned to celebrate the babe's birth, with games and dancing through the night. Kings and noblemen would present the new princess with gifts (and more than a few offers of betrothal.)

And every fairy in the kingdom was invited to give the princess one boon.

A *boon*. The word lingered in Anger's mind, all through the day and the night and the day again. A boon: an irreversible gift, a singular invitation to pronounce rather than suggest. A boon such as he had given her, such as she had been repaying year after year. For blight was pooling from her wood, stunting the crops in the neighboring fields, tainting the lakes until the reeds collapsed and the fish floated to the surface. Now no one rode through her wood without utmost cause, urging their horses lest the evil fairy snatch them away.

A different kind of boon, that.

Was she not a fairy of the kingdom, even if she hadn't received a slip of paper?

Oh she would grant the princess a boon, one worthy of her father. The thought filled Anger's mind until she could not unthink it; it filled in the dark absence of his visit, giving it form and substance as she stroked the marks on her arms and mouthed *boon boon boon.*

She trailed after her sisters on the journey to the capitol, flitting through daytime skies and across broad shimmering lakes, through woods not her own and over fields that ripened in their wake. For once she did not undo the goodness her sisters created; she kept her gaze ahead, her mind's eye on the beautiful terrible thought within herself. A beautiful, terrible thought, but was it more terrible than what awaited the child, with such a man for her father? What torments might he inflict on her, what kind of husband would he force her to accept? A lout from his own lands? Or would he barter her with some distant king for land and gold, no matter what kind of man he was?

It was twilight when Anger arrived at the castle. To a one the guards looked at her in fearful confusion, unsure of whether to admit or bar her, unsure if they could keep her at bay; she let herself savor the moment, that one small, apple-round fairy could so cow them.

Then she suggested they let her enter, and they stepped aside.

Inside all was light: hundreds of candles, perhaps thousands, all burning. A fortune in wax. For the first time Anger understood just what power lay behind royalty: not just the liveried knights riding to every corner of the kingdom, pushing its borders ever outward; not just the battles she knew were waged in distant lands, sometimes painting the sky in her own wood with a haze of far-travelled smoke. It was in the thousands of candles, when so many would never own one; it was in the cascades of tapestry adorning the walls, when so many shared but one rough blanket between them.

The crowd parted for her, the sumptuousness of their clothing almost blinding; Anger resisted the urge to raise a hand to shield her eyes. They looked everywhere but at her. Was she so terrifying? Or perhaps it wasn't fear but disgust, perhaps they could see the bruises through her dress, perhaps they wondered as her own sisters had wondered.

What did you do, what did you do?

The crowd parted, bodies flowing to the far sides of the room as if her taint surrounded her like a cloud. They parted in a wave down the long, long hall, flowing like rivers in springtime when they ran high only to break around the largest rocks. She was a rock now, she could see herself from above, and all the silver and gold was breaking around her. Cutting through it all, the candles and the tapestries, the acres of gilt and velvet and deep-dyed wool, all breaking over the rock that was Anger Anguish Apple.

At last before her a dais rose like a filigree mountain, two towering gold thrones and the golden bassinet between them. On either side her sisters were staring, staring. On their thrones the queen looked merely pale and exhausted, but *his* expression was one of utter shock, one that Anger found herself mimicking. He was so much *older*. The smiling young lad was gone, replaced by a careworn old man on whose lined face was dawning a profound, sorrowful understanding. She had known time was passing, years of it; she had not thought on how profoundly it might leave its mark. For a moment, doubt ran through her, a tremor that echoed back, back, until she was standing in her little cottage with its curtains fluttering in the wind and realizing it was just her and this strange young man—

She raised her chin, banishing the memory back to the darkness. "I am invited to give a boon," she said, and her voice was strong and true. "Every fairy in the kingdom can give one boon to the princess."

"Anguish," one of her sisters said in a low voice—Spring? Seed? She could not say, and in truth it did not matter.

"The princess will be your undoing," she began, her voice ringing out. "All you have achieved, all your value, she will strip from you. She..."

Anger looked down at herself, at her gown spun of her own tears, so many tears, clinging to her body in gossamer sorrow, mottled with the mark of his grasp. "She will take everything from you, using nothing more than a *spindle*."

She looked back up at the king and felt a frisson of pleasure. For his face was a picture of terror, so vivid in its silent emotion that it eclipsed all around it: the gasps and cries and rising clamor of the nobility thronging the room; the ghastly expressions on her sisters' faces; the unholy squalling as the queen dragged the bassinet close, away from Anger's words. All nothing compared to his terrified expression. Like a man staring into an abyss—! That she could create such a thing was a kind of power she had never tasted before, it seemed to make something stir in her belly. She felt as if the darkness in her mind was spreading, growing—

And then a voice said, calmly, "I too have a boon to give."

Crone stepped before the dais, severing Anger's view of the king. It made Anger come back to herself with a shudder, as if she had been bodily struck.

Her sister raised an eyebrow at her, then looked at the king. "I cannot undo my sister's words," she said. "But I can amend them. All that my sister said will indeed come to pass. But afterwards? Something even greater will take the place of all your losses."

There was a roaring in Anger's ears, a sound that wasn't without but within. She wanted to weep, but she couldn't make the tears come; she wanted to scream, but her voice was suddenly a small thing. All she could do was look Crone in the eye and use one of the words a man had called her, when she had suggested his horse throw him into her wood, when she had watched as her wood took him into itself.

"Cunt," she said, and flew from the castle into the deepening night.

Her Words, and Their Meanings

For six months afterwards, the king's men went forth and confiscated every spindle within his borders, burning them in great pyres in the castle yard. Spindles were banned at the borders, and possession of a spindle became a punishable crime. Anger watched it all with interest: had not Crone turned her curse into a gift, wouldn't he welcome such an outcome? Yet still the fires burned.

Anger watched, and waited. But no horses came to Anger's wood, no one disturbed her. Still she waited to see what would come of her words, watching from atop her tallest tree, clutching the large, polished spindle that Crone had given her, long ago.

He came down the overgrown path to her cottage, picking his way through the ivy-choked weeds. On foot this time, leading his horse, his posture erect.

At first Anger did not look closely at the horse, so startled was she that he had come without a retinue. A small, hopeful part of her thought *apology*; a more sensible part of her thought *the spindle*. But then she looked at the horse and saw the slim young girl bouncing in the saddle, her golden braids rippling around her laughing face, and the part of Anger that had dared to hope fell silent once more.

She hid the spindle on a shelf in her kitchen, then put on her dress of tears and unbuttoned the sleeve to show the marks on her arm, as livid and purpling as they had been that day. Calmly she suggested that the clouds occlude the sun: just a suggestion, but he didn't need to know that, and it made for a most dramatic entrance.

She swept out of her cottage, her head held high for she was *Anger*. This was her job, her role, just as her sisters brought the sun across the sky and coaxed the grain from the tilled soil. She walked out, replete in her purpose, and unflinchingly met his gaze.

"What do you want?" she asked.

He took a step back, clearly startled; the movement pleased her. "Only to talk," he said, then before she could speak, "Rose! Rose, come here."

Princess Rose dismounted nimbly from the horse and ran to her father's—no, to the *king*'s side, it was better to think of him as such. A king first, a man second. *Lady, in this moment I am merely a man.* That much Anger remembered clearly, for the lie it was.

He brought the princess in front of him, crossing his arms protectively over her. She looked up at Anger with wide grey eyes, the same shade of grey as the dawn in her wood, not a hint of fear in them. Instead she said, "I'm Rose. Who are you?"

Faced with that small, round face, its open curiosity, the word *Anger* died on her lips. Instead she found herself saying, heavily, "I was called Apple, once."

"That's a lovely name!" Rose clapped her hands. "Apple blossoms are one of my favorite flowers, aren't they, Papa?"

"Yes," the king said softly. "Yes, they are." He took a breath. "Apple, you must undo this." His voice was trembling. "We have just concluded Rose's betrothal to a firstborn prince, a more advantageous match than we dared to hope for. Our joined lands will be an empire greater than anything in the world, and with access to the southern seas our trade will increase beyond reckoning. Would you take all that from our people?"

He was staring at Anger with a singular, miserable intensity, and she understood then: *Crone had the right of it, she knew what I did not.* That her mitigation would have been a true boon to any ruler, save this king.

Rose had wiggled out from beneath his arms. Now, suddenly, her fingers ran along Anger's waist, just skimming the full folds of her skirts. "It's such a pretty dress," she said, frowning a little, "and yet it's a very sad dress, isn't it?"

"Rose," the king said sharply. "Rose, come back here."

"It is a very sad dress," Anger agreed, taking Rose's hand and moving it away. The girl's fingers twined with hers, warm and soft. "Not for princesses, I think." She looked at the king again, but he was staring at her hand clasping Rose's, with its bracelet of bruises.

"You never said no," he whispered.

For a moment she gaped at him, astonished; and then she was Anger again. "I never had to use that word, before you," she spat back. "I didn't know *how.*"

In her mind the darkness shuddered as if rupturing at last, and she couldn't bear it, not now, not like this. She suggested a storm, she suggested her fury be echoed in her wood that was both within and without her, a reflection of its foul mistress—

But then a sound came, light and high, so strange it made Anger pause. She looked down at Rose and the girl was laughing, open-mouthed with delight, as the first raindrops spattered her face. "Rain!" she shrieked, throwing her free arm out. "Rain, Papa! Oh, isn't it love-ly!"

She broke free from Anger's grasp and began hopping up and down, trying to catch drops in her mouth, laughing as they caught in her eyelashes. Anger could only watch as if in a stupor: first those words, then her still-simmering rage, and now this. *Joy,* she thought stupidly, staring at Rose's ecstatic face. Why was there no Joy in their number? Why had she been born Anger, if there was no Joy to balance her?

I think I am Anger, sister
For now

"There is no greater future than the one I have worked for," the king said, his voice driving. "We must expand if we are to quell the threats to our borders. It has taken years to negotiate this marriage. If you cannot undo it, I know you can amend it! Say... say Rose causes me to lose my horse, or a district, or..."

He trailed off, but she did not see his expression; she was watching Rose's face, how in its curves she could see the first hints of the woman she would become.

"Ask me for another boon," she said.

The king recoiled. "What?"

"Ask me for another boon. For *Rose*." The name made Anger's lips round, like a kiss. "Or do not, and bid your empire farewell—

"Give my daughter a boon," he interrupted hoarsely. "Please. *Please*."

Knee-deep in weeds Rose raised her cupped hands to the sky, giggling as she tried to keep the rainwater from escaping between her fingers. And what of her when she grew older, then? What bruises might ring her arms?

Anger took her time with her words, speaking them as much to the small dancing figure as to the king. "The princess will undo all that you have done, with nothing more than a mere spindle. But the greatness that comes after? It too will be her doing, not yours. You will leave no legacy save her."

Rose ran back to her and tugged on her arm. "Apple, Apple, let's dance in the rain!" And when Anger would not dance she ran about, spinning wildly and shrieking with laughter, her gown and hair richly spattered.

She realized then that she had been so distracted by Rose she had forgotten to note the king's reaction to her pronouncement, missed that moment of dark triumph. Now she looked at him and saw only a guarded fury on his face, and she found that she did not care.

Anger shrugged, inclined her head, and went back to her cottage and shut the door on them: on the king, on his horse gently nosing

through the ivy, on the golden figure of Rose who was Joy still dancing as the heavens poured down.

(And would it even matter in the end, Anger wondered? What could a
princess create, when she was nothing more than a bargaining piece
for her father? What could she hope for, save that her betrothed would
be a decent man? Still Anger's eyes kept straying to the spindle Crone
had given her; still she knew that what had been said must come to
pass, even if she could not see how.)

Her Heart

Rose lingered in Anger's memory, sun-bright against the scrim of her
wood. Though she did not consciously decide to do so, again and
again Anger found herself flitting along the castle walls, watching
Princess Rose. Here, she gossiped with her ladies while they tended a
little garden; here, she rode forth to deliver alms; here, she received
her subjects in her father's hall, giving each of their stories her utmost
attention. *Always doing is our princess*, they said in the streets, dab-
bing their eyes. For the time was coming soon for Princess Rose to
leave them: a castle on the southern border was part of her dowry, to
someday become the capitol of the imminent empire.

Had Anger's words somehow created this, added impetus to the
king's negotiations, the better to send away the daughter who threatened him? Yet every spindle had been destroyed; the king's guards
searched every person and cart on the borders to ensure no more
would enter. There was no threat, save for what Anger harbored in her

kitchen. And if Rose left without incident, if the curse played itself out years from now, perhaps a generation hence? That she could reflect so dispassionately on these matters surprised Anger, but only just. It had been many falls of the leaves since the king first rode into her wood. The dark spot in her memory felt almost normal now; she had grown accustomed, even fond, of her weeds and rotting wood and gowns of tears.

Once a bright, golden creature had danced in the rain, and it would be a sorry thing if her words somehow smothered that joy.

No matter that the same was done to you? the voice whispered in her mind.

No matter.

It had been a long time since any dared to venture into her wood, and it was with a sense of inevitability that Anger opened her door and saw the horses crowding the weed-choked path, so hemmed in by the brambles they seemed to form one looming, many-headed creature. The combined patterns of livery and gleaming metal momentarily blinding; she threw up an arm to shield her eyes. For a brief, panicked moment, all her old dreams came back and it was the glistening serpent again, only with one eye dark, the other vibrantly golden.

Then the golden eye rippled, and called a halt, and Anger blinked and saw Princess Rose. She raised one hand in an uncertain greeting while the rider beside her held the bridle of her horse.

"Apple," she said. "We would beg a moment to rest here, and water? Only we were riding and became lost."

Anger took a moment before replying, trying to ground herself. She was no little bird anymore, and this no fearsome beast, only a retinue of young nobles. But the uncertain gesture, the stilted words—

and how could they be lost? Half the kingdom knew the road that ran nearby. You could see the smoke of several villages by simply climbing a tree.

(Rose's hair was, impossibly, even a brighter gold than her last visit. Who gave her that gift? Blossom, Anger suspected. It would like her sister to waste an entire boon on the right shade of blond.)

"Of course," she said, bowing. "My cottage is at your disposal, your highness."

At her words the party began to dismount, the women exclaiming as brambles caught at their skirts, the men looking uneasily at the twisting, stunted trees. A different livery on each—the women part of Rose's retinue, the men clearly linked to the one who now helped Rose down, his arm sliding snakelike around her waist as he lifted her onto what remained of the path.

"If I could refresh myself, inside?" She moved quickly towards Anger; when the man made to follow her she spun about, smiling brightly. "My lord, in this I should be attended by a woman alone."

"Then you should bring your ladies," he replied. A chin that preceded him, a clipped accent to his words. "They say strange things happen in these woods, and speak ill of a fairy who lives in it." He looked hard at Anger as he spoke the last.

"They are fools," Rose said. She swept into Anger's cottage, waving a dismissive hand over her shoulder at the other women, who receded like a flock of injured birds.

Anger followed her, shutting the door behind them. In the dim light all Rose's brightness seemed to vanish. In her place stood a disconsolate girl, shifting from one foot to another, and seeing her wilt so made Anger's stomach clench.

"I will be brief," Rose said. "I don't wish to impose on you. We have imposed too much already, I believe."

Anger just looked at her. Those soft hands twisting, the tremor in her lower lip.

"I leave in a fortnight, and it seemed important..." she trailed off, then began again. "I wanted you to know that I understand, about the curse. Your boon, I mean. I would have done the same if I were you. He should never have..." But words failed her again and she turned away, wiping roughly at her cheeks.

For a moment Anger was stunned: had he told her? What had he said, what did he remember? But before she could think how to ask Rose continued in a shuddering voice, "I—I heard the maids. When they thought I was asleep. Talking about how he was when he was younger, and now—my mother is not well, she, she dreads my departure, she weeps endlessly and cannot sleep. And the maids were terrified that he might *visit* them again..."

She began crying bitterly, and Anger understood then that the king too oozed a taint from his very being, as surely as if he wore the fabric of his violence. Still Rose wept, and she looked around for something to offer her, only to find herself bewildered again: her kitchen was dusty, the jug long empty. Why had she not noticed before? What had she been subsisting on?

Grief, the voice said wisely in her ear.

Still the princess wept, wiping at her eyes with a handkerchief; Anger took an uncertain step forward, hesitated, and said instead, "Your companion. He is your betrothed? The prince your father spoke of?"

The princess nodded, blowing her nose.

"Should I call for him?"

"No!" The word nearly a shout; she took a shuddering breath and wiped her nose again. When at last she had mastered herself she said, "what do they look like?"

"Pardon?" Anger blinked, startled.

"*Spindles.*" She pronounced the word with a hushed reverence. "Only, I have never seen one—that is, I glimpsed one in a painting, but I would not know one if it was placed before me, either to avoid it, or... to avoid it."

She blushed as she spoke, but Anger thought she saw something in her reddened eyes, a gleam of something harder. Wordlessly she went to the shelf, pushing aside the dusty pot and mended bowl to find Crone's gift, as clean as if she had polished it that morning.

"They look like this," she said, holding it out.

Rose gaped, astonished into silence; her hand drifted forward; abruptly she turned away.

"Rose," Anger began, what did she want to say? So many things she could not find words for. "If you want me to, to destroy it—"

But she was interrupted by the cottage door opening, the doorway filled by a large figure in gold-trimmed livery, his chin entering the room before him. The prince's face was smooth and young and glistening with sweat. He seemed to fill the room, blocking out all light. It was suddenly warm; when had it become so warm?

"My lady," the prince said. "I thought perhaps something had happened."

Anger's breath was catching in her throat. He was so close. The spindle in her grasp.

"Nothing save conversation," Rose replied, the bright smile back on her face. "I would have some more time with my dear friend Apple. You may ride on if you like."

"Certainly not." He looked around the cottage, his lip curling. "You will come away now. This place is... *unsuitable*." He uttered the word with distaste.

The smell of him. Had her cottage become smaller? Her breath was catching, she felt dizzy; Rose looked at her in alarm, save that she was suddenly far away—yet how could that be, when her cottage was shrinking?

"In a moment," Rose said, but her voice was muffled, distant.

"Now," the prince barked.

Rose's hands twining with Apple's, her grey eyes like the dawn in her wood, her hair like the breath of the sun from when she was born, all that warm, cradling *light...*

"Rose!" The prince clapped his hands. "Rose, come!"

"Everything will be all right," Rose said softly. Her lips brushed Apple's cheek.

The prince stepped forward, his hand outstretched. Were his eyes blue? Apple begged the chair *fall please fall* and it obediently tipped backwards, making him stumble. With a grunt he swiped for Rose, seizing her wrist and dragging her to him—

and then the spindle was gone from Apple's grasp as Rose spun about and struck the prince in the head with a too-large fist.

He fell to his knees with a bellow. There was a flurry of cries from without and suddenly her cottage was full of people, clamoring and exclaiming, pushing Apple further and further into the corner. Like a wave crashing in, filling every inch of the space. She heard the twittering of Rose's ladies and the muttering of the prince's men and Apple covered her face with her hands and wept, her tears overwhelming her in their sudden bright pain, like some festering thing had been lanced at last.

And when at last her crying subsided, leaving her aching and hollow, she lowered her hands and saw that her cottage was empty, the chair neatly tucked beneath the table once more.

There was no sign of the spindle.

(There was no empire, of course.)

(In fact, there were no marriages at all. Word went around that Rose was quite unfit, with many allusions made to her state of mind, her womanliness or lack thereof, her overbearing father, dozens of stories and speculations boiling down into the succinct *mad bitch*. Which a princess can easily be, if required. Especially if it means ending border campaigns and byzantine negotiations and finally getting back to *ruling*.)

Apple heard the horses, but distantly at first. Not the plodding gait of the lost but a brisk, purposeful trot; still, it gave her enough time to finish her conversation. She had been listening to a large, spreading oak, listening to its requests: a sick branch that needed removing, a pine tree jostling it for some much-needed light. A new thing for her, this listening. Everything had a voice, why hadn't she realized that before? Everything had a voice, and needs, and desires, and she had imposed her own for far too long. She had made enough suggestions for quite a while; it was time to give others a turn.

Dusting her hands, she flitted back to the clearing by her cottage, watching as two horses drew near. Now she heard the gay little bells swinging from their harnesses, a sweet kind of music she had never heard before; it suited the bouncing golden braids of the first rider, a single girlish touch to the otherwise womanly figure.

(Music, Apple remembered, was one of Spring's passions.)

When they drew close Queen Rose dismounted lightly and then hesitated, shifting from foot to foot. "Apple," she said.

Apple inclined her head. Only a little older, but Rose had aged in other ways; such, she supposed, was the burden of rule. Still her eyes were as grey as the first light of dawn; still she carried her brightness within her, as bright as the breath of the sun itself.

"I've been wanting to bring you something." She drew a pouch out of her saddlebag and held it out. "As a thank you."

"A thank you?" Apple took the pouch carefully, reverently. Inside were dozens of small, dark shapes, spheres that tapered to little points.

"Bluebell seeds." Rose looked around with a smile. "I have always loved this wood—it feels so free, and yet so safe. But no wood this lovely should be without bluebells."

Apple found herself smiling as well, as she had not done in some time. "I don't understand. You have nothing to thank me for."

"Other than the means to rid myself of my boorish suitor?" Rose laughed, then sobered. "If you had not spoken as you did, at my birth? I would never have believed my maids, Apple. I would never have been able to see my father clearly."

The words were earnest, she could see it in Rose's face, and yet... "I didn't do it for you," she whispered. "I had no caring for you then. I wasn't even this... I was Anger, in that moment."

"That may be," Rose said. "But you were also brave, and honest, and I am grateful for it."

Apple could only nod. Everything was so wonderfully bright, in that moment; it closed her throat, it seemed to fill her from head to toe, it softened that lingering darkness in her mind to a shadow. Even the pattern of her gown seemed more vibrant, more like blossoms than bruises, though she knew her wrist would be forever marked, just as she knew the shadow would never vanish entirely. Nor did she want it to.

Rose dabbed at her eyes. "I saw your apple trees are blooming."

"They asked to," Apple said simply.

Still Rose hesitated, shifting again; at last she blurted out, "it is a lonely thing to be queen."

Apple looked at the other rider but Rose waved her hand dismissively. "He's to protect me, nothing more. Though we have fewer threats now; everyone wants our textiles, not our antagonism." Then, more shyly, "I would not blame you, if you saw me as you saw my father. Only—only I need a friend? Someone who cares enough to be angry, and brave, and honest." Her eyes were welling again. "I presumed to call, once... and I have thought of you often... Apple?"

Once a thirteenth, apple-plump fairy had believed it was enough to care. Once a girl named Rose who was Joy had danced in the rain.

What are *you?*

Apple took Rose's hand in hers.

A is for Apple, Who is Love

C.S. MacCath

"The boy can see me. Look." Ösp sketched a lesser stave of healing in the air, and it shone beneath the light of an aurora borealis with the same cobalt glow that coloured her galdur bracer. A great auk warbled in the distance, separated from the safety of its colony on Hrisey. It warbled again. Distracted, head tilting toward the sound, she pushed the stave in the bird's direction, and it shot across the valley toward the mountains at her gestural command. "Not hurt," Ösp murmured after a moment. "Lost, I think." Listening still, she sketched another stave in the air, pale fingers flitting in a complex pattern, and sent it after the first. "That should help."

"He might see the staves, at least." Reynir lifted a ring-encrusted hand, his own galdur bracer aglow with power, and pointed at the veil between the worlds where Ösp had thinned it. On the other side, in tidy baðstofur scattered across the Svarfaðardalur valley, families were spending a dark winter evening together. Perhaps they mended clothes. Perhaps they salted or pickled food. Perhaps they told a favourite story.

But in the baðstofa just across the veil from his outstretched finger, there was no such warmth. In that place, a small boy sat alone on a wooden bed, coal black hair covering eyes like an arctic sea, lips trembling as he wheezed. His gaze was fixed in the direction the staves had gone, as if the A-frame wall of his squalid little loft-above-a-barn might be transparent. Reynir was manifestly glad he could not smell the place. "Is that urine in his cup?"

Ösp nodded, a sympathetic frown creasing her lovely features. "Infant urine. His father thinks it good for the lungs." Lightning flashed overhead, and thunder sounded a few seconds later. A rain-heavy breeze lifted auburn curls to her lips. She pulled them away and slipped her hands into the pockets of a grey velvet coat cut short at the right elbow to accommodate her bracer. "Now do you understand?"

"You cannot rescue every broken creature you encounter." Reynir sketched a weather shield above their heads and set the stave spinning with a practiced flick of the wrist. He looked at his twin askance, brow arching. "And even if his father is hálf álfur, the council will never permit you to bring them across." He sniffed, a disdainful flaring of nostrils in a prominent nose, and shrugged a dismissive shoulder in the direction of the veil. "The humans are simpletons now; one god and everything they don't understand is a devil."

"We're half human," Ösp reminded him gently, "and the álfar still have congress with humanity on occasion."

The boy turned his head from the wall and stared up in Reynir's direction, small fingers twitching in the air. After a moment he brought them to his scalp and scratched a cluster of ivory lice. The scratch ended abruptly in a cough; long, hard, and gasping. He fell back against the headboard, a clot of pink phlegm dribbling down his neck.

Reynir grimaced and crossed his arms over a brocade coat cut like his sister's. "Poor thing. And you think an álfur took an interest in old farmer Sigurður's mother? Which religion did she favour, the ancient or the idiotic? And what is the creature's name, anyway?"

Ösp knelt in the grass and placed her palm against the veil. "Possibly. Both, I think, but that was still done in her time. Dagur." Her fingers flexed, eager to sketch the stave that would open the way between the worlds. "His name is Dagur."

Old farmer Sigurður thumped up the stairs from the barn, mumbling to himself with the abstraction of a man who did not expect to be overheard. His son Dagur leaned over the bedside, tipped the cupful of urine through a gap in the floor slats and righted it.

"There's a smart creature," Reynir observed with a wry smile.

"I'm not a creature. I'm a boy," Dagur croaked, glaring up at Reynir as if he were standing at the foot of the bed.

At the top of the stairwell, Sigurður stopped, gaped at the veil between the worlds, and began to scream.

It was a scream that lasted two days, and there was no comfort Ösp could devise for son or father that Reynir would agree to help her offer. Instead, he reminded her that they were the children of two races, the álfar and the humans, brought to live in the hidden world at a time when the goddess Frigg had received their mother's prayer for the safe delivery of her extraordinary twins. They both still wore the iron hammers of Þórr she had tied about their necks with braided locks of her own hair, but they also wore the galdur bracers given to them by their father. The bracers were a powerful sign of trust, smithed of strange metals and arcane knowledge brought from a faraway star long ago. The first rule of that trust was to keep the secret of those who had made them, even though they sometimes still revealed themselves out of ardor, or pique, or some other inscrutable, alien emotion.

But if Ösp could not comfort, neither would she abandon. So the twins kept vigil together, watching Sigurður scream from a greater distance behind the veil, camouflaged by the gap between the worlds.

From twilight to twilight the first day, he bellowed the prayers of the Lutheran Church at the joists, floor boards, and bed frames, at the poorly-cured sheeps' hides peppered with rot, at a drop spindle left in a corner to gather dust.

"Clumsy woman," he spat at the thing, "breaking her neck that way."

At this pronouncement, Dagur rose from his bed, propping himself on an elbow, and bared his teeth at the man.

"She wasn't clumsy," he hissed, all fury and no strength. "You pushed her down the stairs." Then he collapsed with a ragged cough that brought up a child-sized palmful of blood and turned his face toward the wall.

Sigurður ignored him; eyes wide, gaze directed inward at the terrors of the mind. He began to strike himself on the head with a hand calloused by physical labour, raving about the vengeance of the dead and the unwashed children of Eve. A purple bruise bloomed in his bald spot and grew. He lumbered, huge and fearsome, about the baðstofa, sometimes wetting himself or shedding excrement from his trousers. As the hours passed this way, it became plain that he was a man on the fence between madness and guilt who knew nothing about his hálf álfur heritage, whose mind was filled with the very devils Reynir had mentioned, and who had murdered the mother of his son.

From twilight to twilight the second day, Dagur declined into delirium. Shivering under a too-thin blanket, fingers tucked into his armpits, he fought at the end of each breath to begin another one.

"Not a creature," he grumbled once and murmured something about a fine coat. A fever took him, so high that he begged for water. It was never provided. Later, he shot to his feet and cried "Mama, wait for me!" in a frail voice full of grief, arms reaching out until his wobbly knees buckled.

The horses in the barn below were louder in their complaint. Near dawn, they began to kick at the stall doors, demanding in their own way to be fed and watered. Sigurður ignored them as well. He was naked now, having torn through his clothes sometime in the night, but he was still rasping the same prayers yesterday's vocal cords had bellowed. As the pale, winter sun faded to dusk in the outer world, he fell into his bed exhausted and finally slept. Dagur followed him into slumber; lungs rattling, forehead shining with heat. The horses stopped kicking. A grim silence descended.

"They're both asleep. We should go." Reynir held his sister while she leaned against him and dozed on her feet. His galdur bracer was dark, but a powerful stave turned like a clockwork under their feet and the veil together, one that brought them into alignment with the rapid passage of time in the outer world.

Ösp jerked awake and took a step backward. Eyes rimmed in red, palms upraised in a warding gesture, she said, "Wait! I'm going across to give him water, and I won't let you stop me this time." Her shoulders slumped at his wholly anticipated scowl. "I have to do *something*. This is all my fault."

"No." Reynir held up a slender index finger clustered with rings, captivated for a moment by the way they winked in the moonlight. "It is the fault of the álfur who courted a human woman and then deserted both mother and child." He held up a middle finger. "It is the fault of the mother, who never told the child what he was and left him to be educated by that fulminating twaddle pit of a church." He held up a ring finger. "And it is the fault of Sigurður himself, who is busily shaming two different sets of ancestors by breaking his wife's neck and permitting his son to drown in phlegm." He pointed at Ösp. "All you've done is thin the veil in a way that no fully human eye should be able to see. But if you go over there now," he gestured toward the baðstofa, "you will violate our papa's trust, lose your bracer, and likely be cast out of the hidden world forever." Reynir crossed his arms, chin lifting in self-satisfaction. "Then I would have to follow you, and that would mean losing my jeweller. I couldn't bear it."

"But Dagur belongs with us even if his father is..." Ösp searched for a charitable descriptor, "...beyond our help." Her gaze drifted toward the veil, and she paused, eyes narrowing. "Is someone else over there?"

In the outer world, a fleet set of footsteps echoed in the stairwell.

"Sigurður! Sigurður, are you all right? Your horses have kicked the stall doors down and gotten into the grain. One of them is dead of the colic, and I'm afraid for the oth..." The voice trailed off as a tall man of perhaps thirty crested the stairs. Catching his breath, he retched and covered his nose with the sleeve of a clean, homespun tunic.

Sigurður snored in reply like a drunk man sleeping off a binge, his hairy belly rising and falling above a flaccid knob of genitalia.

"Name of Óðinn," the man muttered, noticing Dagur, and rushed to lay a hand on the boy's forehead. "You're burning alive."

Dagur stirred and smiled up at him. "Hello Jón," he whispered. "I saw the álfar. They were here."

"Of course you did." Jón reached back to tighten the thong binding his fair hair into a queue. "I've brought some medicine, so sit up in bed, if you can. I'm going outside to build a fire and melt snow for drinking and bathing." He lifted the boy's wooden cup to his nose, gave it a wary sniff, and jerked his head back in disgust. "And cleaning."

The twins watched him depart and return a while later with an earthenware mug full of steaming water and reconstituted herbs. He had to wake Dagur again, who had propped himself up in the corner between the headboard and the wall.

"We should shave your head, little man, and boil your bedding," Jón murmured, mostly to himself, picking a louse from the boy's eyebrow and pinching it between thumb and forefinger.

Dagur took the mug from his hand. "What did you put in the water?"

"Something to help you breathe and a little honey to make it sweet. Sip it slowly, but drink it all." Jón supported the base of the mug as Dagur lifted it to his lips. "What happened to your papa?"

"He saw the álfar too, and it made him go crazy. Well, crazier than he went after he ki... after mama died." Dagur glanced warily up at

Jón, lifting the mug to his lips a second time. "This is good," he said, changing the subject after a sip. "I was so thirsty. Is there any more?"

Jón glared at Sigurður, teeth clenching so hard a muscle twitched in his jaw, and exhaled with a snort. "It's all right." He turned back to the boy and laid a hand on his knee. "I won't tell your papa what you almost said. You're safe with me. Now, what is this about the álfar?"

The clockwork stave began to fade. The tableau in the outer world began to accelerate. Jón sped out and back again with a bucket of water and soap, bathed Dagur's fevered body, and after a moment of hesitation, shaved his head with a sharp blade. Sigurður slept through it all, covered now by the blanket Jón had thrown over his belly and genitals.

In the hidden world, a bright moon wobbled in the sky and abruptly gave way to daybreak.

"Thank the Gods." Ösp brought her fingers and thumb together in a closing gesture, thickening the veil until it disappeared. "How long have we been here?"

"A few hours at worst. We haven't even been missed, I'm sure." Reynir lifted a booted foot, pointed the toe and flexed the heel, repeated the stretch with the other foot. "It'll be good to take these off." He nodded at the place the veil had been. "What do you know about Jón?"

"No more than you do; that he's kind, that he might be a healer..." Ösp's voice trailed off as she focused on sketching the stave that would permit them to travel home without having to cross two hundred kilometres overland.

A pair of ravens croaked overhead and descended to sweep the landscape, looking for breakfast. Reynir watched them, smiling abstractedly. "He was calling upon the right gods, at least, and he knew how to use a bar of soap. Wasn't hard to look at, either. Can we have him instead?"

"You don't mean that."

"Fine. Can we have him *too*?"

"I'm going to have enough trouble talking Papa into Dagur, especially since we'll be stealing him from Sigurður." Ösp's bracer darkened. A portal opened where the veil had been. On the other side, the sun was rising over Ásbyrgi Canyon and the shining álfur capitol in its shadow. She offered an elbow to her brother. "And he'll have to convince the council even if he agrees with me."

Arm in arm, the twins passed through the portal.

Among the humans, it was said that Óðinn once guided the mighty, eight-legged steed called Sleipnir too close to the Earth, and where his great hoof grazed the ground, Ásbyrgi Canyon came to be. The álfar were not the ancient gods of the North, nor did they worship these holy ones as some of their hálf álfur children did. Neither had they created the canyon with the ship that had brought them to it and transformed into the capitol their descendants inhabited now. Rather, it was as if the álfar had begged permission of the stones, the trees, and the water to abide there. Rugged cliffs held a council chamber, concert hall, and other compartments filled with contrivances that performed enigmatic tasks. Stands of birches bent together with the help of artful silverwork to become dwellings. Tall spires draped in lichen brought water up from beneath the valley floor to rain on the gardens. It was a city only the álfar understood fully, a refuge for people who had transmuted both their bodies and their science to suit the place they had come to inhabit, whose true appearances, names, and histories were only spoken amongst themselves, and whose gods, if indeed they had any, were inscrutable as those who worshipped them and belonged to the distant star from whence they had all come.

So when the twins came to their father with news of Dagur, and Ösp asked him to plead the boy's case at the council meeting that evening, he gave a reply that not even she understood at first.

"There is a clever gyrfalcon with a broken wing resting in the rocks, just there." Vindgnýr pointed at a hollow in the cliff above the pond at the heart of the canyon. He was difficult to look at, especially for his children, who knew what they beheld was the product of his effort and their desire. Just now, he was shifting from a kindly man of middle years, to a warrior, to a being of inhuman majesty watching the bird with luminous eyes. "I don't know how she came to be there after such a terrible break, but I was thinking of ending her life."

"Why, when you could heal her?" Ösp followed the line of his finger, alarmed. The gyrfalcon's spotted wing was spattered with blood, and it hung at an awkward angle over the stones. In a moment of dark reverie, she wondered if the bird would die before it fell or drown in the pond. At least it would be spared a slow death by freezing. In the hidden world, it was a warm, summer afternoon that promised a pleasant shower later. "I might be able to heal her; I've rested enough to use my bracer again. Let me try."

Vindgnýr frowned and settled into the form his wife had loved; a pale man of surpassing beauty dressed in exquisite clothing. He regarded Ösp askance, much as her brother often did when he thought her more human than álfur. "You are never here. Do you not know how to be here? You are my child, after all." He gestured at Reynir, who studied his father with narrowed eyes as if to prevent him from changing again. "He knows how."

"It isn't easy to live in two worlds." Reynir was quick to defend his twin, unwilling to be set above her. "We are both of us doing the best we can."

A song of complex sound and rhythm echoed in the canyon. Vindgnýr tilted his head and listened. "I am called to council," he said after a moment. "Come with me. I will speak for your bird." The gyrfalcon fell. Ösp lifted a hand to catch it with a stave, but her father wrapped his fingers about her wrist. "Leave mine to die."

It landed in the water with a splash as they turned away.

Together they walked through the labyrinth of the city to an island cliff at the centre of the canyon and a stone stairwell sculpted into the rock there. Near the summit, a deep council chamber nestled, where the quiet hum of contrivances droned alongside the sigh of the wind. Neither Ösp nor Reynir understood their function, but the circular stone table and curved benches around it were cut from the cliff itself and chiseled with the likenesses of foxes, puffins, and seals.

The álfar gathered there seemed unaccustomed to the presence of even a hálf álfur gaze upon their proceedings. They were difficult to look at until Vindgnýr joined the group, settling then into pale people of exotic aspect dressed in finery much like his. A brief interlude of conversation followed in the same musical language that had called him from the pond. The hum of contrivances grew louder, and another álfur appeared at the table as if from nowhere, sitting in a chair carved from a tree trunk in the likeness of a hound.

Hands pressed against the cold stone of the chamber wall behind him, Reynir endeavoured not to stare at the newcomer while the álfar conducted the business of the council. She was not actually there, he knew, though Vindgnýr had once explained that no part of the soul as he understood it traveled as she had. Neither was her aspect of his choosing. Rather, she had the air of a woman who had chosen it long ago; a river of silver hair tipped in raven's-wing black, eyes brown as fertile soil above prominent cheekbones, blue tattoos of stylized animals on her neck, shoulders, and arms. An exotic bracer cast in the likeness of a tree graced her forearm, and her fitted vest and trousers were unlike any garments he had ever seen. She was a queen, untouchable to the likes of a hálf álfur barely out of boyhood, so he was glad for both his heart and loins that she lived in some other place.

In time, Vindgnýr stood and beckoned his children to the table. "They would know more about the father and his child."

A narrow-faced álfur with hair the colour of night leaned forward and rested his chin in the cradle of a thumb and forefinger. "Are they beloved of the mountains?"

Ösp exhaled through parted lips and closed her eyes, struggling to comprehend the question for Dagur's sake. But her dark reverie had replaced the unfortunate gyrfalcon with the boy, and now it was he who fell from the cliff into the pond, again and again. *Help me catch him, Mama,* she prayed, fingers coming to rest on the amulet at her throat. In a flash of inspiration, she answered the question with another, eyes blinking open to weigh the álfur's reaction to it. "Was the human woman you knew beloved of the mountains?"

He brightened. "Yes! I was listening to them when they spoke of her descendants. She tasted of salt and iron." The álfur smiled at the memory. "Can the child see?"

By "child," Reynir knew he meant Sigurður. *So this is the deserter.* He grimaced, crossed his arms, and rescued Ösp from another struggle for comprehension. "He can, but he was raised a Christian and fears the álfur sight."

"Christian." The álfur spat the word as if it were a spoiled morsel of food. "Like the man who blamed her for his impotent seed." A light rain began to fall outside the chamber, pattering softly on the stone. He sat up and watched it for a moment. "Well," he continued, still focused on the rain, "I did what he could not, and now the mountains are satisfied."

Ösp leaned forward and braced her hands on the table, grateful for the stone. It was cool, solid, of the Earth. "Fjallavíðir," she spoke the name he had given her long ago, hoping to capture his attention, "I am sad to report that your son is a dangerous madman, and your grandson may be dying. That's why we've come to ask permission..."

"You mean to steal the son from the father." The woman in the carved wooden chair interjected, her voice ringing with authority. "How old is he?"

"I... we do," Ösp stuttered and rose, shifting on her feet, searching for a way to be respectful of the stranger. "And he's young, honoured álfur. Perhaps five."

"Honoured sìthiche, in the language of the Gaels. Bean-shìdh, to be precise." The woman leaned back in the chair and crossed her legs. "Tell me, hálf álfur," she spoke to Ösp but arched a disapproving brow at Vindgnýr, "Is it better to die among the only people you have ever known or watch the only people you have ever known die?"

Ösp glanced from the bean-shìdh to her father and back again. "I'm not... I don't know. I would need to think about it."

"If you cannot answer the question for yourself, why do you presume to answer it for a child you barely know?" The woman did not wait for a reply but turned away from Ösp with an air of utter dismissal and addressed Dagur's grandfather. "I loved them once, not long ago," she said to him with some compassion, "when they were younger and fiercer and believed the world was sacred. So I have heard the call of their lands, winds, and waters to intercede when they flounder. But we are guests here, neighbours at best," she regarded Ösp again and Reynir with her as if they were the product of some awful mistake, "and we know better than to meddle in the course of their development."

Several members of the council began to blur at the edges, as if the bean-shìdh had spoken their true names and called them away from their affected humanity. Vindgnýr sat down again, leaving his children to stand behind him. The language of the álfar rose around them, too sweet for a conversation about the fate of a sick child. In time, the bean-shìdh disappeared, and a chill seemed to depart the chamber with her. The álfar stood.

Ösp gripped her father's shoulder, understanding at last what he had told her at the pond, eyes brimming with tears at the pity on his face. "You already meddle." She gestured at Reynir. "It's why we're alive. It's why Dagur is alive. Please don't abandon him."

"You are very like your mother, whom I loved and do not apologize for it." Vindgnýr wiped the tears from her cheeks with his thumbs and kissed her forehead, blurring as he did until his touch was like the brush of a butterfly wing. "I am sorry for your bird."

Dagur was dying. His skin lay over his bones like a shroud upon a skeleton and his phlegm, when he was able to cough, was bloody. Now and then, he slipped into a fever delirium and called out for his mother, but it was Jón who poured medicine into the boy's failing body while his father was away in the days that followed.

He was packing Dagur's feet with an onion poultice when the magistrate came to arrest him.

"I found these on the table in your house." Magnús Björnsson held up a fistful of papers as if they might contain a murder confession. He was a tall, spare man of thirty-eight years, keeper of the King's goods in Eyjafjörður county, a Lutheran reformer who had brought a loathing of Catholics and sorcerers alike from Copenhagen to Iceland.

"They're healing staves. I drew them to bless the medicine I was making. My father taught me how to do it." Jón rose from Dagur's bedside, a note of rebuke in his voice. "Why were you in my house, and why did you take things out of it that don't belong to you?"

"So your father was a sorcerer." Magnús slipped the papers into the pocket of his cloak and stepped away from the stairwell.

Sigurður took his place and leered at Jón; a bully wielding a borrowed club. "He used them to kill my horses and raise the dead, right here in my house while I was asleep."

"What?" Blindsided, Jón blew the word out with a breath and gaped at the man. A rush of anger dispelled his bewilderment. He turned to Magnús and made a sharp, beckoning gesture. "My father was Catholic, and his father learned how to make those staves from a priest. Give them back."

"Your father was a Papist who prayed to the old gods in his sleep." Sigurður's gaze shifted from Jón to Magnús and back again. There was fear in the hunch of his shoulders, urgency in the audible grinding of his teeth. He stepped away from the stairwell, and two more men crowded into the loft; Ólafur, who contested the boundaries of Jón's inherited land and Eiríkur, who had kissed him long ago in a youthful passion and despised the memory of his mouth.

Jón lowered his hand when Magnús made no move to return the staves and took a step backward, making a mental count of the days since he had seen evidence of Sigurður's instability and violent disposition. Ten. Long enough for the man to agonize about that evidence and deflect attention from it by taking a spurious charge to the magistrate. Long enough to gather support from enemies. He bent to scrub the onion smell from his hands in a bucket of cold water. It was either that or ball them into fists and beat Sigurður into meat for the birds of prey.

"Is this..." Choked with fury now, Jón swallowed hard and began again. "Is this what you've been doing while I've been here looking after your son?" He stood and shook his hands dry, glaring at Ólafur and Eiríkur in turn. "And don't pretend to believe him. You're just here to hurt someone you hate."

"Is he better?" Sigurður bellowed and lumbered to Dagur's bedside, elbowing Jón out of the way and kicking the bucket of water onto the floor slats. He grabbed the boy's arm and shook him awake. "Does he look better to you, Magnús?"

A gust of wind whistled through the baðstofa. Magnús gathered his cloak together, frowning at Jón as if the weight of the Bible hung at the corners of his mouth. "I have read of these things in the book I brought from Denmark. The raising of the dead, the corruption of the innocent, the killing of the livestock, they are all familiar to me."

Sigurður nodded vigorously and dragged Dagur out of bed by his armpits, forcing him to stand. The onions fell from his feet onto the floor. "Tell the magistrate what you saw. Tell him about Jón and the dead."

Dagur whimpered, head rolling on his neck like a puppet's. "Papa, stop. It hurts."

"Sigurður, be careful!" Alarmed, Jón reached around him for the boy.

At a gesture from the magistrate, Ólafur and Eiríkur grabbed his arms and pulled him away. Magnús backhanded him across the mouth, splitting his lip with a signet ring. "Do not touch the child again."

Jón gasped. Blood painted his teeth and tongue. He spat it out. "Sigurður's horses got into the grain and ate too much. They died of the colic. Go downstairs and look at the winter stores. You'll see I'm telling the truth." Adrenaline cramped his stomach as he considered the magistrate's use of the word 'sorcerer' to describe his father. He felt like a man walking across an unfamiliar glacier, could almost hear the cracking of ice underfoot. "As for the rest, I don't know about any dead people." He remembered Dagur's mention of álfar and wondered again what the boy and his father had seen. "I came here that night with a medicine for the lungs. That's all."

"Tell him now, boy! Tell him about the horses!" Sigurður shouted, wild-eyed, and held his son at arm's length like a shield. "Tell him what you said about the ál... I mean the dead!"

Dagur stared up at Jón. Death was in his gaze, ready to claim the one for whom it had come. But gratitude was there also, and loyalty, and love. The boy's nostrils flared, and his lips thinned. He remained silent.

Jón tasted the iron tang of blood, felt the iron grip of his enemies, saw the iron will behind Sigurður's madness. He stared back at Dagur and suddenly knew there was death in his gaze as well, an unexpected guest invited by the servant of an unwelcome god. And if the boy refused to speak, he would be made to suffer in the name of that god for the rest of his foreshortened life. Sigurður would see to it.

So Jón took the burden of suffering upon himself.

"It's all right." He spoke to Dagur in the same gentle, take-your-medicine voice he had used for the last ten days. "Do as he says. You're safe with me, remember?"

Dagur wilted away from his father, hanging forward by his armpits as if he were trying to fall. Gaping, breath shallow, lips blueing for want of air, he wept silent tears that dripped from his nose onto the floor. "I saw..." he croaked. "It was what my papa said. That's what I saw."

Magnús turned to Jón. There was sorrow in his expression and the pity of a butcher over a goat bleating in panic. "It is clear to me now that you are a sorcerer like your father was in his time, and so I sentence you to die as he should have." To the others, he said, "Gather his belongings into a pile outside his house together with anything else that might be burned."

The unfamiliar ice in Jón's mind transmuted into fire.

Sigurður dropped his son back into bed and hastened to help Ólafur and Eiríkur muscle Jón down the stairs.

Dagur collapsed against the headboard in a fragile heap of flesh, eyes round and wet as river stones. "I'm sorry," he wheezed, and there was guilt enough in the words for every man who should have borne it but did not.

Jón grabbed the doorframe and held himself in the room for a moment. "This is not your fault," he told the boy as Ólafur and Eiríkur peeled his hands away. "Not your fault!" he repeated from the stairwell. Down in the barn, he fought back, breaking free long enough to send Eiríkur into the hay with a fist to the gut. The smaller man lurched to his feet and bared his teeth in a cruel grin, but a mask of pious indignation fell over his face as the magistrate descended and bore Jón to the ground from behind.

Outside, the mid-afternoon sun gleamed like a dirty coin behind a mantle of cloud cover. A blanket of snow lay dull upon the ground. Here and there, weeds and shoots of dead grass rose up in brown defiance of the monotony. Grey mountains framed the valley as they had since before the time of settlement, as they would long after his ashes were scattered by the wind. Jón was awestruck by it all, as if no bright summer day, no carpet of wildflowers, no surfeit of waterfalls could ever be quite so lovely.

A team of horses hitched to a wagon waited to bear him away. Two more men waited with it, both of them friends of his enemies and sons of people his father had once treated with herbal medicine and healing staves. One stood and shook out a length of braided rope.

"Do all of you hate me so much?" Jón asked of no one in particular, grief-stricken at the betrayal. "Is there nothing I can say in my own defence?"

There was no reply but the hands of neighbours forcing him into the bed of the wagon and securing him there.

Ólafur and Eiríkur rode ahead on a pair of saddled mounts to comply with the magistrate's instructions. Sigurður sat with the others across from Jón in the wagon, one meaty hand balled into a fist as if he expected to use it as a gag. Magnús climbed into the driver's seat and shook the reins. The horses plodded forward.

A crowd was already gathering when they arrived at Jón's house. His younger, smaller, more literate brother Þorvaldur was there as well, pleading with anyone who would listen while Ólafur and Eiríkur made a pile of Jón's possessions in the snow.

Seeing the wagon, Þorvaldur sprinted to it and grabbed the hem of the magistrate's cloak. "My brother has the right to swear his innocence before *all* of the men in this valley, not just the ones who accused him."

Magnús jerked the garment free with a twitch of the wrist. "This is only done when the guilt of the sorcerer is in doubt," he replied without ever looking at the man, his other hand outstretched to direct the placement of a vertical stake in the pile. "Dig the hole deep enough to hold him upright there!"

"What do you mean? Of course he isn't guilty!" Þorvaldur's voice raised, and the crowd quieted behind him. "My brother can't even read. He isn't smart enough to raise the dead."

Magnús took the sheaf of papers from his pocket and thrust them under Þorvaldur's nose. "It matters little whether or not he succeeded. What matters is that he tried, and these staves are proof of that."

"But..." Þorvaldur spun in a circle, fists clenched in his hair. He stopped abruptly and pointed up at the magistrate. "But you can't execute him without a trial at the Alþingi. That's the law. What you're doing right now is murdering him."

"*I* am the law here." Magnús climbed down from the driver's seat and glowered at Þorvaldur. "What will I find if I search *your* house, son of Rögnvaldur? Did he teach you how to practice sorcery too?"

"Þor... Þorvaldur." It was an effort for Jón to speak his brother's name. He had not given Sigurður and the others the satisfaction of seeing him weep, but he was shaking uncontrollably now, and his voice quavered.

Þorvaldur left the magistrate's question unanswered and went to stand beside the wagon. "I don't understand. Why are they doing this to you, when Papa..."

"Be quiet," Jón interrupted. "There is nothing you can do for me and much for you to lose."

Sigurður leaped out of the wagon, leaving Jón with the other two men, and followed Magnús into the crowd. Þorvaldur craned his neck to watch them go. After a moment, he turned back to Jón and whispered, "But what you do with the staves is no different..."

"I said to be quiet!" Jón hissed and covered Þorvaldur's mouth with his bound hands. "These men want me dead, staves or none." His voice broke on the word 'dead', and he fought the urge to vomit up the salted fish in his stomach. "Listen to me. Give Ólafur the land he wants, and ask one of the women in the valley to look in on Dagur. I don't want him to die alone, and he's close now." The magistrate began to address the crowd, but Jón ignored him. Instead, he leaned down and laid his forehead against Þorvaldur's. "And stay... stay with me until they come. I'm so afraid."

"Name of..." Þorvaldur stopped short of completing the invocation and pressed his palms to either side of Jón's head. "I'm here, brother. I'm right here."

Soon after, Sigurður, Ólafur, and Eiríkur pulled them apart.

Jón had to be dragged to the stake, not because he refused to go, but because he could not walk. They bound him there, surrounded by the table where he had mixed Dagur's medicine, the bench he had built from a fallen tree, the bed linens. Neighbours added to the pile, some out of malice, but most out of pity. It would be better if he died of the smoke and not the flame.

The sun broke through the clouds and began to set. Jón looked up, too terrified to pray, and voided his bladder.

Magnús shoved a burning torch into the pyre.

It was then that Jón finally wept; throat rasping, shoulders heaving with sobs. A lick of flame singed the hair on his calves, stung his flesh, flickered away for a second. Smoke rose from the linens. Fire settled into the wood. His feet began to burn, to blister, to blacken. He screamed and sought Þorvaldur in the crowd, a place of love to rest his eyes until they failed him.

What he found was a window into summer and a richly dressed man with an eldritch expression on his face.

Ösp bolted through the veil to Dagur's bedside, slipping in a pile of cooked onions nearly frozen to the floor in a spill of water. She kicked an overturned bucket on the way to a hard landing at the edge of the bed. Her galdur bracer chipped the frame and marked her wrist with a red welt. She cried out.

Half-uncovered in the bitterly cold baðstofa, Dagur did not move, and indeed his breath was so shallow that for a moment Ösp feared he might already be dead.

"Are we too late?" she wondered aloud, removing her coat to throw it over the boy's emaciated body. It had only been a day by her count; an evening meal with her father and brother after the council meeting, a restless night of too little sleep and too much worry, an hour to persuade Reynir that they should offer Dagur a measure of healing even if they were forbidden from offering him a home. But it had been almost a fortnight in the outer world, long enough for a father to warm the home his son was dying in, to say nothing of any succour he might have provided. A knot of loathing for Sigurður uncoiled in her belly.

"Not yet, I think," Reynir observed, peering over her shoulder. "But do it now, before he wakes, so we can leave unseen." A perfume of birch and poppy clung to his clothes, sweet counterpoint to the odour of onions. "Are you all right? Your wrist is bleeding."

Ösp nodded by way of reply and sketched a greater stave of healing above Dagur's chest, pushing it through her coat and into his body with a palm down motion. "I cannot mend the damage to his lungs; only Papa and his people can do that, but I took the disease. It will have to be enough." She rose gingerly to her feet, took the blanket from Sigurður's bed and leaned down to trade her coat for it.

Dagur reached up and grabbed her fingers, eyes opening, lungs expanding in a deep breath. "Save him." The words were like a sigh of wind, the creak of a stair, the demand of a ghost.

"Who, poppet?" Ösp covered him with the blanket, slid into her coat, and sat down again.

"Does he know a decent jeweller?" Reynir muttered behind her and cursed.

"Papa made me say you were dead and he brought you back to life, and another man called him a sorcerer." Dagur began to cry in the way of a broken-hearted child before an evil he cannot hope to comprehend. "They're going to do something bad to him now, and he said it's not my fault, but I know it is."

"Jón." Reynir inhaled the name and turned toward the stairs, his arm already raised, a cobalt stave taking shape before his fingers.

"Where is he?" Ösp gathered Dagur's small, cold hands into her own, the bean-shìdh's words ringing in her mind like an indictment. *We know better than to meddle in the course of their development.*

Dagur pulled his hands free and sat up. "Across the valley. They're burning all the stuff in his house. That's where they took him."

Ösp gasped and jerked around toward her brother, but Reynir was already gone. The veil closed like a curtain behind him.

She turned back and planted her fists on either side of the boy's legs, auburn curls tumbling over her shoulder, jaw set in a mulish line. "Tell me, poppet, and tell me true," she began urgently. "Is it better to die among the only people you have ever known or watch the only people you have ever known die?"

A billow of smoke in the air. A stench of cooking flesh. A howl of agony. These were the beacons Reynir followed to Jón as he skipped from the hidden world to the outer world and back again. The Christians had made a spectacle of him and watched it now in a semi-circle around the pyre, transfixed, devils in a hell of their own making. His feet were not visible in the flames, but his clothes and hair were burning away, charring the skin of his arms, chest, and face.

"Name of Óðinn," Reynir whispered, remembering Jón's tall, broad-chested beauty, the deep timbre of his voice, the well of good so evident in his character. He stood across from the man behind the semi-circle of devils and held the veil open against all common sense, a clockwork stave turning beneath him while he scanned the pyre and the wintry valley beyond for a way to mount a rescue that would not betray the álfar.

Finding none, Reynir scanned again for a way to help Jón die, grief and rage coursing through him like an ichor in the blood. Now and forever, he would hate them, swore the hatred in his heart like a vow. Sigurður, who rocked from foot to foot near the blaze. The well-dressed man behind him bearing the countenance of a judge. The two men at his side. The spectators. Their children. Any person who would ever call upon the Christ in the long lifetime given to him by the inheritance of his hálf álfur blood.

Ösp ran toward Reynir in the hidden world, Dagur riding on her hip, arms wrapped about her neck. Outside the clockwork stave and out of sync with his perception of time, they appeared to move in slow motion until Ösp saw the open veil and skidded to a stop inside the stave. "What are you doing?" she hissed. "Someone might see you!"

Dagur tilted his head, distracted from an awestruck survey of the summery landscape. "Who is screaming?" His eyes widened, and his chin began to tremble. "Is it J-Jón?"

By way of answer, Reynir lifted a hand without ever looking away from the outer world and sent the child a stave of sleeping.

Dagur slumped into Ösp's shoulder and began to snore.

"I've found him." Reynir's hand remained in the air, splayed open in a warding gesture. He shuddered and continued in a flat, quiet tone. "Take Dagur to Papa right now. Tell him Sigurður and the other Christians are burning people alive, and you're afraid they might do the same to the child."

Ösp shrank away from her brother as if the words had been a physical blow. "No. No," she repeated, gathering her wits, and strode toward the veil holding Dagur against her body. "They're just burning his things and making him an outlaw. It's awful, and we should help him, but it was done in Mama's time, remember?"

The scream was louder now, a hopeless wail rising from a ragged throat.

"Stay back." Reynir's breath was shallow, and his lips were drawn in a grimace. "Please, for your own sake."

Ösp stepped around her brother's outstretched hand to stand at his side and turned toward the veil. A strangled sound escaped her throat, and she stumbled backward. Reynir caught them both, sister and child, from behind. "Oh, Gods," she whispered from the hollow of his embrace. "Is there nothing we can do for him?"

Reynir pressed his cheek against the crown of her head and permitted himself to weep. "No. It's bad enough we've stolen Sigurður's son."

"It takes hours to burn a body."

"I know, but he won't last that long. I promise."

As if he had heard Reynir's assurance, Jón's hopeless wail faded into the relative silence of a crackling fire. Ösp looked out to find him looking in at Dagur, an expression of mingled agony and wonder on his face. He blinked once, twice, and collapsed into unconsciousness.

Reynir lifted a hand, closed the veil, and dismissed the clockwork stave.

Behind them, a songbird twittered from a fruiting crowberry bush.

Ösp buried her face in Dagur's neck and keened, long and low. "This happened because I meddled," she said after a time, lifting her face to the sun and wind. "The bean-shìdh was right."

"Great fucking gods of my ancestors! What happened out there was not the result of meddling, and it was not the fault of a sick child." Reynir turned her in his arms and laid protective hands on her cheek and Dagur's back. A rush of dark emotion washed over him like a storm tide. "Don't you think the people who burned Jón at the stake ought to be the ones held accountable for it?"

Ösp leaned forward and kissed the tears from his cheeks, the loathing in her belly rising like a serpent to greet the vengeance in his eyes. "I do," she began, her voice trembling under the words, "but the hour is late in the outer world, and time moves swiftly there."

Reynir nodded once, a sharp dip of the chin. For a moment, he was much like his father, difficult to look upon. Then his countenance settled into a thing so forbidding he might have been the messenger of a wrathful álfur god. "I have Christian devils to visit while they sleep."

Ösp stepped back a pace and adjusted the sleeping boy on her hip. A herd of wild horses thundered across the distant green, their manes whipping like flags of ivory, copper, and black. Several foals were among them, gambolling after their parents. "Be just," she counselled quietly, watching. "Spare the innocent."

"Just. Yes." Reynir followed her gaze, a malevolent smile growing on his face. He buttoned the wooden toggles of his coat and straightened his collar.

Ösp turned as her twin opened the way to Ásbyrgi in the place where the veil between worlds had been. Dagur slept on, unperturbed, his breathing deep and even. "I'll come back if Papa lets me keep my bracer," she said, stepping through. "Save Sigurður for last."

Be just, Reynir told himself as he stood beside the beds of sleeping children. *Be just,* he repeated over the heads of their families and neighbours. And he was, even when loathing for them poured out of him like a vomited poison.

It was difficult to inflict the thing these humans called an elf shot. A powerful stave like the one he had used to sync time in the two worlds, its purpose was not to kill, but to sour luck. The young daughters and sons of the devils would wake in the morning, eat a bowl of hot grain, feed the horses, play in the snow. But the devils themselves would stumble over a root and break an ankle, miss the ladle and dip a hand into boiling soup, fall over the side of a fishing boat and drown on a calm day, die of a heavy tumour in the bowels. Unlucky, they would be called as the years passed, but they would live.

For a while, anyway.

Ösp found him spent in body and spirit, leaning against the barn door below Sigurður's baðstofa. A low, full moon brightened the jewels on his fingers, but the hem of his brocade coat was dusted with soot and spider webs.

"I was hoping you'd come." Reynir yawned and held up the forearm bearing his galdur bracer, now dark. "Sigurður stayed to watch the pyre burn out and dispose of Jón's remains. He should be along soon. Is Dagur with Papa?"

"Yes, and he sent me back to make certain you had a way home. I told him what you were about, but all he said was that an ethic of non-interference demands the restoration of balance upon occasion." Ösp laughed a little, not a merry sound, but one of relief. "I don't know what he'll say to the council, but under the circumstances, I doubt we'll be banished. Fjallavíðir might even be on our side; Dagur is his grandson, after all." She gestured at the barn door and bared her teeth in a venomous grin. "So, shall we go upstairs and wait to push a wounded bird to his death in the service of balance?"

Reynir took her offered elbow and drawled, "You are your father's daughter after all, aren't you?"

Ösp laid a hand on his arm and led him inside. "I most certainly am."

Author's Note:

In 1625, a farmer named Sigurður accused a man named Jón Rögnvaldsson of raising ghosts and killing his horses. A small boy unrelated to either man blamed Jón for the illness he was suffering. Magistrate Magnús Björnsson, educated in Copenhagen about the problem of witchcraft, came to investigate the case. He searched Jón's house in the Svarfaðardalur valley and found pieces of paper with magical staves written on them. These, along with the accusations, were enough to convince him that Jón was practicing sorcery, as it was called in Iceland.

From here, accounts of the incident diverge. Some indicate that Jón was never given a trial, while others indicate that his brother Þorvaldur spoke at a trial in his defence. Still other accounts indicate that Jón admitted to practicing sorcery, though he flatly denied having ever harmed anyone with it. In any event, the result was the same; namely, that Jón Rögnvaldsson was the first person to be burned at the stake in Iceland for engaging in practices only recently criminalized by the Reformation.

So while the story I have written here centralizes the álfar (also called huldufólk and elves), I have endeavoured to honour the spirit of Jón's story, the world he inhabited, and the way it changed around him to his detriment. He was a real person who suffered a horrible death, and I would have him remembered as more than a fictional character.

B is for Burned

Jonathan C. Parrish

So, this is a story about how I fucked up. I disgraced my kin, spoiled our economy and undermined my own earnings potential, all because I overestimated my abilities. Full disclosure, this happened quite some time ago, but I am still dealing with the after effects. I am not using my real name; nonetheless, if you have read my previous stories you can probably figure out who I am.

I was young, only a few hundred years, and paper thirsty. I had yet to land my first mark—hadn't even gotten so much as a rain wish within earshot. I wasn't the last of my cohort, but I would have given almost anything for even a mild regret.

Enter desperate lady (DL). She wanted to be younger and I just happened to be on call when her request came in. Most people with this kind of request are level 4 narcissists, and given the right combination of early desire and delayed dismay, the potential profits are huge. Outstanding!

Standard fees in a situation like this are tied to the length—2:1 servitude ratios are common (e.g. 2 years servitude for every year of "youthenizing" (not the official word, but the one we used in training and one of my favourites!)). The ideal was to get them hooked with a year or two and then try the "land and expand," to get them to trade in for bigger and bigger payoffs. Servitude was the primary driver of retirement income.

She wanted to knock twenty years off. 20 years! That was a giant payoff and a major résumé booster. I tried not to reveal my glee when I asked for 40 years servitude, to begin 40 years after the contract was signed.

"That won't do," she said. "Is there anything else I can trade? Someone else, for example?"

Third party trades are tricky, as consent becomes a major sticking point, and we all avoid it when we can. The biggest issue is that third parties have to sign—but there is a loophole with unborn children as their consent derives, according to our standing contract law, from the parent. Child trades are white whales—dangerous sometimes but *always* lucrative. Well, at least they used to be.

I explained that I could trade for her next child and she paused a moment before agreeing. That pause was important—her regret was going to set me up for hundreds of years.

As I was writing the contract, I had an idea that she might want to make it "open ended" so she could continue to trade in children and receive a twenty year age-reduction coupon for each. It was a long shot but worth a try. She agreed, so I added "for every unborn child." I figured after a couple she'd have enough regrets to seek a hero loophole but by that time I'd be set and not have to worry too much. Contract signed, bim bam boom, 20 years of youthenizing granted with the expectation of payment at an unspecified point in the future with the first child. She was happy, I was happy. I was moving up!

A few years later, tax forms were flagged indicating that she had a child dependent and so I dutifully showed up to claim the terms of the contract. With surprisingly little fuss, she turned the newborn over to me, I signed a receipt and I took it to central for processing.

The comptroller was impressed, and asked to see the paperwork. I turned it over and his eyebrows rose at the open-ended wording in the contract but he stamped it and said they'd deploy the monitors and I'd receive statements every five years. Babies are high-value assets, and I received a sizeable lump sum, but the big payoff should be in five years when her regret had kicked in. Given the expected size of the payoff, I didn't even try to work to secure any new contracts.

Five years later my statement was far smaller than I expected. Still, it was something and I was pretty happy—I assumed the next one would be better. Five years after that, I got a statement for less than a quarter of the first amount. Assuming it was an error, I headed down to central to talk to someone. I talked to the guy at the front desk and he sent me to a manager's office. I was feeling optimistic—they must have realised they messed up and now were gonna straighten out my account, right?

Wrong. The look on the manager's face was not happy.

"Is this your contract?" He pointed to the copy of my contract on the desk. I happily stated that it was and asked if there was an issue.

"Yeah, there's an issue. What the hell were you thinking when you wrote this up? Did you check it with anyone?"

I admitted I hadn't, but as it was a standard contract I hadn't thought it was necessary.

"No open-ended contract is standard. Your mark has been cashing in a lot of babies."

So where was the problem? From my end that should just increase earning potential, right? Rate multiplied by time equals yay!

"A lot of babies..." he continued. "So many babies, in fact, that the baby value index has significantly decreased. You have devalued them to the point where all baby deals are no longer cost-effective. You've noticed a drop in income, I assume."

I mentioned that was why I was there. I asked him to explain the number of babies, I mean she shouldn't have been able to manufacture much more than one a year.

"After auditing her account, we noticed some inconsistencies in terms of pedigree, and we determined that not all of the babies were genetically descended from her."

I could feel the heat rise up the back of my neck. *Shit.* Two implications. One, I had said "for every unborn child" and not specified her own. Two, she was trading other people's children freely, so she might be a psychopath. Don't get me wrong, I didn't personally care what she did but any reduction in remorse was going to significantly impact my D revenue stream.

"Can we argue that the spirit of the contract is violated? I feel consent is an issue here and that we'd have good grounds for refusal of children."

"That's true, but we have just begun gathering documentation. I'm going to need any documents you have in your possession that you have not provided us yet so that we can begin proceedings."

Many of you might think, "Ok good, so once that was resolved it was fine." Right. Well, it's a nice sentiment but if that happened I wouldn't be telling you this story, or whatever this is. Turns out, she might have been better at contract law than most of us, better than me anyway. When central argued that consent was being breached, she countered with precedent. Precedent that had been approved by me, complete with full paperwork of acceptance, because not a single one of the babies had been her direct descendants.

That could have been the end of it, and for some it was. But central had to re-adjust the child currency indices to adjust for what was a sudden baby glut, and they also had to find a way to dispense with those babies. Their solution was to create a storage facility and I was given the dubious distinction of being the fairy chosen to care for them, "until such time as the terms of the contract have expired."

TL;DR: I thought I was super-awesome at contracts and turns out I super-sucked, and I almost bankrupted the entire wish economy.

Footnote: Added for those of you not familiar with the business: "rain wishes" are transient, throwaway wishes, like: "I wish this rain would end" (hence the name) and usually paid a trinket. Contract makers have two earning streams that we indicate as P and D streams: P streams are the *physical* items identified in the contract and can be sold and traded, D streams are not as defined but come from the *distress* associated with loss of the item or costs of the contract. D streams are significantly more important in status and earnings.

C is for Contract

Jeanne Kramer-Smyth

The metal of the hatch door squealed under the assault of razor sharp claws. Naqi-12 curled her upper fringe to block out the sound. It certainly didn't help her concentration.

"Did you see what they did to me?" asked Zee-47, examining the claw marks oozing orange fluid on her torso. "Can they cut through the metal?"

"Maybe," Naqi-12 turned away from the tiny fierce face, all hard angles and teeth, mashed against the hatch door window. "What do we do?"

"I told you we should never have landed on Earth. That place is infested." Zee-47 circled around Naqi-12.

"You did. You told me. But I thought the shipment was worth it." Naqi-12 kept her eyes on the interactive diagram of their long-haul ship, studying the spread of the small aggressive Earth creatures. Most of it flashed red, casting a warm glow on the multicolor enamel mosaics that covered the curved surface of the walls and ceiling. "You were right. I was wrong. How do we turn this around?"

"Can you get an external connection?" Zee-47 swayed beside Naqi-12, staring at the screen.

"I tried." Naqi-12 used her longest tentacle to tap the com button on the far panel. The hiss of white noise filled the small room for a moment before she turned it back off again. "I've been trying every five minutes, but we are out of range for live calls and it seems like a waste of energy to start leaving messages. Besides, if we pay for an exterminator to come out we are going to lose any profit we might have made this trip."

"Ok. So we are on our own." Zee-47 glided back to the hatch door window, holding herself still as the grimacing creature banged on the transparent panel inches from her face. "But definitely not alone."

"Look at this." Naqi-12 shifted the feed from the cargo hold onto the main screen. "What are they doing?"

Zee-47 turned back to the screen. "Are they trying to open it?" A swarm of the tiny winged creatures were clustered along the edge of the largest crate. "What is in there?"

"It is labeled 'Fatum Aurum'." Naqi-12 read off a side screen.

"Is that what it says?"

"Yes. Do you understand it? You know I never bother reading the manifests when we get these consolidated shipments."

"It is an Earth language, I think," Zee-47 said, "Vessel, translate Fatum Aurum."

"Earth Latin. Literally, weird currency. More precisely translated as fairy currency." The ship's voice was melodic. Naqi-12 still had it set to the Proxima Centauri accent she found most comforting.

"Fairy currency?" Naqi-12 repeated, "I still don't understand."

"I don't either." The cloud of tiny winged creatures scattered to the corners as the huge crate exploded, shards of composite packaging flying in all directions. Zee-47 turned the cargo bay lights on full. When the cloud of debris cleared, a large creature with wings sat on the floor stretching two pale appendages. "It is similar to the Earth humans we encountered at the port, but I do not believe any of them had wings."

"I agree." Naqi-12 pulled up diagrams of human adults on a side screen. "Human-like, but not human."

"Are there any more crates with the same label or markings?"

"Oh dear." Naqi-12's tentacles flashed an embarrassed moment of bright yellow.

"What?"

"Would half the cargo be an alarming amount? I bet if I did the math, it would be 49%. Just little enough to not trigger declaring it too big to be part of a consolidated shipment."

The creature stood and looked calmly around the cargo hold. The tiny winged creatures clustered around it, some landing on its shoulders and arms - others circling its head. It strode across the cavernous space toward a stack of large crates with the same markings as the container it had broken out of.

"Naqi-12, how many? Precisely."

"17."

They both swiveled to stare at the cargo feed, hypnotized by the movement they could not stop.

"17." Zee-47 repeated. "This is only going to get worse. I feel like this has changed from an infestation to a hijacking. Or a mutiny. Can you mutiny if you aren't a member of the crew?"

"No. You can't mutiny if you aren't on the crew. I think this definitely would have to be classified a hijacking."

"Got it." Zee-47 nodded before covering over her face with her upper fringe. "Hijacking it is."

"If we are being precise, I would say at this point they are only stowaways."

"This is not the time to argue over semantics." Zee-47 gestured at the screen. "This is the time for *how do we get rid of the things with wings?*"

"Got that out of your system?" Naqi-12 asked quietly.

"Yes." Zee-47 settled her fringe down again, her voice back at normal volume.

"We could open the cargo bay door and space them?"

"That would only take care of anything in the cargo hold that's not tied down—what about the ones still in the boxes? Or the small ones still trying to get in here?"

"At least it would stop that big one from opening more boxes."

On the screen, the Earth human with wings crouched on top of the largest box in the hold. It gripped the lid and its wings blurred as it rose up off the lid and pulled. The box shook, but the lid held tight.

Naqi-12 navigated to the emergency control screen, methodically sealing off the part of the ship they hid in, while opening everything else they could manage to connect. With a look to Zee-47, who blinked in agreement, Naqi-12 disengaged the large outer doors in the main cargo bay.

The creature on the box held tight as its body was pulled toward open space and the tiny creatures were sucked out as a cloud into the blackness beyond.

They joined hands and a few caught the edges of the doorway. Naqi-12 adjusted the feed cameras just in time to show them pulling themselves down onto the outer skin of the ship and clawing their way across the surface. The Earth creature still clung to the large box.

"It isn't letting go." Zee-47 tapped her tentacles. "Why isn't it letting go?"

"It is clearly very strong. And they," Naqi-12 waved at the screen, "don't need air."

"Well, close the bay then. At least that puts more of them outside than in."

"Step one, reduce the number of problems." Naqi-12 closed the cargo bay door and cycled the air pressure to return. The Earth creature let go of the crate. Its wings fluttered, raising it up a few feet before it landed lightly on its lower appendages. It moved to the cargo bay door and ran its upper appendages along the seam of the now sealed portal. Zee-47 entwined one of Naqi-12's tentacles in hers as they watched. "We need weapons." Naqi-12 admitted quietly.

"You wouldn't let me use any of our cargo space for weapons."

"Okay then... things we can *use* as weapons." Naqi-12 withdrew her tentacle from Zee-47's, her skin shifting to a darker anxious blue as she glided across the small room. "There has to be something. Do we have any tools? Or poison?"

"The welding kit is... " Zee-47 pointed back to the monitor. ".. in the cargo bay."

"Of course it is! What else?"

"We could use the escape pod."

"I am not giving up everything we have worked so hard for."

"Unless they are allergic to our food, I don't know what else to suggest."

Naqi-12 toggled on the intercom into the cargo bay. "What do you want from us?" she shouted.

The Earth creature stared up at the speaker in the ceiling. Its wings blurred as it lifted itself up to just beneath the ceiling, running the flexible tips of its upper appendages across the speaker grill. It pushed its face close and a quiet jumble of melodic sounds came out of the speaker in the room they were trapped in. The ship's computer did not recognize the language and could not translate.

"Hello?" Zee-47 said hesitantly into the microphone.

"Hell low?" the creature repeated, its wings working hard to keep it close to the speaker.

"Naqi-12, cycle a translation of this through all the Earth languages we have available." Zee-47 waited a moment then said, "Hello, my name is Zee-47. What do you want?"

After a few beats of silence, the ship's computer began transmitting translations of Zee-47's words in different Earth languages. The winged creature lowered itself to the floor of the cargo bay, folding its long lower appendages beneath it but watching the speaker attentively.

The ship's computer generated the phrase over and over, working methodically through the known languages of Earth in its data stores. They swayed half in stasis as the words flowed over them. They were startled to alertness by the creature zipping up to the ceiling and banging on the speaker.

"Computer," asked Naqi-12, "what language was the last one you used?"

"Scots Gaelic. Spoken by a small percentage of residents of the British Isles on Earth."

"Computer, please translate into Scots Gaelic." Naqi-12 paused, taking a deep breath before continuing. "Please explain your presence on our vessel."

"We require transport." The Earth creature responded to the speaker's grill as the ship's computer translated in almost real time now.

"My name is Naqi-12, what may we call you?" Naqi-12 asked before adding. "You do not need to be where the voice comes out in order for us to hear you."

"You may call me Fenella." It floated back down to the floor, but kept its eyes on the speaker. "We must be taken."

"Taken?" Naqi-12 looked to Zee-47, who shrugged her upper fringe. "The smaller winged ones who released you from the crate have harmed us and taken over our ship."

"They wait to join me." Fenella moved back to the cargo bay door, touching the seam with its upper appendages.

Zee-47 pointed to a side monitor that still showed the outside of the ship. The small winged creatures were still out there, but now they clustered on the other side of the door as if they could sense their larger compatriot reaching out for them from inside the ship.

"Can you keep them from harming us or our ship?" Naqi-12 asked.

"I can," Fenella turned back to the speaker, its wings lifting its feet just off the ground as it nodded its head urgently. "Not to harm. Not to damage. It is vowed."

"Well, if it is vowed - what could go wrong?" Zee-47 mumbled under her breath.

"You will need to hold onto something when I open the door." Naqi-12 carefully avoided looking at Zee-47.

Fenella looked around the space before moving quickly to wrap its upper appendages around the vertical braces at the rear of the cargo bay.

Naqi-12 opened the cargo bay door again. The tiny creatures clung to the skin of the ship just outside. They clambered across one another, using their sharp claws to hold fast to the surface and not be pulled back out into open space.

Naqi-12 used the external cameras to verify that they were all safely back inside before she closed the door. As the air pressure was re-established, the air in the cargo bay was filled with the blur of tiny wings.

"We are grateful," said Fenella as they landed on and around it. "We must seal our pact and discuss our transport needs."

"And you vow no harm to us?" Naqi-12 had pulled up a running analysis full of text and symbols on a side screen. She gestured for Zee-47 to read what she had found.

"We agree not to harm or damage you or your vehicle. It is vowed."

"Thank you." Naqi-12 toggled off the microphone. "There, it is done."

"What?" Zee-47 asked, skimming screens as the flashed past. "How can you think we are safe?"

"These are the symbols and words from the containers. We have a number of chronicles documenting the rules that govern these creatures. A vow is inviolable to them, it cannot be broken. We are safe."

"You are certain?" Zee-47 turned to Naqi-12, entwining tentacles. "You are willing to risk our skin and ship based on this?"

"Yes." Naqi-12 waved her upper frill with joy. "Yes, this is our answer. Let us go meet our new passengers."

They checked the air balances before disengaging the hatch and moving through the brightly-lit corridors to the cargo bay. Up close, the creature called Fenella stood only half as tall as Zee-47 and Naqi-12. It approached slowly, the tiny creatures hovered just behind Fenella. They did not flash their fangs or brandish their claws.

"I am Naqi-12 and this is Zee-47. We own this vessel and are not accustomed to non-negotiated intrusion." The computer continued its job translating.

"Greetings. I am Fenella." It touched its upper appendages to each other and leaned its torso forward while dipping its head toward the floor. "We must be taken."

"Where must you be taken?" asked Zee-47, keeping her voice steady.

"Earth is no longer safe for us. We must be taken elsewhere. We can pay for our passage." Fenella gestured to the crates. "And I can heal the damage done to you." It used its wings to lift off and hover in front of Zee-47. Fenella's upper appendages glowed white as it brought them close to Zee-47's torso. As the glow illuminated the claw marks the raw edges smoothed and fused together.

"It is healed!" Zee-47 touched her torso where the marks had been, feeling along her skin with her longest tentacles. "Thank you."

"You should never have been damaged. My small friends can be fierce when seeking to protect me."

"Are there more like you in there?" Zee-47 pointed toward the crates. "Or are they full of currency?"

"There are three more like me. 5,000 more small folk. And a great amount of Fatum Aurum."

"We are not outfitted to be a passenger transport," Naqi-12 said, "but perhaps we can provide something temporary here in this space."

"And we will need to see this Fatum Aurum currency to judge its value on the intergalactic exchange," added Zee-47.

"Our currency must be used quickly once leaving our control, but if exchanged within an Earth day it will appear as valuable local currency."

"What happens after one Earth day?" asked Naqi-12.

"It is a short lived currency. You will want to have continued on your way quickly before that."

Naqi-12 and Zee-47 looked at each other and silently fluttered their frills in agreement.

"How do we seal a formal pact between us?" Zee-47 asked.

"First we shake hands." Fenella reached forward with one of its upper appendages, looking curiously now at Naqi-12 and Zee-47's upper tentacles. "Or in our case, touch appendages."

Naqi-12 and Zee-47 reached forward with their primary upper tentacle until all three touched.

"We would like a vow of no harm to us or our vessel. And a vow of payment for sustenance, ship fuel, and our services." Naqi-12 stated formally. "In return, we vow safe transport to agreed upon destinations and to provide sustenance."

"We require infrequent sustenance and have brought some supplies with us, for we knew not how long our travels would be. We agree with your terms. We declare you our good friends and neighbors. With our vows our pact is sealed."

Fenella's appendages glowed a bright blue where she touched Naqi-12 and Zee-47's tentacles, sending a strong, but not uncomfortable, tingle along their skins' surface.

"With our vows our pact is sealed." Naqi-12 and Zee-47 repeated.

With these words ringing through the cargo bay, the air began to shimmer. Fenella moved to the center of the space and began to spin. The creature's body glowed as it rose up, the small folk moving to surround it. Naqi-12 and Zee-47 watched with wide eyes as the metallic impersonal cargo bay transformed into a cheerful space dominated by green terrain and bright blossoms. Fenella landed lightly, reached for their tentacles, and led them in a dance through their new home as the small folk made music all around them.

D is for Diplomacy

Pete Aldin

A reminiscence of William Edward Duigan,
being a true and accurate account of the happenings near
Hawkesbury,
in the Colony of New South Wales,
upon the eighteenth day of January
in the year of our Lord 1856

Our poor, ailing milk-cow Lisbeth lay on her side in our high pad-dock, the cleared field that ringed the hilltop in the direct centre of our holding. Her "bed" was a wide and natural ledge in the hillside. All thirty-three of her sister animals had gathered at the lowest point of the field, calves and mothers sequestered against the fence behind the dam we'd dug to capture water from the stream on the other side of that fence. I'd been a mere boy during that digging, all of three years old, but eager to cart dirt, to help. This was back when our cattle had numbered but three, when both Da and Ma were naught but former convicts, struggling hard to make an honest living. Now, mere days after my fourteenth birthday, they were seen as respectable members of local society, a fact they treasured among their best accomplishments, along with raising a son destined to study the sciences.

On this day, the day that the old woman looked over our unwell beast, I was fourteen, broad-shouldered, and with a broad and curious mind that stood me in good stead to study those very sciences in future. I watched her keenly. She was dressed all in patches of cloth. Wool. Linen. Silk. Stitched together into blouse and skirts and gloves, covering all aspects of her skin except that creased and drooping face of hers. My parents did not know her name. To them, and to the population of farmers, traders, convicts and artisans throughout the Hawkesbury district along the Glendale River, she was known only as the old woman. (Though some called her *witch*, it must be said). Despite the fierce heat of this January late-morning, she had gathered her hair beneath a woollen bonnet. And she kept on muttering the same string of nonsense words as she worked: "Reveal thissen, small spear, if thee be 'ere within."

As she muttered her nonsense, she moved around and around Lisbeth with one gloved hand scratching at her own pointy chin, and the other feeling the animal: along her ribs, under her jaw, the length of her tail, udder, fly-ridden ears.

Once in a while, Lisbeth would let out a quiet and short-lived lowing at the old woman's ministrations, before lapsing again into silent misery. By way of contrast, the woman cooed and hummed in lively fashion as if she had pigeons and bees inside her all at once.

It was my mother who had invited her. Not my father. Whenever her back was turned, Da would mimic her squint-eyed face and bow his back and nudge me with an elbow, making me bite down on the laughter that threatened to spill from my mouth. By the time she had completed that circuit around the ailing animal, Da would be standing straight and respectful again as if he had never made sport of her. It seemed to me each time that he could have mocked her with impunity since she never so much as glanced our way. In point of fact, since the moment my Ma had pressed coin into the woman's hands and bade her precede the manfolk up the hill, the woman had not once acknowledged us.

Da's discourteous impersonations were doubtless to take his mind off the heat and the boredom. Despite his constant good-humour, he had never borne colonial summers well. He was not born to it as I was. Originating in County Cork, a vivid world of green mystery to me, six months by ship had brought him to the sunburned brown and greys of the Colonies, and each summer and autumn here served him with five months of misery. Marooned once his sentence was served, without money for a passage home, he found himself in love with another freed convict. A plot of land and grant of money from government allowed them to start their farm. And then came a child. Unlike his parents in so many ways. Born to love the heat and the washed-out colours. Me.

This was the subject of my thoughts as the woman commenced her thirteenth circuit around Lisbeth. Shaking myself from reverie, I drew breath to ask what on earth her odd behaviour was intended to achieve. My Da's hand applied a brief and warning pressure upon my arm. He gave me a small grimace and shake of his head by way of discouraging inquiry. I felt of course that my inquiry was warranted and justifiable. Yet I loved my Da, so just as the cow had lapsed back into silent misery, so did I (although I itched with impatience and boredom).

I should have had more compassion for the beast. As a young man, however, I was selfish. Just as my father was sensitive and patient.

So sensitive was he toward my situation that he began another interpretation of the woman hoping to provide a modicum of amusement. Once again, I forced back a snicker.

Then the old woman raised her voice.

"I'm aware o' thy antics," she said, her back fully to us. "Thou be makin' skit o' me."

Since she too had come to these lands as a convict, it had not surprised me that she be English. However, her words were flavoured by an accent and dialect I had not heard before.

Caught in his transgression, my father turned a chagrined face toward me, his mouth forming a wide O of surprise.

The woman continued, "Just as I'm aware o' t'fella behind thee both."

Da and I exchanged a frown and turned.

Sure enough, a man stood a few yards behind and downhill of us.

Trooper Enwright.

How he'd passed across the brown and brittle grass without alerting either of us to his presence was as much a mystery as the old woman's awareness of shenanigans happening behind her back. Enwright was known locally as a big bastard. (I do hope the reader will pardon my language). To be precise, Enwright was a tall man and wide. He carried a short sabre on one hip and a revolver on the other. The latter weapon was something of a novelty at the time and my attention was instantly drawn to it. Despite the rarity and cost of revolver bullets, the trooper had something of a reputation for using them liberally, sometimes upon wildlife and sometimes upon Natives.

"Good morning," Trooper Enwright said to my Da. Me, he ignored.

He took off his dark blue cap revealing greying hair so limp with sweat that the breeze could not shift it.

Peering past him and squinting against the sun, I made out his two horses near the copse of wattle trees on the other side of the creek. His tracker Gunung was distinguishable standing with them, a musket slung on his back as he watered the animals.

The tracker was a Native, though native to lands far south of Hawkesbury near the colony of Melbourne. Enwright, it was said, had Gunung "imported" from there, providing him with a tracker who bore no sympathy for the Blacks of *our* regions.

Through the morning glare, I also perceived three more shapes pressed into a crouch behind the horses. Natives, like Gunung. But also not like Gunung. I could not see the chains that held them, preventing their flight back across our property and into the forests but chains there would be. The thought of them shackled like convicts made me sick to my stomach.

"Top of this good morn to you too, Mr Enwright," Da responded. "You've walked a long way up this hill, sir. We could have come down to speak with you."

"No bother, Duigan. After six hours spent on a horse, a little walk has helped stretch my legs." His eyes shifted to the old woman. "Trouble with your animals?"

"Oh, just this one." Da took a small step sideways, blocking the trooper's view, discouraging further examination of either the cow or her arcane physician. "And how can I be of help to you, sir?"

Enwright leaned left, still interested in the woman, but he came to business smartly enough. "My tracker's horse has thrown a shoe. Probably the rider's fault and not the animal, though I can't work out how he caused it. Always buggering up something, these Blacks. No matter. I was told some years back you're a competent smith? I need a new shoe..."

Da rubbed at the stubble across his throat and scrunched his face in thought. "Well, sir. Hm. You see, it takes some time to fire up the forge. And this is fair hot weather to be smithing. I could send Will here into town for a farrier and a loan horse."

"Damn it, man," spat the Trooper, his cursing unmindful of either me or the woman uphill of us. His face was red with more than just the sun. "It'll take the boy days to get there and back. I want to be gone by tomorrow. I'll pay you fairly. Gunung will be walking the whole way, since the wretched savage caused this predicament. But the horse is my personal property and I'll not see her lamed wandering this godless wasteland when there's a perfectly capable smith who can see to her wellbeing."

Da was already making reassuring gestures long before Enwright completed his ranting. "Not to worry, not to worry. I shall get to it right now, sir. If you'll follow me back, we'll take a look at the damage done and see if we can resmelt that shoe."

He moved down the hill and Enwright followed. "And my own boots need some retacking, if your wife has time to see to that."

"Yes, sir."

"Also I'll need food for my tracker and me too," the trooper said. "I'll pay you."

"Of course, sir, of course, we'll find something in the larder for you. Something for those prisoners of yours too."

"No food for those bloody wretches! Bugger them!"

Enwright's swearing caused my Da to glance back toward me in embarrassment and I turned my face up toward a passing cloud, pretending I had not heard. When I looked back, they were several yards further on and neither man was talking.

"No food for his prisoners," I said and shook my head in disgust. I tried a little bad language of my own: "What a big bastard he truly is."

A tugging at my sleeve startled me and I swung around.

The woman.

I had forgotten her presence, if that can be believed. Her gaze rested, not upon my eyes as one would expect, but upon my chest. It was as if she could not raise that gaze any higher, or as if there were something inside me she could see.

In her youngish voice, the old woman said, "Elfshot."

Having never heard such a word before, and being unfamiliar with her accent, my mind made sense of her sounds by thinking she had asked me, "'Ave shot?"

"Er, no," I stammered. "No shot here. My Da's gun is down in the house." I wondered did she want us to put Lisbeth out of her misery.

She startled me again by striking me in the chest with the back of her hand, and none too lightly. I staggered, taking three or four steps to find my balance on the hillside.

"Not musket shot, fool lad," she said with mouth twisted up so that her stained and rotted teeth were visible. She pronounced her diagnosis more carefully this time. "Elf-shot. *Elf.*"

I frowned, not knowing what she meant. Elf seemed but one more strange word in the mouth of a woman who knew many.

"May be I can I fix it," she continued. One gnarl-knuckled thumb and forefinger ground together as she held them to my face. "Hast tha more brass tha can give?"

By way of reply, my frown deepened.

"Fagh!" she spat when it was clear I wasn't following her meaning. She brushed by me and waddled downhill, leaning on the polished gumtree branch she used for a cane. "Owt to be gained talkin' wi' fool lads. I'll tell ee Mam." She paused a moment to get her balance before raising her stick to the sky and proclaiming a loud string of completely unintelligible words. From the bottom of the slope, the two white-skinned men turned back to regard her curiously. Enwright made some joke about her, and climbed the fence laughing loudly.

My Da, I noted, did not laugh.

I returned to the relative cool of our homestead after an hour of chores about the farm, having eaten the rough lunch of biscuits and dried river fish my Ma had packed for me in the morning. Closing the door fast behind me to keep out windborne dust and heat and flies, I doffed my cloth cap and mopped my forehead with it. In the dimness within, and with my sight still white from the sun's glare, Ma was a soft blur at the table. From her movement, the scent of butter, and the soft smacking and squelching sounds, I could tell she was kneading dough. That seemed a fine activity to me for, being a young man, I was ever hungry, a bottomless pit for food of any kind, but especially bread.

Blinking in the gloom (Ma had only a single candle to work by and the shutters were drawn against the summer day) I made certain that the old woman was absent before venturing a question.

"What did she tell you?"

Ma sniffed. She said, "She has an answer to the problem of our cow."

"And it is?"

"None of your concern, now. Have you cleared the brushwood from the western fence line?"

"Yes, Mam. But..."

"And the fallen tree from upcreek?"

"Did that yesterday. The woman said to me something like *elf* and *shot*. She speaks like a magpie, so I've no idea what she meant."

"Now, now, young rascal. I'll not have you speaking of her like that." The words were stern, but the tone was light.

I grinned, happy to get away with the insult. "Well, then, did you understand her?"

Another sniff. Another smacking of dough on board—I could see it this time, my vision adjusting. Eventually she said, "I did."

My impatience was back, but because of my great affection for my Ma, I stowed it away deep and asked as lightly as I could, "Can you please tell *me*, then?"

"I've told your Da and that's all that matters. Now, clean those hands and you can help me here."

I made no move toward the wash basin, remaining with my back against the door. It was warmed with the sunshine from the other side. "And what did Da say?"

"Never you mind. Wash your hands."

I took three steps toward the wash basin, then stopped. Those hands that so concerned her I rested on the back of a chair. I tried again, "What is elfshot?"

This time the dough was flung to the board with a loud thud. "You've nothing better to do than pester me with this?"

I grinned again. "Nope."

Her scowl melted as suddenly as it had arrived. "Rascal," she whispered and plunged her fingers into the blob of dough, busying herself. "Very well. I suppose you *should* know about such things, being of Irish blood after all. Let's only hope your mind is more open on the subject than your dear father's. It seems our woman believes that the cow was hurt by... by the little folk."

It was my mother's turn to say things I couldn't understand. *"Little* people? Who are they?"

She sighed, wiped her fingers on her apron and sat upon a stool. "Pour me a water will you?" When I had done, and passed it to her, she said, "There's a good lad. Well, then. Your father and I grew up in Ireland where he was an educated man and I an educated woman. Not that this made us any richer with the English being the way they are. Poverty and restriction forced us both into acts that we regretted in more ways than just the punishment. Any way. You know the story of our deportation here. What you don't know is much of the lore of our homeland. Both of our families produced good Catholics, as I hope we have produced in you, son."

She fixed me with a stern look until I said something pious that I don't remember now.

Satisfied she went on. "But whereas his family rejected all of the old ways and the old stories out of hand, mine did not. Many a time, my *Maimeó*, my grandmother, would regale me with tales of old, and with ancient remedies for all sorts of ills. A frequent subject of our conversations were the little people. I was fascinated by them. In the old days before Christianity came, you see, before the British came too, our people believed they lived side by side with another people."

"Like we do here with the Blacks," I chimed in.

She cocked her head and rubbed dough on her chin as she thought about that. "Similar. But not the same. No, actually, not the same at all. Those poor souls."

Ma kept a small nativity figurine on the mantle. She faced briefly toward the Holy Family while crossing herself. I wasn't sure if she did it with the Enwright's wretched captives in mind or because there was something she feared that had to do with the story she was telling me. "The little folk I'm telling you of are the ones we also called fae. The English in some parts—like where *she* hails from—called them ælfe. Elves."

She sighed and drank from her cup, wiped at her mouth. Keeping my silence, I waited until she was ready. There was a gravity about her mood that fascinated me as much as the subject matter.

"The fae, the elves, are not something I particularly believe in. I mean, I did at one time. As a child. But I grew out of that belief. And upon my confirmation, well, I renounced such things. Much to my parents' relief, and my *Maimeó*'s irritation. And fae were something I gave not a thought to when I called on the old woman. But when I saw the state of young Lisbeth, well, my grandmother had uncanny ways for curing everything from a bad cough to a chicken's inability to lay. Except for that dreadful, *dreadful* accent she has, our old woman reminds me very much of my *Maimeó*. And it's her belief that the elves, the little folk, are behind Lisbeth's ills."

I scratched at my cheek a while as Ma emptied her cup in small sips. When she set it by the bread board, I said, "What do they look like?"

She stood with a little groan as she stretched her back then flexed her hands. "As their name suggests, they're little and they're folk." She smiled and picked up the dough. "So I'm told."

"But—"

"I'll tell you what, my son. The one with all the answers is the one who truly believes in the creatures. Why don't you go take *her* a cup of water and see if she'll fill that fine young mind of yours with more knowledge?"

I frowned a moment, thinking she wanted me to go all the way to the river, then along the local valley, past the township and finally to the hut the old woman lived in. Then it made sense to me. "Oh, she's still on our farm? Why?"

Ma shrugged and slammed the dough down on the board. "Looking for herbs she thinks might give our Lisbeth a fighting chance at recovery. Take her an apple too. Make her more inclined to answer you."

I glanced at the triangle of apples piled beside the Holy Family on the mantlepiece. Reluctantly I took one. Our last three apples for the season and I'd been hoping that Ma would bake them one of these nights. Taking one meant dividing two between three people: not the kind of mathematical problem I enjoyed solving.

Trudging to the door, I paused with a hand on the knob as my Ma spoke one more time.

"Maybe take that back to her too. That's what she says she pulled from within Lisbeth's leg." I followed her outstretched arm to the rocking chair by the door. A small rock sat in the middle of the cushion. I picked it up with the hand that held no apple, opened the door and ducked outside, in my haste slamming the door and provoking a cry of annoyance from Ma.

"Sorry!" I called.

I stepped from the veranda into full sunlight. Flies swarmed me but accustomed to them, I let them roam my face and buzz about my ears.

To my left and two hundred yards away, wattle trees and a few young gums marked the line of the creek. The prisoners were visible there, slumped together in the shade. Near them, Gunung had a small campfire going and I think he had a billy on, making tea.

To my left and from the other side of our small barn where Da had his smithy, there came the clank and bang of iron on iron.

A kookaburra cackled from somewhere along the creek.

Up on the hill, Lisbeth was vaguely distinguishable as a brown blotch of different hue to the other browns around her.

The woman was not in sight, but I would find her. By the angle of the sun, the time was around one o'clock, which allowed me plenty of daylight in which to search for her. I had forgotten a mug from inside, but figured she could drink direct from the creek if she was thirsty. Just like the unfortunate Blacks had done. She was getting one of my apples, and she'd already cheated (or so I believed) my Ma out of one or more coins.

I held the stone she had brought my Ma up close to my face. It was half the length of my thumb, sparkling with tiny dots scattered throughout, perfectly symmetrical, sharply pointed and smoothly polished. I grunted in surprise as I recognised the shape from English story books.

Very strange, I thought.

It resembled strongly an arrow head.

I searched inside all the folds of land in our property, the dales and the scattered copses of trees and the struggling apple orchard. I even looked around the backside of that hill and out into the bush we hadn't cleared. No sign of the old woman.

None, that is, until I returned back around the hill and toward the creek. I found her squatting there in imitation of Gunung. The captives seemed to pay her no attention, their focus uniformly upon the dirt and twigs before them. When I saw her, I stopped in amazement, wondering how she could have evaded me on such open, sparsely-vegetated land and circled back to the wattle copse. And why on earth was she consorting with Enwright's Tracker? Better to keep her distance from anything that belonged to Enwright.

I drew nearer around the hill and saw that she had a pot she must have borrowed from Ma on the fire going on the fire. Gunung's billy was sitting in the dirt and he was sipping from a tin mug, watching her. Approaching the fence and I could hear that the Tracker was talking.

"Yeah, that's good, missus," he said as I reached the other side of the creek from them. "My mob down south, they use that stuff too, eh."

The woman nodded and stirred and said nothing in reply. Gunung chattered on about the medicinal properties of different bush plants while I navigated my way across the fence and down one creek bank, across the sluggish and shallow flow of water, and up the other side. I smelled unpleasantness, a sour stench like wet clothing left sitting too long.

When he noticed me, Gunung fell silent and dipped his head, concentrating on his tea.

I said, "Mr. Gunung, no need to stop talking on my account."

"Allgood, mister," he returned, his eyes downcast like those of the captives. "I been talkin' too much anyhow."

"My Ma said to bring you this," I said and offered the old woman the apple. Whatever she was brewing smelled so much the worse for being nearer to it, though the breeze blew it and the smoke toward the captives. The concoction looked like a broth containing leaves of some sort.

She took the apple and inspected it with a wry smile forming. "Thirty-one year ago, I were sent here for thievin' such as this. Now thee be givin' it me. Ee, but life's a funny thing."

Surprising me yet again, she tossed it to Gunung. The tracker, while appearing not pay no attention, snatched it deftly from the air.

"Quarter that," she told him. "Share it wi' thy kinfolk."

Gunung pulled his short-bladed knife from a sheath on his belt and set about complying.

I took opportunity to sneak a glance toward his "kinfolk" as she had called them: two skinny men and one skinny woman, all completely naked but for the hobbling shackles on their ankles. Immediately embarrassed and ashamed I snatched my gaze away. Ma would not approve of me seeing any woman exposed.

But though I made my eyes busy inspecting nearby blooms of wattle so starkly yellow against this sun-washed landscape, the impression of all three captives remained clear upon my mind. The contrast of deep brown flesh against the rust-brown and dirty grey of their shackles. Their downcast eyes though large and sad, it must be said, so very beautiful with long thick eyelashes. Softly featured faces and kind. One man, I had noticed, had bled from a forehead wound and it was now dried and attracting flies.

"What's that stuff?" I asked, trying to distract myself from their plight.

The old woman grunted and picked up her stick. She used it to lever herself upright, waving off my offer of assistance. "Grab thee that branch there and take t'pot from t'fire."

As I moved to obey her, she shuffled close to Gunung. She spoke to him then, in laboured strains of what *I* thought of as normal English. "These three prisoners might not speak your family's language, son. But they share many things in common with you. From far south of here, you might be. They are yet your people. And you are strong, son. They need you." She startled him with a single and gentle stroke to his beardless cheek by the back of her hand. When he stared up at her frankly, breaking the taboos that many of the Natives shared about locking gazes, she said sternly, "And you do not need white men."

She had me follow her up that hill once more. The pot was heavy; my arms ached with its weight and with the awkward way I had to hold the branch under its handle. It reeked worse the longer I carried it. I had thought it broth, but it had thickened now like porridge. Like paste.

When finally I was able to put it down close to Lisbeth but far enough she would not accidently kick it, I gasped with relief and swung my arms about then massaged my forearms.

The old woman slipped off her gloves, revealing pale and much-scarred skin loose over the bones within it. She drew her wooden stirring spoon from a fold in her clothing, dipped it in the potion, sniffed it, touched it to her lips, grimaced. "Too hot yet."

The spoon dropped into the pot and the woman eased herself down on the lip of Lisbeth's resting shelf.

While I still manoeuvred my joints and muscles to ease their pain, I checked on Lisbeth, going around to her face. She was still on her side. One eye turned up to me; a tear leaked from it. Her ribs rose and fell with a breath.

"Close enough to death, lad," called the old woman. "Needs to drink but can't bring hersen to walk to t'dam."

"So you said she was elfshot."

"Aye."

"Well... I mean..."

She shushed me then, slashing her walking stick at me through the air. I fell silent. Her head twisted toward the top of the hill and then her body followed as much as age would allow it. A few seconds later, she whispered, "Thou hear it?"

I frowned, concentrating. Did she mean the hiss of wind of grass, the buzz of the passing bee, the faint birdsong from down in the wattles?

"Not those things," she hissed. Her seeming knowledge of my thoughts caused me to flinch. She stabbed the stick toward a point forty feet up the slope. "*That.*"

But I heard nothing. Nothing save the things I have already mentioned here.

"Lad, at thy age, thou should still have the ear."

"For *what*?" I asked in a quiet voice, for though I could not hear what she did, I was convinced by her manner there was something indeed to be heard.

"There," she said and pointed the stick again. "That little knoll wi t'slightly greener grass."

"What about it?"

"It's where they live. It's where they sing."

I gawped. "The..." I dropped my own voice to a whisper. "The little folk?"

"Aye."

I strained my eyes, seeing nothing but the *knoll* as she had called it, a lump of soil and grass, like the dozen or more other lumps of soil and grass across the face of this hill. Nor did I hear what she heard.

"What are they singing?" I asked.

She faced forwards, but listened a while longer. "They're askin' why they were brought here so far from their home. And when finally they found a quiet place, why did 'you' follow and disturb them."

"Who's 'you'? Who followed them?"

"Thee, fool lad. Thy family."

"Oh. They sang that? They sing *English*?"

She shook her head. "Gaelic."

"You speak Gaelic?"

"I *understand* it."

"Well, what do they mean we followed them and disturbed them?

"Fagh! I can't ask them, lad. If I give sign that I see or hear them, they'll tell me nowt and likely shut their mouths. Which means thou should stop starin' at them too."

"Can you *see* them?"

"No."

"Oh. But you hear them."

"Thy curiosity gives me hope for thee. Never lose it, lad." She stretched out to pluck at grass, sniff it and crush it between her wrinkled fingers, allowing the breeze to carry away the remains. "Here be my best guesses on the matter. I'm guessin' they got here early in the piece. Perhaps that god-be-damned first fleet, perhaps later. They're very cross at bein' brought here. But they found a nice quiet place to settle out here until thee and thine came along. Until thy croft expanded and thy cows procreated and wandered up this hill and—" Here she poked her stick at a dried cow pat "—and shat liberally upon the very landscape where the elves like to play." She paused to knock dung from her stick.

"Play? Are they children then?" I came over to crouch beside her.

"Smartest question thee asked thus far." She reached up and patted my hand with some warmth. But clarify, she did not.

I thought I would try my hand at coarse language again. "How the hell did they get here though?"

Rather than reprimanding me for the swearing, she shrugged. "That I'd love to ken, lad," she replied. "Surely, I would. Perhaps they were investigatin' a ship that stopped at an Irish port. Perhaps they became interested in a rum keg, drank a little and slept t'journey."

We sat a while, her cocking an ear uphill, me trying in vain to hear it too. Eventually, she shook herself and gestured to the pot.

Reading her intention, I roused myself and went to lift the spoon. I carried it to her bearing a glob of the paste.

"Thee won't try it?" she asked.

I stared back aghast, uncertain as to how to decline without causing offence.

She cackled and took the spoon, stuck her tongue into the middle of the paste. "Fine, fine." She handed it back while she got herself upright. Then she dipped spoon into pot and withdrew a larger portion of the muck therein. "Carry t'pot here, lad."

I followed her to Lisbeth's hindquarters.

She tipped the muck onto a wound I couldn't see. In an official tone, she began thus: "Whether it were the ēse's pain or the shot of the ælfe or a wounding by hægtessan, then now, dear beast, I will help thee." As she spread it around the wounded area, stroking Lisbeth's belly with her free hand, she intoned, "This for thee as remedy for the pain of ēse." The spoon dipped again to the kettle and she spread more brew onto Lisbeth's thigh in an even larger circle. The cow did not complain or startle. "This for thee as remedy for the shot of ælfe." A final time, the spoon returned to the pot and she repeated her action, saying, "This for thee as remedy for the wounding by hægtessan." She indicated for me put down the kettle and she dropped the spoon into it. Her clean hand moved to Lisbeth's head to pet her gently. "This will help thee. Run thou around this mountain top. Run around the fields. Move free. Live long. Be healthy. May the Lord help you."

The rite complete, the old woman stooped to wipe the leftover paste from her fingers. "Thou and thine be lucky the elves wanted only to hurt thy cow and not kill her outright. However, best thou appease the little sods. Get thee some cream or buttermilk and leave it up by t'mound there." She indicated the knoll. "All will be well by morn, lad. Mark my words." Her clean hand thumped me none to gently in the gut. "And make sure thou never ever stop listenin'."

With that, she departed our hill and our property, leaving me staring after her with a heavy, stinking kettle to clean and so very many questions in my mind.

My parents allowed me to sleep outside that night with the cow.

I wanted to observe Lisbeth's recovery, if recovery there would be. And also, it must be admitted, I wanted to see if the night's quiet would break with snatches of the little folk's song. Perhaps they would make an appearance at the dish of buttermilk I'd left by the knoll.

The lump of earth the old woman had identified as their home was three feet high and not much broader. Up close, there was no sign of its habitation by tiny people nor by non-arcane animals like wombats.

Just a heap of dirt. And for the moment, the buttermilk was serving no one besides the local population of flies and black ants.

There was always the very good chance, I thought, that the old woman was a trickster, offering falsehoods and false hopes in exchange for an apple and a pair of shillings.

As the sun set, Enwright sat by Gunung's fire. To my disgust—and my Ma's, I am certain—he drank steadily from a brown bottle he had pulled from his saddle bags, singing bawdy ditties. His boots were off and occasionally he would take one up to inspect the sole as if he didn't trust my mother's working. Meanwhile, his captives huddled together. Gunung was nowhere to be seen, but Enwright seemed untroubled by this; I guessed the man was collecting local food. The Natives always seemed to find things to eat where we white fellas saw nothing but trees and grasses.

With my Da's help, I set two small campfires into the hillside. Though the night was warm, there'd be cooler hours before dawn. Also there were snakes to keep away, though they rarely venture into the open nor up hills. After Da brought me supper, he topped up the buttermilk—to humour my Ma and me—then sat a while, entertaining me with tales of Enwright's fussiness over the horse's shoe and with news of the wider world the Trooper had mentioned. Eventually, Da retired for the night. I cracked sticks from the pile of kindling, or used them to tap rhythms against the water pot I'd kept in case the campfires spread to the grass. I hummed hymns I learned in Mass and songs of Ireland my Ma had taught me. A huge owl startled me when it flapped past in the dark. I lay on my back and counted stars. I fell asleep.

Sound woke me. An eerie intonation, carried by several voices. Upon the air I tasted Lisbeth's animal-stink and the smoke from my campfires; the irregular surface of the hillside poked my spine and ribs in discomforting ways. Blinking gummy eyes, I sat up seeking the source of that compelling music.

The fae? I wondered. The elves?

But, no. The chanting came from the creek, from the deep shadow beneath the wattles.

The captives were singing.

I had not heard Natives sing before. It was, I must report, mesmerising. I confess that I could well have sat there the rest of that night listening to it. However, mere moments after it had awoken me, their vocalising was cut off sharply by a shout from Enwright. His drunken, uncouth mutterings followed for several seconds before the wattle grove lapsed again into silence.

And that was when I heard the other sound. The kind of bass-toned fluttering I might make by running a stick along fence palings. Bardi moths made such noise, whenever those huge insects came into our house attracted by light.

I turned my head ever so slightly toward the fire and my gaze caught upon Lisbeth's great eyes staring back at me. She was standing. She seemed calm. In fact, she seemed *well*. But she was not the source of that fluttering sound.

What I saw next—I will never know: was it dream, was it a trick of poor light and sleepy eyes, or did I see what my mind and memory still insist I saw?

The furiously beating wings did not belong to moths.

The beings hovered in a cluster right between the campfires. There were seven of them and their tiny faces were set on the wattle grove below us. Each had a body no longer than any of my fingers. And they wore clothing of sorts, its design reminiscent of nothing I had seen before or have seen since. I blinked my eyes to focus better, squinting: yes, they appeared as enraptured by the recent Native music as I had been. I wonder now: were they hoping for its return?

And in the humming of their wings, I now heard more music, chords. And beneath it, ever so faintly, I heard singing. Their mouths moved in unison.

One of them (a female) noticed me noticing them. She flew immediately out from among her kin, a scowl defiling the innocence formerly upon her features. She said a single word I didn't know, and flew directly into my face to strike me on the nose.

I awoke later.

Dawn was a smudge in the east. One of my fires had burned out and the other was coals. I added kindling, then logs, wrapped my blanket about my shoulders and sat beside it while the fire caught.

Lisbeth was gone. A moment after I realised this, I saw her down among her herd by the fence. This made me smile.

Remembering, I searched the air around me for signs of the little folk and strained my hearing for the sound of wings. Using a stick from the fire as a torch, I went up to check the mound the woman said was theirs. It appeared as quiet and unremarkable as it had earlier. The dish of buttermilk was empty, but other creatures might have lapped that up. My only proof of the elves' existence in that moment was one shaky memory, the healing of our cow and the sharp stone the old woman had given my Ma.

More than a little despondent, I returned to the campfire and lay by it, returning to a sleep troubled with dreams.

In the morning, Trooper Enwright was dead.

He lay flat on his back, head on his saddlebag, blanket pulled up to his nose.

His horses, his man and his captives were gone. And never were they seen again.

Stories persist from this event, even today. Perhaps you, Dear Reader, have heard them?

Some believe that Gunung rebelled and murdered his master in his sleep, hit him with a rock, or stabbed him in the heart. Then he followed the other Blacks into the night, carrying away the white man's goods. Those who believe this take no stock in the facts: his horses and their saddles were taken, but the rest of his goods remained, including his revolver; no wound was found on Enwright's head, no stab wound on his body and there was no indication around his neck of stranglement.

"Then," others claim, "he was smothered." And yet the ground around him was undisturbed as would be expected in a struggle, since no man would accept suffocation without a fight.

Others say that Gunung poisoned Enwright's tea. But that belies the common knowledge that Enwright (fearful of such treatment from the Blacks he so despised) always had his Tracker drink from the same billy a full half hour before he would touch it himself.

Of course these stories persist. Because it is only now that I inform the world of the truth, of what I found on (or rather *in*) the Trooper's body.

Under pretence of checking him for snake bite, I did what I had seen the old woman do with Lisbeth: I ran my hands along the exposed areas of the man's skin. Until my hand caught upon a lump, so small I almost missed it. Just below the collar of his shirt and along the triangular muscle of his shoulder, something inorganic and tiny protruded from the flesh. Between my fingernails, I seized it. Tugging brought it loose. I turned it over in my hand. Not much larger than a splinter someone might get by bumping against a fence: but this was stone. The size of the moon on my smallest finger's nail.

And perfectly shaped.

Like an arrow head.

E is for Elfshot

Steve Bornstein

"Storyteller! What a surprise, how nice! What can I do for you?"

"I think you have that the wrong way around. I have a tale for you, a short one but one I think you'll find enlightening. May I join you?"

"Of course, of course! Please, this way."

Taeden drew his wool cloak tighter around himself, trying to shrink into it to hide from the people in the street. He wouldn't have come here to Bradon if Valkanyr hadn't insisted on it. After all these years he still felt awkward in this skin, this human body. He hated being around other, real humans, sure that at any moment someone would see him for what he truly was.

"Nobody cares," the avatar walking next to him said dryly. "You're just another human to them, as I am."

Valkanyr's avatar did look like a perfectly ordinary human, it was true. No fancy clothes or beautiful features to stand out, just brown hair and eyes and mildly pink skin, dressed in a drab shirt, breeches, boots and a cloak. Taeden supposed he and the avatar might even be mistaken for father and son.

But Taeden could feel the power radiating from the dragon's avatar like heat from a furnace. How dead to mana all these humans must be to not sense it. He was still unsure if the dragon somehow actually inhabited the construct or was simply directing it from afar.

"I don't care," he muttered, warily eyeing a group of children running past. They kicked a crude ball between them as they fussed their way down the cobblestone street. "They feel so empty inside. I feel like they would want to eat me."

Valkanyr barked a laugh. "Is that so! If it's being eaten you're worried about then worry about who we're going to see, not any of these cattle."

Taeden snapped his head back to glare at Valkanyr. "What?" he cried. "You said he'd get me home!"

The avatar didn't even blink at the outburst but simply strolled along with the same calm smug smile it always wore. In that respect it resembled Valkanyr-the-dragon very much. "Oh, he will, never you doubt that." It slowed in front of a shop and nodded, and Taeden turned to look.

"Curios" the sign over the door read, the letters curling and moving in glittering silver. Taeden could see the tiny bit of magic that made the letters stand out from the wood like that. Underneath the shop's name "Bharidh Ghalaigh" was written in Sitir, the language of the Kin.

He turned to Valkanyr. The avatar was looking at something through the shop's window, craning its neck as if to look deeper inside. "We're going to see a Kin?" Taeden liked this idea less and less. Magically powerful and arrogant about it, none of his few interactions with Kin had gone very well.

"Mmmh," was all the avatar said before pulling open the shop's door and ushering Taeden inside.

The shop was cramped but clean and organized. Shelves were crowded with jars, books, bits of stone and crystal and other materials valuable for their magical uses. The shelves themselves were crowded together too, separated only by narrow walkways. Taeden followed Valkanyr down an aisle to the shop's counter, half-hiding behind the avatar. The store was quiet except for the sound of their boots on the stone tile. Was the shopkeeper out? Taeden didn't like this; it felt too much like an ambush.

Valkanyr simply stopped at the counter and waited. Taeden glanced around and paused, about to ask the avatar what it was up to when a tall Kin dressed in a long ornate mage's robe emerged from the darkened doorway behind the counter, glaring angrily at Valkanyr with piercing cerulean eyes. He was beautiful by almost any standard, tall, almost willowy, with perfect skin, long platinum hair and an aquiline nose.

He and Valkanyr locked gazes for a heartbeat before the Kin sighed in something between aggravation and resignation. He looked away at the front of the shop and flipped his hand in the air, curling his fingers. Taeden could feel the shopkeeper draw mana from the manastream and spin the energy, shaping it to his will before casting it at the door and window. He looked to follow the spell and saw it settle there like a wall. Some sort of shield, perhaps?

"What?" the shopkeeper deadpanned, looking back at the avatar.

"How rude," Valkanyr replied cheerily. "Do you greet all your customers like that?"

"I scarcely think you're here to purchase something," the Kin replied. Taeden felt a little relief that the angry shopkeeper hadn't noticed him yet—he didn't like the way this felt. If it wasn't for Valkanyr's promise to get him home, he'd have already slipped out of the shop.

"Mmmh," the avatar said. "No, I'm not. I'm here to put you to task. You've a mess to clean up."

The shopkeeper snorted. "I've not made a mess, as you so gently put it, in quite some time, wyrm."

Taeden's heart skipped a beat, sure the insult would spark violence, but if the avatar was offended by the term it didn't show it. Who was this Kin to be so casual with what he obviously knew was a dragon?

Valkanyr took hold of Taeden's elbow and pulled him around to the counter to face the Kin. "True. You made this mess quite a while ago."

When the shopkeeper turned his blue eyes on him Taeden's unease went from vague to acute. Where Valkanyr's avatar felt powerful this Kin was altogether something else. Where Valkanyr felt like the potential to wield power, the Kin before him *was* power. If the dragon could spin up a fireball then this Kin was a fireball wrapped in a gold-threaded mage's robe, a towering presence in the manastream that didn't at all match the person standing on the other side of the shop's counter.

Taeden's breath caught as the Kin leaned over the counter to sniff at him like a hound after a chunk of meat. The Kin narrowed his eyes at the avatar and growled. "What is this?"

What, Taeden thought. *Not who.* He tried to shrink away from the counter but Valkanyr held him fast. In one smooth motion the avatar reached over and pulled Taeden's cloak from his shoulders, casting it to the floor in a heap.

Taeden cringed as he felt his gossamer wings unfold and reach for the light, spreading out in a delicate web of golden threads. They cast a soft warm glow like the morning sun rising over his shoulders.

"Congratulations, Alcreagh," Valkanyr lilted at the Kin. "You created fae."

Alcreagh's eyes shot wide and he took a step back, hissing like a cat.

Taeden squeezed his eyes shut and pulled harder at Valkanyr's implacable grip. He didn't know what Alcreagh really was, but he definitely wasn't Kin. "This is wrong this is wrong this is wrong," he whined.

"Drayshit," Alcreagh spat. Even through his panic, Taeden could hear how the not-Kin's growling voice was suddenly different, with a strange echo to it like he was speaking inside a much larger, emptier room. "You think I wouldn't know if I'd made a fairy?"

The change in Alcreagh's timbre fed Taeden's rising panic, fueling it. He had to get out of here. Now. "Please let me go please please please..."

"And yet clearly you don't," Valkanyr said, thoroughly unruffled at Alcreagh's continuing outburst and Taeden's whimpering. "You channeled so deeply into the manastream during your attack on Baydryn's keep that it corrupted her portal and dumped out Taeden here."

Getting home wasn't important anymore. Surviving was. Taeden wriggled and yanked as hard as he could, trying to flee, but Valkanyr's grip held him fast. "I don't want to be here anymore I don't want-"

"Silence." Alcreagh's word was calm in Taeden's ears but thundered inside his head. It stabbed into the core of Taeden's mind and grabbed it in a fist, cutting off his voice like a waterfall over a candle.

The fairy opened his eyes in shock, his mouth caught agape in mid-babble. Where the tall Kin once stood was now some nightmarish creature, a head taller than before and much more muscular. Glowing coals had replaced cool blue eyes, fine platinum hair was now a mid-night blue mane, and alabaster skin had become a black hide stretched tight over muscle and sinew, gleaming oily in the light of Taeden's wings. Glittering black claws gripped the edge of the shop's counter as what was once Alcreagh snarled with a mouth full of razorteeth.

"Taeden," Valkanyr purred, sweeping his free hand at the creature. "I present to you the Beast of Navarr, the Slayer of Dragons. The Scourge."

The Scourge? Here, right in front of him? The monster who had terrorized the entire continent for years, was now masquerading as a simple Kin shopkeep? Taeden's head swam and knees weakened. If it wasn't for Valkanyr's grip on his arm, he'd have slumped to the floor.

He could barely breathe. The Scourge's presence was overpowering now, a vast connection directly into the manastream that had been Taeden's home until it had spat him out into this corporeal form. He couldn't imagine how the creature had hidden all this earlier.

He suddenly wondered if this actually was Valkanyr's plan after all, to have the Scourge eat him to send him home.

The Scourge stared at Taeden for a long moment, long enough for Taeden to think the idea even more likely, before those baleful red eyes swiveled to the dragon's avatar.

"Now that you've had your grand moment," the Scourge rumbled, lip curled, "what would you have me do with it?"

Gobble him up, Taeden expected the avatar to say.

"Him," the avatar said, a tinge of exasperation leaking into his usually confident tone. "Return him to Baydryn's portal and send him home."

Taeden let out the breath he hadn't realized he'd been holding.

The Scourge folded his arms, long talons tucking themselves against his broad black chest. "Baydryn would much prefer a visit from you than I," he said, eyebrow quirked.

Valkanyr snorted. "I'm sure she would," the avatar said, "but you have much more to gain from this quest than I."

"And what would that be?"

Valkanyr's smile widened slightly. "I'd rather not ruin the surprise for you." The Scourge dipped his chin slightly and the avatar continued with a quiet chuckle. "Honestly, Alcreagh. If I still bore you ill will after all this time, do you think I'd go through this sort of charade?"

Taeden's panic finally began to ease and his thoughts clear. Alcreagh was a Kin name; it meant "Windspinner" in their Sitir language. So that hadn't been just a disguise earlier? The Scourge actually was Kin? The Kin mostly kept to themselves in the mountains and forests they called the Homelands, insular enough that they had maintained their neutrality even during the Scourge's war that had swept the rest of Navarr. Was he suddenly privy to some kind of Kin/dragon conspiracy? And what sense did that make when the Scourge's main target had been the dragons themselves?

"If it amused you, yes," Alcreagh muttered, and surprised Taeden with a chuckle of his own. It rolled like distant thunder.

"Fair enough."

"Taeden, is it?"

Taeden blinked and looked up at Alcreagh. Even now that the situation had calmed and furies quieted, Alcreagh was still the Scourge. He could probably raze the whole city of Bradon without much effort but here he was chatting in a quiet magic curio shop. It didn't seem real. "Ah, uhm, y-yes?" he said, then added, "Ser?"

Alcreagh's lips curled in a half-smile at the honorific, showing off a sharp fang. "Be at ease, boy, nobody's dying today." He looked at Taeden for a long moment, tipping his head to one side and then the other, then turned back to Valkanyr with a resigned sigh. "Very well then. I'll see the fairy home."

"Without killing Baydryn," the avatar said, raising a finger for emphasis. Alcreagh's mouth twisted in distaste and Valkanyr continued. "I don't care. You will not use this as an excuse to settle old scores. I don't have to remind you what will happen if a dragon suddenly shows up dead with a hole punched through her chest."

"You'd know about that, wouldn't you?" Alcreagh rumbled coolly, and Taeden was shocked to see the smile finally sour on Valkanyr's face. He wasn't sure the dragon or his avatar could frown at all, but there it was.

"Into the back, boy." Alcreagh waved Taeden behind the counter and gestured back through the doorway he had emerged from. "Your first chore is to find me a bucket so I can spin some *Change*. I can't go out in public like this. You," he said, gesturing at the avatar and then at the door, "find yourself out. I'll let you know when the deed's done."

Valkanyr's smile returned and he gave Taeden a brief bow. "We part ways here, lad. I leave you in the best hands I know. Other than my own, of course."

Alcreagh snorted.

Taeden put on the bravest smile he could for the avatar, but he could feel his mouth quiver and tremble at the edges. He was feeling more dazed than brave, but the dragon had gotten him this far. Surely he wouldn't have gone through all this just to doom the fairy. He had to believe this would work out. It was all he had left.

It only took a day for Alcreagh to make the necessary arrangements. Once he'd spun *Change* and returned to his more normal appearance, the Kin had closed his shop and mobilized the neighborhood runners to gather supplies, leaving Taeden alone in the shop's quarters.

Alcreagh lived comfortably, by himself if Taeden was to guess. Kin were given to displays of extravagance but Alcreagh's home was much more restrained than he'd expected. For a monster who had destroyed and pillaged for years, Alcreagh's home was remarkably free of the spoils of victory. Taeden felt a little guilty at his disappointment.

They rode off before sunrise the next morning. Bradon stood on the edge of the Barrens, Navarr's great central desert. Taeden remembered stumbling across the wastes after he'd emerged from Baydryn's portal, wandering for days before a passing caravan of traders had rescued him and taken him to civilization, dropping him at the trading nexus of Asmara. He'd managed to live there among the street urchins, trying to figure out the rules of this world and how he might return home, before another of Valkanyr's avatars had found him. There were some who could sense he wasn't a normal boy and seemed far too interested in him for his comfort but he'd always managed to evade them until Valkanyr had caught him unawares. Luckily the dragon's intent wasn't malign.

Alcreagh had kept to himself after Valkanyr left, treating Taeden like a package to be delivered. He only spoke to Taeden to give him orders; sit there and wait, eat, sleep, help him pack the drays, leave. He waited to see if Alcreagh would warm up to him once they got out into the Barrens by themselves, but after several hours of swaying in the saddle of his dray to the sounds of rubble crunching underfoot and watching Alcreagh sitting ramrod-straight on his dray up ahead, it was clear he'd have to take the initiative.

"So... You're the Scourge, then?" Taeden closed his eyes and cringed. He'd never quite figured out all the social rules of speaking here, but he knew enough to hear how awkward that sounded.

Alcreagh tilted his head slightly without turning around to face Taeden, as if listening for something more. "You've questions," he said quietly, his smooth Kin voice free from the harsh growling of his monstrous form. "Ask them."

Taeden bit his lip. "I'm, ah, not sure where to begin."

"Pick one."

Taeden didn't know how many days this trip would take, but judging by the mountains in the distance he assumed it would be more than an overnight journey. He didn't want to offend Alcreagh and risk another outburst like at the shop but he didn't want to pass the trip in silence either. The fairy took a breath to muster his courage. "Are you afraid of me?"

Alcreagh snorted loudly. "Whatever gave you that idea?"

"The way you reacted when you saw my wings."

Alcreagh grunted. "Not my finest moment, no." He paused. "For as long as mana has been known, there've been those who want more than the sips of power we can take from the manastream. And even though mana and its use is a fact of life, so little is known about where it comes from. Nobody can breach the stream's barrier, and trying to draw too much from it can have disastrous consequences. We know of the manastream, but we do not *know* the manastream. However, a manifested fairy can be used as a kind of conduit to draw almost unlimited power from it," he said, reaching up into the air and closing his fist. He turned and looked back over his shoulder to consider Taeden with an eye. "You're not the first fairy to manifest on Estica. The world has seen a few of your kind. But every time one arrives, it inevitably leads to misery and war. Despots and mad mages would level mountains and burn cities to get their hands on the likes of you and when they do there's a great deal of bloodshed before they're brought down. You, yourself, do not frighten me. It's the upset to the balance of power that you represent that's frightening. The simple fact of your existence here is frightening to anyone with enough sense to know that."

Now he understood the hungry looks he'd gotten in Asmara. He knew the few who'd sensed his nature had wanted him but didn't know why until now. Would the traders of that caravan have killed him outright if he hadn't draped a scrap of ruined tapestry over himself during his escape from the wreckage of Baydryn's lair? The hairs on the back of his neck stood up as he realized just how lucky he'd been to last this long.

He also understood why Valkanyr had brought him to Bradon. Alcreagh—the Scourge—was more powerful than Taeden could ever hope to be. It would be like offering a songbird to a wolf after it'd feasted on a dray; Taeden simply wasn't worth the effort. Taeden wasn't sure how he felt about Valkanyr relying on Alcreagh's apathy, but at least he felt safe as long as he didn't think too hard about all the horrible things Alcreagh had done and could still do.

"You don't like Valkanyr, do you?"

Alcreagh snickered softly, just loud enough for Taeden to hear him. "We have a mutual respect for each other," the Kin said without turning around. "But I don't seek him out, no."

"He treated me well and offered to send me home." Now he understood why the dragon had been so keen on the idea. Taeden paused a beat before continuing. "Is it because he's a dragon?"

Alcreagh was silent for a moment before giving a little tug on the reins, slowing his dray to let Taeden catch up. Once they were side by side he spoke, looking over at the fairy. Even dressed out in shapeless desert robes, the Kin still struck a regal figure. "You're lucky he's the one who found you. Few dragons are as restrained as he."

Taeden could feel a subtext to Alcreagh's words, but if there was a story there Alcreagh wasn't being forthcoming. He listened to the dray's hooves crunch along for a moment before continuing. "How do you know him?"

The Kin turned, looking away to scan the horizon before returning to Taeden. "Valkanyr is the one who got away, the first dragon to escape my wrath and reveal my existence to the rest of them."

Taeden wasn't sure what answer he'd expected, but that was definitely not it. The two hadn't seemed like mortal enemies back in the shop. "You- He-" he stuttered, blinking and trying to wring understanding out of what Alcreagh had said. "What?"

The Kin smiled thinly. "I was living in a ruined dragon's keep, using his library to teach myself how to control my powers. A flight of dragons came to visit him but found me instead. I killed three of them before Valkanyr managed to *Gate* away."

Taeden's blood ran cold at the nonchalant way Alcreagh spoke. There was no more emotion in his voice than if he was discussing the weather. What was he doing here, riding into the desert with this monster? Dragons were universally feared and respected, but Alcreagh spoke of killing them as if they were merely pests.

Alcreagh glanced aside at Taeden's silence. "Oh, I'm past all that now," he said, looking away again at the horizon.

A shiver ran down Taeden's spine. He might not be in imminent danger, but he still felt like he was sitting next to a powderkeg. Still, the conversation seemed to be going well, better than he'd expected, and before he could consider the wisdom of it he asked, "Why did you do it?"

Alcreagh lifted a perfect eyebrow. "It?"

"Your war against the dragons and everyone else."

Taeden saw the Kin's brow tighten slightly and his mouth thin. A long moment passed before Alcreagh finally spoke. "The dragons—*a* dragon—took something from me, something that could not be replaced, and I decided a price needed to be extracted."

Taeden tried to imagine what could be so valuable. He'd arrived in this world many years after the Scourge's campaign had started and it was several more years before it abruptly and mysteriously ended. Alcreagh had left a trail of destruction across Navarr that'd more than earned him his moniker. "You did it... for revenge?" the fairy wondered. "What... W-why didn't you ask the rest of the Kin for help? What could be so valuable to cause such misery?"

Alcreagh looked away and scoffed, the sort of harsh sound usually reserved for scraping filth from the bottom of a boot. The Kin's lip curled as he sneered around clenched teeth. Taeden saw his cheek flex and thought he could hear enamel scraping against enamel. Alcreagh's leather gloves creaked around the dray's reins. For an instant Taeden was sure Alcreagh was about to transform again into the horror of the Scourge but the Kin took a long, deep breath and slowly relaxed.

The fairy dared not speak, too frightened to look away from his escort.

"Everything," Alcreagh growled, enunciating each syllable as he stared into the distance.

It was after sundown before either of them spoke again.

Taeden had resigned himself to spending the rest of the journey in silence—he didn't want to upset Alcreagh and appreciated what the Kin was doing to help him get home, even if he still couldn't quite reconcile what was going on. Part of him wanted to turn and whip his dray and flee this entire situation, but the thought of someone else catching him, someone else with less benign intent, chilled him. He didn't know what the process of acting as a mana conduit entailed, but he didn't imagine it was pleasant.

For him the safest place in the world was at the side of the worst evil it had ever seen.

Was it wrong to accept help from someone who had done such harm when they were apparently reformed? At what point does punishment end and forgiveness begin? What does atonement for that much wrongdoing even look like? Taeden didn't know the answer to any of those questions.

They'd stopped to make camp for the night against a pile of boulders. The drays were staked on one side of the fire while he and Alcreagh settled across from them, against a tall flat slab of granite. The fire was warm against Taeden's face and cast an orange glow across the sand and rock. Alcreagh had spun the fire into existence with a brief flick of his wrist and now waved the supper pot onto the flames with a casual sweep of his fingers.

Taeden was watching the flames to take his mind off his mood, enjoying the way the little trickle of mana fed the spell that kept them alight and wondering how it all worked, when Alcreagh broke the silence.

"Tell me of your home."

The sudden sound of Alcreagh's voice gave him a start. The fairy jerked and looked over where Alcreagh had settled with his back against the boulder to find the Kin staring at the flames as well. "Uhm. It's... It's not like this."

Alcreagh didn't say anything, but the little smile Taeden could see on the Kin's lips encouraged him. "It's... It's not physical like this, I mean. Things are as we want them to be but here things are as they are."

Alcreagh turned to look at him, brow creased. Taeden struggled to find the right words. "We just..." He waved his hands in the air. "...And it is!"

Alcreagh slowly waved his hands in the air. "You just...?"

Taeden sighed in frustration and let his hands fall back into his lap. "I'm not sure how to explain it." He thought back to the way the Kin had explained his value here, and the strangers he'd met who had wanted to take him. "There's no strife like there is here. People here... want, but we don't. The world responds to us. Our desires manifest themselves."

Alcreagh sat up straight and leaned in a little, shuffling his desert robes. "So you don't actually have to spin the mana?"

Taeden shook his head. "No, it just is. The world responds on its own. Sometimes a passing memory will draw out a place, but if we don't like it it'll go away."

Alcreagh closed his eyes and shook his head as if to clear it. "A passing memory? What?"

Taeden nodded eagerly as he began to grasp how to explain it. It felt good to talk like this, without all the menace and pretext. Just thinking about home was lightening his mood. "Memories, yes. That's where they live. Your memories are there. Well, not just yours, I mean everyone's memories. They sort of float around, like the clouds do here but there really isn't a separate sky and ground like there is here. But... But I can feel how tightly connected to the manastream you are. You mean you don't know this already?"

Alcreagh was watching him intently, motionless. Taeden had seen that look in Asmara once, on a sandsnake stalking a bird. He leaned away a little bit, unnerved. The Kin blinked slowly and looked somewhere past him. "I've had a contentious relationship with my memories since I became the Scourge," he murmured, pausing a beat before adding, "This explains a great deal."

Taeden had just assumed Alcreagh had always been the Scourge, but now the Kin was talking about it like it was a mantle. More importantly, it was obvious that telling Alcreagh about the way memories inhabited the manastream had jarred the Kin. The fairy sat up straight and slid over towards Alcreagh's side, feeling the Kin's latent power loom over him again as he got closer. "Can you not see them? No, wait, you obviously have a memory. What is it about them, then?"

Alcreagh was still staring into the distance, slowly shaking his head. Taeden wasn't even sure the Kin was listening to him anymore. He didn't think the news had been that shocking. He leaned in to peer at Alcreagh's motionless face.

Was the Kin in some sort of trance? He reached out to touch his hand, suddenly worried he'd somehow injured him. "Are—"

"papa! papa!" his father looms over him with a grin and scoops him up. he throws his arms wide and laughs as the world spins around him.

his mother lays her hands over his, helping him hold the bow and draw the string back. she presses in close. he's warm, loved, and safe in her arms. they release the string at the same instant and the arrow flies true.

despite being younger, his brother is almost as fast as him. they race through the forest, trees whipping past at a breakneck pace. he dashes out of the woods and launches himself from the top of the hill just ahead of his brother, listening to his laughter echo his own as the pond rushes up to meet them.

the sharp tang of blood scents the cool night air. he catches up to his brother as the younger kin draws his arrow from the boar, ecstatic after his very first night hunt. "i'll never forget this," he's told, the boy's eyes shining in the moonlight.

"help! no!" a dragon looms over him with a grin full of teeth and malevolent promise and scoops him up. the world goes black.

years pass, captive to an unending string of tortures and trials at the dragon's whims. it is pain, it is suffering, it is misery he cannot escape. he tries to end his life but the dragon saves him and redoubles his violation.

years pass, and finally the dragon makes a mistake, a fatal mistake. he breaks free, the raw power of the manastream surging through him, and slays the dragon. he flees home, somehow knowing the way.

his brother looms over him with his bow drawn as he begs for help, the moon casting his brother's shadow across him. he is no longer welcome there. "unclean," his brother hisses at him. "you are forgotten."

years pass as he hones his newfound powers, bent on revenge, fueled on by the loss of his home and family, as if he could somehow fill the yawning emptiness in his soul with the carcasses of dragons.

they arrive before he's ready but he dispatches them easily. one gets away. his campaign begins, slowly at first but with increasing fury, slaying dragon after dragon, attacking their allies, giving no quarter, his wrath driven by his thirst for vengeance.

he looms over the deathbed of his father with a grin full of teeth and malevolent anticipation, waiting for him to die, but his father begs for forgiveness rather than mercy. he had been cast out to save him from death at the hands of those who thought him cursed, for shameful reasons, ill-advised and without any thought of consequences. he realizes in warring against the dragons he has become the very thing he despised, and in doing so has created a world the antithesis of everything he wanted. in full view of his mother the queen, brother the prince, and the rest of the kin royal court, his father the king apologizes for his banishment and recants his disownment, returning him to the ranks of the kin. "i love you, and i am sorry," the king tells him, his last words on this world. before he can answer the king evaporates into nothingness and his heart breaks again.

the war ends that day, but despite his emancipation he can never return to his family and station. he returns to the old battlefields in disguise, working to repair-

Taeden gasped for air and grabbed at his chest, sobbing, fingers digging into his robes, trying to feel for the gaping hole he was sure was there. Pebbles dug into the side of his face as he squirmed, clinging to his tear-wet cheeks. He coughed at the dust caught in his throat. The ground here looked just like it had at Thessac, when he'd surprised a relief caravan and burned it-.

No. That wasn't him. Was it?

His heart hurt. He wasn't injured but his chest still felt empty, like a huge claw had ripped a gobbet out of his soul and left the ragged edges raw. Weeping, he pushed the back of his hand across his dirty face, wiping sand and snot from his nose as he slowly got up. He was empty and alone and would never see his mother or father or brother again-.

No. That wasn't him.

He rolled over and slowly sat up, the gentle light of his wings casting an extra set of shadows across the blasted face of the boulder. The light gleamed off the smooth glass curve set into it that continued onto the ground, describing part of a small perfect sphere. Over his crying he could hear the agitated dray honking and calling but looked instead at the slowly stirring creature on the other side of the gleaming crater. The Scourge.

How could he be looking at himself? No. That wasn't him.

But he'd been Kin for years and the Scourge for even longer, after the dragon Rhaedon had taken him and-.

No. No, he was fae. He was Taeden. He hiccuped and sniffed, wiping at the mess of his face and panting, trying to calm himself and wake from this nightmare. "I'm Taeden," he whispered to himself,

hugging himself tightly to make sure he really existed, trying to remember when he'd not been an engine of destruction. "I'm Taeden."

The Scourge grunted as he pushed himself up onto an elbow, rolling over and looking back at the fairy. Taeden flinched as those
glowing crimson eyes fell on him then looked away. The hulking
black shape got to its feet and carefully stepped to the edge of the
shallow glass bowl, firelight playing across curves of rippling muscle.
He tested the edge with a marbled hoof, breaking off a chunk with a
grating crunch, then slowly moved around the rim towards the fairy.

Taeden watched him come, shivering and trying to calm himself
with slow deep breaths. He was Taeden. He was fae, not Kin. Not the
Scourge. But he understood now. He hadn't lived Alcreagh's life, but
he'd experienced it all the same through the storm of memories. He'd
been there for every moment, from being swaddled in silks and waving his pudgy hands at his mother to glaring at the avatar who'd
brought some frightened boy into his shop. All the joy, the success,
the promise, the love, the pain and failure and ruin and emptiness,
he'd seen it with his eyes, heard it with his ears, felt it in his heart.

The Scourge stopped over him, silhouetted in the light of the fire,
and the memory of Alcreagh's brother looming over him as he was
banished suddenly sprang to Taeden's mind. Taeden felt his throat
start to tighten and eyes burn as tears began to well up. "It hurts so
much. I'm so sorry," he croaked, squeezing himself harder. Sorry for
what had happened, just now and years in the past.

Blade-sharp hooves ground across the sand as the Scourge lowered
himself into a squat next to Taeden. The fairy could feel the familiar
surge of power close again and was closer to that monstrous face than
he'd ever been but it didn't frighten him anymore. He knew it now,
what it was like to wear that glistening black hide and wield that terrible power and feel the aching loss that drove it. It was like looking at
himself.

The Scourge considered him for a long moment, silent and motionless, the only sounds the crackling fire and the sniffles of the fairy. His

brow relaxed a bit and Taeden suddenly realized he could read the expression, the way the sharp eyebrows tilted, long nose flared, bestial lips pursed. Through the terrifying visage he could see it change from guarded to actual warmth, even kindness. "No need to apologize. I hope this has answered your questions," he said in that echo-voice, one side of his mouth quirked in a gentle smile.

A single sobbing laugh burst out of Taeden before he caught his face in his hands and his emotions took over again. How could anyone have survived all that Alcreagh had been through? Just the memory was too much to bear, he couldn't imagine what it had been like when it had actually happened. He felt like he could cry until he withered to dust and still not be free of this misery.

"It's all right, I have you," the Scourge murmured, and Taeden felt himself lift into the air. He gasped in alarm and for an instant thought the Scourge had actually picked him up and whatever had happened when they'd touched might happen again, but when he looked up he saw those strong black arms to either side of him, lifting him by mana alone. The fairy tucked his face back into his arms and curled up in a ball, gently weeping into the sleeve of his robes until sleep finally claimed him.

Taeden awoke in his bedroll the next morning, surprised to find himself cleaned up and dressed in a fresh robe. The memories still rattled around in his head, still roiling but settling like bubbles rising into the foam of a beer. Not all of them, though. Something about last night was niggling at him, like he'd forgotten something and was trying to remember it. He closed his eyes for a moment to reaffirm to himself he was who he was, then slid to his feet.

Alcreagh was back to his Kin appearance, just dishing up breakfast. Taeden took the bowl from the smiling, silent Kin and watched, bewildered, as Alcreagh sat on a rock to sift through his stew. Sometime, while he slept, he'd been cleaned and given a change of clothes, and now he was being happily served breakfast. Was this the same dour Kin he'd been riding with? He looked back at the glassy scoop taken out of the boulder and ground to see if he'd imagined the entire event. It was still there, smooth brown like melted caramel defining the shape of a globe.

"Do you know what happened last night?" Alcreagh asked quietly. Taeden looked back to find the Kin watching him rather than his food. The fairy shook his head, alarmed that Alcreagh might blame him for doing it on purpose.

"Neither do I," he said, watching Taeden for another beat before returning to his meal. "Some kind of interaction with the manastream, perhaps. I suspect our situation is a unique one." Alcreagh took a spoonful of the stew and chewed thoughtfully.

A fairy and a... whatever the Scourge actually was, meeting like that? Unique was an understatement.

Taeden slowly sat to join him. The psychic wound still hurt but it was a dull ache now, a fading pain he knew would eventually vanish and leave behind only the memory of itself.

They ate and then broke camp in silence. Taeden still wasn't sure what to say to the Kin. What do you say to someone whose entire life you've just experienced for yourself? He knew the answer to any question about Alcreagh he might ask.

He spent the morning ride settling his thoughts. He knew Alcreagh—the Scourge—better than anyone else would ever know him, human, Kin, or dragon. He didn't know if it excused what the Scourge had done, but now he understood why he'd done it.

But still there was something that evaded him, something about those alien memories he couldn't quite put his finger on, like there was still a blurry line between Alcreagh's memories and his own.

It was another day and a half before they reached their destination. Taeden and Alcreagh didn't dare touch each other again but neither did Alcreagh keep his distance from the fairy. What had started out as a grudging chore for the Kin had become friendly, almost loving. Taeden was glad for the change in attitude, even if he didn't really understand it. It wasn't until they'd arrived at the mouth of the cave that was Baydryn's lair that he dared mention it.

"I'm glad you came with me," he said, then closed his eyes and sighed. That didn't come out right at all. "I mean, I'm... I'm glad this wasn't..."

Alcreagh's chuckle got his attention. "Thank you." The Kin finished belting down his dray's saddlebags and staked the reins to the ground before turning to the fairy. "You've given me something nobody on Estica could: the chance to be understood. I suppose Valkanyr was right," he said with a grudging lopsided smile, "I had much more to gain from this quest than he."

Taeden felt his apprehension melt away and grinned back. "Oh, I'm glad. I'm... I'm sorry about..."

Alcreagh held up his hand. "I know, and thank you," he said, cutting him off with a patient smile. "Now let's get you home."

The fairy turned to consider the cave's entrance and the darkness beyond. The roof of the opening loomed dozens of feet above them. He remembered stumbling into the light, chased from the cave by the smoke and noise of battle, wondering where he was and where to go. Now it was deathly quiet, by all appearances abandoned.

Alcreagh stopped by his side, peering into the cave's mouth with him. "She's still in there, if that's what you're wondering. This won't be easy."

Taeden looked up at Alcreagh and that nagging tickle in the back of his mind returned. There was something else familiar here besides Baydryn's cave. "What do we do now?"

Alcreagh looked down at him. "Do you remember where the portal is?"

Again, that feeling. He shook his head.

"Then we'll have to hope we find it before she finds us. Come along, quietly now."

They quickly left the light behind as they crept into the dragon's lair, slipping around a bend into total darkness. He felt Alcreagh's hand on his sleeve and stopped, and a moment later the lair's walls sprang to life around him in shimmering false colors, worn smooth by dragonhide scraping past it. "Allsight," Alcreagh murmured, drawing his hand back from in front of Taeden's face. Errant glittering wisps of spent mana evaporated off the Kin's fingertips. Again, unattached familiarity teased at him.

The tunnel's floor sloped down slightly as it wound deeper underground, eventually opening into a large cavern. Riches were strewn haphazardly across the floor, gold and gems, coins and treasures piled like glimmering hills. The walls and ceiling of the tunnel peeled away and disappeared to either side and overhead, vanishing past his magically-augmented vision. He couldn't remember if the cave was really as big as it seemed or if it was just a trick of the *Allsight*.

Alcreagh prowled into the cavern in a crouch, sneaking up to a mound of golden bars and kneeling behind it. Taeden followed close behind, peering around for the tall stone ring he remembered falling through. The Kin made a tiniest of sounds and *Change* evaporated from him like dust in a lazy breeze. His fair Kin features, even his clothing, cracked and peeled away in bits and pieces rising into the air before disappearing to reveal the Scourge beneath. It was the first time he'd actually seen Alcreagh change forms.

That was it. That's what'd been bothering him since the memory storm. He'd seen this kind of effect before, in Alcreagh's memories when his father evaporated on his deathbed, and suddenly realized he'd recognized the face.

"I know your father!" he blurted out, then gasped and clapped his hands over his mouth.

The Scourge spun around. "Quiet!" he hissed, red eyes glowing.

Taeden looked back at him over his hands, eyes wide with horror at what he'd just done. He looked left and right, and when nothing started exploding he murmured through his fingers, "I know your father."

"Of course you know my father. *I* know my father, you're remembering him through me."

Taeden shook his head and slowly peeled his hands away from his face. "No, *I* know him. You Kin call it Ascension when your mage-king dies but that's just them joining the stream. They all do it. Sometimes they'll eventually move on but Aifeal's settled in, he likes it. I know him!"

The Scourge's face slowly relaxed as realization dawned. "You... My father–?"

The musical sound of a million gold coins avalanching across the floor interrupted him. A great green dragon slid out from under a mound of treasure, sharply angled head rising above them. One eye was ruined by a horrid scar but the other great yellow eye turned to face the pair. "You!" she shouted, loud enough to make Taeden's ears ring.

The dragon's head reared back and the Scourge leapt to his feet. "Down!" Just like in the shop, the Scourge's single word tripped a switch in Taeden's head and his legs collapsed without a thought, dropping him into a heap at the monster's feet. He saw those broad black arms sweep in a pattern and then cross just before the entire cavern disappeared behind a roaring wall of fire. The Scourge grit his teeth but the bubble held, incinerating dragonbreath blasting and swirling around them but never quite reaching them.

The flames abruptly stopped and the Scourge pounced, unceremoniously grabbing a handful of Taeden's smoldering robes and leaping into the air. The pair landed in another pile of coinage and slid to the bottom, the fairy tumbling away in a sprawl. The Scourge landed on his feet, bracing himself with a taloned hand.

The ground shook under Taeden's bottom as he batted at the guttering flames along his robes, then ripped them off entirely when the cloth began to catch in earnest. His wings spread out behind him, highlighting him in a warm golden glow. He began to pant in rising panic. Here he was, naked in a dragon's lair, so close to finally returning home, and it might all end in fire and blood.

"I knew you weren't dead," the dragon said, her voice echoing around the cavern. The quaking of her footsteps grew stronger. "That old bastard Figarl claimed he'd gotten you after you put Winterkeep to the torch but I knew, I knew! Owes me my weight in astrals now, he does!"

He was going to die here. All that hiding, all that luck, all for nothing. This is where he would end. Tears began to well.

The Scourge leaned in close to him. "I spotted the portal. It's behind us, straight that way against the wall." A glittering black talon showed the way but his wide eyes were locked instead on the direction the dragon's voice was booming from. "Taeden!" he hissed. "Look at me!"

The Scourge snapped his fingers and a burst of light startled the fairy back to the present. Baydryn's voice boomed off the walls. "And who's that with you? They smell delicious!"

Taeden glanced back in the dragon's direction with a whimper. "Listen to me," the Scourge said under his breath. "To me!" The fairy looked back at the Scourge with watering eyes, trying to find solace in that savage, determined face. "I will get you out of here. I promise. Do as I say."

Taeden nodded and swallowed just as Baydryn's head swooped into view over the top of the hill of coins. Even the dragon's gasp of surprise sounded huge. "A fairy?! You brought me a fairy?!"

"To the portal! Now!" The Scourge spun to face Baydryn and slammed his palms together. The shockwave skipped off the top of the hill, blasting a shower of coins up into the dragon's face and making her reel back with a thunderous stumble.

Taeden spun and scrambled away from the dragon, feet slipping on coins underfoot. He could see it now, just barely on the edge of his *Allsight*, the stone ring set into the wall of the cavern.

"I will have my prize, Slayer!" Baydryn roared, charging towards the both of them. The Scourge planted his hooves and stood his ground, fingers, hands, and arms all moving as he called up a surge of mana to spin *Barrier*.

The wave of power almost knocked Taeden off his feet. He'd never felt that much mana wielded here, ever. It was like a bucket of ice water in his face. He looked back in time to see Baydryn hit the *Barrier* at a full gallop and fetch up against it with a tremendous thud, wings splaying awkwardly. The dragon roared and clawed at the wall of magical force while the Scourge pushed back, a tiny black figure braced against nothing with the great green beast unable to cross the last few feet to rend him apart.

Taeden could feel more and more mana pouring into the fight through the Scourge, but even so it was just barely holding back Baydryn's fury. There was a crack of lightning behind him and he turned in time to see the portal spring to life, white light flowing across its face like water. Another surge of mana hit him but where the Scourge's channeling wanted to push him away like a wave, the portal was welcoming, gently drawing him closer.

The portal had opened again and home waited just beyond.

Baydryn's indignant screech shook the walls. "No! He's mine, I want him!"

Taeden stepped closer to the portal's edge and began to glow himself, outlined in white, his wings gleaming brighter than the dragon's hoard.

Sparks flew as the Scourge's hooves began to scrape backwards across the granite floor, shoved by the dragon's raw strength.

Taeden's corporeal form began to dissolve, bits of him peeling away and evaporating back to mana in silvery threads, floating back through the portal to the manastream that had birthed him. He held his arms out and turned back to take a last look at the Scourge and his old nemesis locked in battle.

The Scourge turned and met his eyes and Taeden saw determination, then shock, then desperation. "No! Wait!"

There was no waiting, not now. He was going home.

Baydryn raged and screamed, tons of muscle clawing and pounding at the *Barrier*.

The Scourge's muscles bulged and flexed under the strain. "Tell him!" he shouted over the din. "Tell my father I love him! And I forgive him!"

Taeden smiled at the Scourge, even as the smile itself dissolved away to nothingness. "I will," he said softly, and then even that trailed off into vapor and wafted back through the waiting portal.

The Storyteller folded his hands in his lap, his tale told.

The Kin across from him stared at him, one hand pressed over his mouth, glimmering tears running down his perfect cheeks. It took a moment before he found his voice. "He is well?" he asked, resting his hand again on the marble table.

The Storyteller nodded. "You would be proud of him, Aifeal. He's done much to undo the damage he's caused, as much as anyone can. I know, I've seen it."

Aifeal nodded shakily and cleared his throat, conjuring a bit of silk cloth to wipe his eyes. "That, and this, means a great deal to me, more than you can possibly know. Thank you."

Taeden smiled, his golden wings glowing warmly.

F is for Family

Stephanie A. Cain

With a final glance in the rearview mirror, Lucy Ruiz tucked a stray hair behind her ear and turned off the ignition. She was never comfortable in downtown Indianapolis after dark, but she was never entirely comfortable *anywhere*, so she might as well make a difference in the world while she was at it.

"Lucy! Thank you so much for helping out!" Lucy turned to see Tina, the woman who coordinated their church service teams. She was a short woman with a big heart and the shout of a drill sergeant.

Lucy forced a smile. She hated that she couldn't volunteer much in March and April but, as an accountant, she routinely worked eighty-hour weeks during tax season. "It's nice to be back at it."

Tina looked relieved. Lucy aspired to have a place for everything and everything in its place, but Tina was hyper-organized in a way Lucy couldn't imagine.

"I'm just glad to have you back," Tina said. "We're trying to get all the homeless kids to come to the shelter tonight. There's a doctor doing clinic hours, and she's agreed to stay as long as there are kids to treat."

Lucy straightened, nodding. "I'd better get at it, then. Who am I working with?"

Tina winced and handed over a map. "I've got your blocks marked, but..." She bit her lip. "The flu season's been brutal. We're running a skeleton crew. I hate sending anyone out alone, but—"

Lucy held up a hand before Tina could elaborate. "It's fine. We just won't tell my brother." Jacobo, an officer with Indianapolis Metropolitan Police, would have a stroke if he found out. Backing out would leave some kids without help, and Lucy couldn't do that.

Tina mimed zipping her lips, though she looked uncertain.

"It's fine," Lucy said again, trying to reassure herself as much as Tina. "Jake's a cop, you know I can handle myself." She looked down at the map and saw she was heading for Mass Ave. Tina had given her a well-populated street to begin on, at least. There would be plenty of people, so it was bound to be safe.

Lucy was halfway through her assignment and had sent four teenagers and a boy who couldn't be more than ten back to the shelter when she heard a voice raised in anger down an alley. The hair prickled on the back of her neck but she forced herself to turn away. She couldn't afford to get caught in the middle of whatever that was.

A yelp split the night and before she knew what she was doing, she was halfway down the alley. It smelled like urine and sour produce and her feet stuttered to a halt as she realized what a bad idea this was. She would have turned around, but the yelp came again.

The cold voice spoke again in a language Lucy didn't know with harsh consonants and a crispness that made her hair stand on end.

Another yelp—this one drew out into an agonized howl. A surge of rage hit her. Lucy shouted, "Freeze!" without thinking and ran down the alley toward the noise.

Her thoughts were surprisingly clear. *I've gone crazy,* she told her-self. *I'm going to get myself killed in an alley and Jacobo's going to have to tell Celia and then he's going to come to Purgatory and drag me back just to kill me himself.*

Then she was standing in front of the most stunning man she'd ev-er seen. He had long, white-blond hair and glittering silver eyes, high cheekbones and upswept brows. She had a moment to wonder how she could see him so clearly in this alley—the moon was full, but it was dark back here—and then she realized two things.

First, he was glowing.

Second, he was entirely encased in ice.

Lucy drew up short, heart thudding against her chest. *I really have gone crazy.* The man was looking directly at her, and his eyes might be the coldest thing she'd ever seen, colder even than the ice that held him in place—and how was that possible when the weather was in the sixties? What was going on? Lucy stared at him so hard her eyeballs hurt. She could *feel* how much he hated her.

Something shadowy moved behind him and Lucy jumped back, ut-tering a noise that, to her embarrassment, was more than half a shriek.

Before she could fumble for a weapon—trash can lid, discarded shoe, anything—the shadow resolved itself into a hunched back, low-ered head, and drooping tail. A German Shepherd slunk out into the glow cast by the ice man. Its brown eyes were on her. When it saw she was looking at it, it crouched even lower, but its tail gave a hopeful wave.

"Was he hurting you?" Lucy asked. The words felt funny in her mouth. She frowned, licked her lips, and swallowed. "Poor thing, come here," she added, and this time she almost sounded like herself, though her voice was shaking. So was the hand she stretched out to the dog.

The dog slunk in a half circle around the man's back and then a cold nose touched Lucy's fingers.

She stared down at it in bewilderment. What on earth was she supposed to do with this? A frozen man and the dog he'd been shouting at and probably beating.

Warmth curled around her fingers and withdrew. When Lucy looked down, the dog's tail was wagging. He looked up at her and opened his mouth, letting his tongue flop out.

"Damn it," Lucy sighed. "All right. We'll... Well, what do I do about this fellow, though? I can't just leave him here."

The dog gave her a very direct look—odd, considering how tentative it had been a moment ago—and turned to look at the ice-man. Then it lifted its leg and peed on the man's ankle.

Lucy let out a shocked laugh but the man's eyes burned with augmented rage.

"All right," she said. She wasn't sure whether she was saying it to the man or the dog. The man, she decided, and glared at him. "I suppose I *can* just leave you here. You deserve it, if you would hurt an innocent dog." She looked back at the dog, who wagged his tail again. "I'll figure out what to do with you tomorrow."

She turned her back and walked away, the dog trotting at her heels—slightly out of arm's length, but clearly happy.

He trailed her as she finished her assigned route, netting a teenage girl who'd darted away from her earlier. When the girl saw the dog wagging its tail behind Lucy, she crept out of the shadows and gave him a tentative pat.

"Who's a good boy?" Lucy said, giving the dog an affectionate ear rub. "Yes, you are. Nice job winning her over, you *good* boy."

He barked once. When they reached her car, he jumped into the passenger seat as if they'd always been friends. She drove home, trying to put thoughts of the ice-man out of her mind.

Lucy woke up curled into a ball and shivering, which wasn't surprising considering the horrible dreams she'd had. A giant with glowing eyes chased her down dark alleys in the middle of winter. When she reached a dead end, the giant had shouted harsh words at her and turned her into a living statue made of ice. She'd watched as the man looped cold iron around her wrists and neck—and then the dream reset itself and she was running in a dark alley again.

She groaned and covered her eyes for a minute, squinching them closed so tightly she saw sparkles behind her eyelids. She'd nearly drifted off to sleep again when her alarm went off.

Jolting upright, she stared around her. Her bedroom looked like it always did at seven in the morning: the sun sneaking in between the louvres of her blinds, the pale yellow walls reflecting it so the room almost glowed. Lucy had never been a morning person, but she'd read that natural light and warm colors helped people wake up more easily, so she'd painted her room several years ago when Indiana adopted Daylight Saving Time. Jake and Celi had laughed at her, but it *did* help, even if it was just psychological, so Lucy had the last laugh.

"What the—" shrieked Celi from the living room. Hard on her shriek was a male voice offering garbled apologies.

It wasn't their brother's voice.

"Josefina Lucia Ruiz!" Celi was even less of a morning person than Lucy, but she sounded disturbingly awake.

Lucy jumped out of bed and dashed out to the living room, forgetting she was wearing nothing but panties and a long t-shirt stolen from her last boyfriend.

The naked man who stood in the living room, trying unsuccessfully to wrap a loose-knit afghan around himself, made her remember as he looked at her and went scarlet. "Sorry, oh, God, I'm so sorry," he mumbled, averting his gaze.

"*What* the hell," Celi said. She was wearing a frilly nightgown that made her look even more delicate than she usually did—a deceptive look, because she made her living hauling around computer equipment and spent some of her free time doing some insane fitness routine that Lucy thought more appropriate to the US Army than a petite computer nerd.

"I can explain," the man said.

Lucy stared at him. "Where's my dog?" she blurted.

"Your *dog*? We don't have a dog." Celi propped her hands on her hips.

"I did last night," Lucy said. She marched up to the man and poked him in the chest. "*What did you do to my dog?*"

He coughed and took a step back. "I can explain," he said again. Lucy couldn't help noticing the chest she had just poked was nicely muscled, which the afghan did little to hide.

"Then start explaining. I didn't rescue that poor thing from the ice-man just to have some—some—malefactor break in and steal him!" She poked him in the chest again.

"Lucy, the man's naked!" Celi howled. "Who breaks into a house naked to steal someone's *dog* that she doesn't even *have*?" She frowned. "Did you say *ice-man*?"

"Please," the man said, rubbing the red spot that was forming on his chest. "Let me explain."

"Call Jacobo," Celi said, at the same time that the man added, "Please don't call the police yet."

Lucy stared at him, really taking in the fact that yes, afghan notwithstanding, he was entirely naked. Then she looked back at Celi, feeling her cheeks getting hot.

Celi's expression slowly changed from outrage to amusement. She looked from Lucy to the man and back to her sister and clearly decided not to ask. "You know what? This is your situation to deal with. But if you need someone to punch him, call me, Lu. You're a better shot than me, but I hit harder." She punched her sister lightly on the arm. "I'm going to take my lifeblood back to my room and leave you two alone."

Hefting her coffee mug, she went into the kitchen. There was the sound of coffee being poured and then Celi came back through, smirking faintly. She darted a look at Lucy and made a sound Lucy thought could be properly termed a cougar growl. Lucy's face heated so much she thought she might catch fire. She was absolutely *not* in the habit of bringing men home with her, so it wasn't at all fair Celi would act like she'd hooked up last night.

Then again, Lucy couldn't deny how attractive the guy was.

Or that he'd probably done something horrible to her dog.

"Um," she said. She couldn't quite lift her gaze from the side of his neck, where she could see a pulse throbbing. She didn't want to meet his gaze until her cheeks didn't feel so red. What she did want to do was poke him again and ask where her dog was, but since that hadn't gotten her any answers the first two times, she just folded her arms across her chest.

"I am so sorry," the man blurted. "I meant to stay awake until I changed back and then just let myself out. I must have been more worn out than I realized. If I'd known you were living with humans..." He trailed off as he realized Lucy was boggling at him.

"The—what? I'm living with—*what*?"

"Humans? Er, mortals. I mean." He stopped talking and lifted a hand to rub the back of his neck, then hastily dropped it as the afghan drooped in front.

"I—"

"My lady," the man added. He sketched a bow and then clutched again at the afghan.

"*What?*"

He paused in the middle of tucking the afghan in a strategic place. "I'm sorry. I don't know the correct term of address. The pack doesn't spend much time mingling with the Courts."

Lucy's head was spinning. She huffed a sigh. "If I had any idea what you were talking about, it would help. I mean, I know you're speaking English. I know what all those words mean. I just don't know what they mean in the order you're putting them."

The man's brown eyes warmed suddenly, looking almost golden as he smiled at her. "I have forgotten my manners. I am Theodore Smith, of the Eagle Creek Pack. Most people call me Theo."

"Theo," Lucy echoed faintly. "Er. I'm Lucy. Um, Josefina Lucia Ruiz, technically, as you no doubt heard my sister shriek."

Their eyes met, and suddenly the situation as so absurd Lucy burst out laughing. A moment later Theo joined in her mirth.

It was several minutes before Lucy could gather herself enough to ask, "Would you like some coffee?"

"My thanks, lady," he said, and she drew up stiffly. The words sent an odd feeling through her, like someone had taken the edge of the world and shaken it like a bedsheet. It made her skin ripple oddly.

"Lucy," she said. "Please. Just—Lucy."

Theo nodded. "Lucy," he said after a moment, and her name on his lips was as intimate as an embrace. She blushed.

"Coffee," she said, and led the way to the kitchen. Halfway there she remembered her pantsless state. Her steps stuttered and then she forced herself onward, pretending there was nothing amiss. If she pretended, maybe he would pretend too.

She poured coffee for both of them and then excused herself as he leaned against the kitchen counter, sipping. Fleeing to the bathroom, she grabbed her brother's bathrobe and then darted into her bedroom long enough to pull on a pair of leggings. Catching sight of herself in the mirror, she realized what a wreck her hair was and took a moment to scrape it into a messy bun.

When she returned to the kitchen, Theo was inspecting the family photos hanging on the wall next to the refrigerator. He turned quickly, his expression changing to one of relief as he registered the bathrobe in her hands.

"I'm really sorry," he said, setting his coffee on the counter. "I hadn't intended to be away from the rest of the pack when the change hit, but I got a call from—well, I thought it was one of my packmates, but it turned out to be that guy you frosted. I'd heard the Winter Court was restless, but this..." He shook his head.

Lucy held out the bathrobe. "Again with the not making sense."

He glanced over his shoulder at her as he shrugged into the bathrobe. He was stocky in a muscular way, but fairly short, which meant he was swimming in her brother's linebacker-sized clothes. "Sorry. You might want to finish your first cup of coffee before I explain. I can tell you're less of a morning person than I am."

The grin he gave her was disarming. Lucy scowled back at him. "I'll drink faster. Sit down and explain."

He sat obediently across from her, curving strong-looking hands around his coffee mug, but he seemed to be studying her, perhaps gauging what he could say that she could understand, perhaps gauging just how much nonsense she would put up with before she threw him out.

Thankfully, he waited until her mouth wasn't full before he spoke.

"I'm a werewolf." His voice was flat, the statement bald.

Lucy's mug clunked down on the table as she set it down hard. She opened her mouth, trying to find words—and then closed it again.

"Last night was the full moon. You knew that, right? You must have known that. You came to my rescue so quickly when the change hit. Of *course* he waited until I was incapacitated," he muttered.

Lucy's mouth opened again and she stared at him.

"Or... you didn't know?" Theo turned his head, watching her askance. "You were following the Unseelie taint, perhaps."

Lucy slumped back in her chair, gaping openly.

Theo cleared his throat. "I apologize. I'm not explaining very well. I am a werewolf, a member of the Eagle Creek Pack. We usually gather during the full." He paused. "We don't bite people. We don't lose control during the full. We can't deny the change, but we retain our own minds. We know what we're doing."

Lucy tried to find words but only managed to squeak in an indignant manner. This whole morning had been entirely insulting! To wake from bad dreams to her sister shrieking and a mostly naked man in her living room—and then to have said man try to convince her he was a werewolf! It was beyond imagining!

"Surely you know about werewolves."

Don't call me Shirley, flashed through her mind, a ridiculous callback to her brother's favorite movie. She suppressed a mad urge to giggle. "Werewolves."

Theo's dark brows drew together. "I would have thought one of the gentry would be more knowledgeable about the other races. Especially one sharing living quarters with humans—mortals. Are you under a geas? Or some compulsion? Have you been cursed?"

Lucy realized suddenly that she was breathing so fast she was in danger of hyperventilating. "I don't know what gentry means," she said. "Or geas." She huffed a noise that was halfway between laughter and despair. "I don't *think* I've been cursed, but who knows? At this point I'd probably believe anything."

Theo tilted his head. "And yet you don't believe werewolves?"

Lucy buried her face in her hands. "I thought you were a German Shepherd," she said, her voice muffled.

To her surprise, Theo started laughing.

Lucy's shoulders tensed and the laughter broke off. When she straightened, though, there was a clear light of mirth in his golden eyes.

"I cry you mercy, lady," he said. "A German Shepherd." His eyes crinkled pleasantly in amusement. "And here I was thinking I'd pass for a Malamute at least."

Lucy blinked at him for a moment and then dissolved into laughter. It was uncomfortable laughter, wild and tinged with hysteria, but it released some of the tension. When she wiped her eyes a few moments later, she was breathless but more relaxed.

"All right, Mister Theo Not-a-German-Shepherd Smith of the Eagle Creek Pack," she said. "I'm pretty sure that I'm an accountant who just rescued a dog. You seem to think otherwise. Can you explain why?"

Theo was grinning at her. "I'm happy to. Or to try, at least." He glanced down at his borrowed bathrobe. "But could you please get me some real clothes first?"

"All right, I can almost—*almost*—see werewolves," Lucy finally admitted. "I've met Braxton Wolfe, and I always thought there was something odd about the way Chloe went off him briefly. I'm guessing that's when she found out?"

"Wait, you're friends with Chloe?" Theo smacked his forehead. "Of course you're friends with Chloe. You're *that* Lucy. But she never said you were—"

"I am absolutely not whatever you think I am," Lucy interrupted firmly. "I know who my parents were, and my older brother would have been seriously glad for any opportunity to try to convince me I was adopted. Trust me."

Theo's golden-brown eyes were steady on hers, though his brows drew together. "But... I mean..." He paused and darted a glance to the clock and then back at her face. "You don't smell human." His lips twisted in an apologetic grimace. "I know plenty of Fae, but I've only encountered a couple who were high court. Though honestly..." He shrugged. "Your scent has that same... that same... *j'e ne sais quois*. I would bet my car that you're high court Unseelie."

"I can't be high court Unseelie, I'm *Catholic*!"

Theo's eyes widened and then he laughed. "That doesn't really rule it out. All of the Unseelie acknowledge Christ, and some of them even worship him. That's why a lot of protective measures against the Fae include crossing yourself and speaking the Lord's name."

Lucy sighed and opened her mouth, but Theo held up a hand. She folded her arms across her chest and glared at him.

"Look," he said, "I really do need to check in with Braxton. He's going to want to know what happened so he knows to watch out for more Fae tricks. That fellow last night wanted me for the winter queen's hunting pack." He rubbed a hand through his hair, scowling. "That Unseelie lord's actions last night violate the Crossroads Accord which has protected peace since the capital moved from Corydon to Indianapolis."

That was all very interesting, but Lucy didn't know what any of that had to do with her. "Your point?"

He gave her a rueful grin. "Sorry. Let me go see Braxton and get some of my own clothes. Then—could we meet somewhere? The Central Library maybe? That's where I work."

"Wait, you're a librarian?" Lucy found herself grinning. "A werewolf librarian?"

Theo's brows and mouth drew down into flat lines. "Werewolves can be nerds, too."

Lucy started laughing. "I suddenly want to call you Remus Lupin. That's... okay, that's kind of awesome."

Theo rolled his eyes. "I promise, my clothes are way less patched than Lupin's," he said, and then coughed. "Partly because I have no idea how to patch clothes."

Lucy just giggled.

"Okay, so can you meet me at the library? It's already open by now, but I always try to get the day after the Full scheduled off, so I'm not expected in. Say... eleven o'clock?"

"Why are we meeting?" Lucy said, and then regretted it. She'd been hyperaware all morning of just how nice-looking and fit he was. She didn't want him to think she wasn't interested in spending time with him, because she wasn't one-hundred-percent convinced of his sanity.

"I want to do a little bit of research," Theo said, "but I'm pretty sure I can show you some stuff that'll convince you I'm not crazy."

The weird echo of her thoughts made her narrow her eyes. Theo laughed.

"No, I don't have mind-reading skills. But I have an exceptional sense of smell, so I can tell you're skeptical. And logic tells me that I wouldn't believe it if I weren't currently living it, so." He shrugged.

Lucy sighed. "Fine. It isn't like I have anything more pressing, anyway."

Theo's lips quirked. "Um. Does the bus run anywhere near here?"

Lucy rolled her eyes and reached for her keys. "Just tell me where to drop you off. I invited an unknown German Shepherd into my car last night. I shouldn't be squeamish about an unknown man this morning."

Lucy arrived at the library ten minutes early so she would have time to change her mind. Her hands had been shaking since she dropped Theo off at his apartment. What was she doing meeting some random guy so he could try to prove to her that he was a werewolf and she was a fairy?

Except... she'd definitely come home with an animal that probably *had* been a wolf, and woken up with a naked guy in her living room. That seemed pretty decent proof, unless the wolf had been trained to open doors and let his owner inside to run some crazy scam. But seriously, what kind of scam could this even be? Theo hadn't even asked her for anything except coffee and a ride home.

While she waited in the front lobby for Theo to show up, she pulled out her phone and texted her friend Chloe. *So you're engaged to a werewolf and didn't tell me? Major foul, dude.*

She stared at the dots indicating that Chloe was typing a response, a grin tugging at the edges of her lips as the seconds ticked by and Chloe still didn't send an answer.

Finally she sent, *Sorry? How did you find out?* which was definitely a shorter response than the length of time it took her to answer. The grin won as Lucy thought about how many responses Chloe must have deleted before settling on that.

Met Theo this morning. In my living room. After rescuing a stray dog.

Chloe sent back a laughing-crying emoji in response.

You and I are going for drinks very soon, Lucy sent, and then looked up as Theo's voice said her name. He sounded relieved. That she'd showed up, maybe?

"So... hi," she said, giving him a smile that felt weird on her face. She wondered suddenly if he would think she'd dressed up for him, with her favorite red sweater, black pants, and knee-high boots.

"Hi. Come on back to my office," he suggested. "There's a database I need to access."

"This is insane. There's a fairy database?" Lucy shook her head. "I can't believe this."

Theo pursed his lips. "You keep saying that, but you're here."

"I just—I—I'm so confused," she blurted.

Theo smiled, his brown eyes warming to amber as he held the door for her. "It's okay," he said. "I imagine everything about today has been pretty confusing."

"Well, Chloe vouched for you, so even if you're confusing me, I guess I can trust you," Lucy said. "I mean, I wanted to trust you anyway, but..." She trailed off, wondering if her careless words would hurt his feelings.

But his smile widened. "Smart move, checking my references. I suppose I shouldn't be surprised, considering your brother and friend are cops, but I'm glad. The way you charged in last night to save me..." He shook his head. "I've never seen anything so brave—or reckless."

"If I'd known what it was going to get me into, I probably wouldn't have," Lucy confessed.

Theo snorted. "Please. You spend your free time wandering around downtown helping homeless kids. I think you probably would have charged in just the same."

Lucy felt her face heating up. She ducked her head and followed him without replying.

When they reached his office, he sat down and started tapping away on his computer. "Pull up a chair," he murmured.

When Lucy settled in beside him, she saw he was searching a newspaper database. Then she looked at his search term. "Hey, why are you researching *me*?"

"Because I have an idea to figure out who you are," he said.

"I *know* who I am," she whispered furiously. "I'm Lucy Ruiz."

"Except you're also gentry," he said. "There's no getting around the scent of your magic. Or the way you froze that Unseelie lord."

"Froze—" Lucy broke off and took a couple of deep breaths. "I did not freeze him. He was frozen when I got there."

"Because you shouted at him," Theo said. "I've made a study of Fae speech, because I get a surprising number of Fae patrons here. You shouted at him to freeze, and your magic took it literally."

Lucy stared at him, her thoughts swirling. "Freeze..." She dropped her head in her hands. "Sweet mother Mary. I've spent too much time around Jake and Chloe."

Theo chuckled. His fingers rested on her shoulder for a few moments. "I'm glad," he said. "If you'd yelled stop, it's hard to say how long it would have lasted."

Lucy lifted her head and blinked at him. "Do you think that guy is still frozen?"

He shook his head. "Braxton and Elliott headed down to check. They texted me that he was gone, but they could smell the Fae magic all over that alley. And *not* just his," he repeated, looking meaningfully at her.

Lucy sighed. "So why are you searching a—a human newspaper database, if you're so convinced I'm not human?" She gestured at the computer screen. "Shouldn't you be asking some Fae loremaster or something?"

He grinned. "I could, but frankly she's hard to find. Anyway, I speak database." He turned back to the computer and typed in a few commands... and the language on the screen changed from English to a script that was somehow both flowing and spiky. Lucy couldn't read it, but Theo obviously could.

He clicked a button and typed something into what looked like a search box.

"Okay, what—" Lucy began, and then as the page reloaded, the results came back in English. "What just happened? That wasn't English."

Theo glanced over at her. "It still isn't. You can read that?"

Lucy blinked. "Yeah. It says Eluciara Winter."

Theo clicked the first link. The story that loaded featured a picture of a haughty-looking woman with black hair and sharp cheekbones. Something in her face made Lucy's throat tighten.

"That's it." Theo sounded satisfied. "I thought I remembered something about one of the ladies of House Winter losing a child. I know it isn't done, but—how old are you?"

"I... um. I'm thirty-two." Lucy shook her head, staring at the woman. Her eyes were ice-blue but her skin was as dusky as Lucy's. "Who is she?"

"If I'm right," Theo said, "She's your birth mother."

Theo printed several articles and set them on the desk in front of her. Lucy rested her fingers on the papers without looking at them. She wasn't sure if she ever wanted to look at them.

"Why are you doing this?" she asked, not looking at Theo either. Her voice sounded very small to her.

Theo sighed. "The pack has a rule that any newly-turned wolves can't be left untrained. We have to teach them how to adjust to their new abilities and limitations. We have to make sure they'll be able to survive on their own, even if they decide they ultimately don't want to stay with the pack."

Lucy sneaked a glance at him. His brows were drawn together in concern, his gaze steady on her face. She looked back down at the papers on the desk. "I'm not a werewolf," she said, her voice small.

"It's the same concept. Last night, you instinctively froze a guy. I don't blame you. In fact, I'm grateful to you. You kept me from being enslaved by the Wild Hunt. But you can't go around randomly magicking people on accident. It isn't safe. Not for you, not for the mortal population of Indianapolis, and not for the supernatural community at large."

"You think I'll accidentally pick a fight?" Lucy didn't like to think of her parents not being her birth parents. She looked like her siblings and her parents. How could she be adopted?

"You might. Or you might overextend yourself. I'm not an expert on Fae magic, but I think it's possible. And the thing is, if you accidentally use magic on someone who isn't part of the supernatural community, you could out us to the world in general."

Lucy sighed. "This sucks."

"It doesn't have to." Theo smiled at her. "Why don't you go home and read what I found? Then call me when you're ready and we can figure stuff out."

"No." Lucy frowned at him when he gave her a wide-eyed look. "No, I'm going to deal with this today. I don't want to stew over this. What good will it do to sit around wondering if you're right? I need to know."

Theo nodded slowly. "All right. I'm going to leave you alone to read through these, okay? I'll be back in a few minutes."

Lucy took a deep breath and lifted the first article.

The upshot was that Lady Arborage of the House of Winter had gone missing for a time in the mortal world thirty-some years ago. When she disappeared, she was with child. When she returned to the Unseelie Courts, she was not. The child had never been found, and Lady Arborage had never spoken of what happened in the mortal realm.

Some of the articles had background information on House Winter, and others mentioned Lady Arborage's estranged husband, who was apparently another Unseelie lord. None of them mentioned any siblings.

By the time Theo came back, Lucy thought she had control of her breathing again. Her head was still spinning, but she sat straighter, hoping to hide it.

Theo held out a bottle of water, which Lucy took gratefully. She sucked in a breath and finally said, "You think this Lady Arborage is my mother?"

"I've never met her, so I can't speak to her scent, but she has a physical resemblance to you." Theo ticked his points off on his fingers as he spoke. "You're the right age. You have magic that feels like House Winter."

"She has blue eyes," Lucy protested.

Theo met her gaze steadily for several seconds and then touched her chin. Lucy's heart tripped over itself and surged into her throat before she realized he was holding up a small mirror. Was that why he'd left, because he had known she would protest? She blinked sev-

eral times, not looking away from his compassionate gaze. Not wanting—despite her earlier assertion—to know.

As the compassion in his eyes changed into something that looked
suspiciously like pity, Lucy jerked her gaze away and looked at herself in the mirror. For a single heartbeat she met the same brown eyes
she'd always seen. Then, like melting snow, the brown dissolved into
an icy blue.

Lucy swallowed. Her heart was pounding in her chest and she
couldn't quite catch her breath. Her fingertips tingled. She wondered
if she was having a panic attack. She licked her lips and finally whispered, "What now?"

"Now we visit Lady Arborage."

Lucy swallowed, grateful that he'd said *we* and not *you*. "How do
we even do that?"

"Like I said, I've interacted with quite a few fairies over the years.
It's my job to help people research, so I don't really create the burden
of debt when I help fairies find things—but on the other hand, the
good neighbors hate having things unequal. If you do one a good turn,
they owe you a debt, and things feel unbalanced to them." He frowned
and scratched his temple. "For that matter, I shouldn't have thanked
you. It isn't done, and even though you thought you were human, I
didn't. I'm sorry about that."

Lucy frowned back at him. "*That's* why it felt weird when you said
it?"

"Did it?" His frown turned into a smirk. "There, then. More proof."

Lucy rolled her eyes. "So you're going to help me arrange an introduction to this Lady Arborage? How? And when? And—"

"One question at a time," Theo broke in, chuckling. "I have a
friend connected to the Unseelie Court. I called him before meeting
you here, and he gave me some guidance on how we can find Lady
Arborage. I didn't tell him why," he added hastily.

Lucy quirked an eyebrow at him. "That was a little presumptuous."

Theo shrugged. "What can I say? I'm brash, impetuous, and over-bearing."

She snorted. None of those words seemed to describe him. Then again, she knew most people didn't think "insecure," "misfit," or "out of place" were phrases that described her. She'd constructed her armor with power suits and high heels, carefully styled hair, and perfect lip-stick. On one hand, she knew it kept people at arm's length. On the other hand, it kept people from seeing how awkward and out-of-place she always felt.

"I'm sorry if I presumed too much," Theo said, and Lucy realized she'd been sitting without speaking for several minutes.

"No," she said. "Sorry. I was just thinking."

"It's a lot to take in."

Lucy nodded. Eluciara. It felt odd, but it settled over her shoulders like a mantle. Maybe she was Eluciara Winter. Maybe that would ex-plain why she always felt so out of step with the rest of the world. Only with numbers did she ever feel comfortable.

"So where are we going?" Lucy asked.

"There's a Faerie gate in Irvington," Theo said.

Lucy huffed. "Why am I not surprised?" Irvington was notoriously proud of their haunted history, which included Masonic Lodge #666 and a house where serial killer H.H. Holmes murdered a young boy, as well as plenty of other urban legends.

Theo grinned. "The Kile Oak. It's on Beechwood Avenue. It's four hundred years old, and when you get there, you feel like you're walk-ing into a different world." He paused. "Which you are, I guess."

"A gate into Faerie," Lucy repeated. "I can honestly say that's something I never thought I would say."

He gave her a wry smile. "Do you want to drive, or would you like me to?"

It might be safer for her to insist on meeting him there, but based on the way her hands were shaking, Lucy wasn't sure it would be safe for her to drive anywhere. "I'll let you drive."

When they pulled up in front of a charming green picket fence, she had to agree—it *did* look like something out of a different world.

"Okay, so... what next?" She looked down at her boots. At least they were practical enough for walking. Somehow she didn't think Faerie would be hospitable to three-inch heels.

"Now we see if Faerie is feeling friendly today." Theo gave her an encouraging smile. "Come on. I'll be with you the whole time."

The Kile Oak was the largest tree Lucy had ever seen. It had to be at least five feet in diameter, its green branches spreading over them like a shelter. She found herself holding her breath and had to remind herself to inhale.

"Are you sure we're allowed to be here?" she whispered.

Theo nodded. "I'm pretty sure the moment you touch that bark, the tree will open the gate for you," he said. To her relief, he was barely speaking above a whisper himself.

She looked doubtfully at him, but walked at his side to stand in front of the tree. She stared up at it, feeling insignificant, and bit her lip. Her fingers itched to reach out to the tree, to see if what Theo said were true. Could there be another whole world where she truly belonged?

As soon as she realized what she was thinking, Lucy clenched her fists. She belonged *here*, in Indianapolis, no matter how she felt. She belonged with her brother and sister, in the home where their parents had raised them. She belonged with her friends, as a member of her church, as a volunteer helping homeless kids get healthcare and meals. She belonged at her accounting firm.

Didn't she?

Theo must have sensed her hesitation. Strong fingers curled around her left fist, gently unclenching her fingers. "You don't have to choose," he said quietly. "If you don't want to do this today—"

After her initial shock, thinking he had read her mind somehow, Lucy shook her head. "No. Either way, I need to know."

Theo nodded. "Then let's find out together," he said, and tugged lightly at her hand.

Lucy let him lift her hand, stretching it out in front of them, but when their hands were still at least six inches from the oak's bark, Theo let go. She glanced sideways at him, her heart thudding in her chest.

"I can't make the decision for you," he said, smiling. "But I'll be here when you make it."

Sudden gratitude swamped her. He would let her back down if she wanted to. She could turn around, walk away, and go back to her comfortable life.

Not comfortable, whispered a cold little voice in her head. *Isn't that the whole point of volunteering downtown at night? Isn't that the point of armoring yourself with business suits and expensive lipstick? You aren't comfortable because you don't belong here.*

Lucy sucked in a breath and reached out, the bark scraping against her fingertips—

—and energy jolted through her as if she'd been struck by lightning. Before she knew what she was doing, she had taken several steps forward, feeling her fingertips sink *into* the bark. She heard Theo yelp behind her, then something gripped her elbow just as another force grabbed her hand and pulled.

Lucy tumbled into the tree, *through* the tree, and fell, breathless, onto a cold, soft surface. *Snow.* A moment later a shaggy wolf rolled onto the snow behind her. She only stared at it for a moment before turning her attention back to the bright world around her.

The shade of the Kile Oak was gone. A fuzzy, white sun shone down on her, its light reflected back by the seamless snow that spread around them. Lucy shivered automatically and then realized she wasn't cold. She huffed a laugh, watching her breath rise in front of her eyes, and spun in a circle.

"It's so beautiful," she whispered.

A warm, wet nose pressed into the palm of her hand. Lucy jerked her gaze away from the world around her. She knelt, somehow unsurprised that the snow didn't soak through her jeans. "Theo," she breathed.

The wolf looked at her and whined.

"Are you stuck? I mean, did—something *make* you a wolf?"

He whined again. Apparently telepathic communication with werewolves wasn't an Unseelie talent.

Lucy sighed and stood up. "Do you know where I should go?" Theo pressed against her hip and she buried her fingers in his ruff. She immediately thought she shouldn't have, that she was being too familiar, but Theo leaned harder against her for a moment.

Lifting her chin, Lucy gazed around them at the white-limbed trees nearby. Nothing looked familiar, but everything *felt* familiar. She narrowed her eyes, exhaled enough to see a thin spiral of breath on the cold air.

"I am seeking Lady Arborage of House Winter," she said aloud.

A sudden breeze danced around her, teasing at her hair and lips. At its touch, Lucy's lips chilled and she smiled. "Yes, carry my words to Lady Arborage. I would speak with her."

The breezes whisked around Lucy, ruffling her hair and clothes in what felt like excitement. Theo barked at them, making Lucy laugh.

She settled a hand on Theo's head. "They were messengers. I don't know how I knew, but I could just tell." Theo tipped his head back and swiped his tongue across her fingertips. Giggling, Lucy jumped and then gave him a reproving look.

"I'm glad you're with me, but don't make me jump. I want to look at least a little dignified if the woman we're meeting really *is* my mother."

Theo lowered his head in exaggerated shame, which made Lucy want to swoop down and plant a kiss on his doggy nose. *Except that nose doesn't really belong to a harmless dog, does it?* whispered a voice in the back of her mind. *You would be kissing the nose of Theo Smith. A librarian.*

Lucy shoved the thought away, not wanting to consider the implications. "Come on," she said, lifting her chin. "We might as well follow it."

She didn't bother questioning how she could follow an errant breeze; there were enough questions swirling around in her head as it was. She merely followed, and after they had been walking for a time, she saw the white towers of her destination.

"It looks like the White Witch's castle," she muttered, wondering if Theo had grown up reading the same books she had. "I hope we fare better than her subjects."

But you are no subject, whispered the wind.

Lucy straightened her shoulders and began walking again.

What am I? she wondered. She knew Theo's opinion—that she was a long-lost daughter of the Unseelie Fae House of Winter. She'd tried to convince herself not to believe it... but the tree had brought her here. The cold didn't bother her. She understood the message carried on the winter wind.

She might be Lucy Ruiz, but she was also someone *more* than Lucy Ruiz. She didn't know what that might look like, but if the towers of House Winter were any indication, it was beyond anything Lucy had imagined.

The gates to the keep opened when Lucy looked at them. She hadn't expected it; she had, in fact, slowed her steps enough as she approached that Theo outpaced her. But as soon as she looked up at the heavy stone doors, they swung inward, inviting her to keep moving.

Theo glanced over his shoulder at her. Lucy shrugged. "This is your fault, you know," she said. "You know just as much about what's happening as I do."

She couldn't help grinning—just a little—when he ducked his head and moved forward again without looking at her. His tail was tucked close to his butt, though his ears were perked forward. Lucy was no expert in canine body language, but she was pretty sure that a tail that wasn't wagging meant the canine in question wasn't excited about whatever was happening.

She half expected the courtyard to be filled with stone statues, but the clean swept cobblestones and large, crystalline windows were indications that perhaps she wasn't entering the keep of Jadis, Queen of Narnia, Chatelaine of Cair Paravel, and Empress of the Lone Islands. All the same, Lucy's steps faltered until she came to a halt just a few feet from a fountain in the center of the courtyard, frozen in the midst of a shower of ice crystals.

The breeze whispered around her ears, whipping her hair against her skin and bringing tears to her eyes.

Theo paced in a circle and then came back to press against her leg again. His golden eyes fixed on Lucy's face. She felt restless and irritable suddenly. Why was she supposed to have all the answers? He was the one who had told her she wasn't human. She glowered at him and then felt guilty when he crouched and tucked his tail between his legs.

"This isn't fair," she muttered at him. "I never asked for this."

"Never asked for what?"

The woman's voice was low and husky. It sounded nothing like her mother's voice, but it made all the hair stand up along Lucy's neck and wrapped her as securely as an embrace. Lucy shivered against the urge to relax into that voice.

"I never asked to be different," she replied, not turning. Her voice was harsh in the snow-softened courtyard. "I never asked to be special."

"Doesn't everyone want to be special?" the woman asked. She didn't move into Lucy's field of vision. "Is that not the eternal struggle of the mortal races, to find something that distinguishes oneself from the others of one's race?"

Lucy scowled. "I've spent my whole life wishing I fit in better," she said. If she had questioned whether or not the woman speaking had power over her, it was abolished in the face of Lucy's unrestrained honesty. "I've never been smart enough, pretty enough, Catholic enough, or Hoosier enough. My sister is a lesbian and she fits in better than I do. No. Humans don't want to be distinguished from the rest. We want to fit in."

The woman chuckled, a warm sound entirely unlike Lucy's expectations. "My child, you are not human, and you were not born to fit in. Why should you wish to? You were born to wield power."

Lucy spun around, hands clenching into fists. She stared at the beautiful woman who stood before her, black hair swept up into an intricate coronet of braids.

"Then why did you leave me there?" she demanded. She didn't recognize her own voice. It was swollen with anger and grief and fear.

Theo didn't make a sound, but he pressed hard against her legs. She felt, suddenly, an overwhelming sensation of strength coming from him. Lucy dug her fingernails into her palms and prayed she wouldn't cry, which was her usual reaction to rage.

Lady Arborage—for the woman facing her could be no one else— lowered her head. She wore a flowing, ice-white gown; the sleeves fell down to cover her clasped hands. Lucy's birth mother had skin as dusky as her own, but it had alabaster undertones where Lucy's family had always had ochre. Her hair was blue-black instead of the red-black of the Ruiz family. Her cheekbones were high and looked sharp enough to cut, though Ruiz women always had round faces.

Lucy went very still in the sudden realization that she was, certainly, this woman's daughter. All the tiny details of her physical appearance, which had never quite matched with her sister or mother, were explained in Lady Arborage's face. It left her breathless.

"I never meant to leave you," the woman—her mother—said. "I was lured away from our seat of power. I dealt with the one who misled me, but the effort weakened me badly. My magic was nearly drained when my time came." Her voice was soft, barely more than a whisper. "I was forced to choose between bearing a living child and leaving her in the human world, or sacrificing my daughter's life to preserve my own strength for the return."

Arborage lifted her gaze to meet Lucy's, and her blue eyes were so cold they burned. "I chose to bear a living daughter and leave her in the hopes I would one day recover her."

Lucy felt as if her blood were freezing in her veins. She wanted to deny the woman's claim. She wanted to reject Lady Arborage in punishment for all the years she had felt a misfit in the human world. She wanted to set something on fire and watch it burn to the ground.

She wanted suddenly to hug her parents—her *real* parents—to look at the photo albums of her childhood and hear her mother singing "Duérmete, mi niña" in her husky alto. She wanted to argue with Celia and have Jacobo offering her unsolicited safety tips.

"I am Josefina Lucia Ruiz," she told her mother, her voice low and deadly. "I may not be mortal, but I'm still me."

Theo leaned harder against her legs. He could understand what she was saying, she remembered. He knew the choice she was making. Or maybe he didn't. Maybe he thought she was still in denial. But Lucy knew the blood that flowed through her veins. She *was* Unseelie, of the House of Winter. But that didn't mean she wasn't Lucy Ruiz. That didn't mean her life had been a lie.

"I am Lucy Ruiz, and I choose the family that raised me."

Lady Arborage seemed to sag, her shoulders slumping and her frame shrinking into itself. Her blue eyes met Lucy's gaze and held it, a deep sorrow in them. But she didn't argue.

"I'm glad I know the truth, I guess," Lucy said after a moment. "But it doesn't change anything."

"Doesn't it?" Lady Arborage's voice still sent shivers down Lucy's back. Lucy tensed to keep from shrugging the sensation away.

"Not really." Lucy took a deep breath. Maybe everyone went through life wondering if they really fit into the life they'd been born into. Maybe everyone wondered if they should have been a poet or an actress or a nuclear physicist instead of an accountant. Maybe everyone wondered if they had made the wrong choices in life.

Maybe they did. But Lucy was the one who had to decide now.

"I grew up in Indianapolis, in the Ruiz family. Maybe I have a heritage I didn't know about. Maybe I have talents or powers I didn't know about. But here's what I do know." Lucy curled her fingers into Theo's fur. "I'm good at accounting. I love Jake and Celi. I want to keep trying to get homeless teenagers off the streets. I may have a small life that doesn't always feel like it fits me. But it's *my* life. And I choose to live it."

Lady Arborage lowered her head in acquiescence, but Lucy would swear that her birth mother's lips were curled in a smile. "Always know that you may call on me, Eluciara," she said softly. "There will always be a place for you in my heart."

Lucy sucked in a breath and opened her mouth to say thank you, then remembered what Theo had said about not thanking the Fae. Would it offend her mother if she thanked her? Maybe someday she would want to know more about her blood heritage. Maybe someday she would want to understand why her words were enough to turn a man to ice. She was born of winter. There was no need to burn the bridges she might one day need to cross.

"I will hold that knowledge dear," she said quietly. A hundred questions tumbled over each other in her mind, but she wasn't sure how long she and Theo had been here, and stories like Rip Van Winkle made her leery of staying too long. She drew in a long breath. "For now, farewell."

Fingers buried in the fur of her werewolf, Lucy Ruiz turned her back on Faerie and began her journey back to the mortal world.

G is for Gentry

Suzanne J. Willis

Thomasina – a woman with an empty space where her heart should be

"Speak to her," the voice said.
"To who?" I asked. There was no-one else in the room.
"You know who."
I had made it here through a doorway unknown. What was one more step into empty air? I took a deep breath and began, hoping that it would be enough...

Anyone who believes that faeries are wee, golden-haired creatures with dragon-fly wings and sweet intentions has never met a real faerie. Never crossed the borders, or pushed through the back of the cupboard, or crawled through a strange, crooked doorway in the base of an old tree, into the realm where the fae live. If they had, they would know what real faeries are; the hags and the dragon tamers, the goblin-children and wind riders. The Heart Keeper.

Of course, you don't have to cross anywhere to find the Heart Keeper. She and her ilk are still criss-crossing from their lands into ours. Human hearts are far too tempting for them to stay put and wait for the brave, the silly, the lucky and the believers to seek them out. Oh, not the organ of muscle and ventricles and electric impulses that keep our fragile bodies going. No, it's much more gruesome than that. Their taste runs to *real* hearts, where we keep our desires and fears and love. Strange things they are, too, and each one a different shape and size depending upon its owner.

Small and gentle as seahorses, hiding in a kelp forest of shyness; cumbersome sailor's chests full of scrimshaw love notes in language unfamiliar; ordinary teacups holding witches' brews of forgotten dreams and hope.

Whatever their measure, they all beat in the same manner. Like burning wood, alight from within, red and white heat moving through them in shifting light. Sparks find their way out, here and there; flames shoot out from the scars of old wounds, licking at the cold air.

These were things that I knew, knowledge that had reached for me across the borders, long before I found myself before the hearth of the Heart Keeper, looking for my own heart that she had stolen from me years before.

Venya – a wildwood faerie. The Heart Keeper.

Human hearts belong in Faerieland. We Keepers don't have mothers or fathers. So there is no-one to teach us this, but we are born with those words on our tongues. They are the very first words that we speak. For the first century or two, I believed it. But I made enough mistakes in that time – do you know how difficult it is for a faerie to admit she has made mistakes?–to know that not all of them should come this way. It's the people who can live quite happily without their hearts that are the best and worst to steal from. The ones who don't even recognise its absence. We *need* them, but too many will irrevocably breach our worlds.

All hearts call for their owner. That's part of the pleasure of taking them. A thin sliver of longing connects the two parts that make a person whole. Some hearts sing softly as evening falls, while others whisper storm words at the height of summer. Others still send snowflakes or raindrops that wisp across the skin. But those whose owners have forgotten them entirely sit silent and cry quietly from time to time. They are the ones that I have learned to use for the most secret of faerie things. From them are born the doorways between Faerieland and the ordinary world.

Thomasina

I can tell you the exact day when I first realised that my heart was gone. It was hot, the middle of summer, and the wind swirled off the ocean in briny updrafts. A flock of northern kites circled on updrafts, watching the ground. I began to walk and it was only when I had gone the full three blocks toward the beach that I realised they were watching *me*. Had followed me the whole time, calling to me.

I knew, without a shadow of a doubt, that my heart sent them there, to tell me it was waiting for me. For the first time, I keenly felt my loss. The kites called above me, a hollow song that sounded like the end of the world. I bumped down onto the ground, watching them and remembering the long-ago night it had been stolen from me. Until that moment, I had always thought that the memory was just the fanciful imaginings of eight-year old child.

I had woken suddenly, in the still darkness of the small hours that I now know can stretch on forever. The rocking chair in the corner of my room was gently rocking back and forth. At first, there was just a faint outline of *someone* sitting there. The chair moved back and forth, hypnotic. As I drifted in and out of sleep she came into view, flickering like an old movie, silvery and indistinct. Her hair moved about, as though snaking in the wind. Or was it the gentle writhing of snakes? I smelled earth after the rain; smelled the thunder and storms of Faerieland, although I couldn't tell you how I knew that. That untamed creature sat and rocked in my chair. Then she smiled at me.

In that smile was an invitation. She stretched out her hand.

Come with me, she said.

Even in dreams, that is a scary prospect. I shook my head and her smile faded as I fell asleep again. The next morning, my mother told me I looked pale, and I felt *odd*, although I couldn't quite say why.

I never slept through the night again.

And if the kites hadn't found me that day, years after that strangest of nights, circling overhead and calling out sadness, I might never have known why

Venya

Human hearts taste like faerie food. Although part of being the Keeper is to stop those precious kernels from falling into the hands of other faeries. I haven't always been successful, but that wasn't *always* a mistake. Long ago – longer than three of your lifetimes – the Autumn Queen decreed that at the solstice feast, the heart of a babe was to be joined with lightning from the Dark Music mines. That dish was hers alone to consume. Afterwards, she danced the rowan-tree waltz. It was marvellous to see her, moving like a tree bends in the tempest, like the willow sings to the waters flowing under it. The waltz meant that for the next year, no rowan tree branches could be used by people to escape dancing in a faerie ring. Although why they would want to escape, I don't know.

Then came the year when, instead of a babe's heart, that of a dying miser was used instead. There was something just as magnificent in watching the Queen try to dance within the enormous circle of *amanita muscaria* mushrooms as she grew thick roots into the earth and sprouted red berries from her slender branches that spread outwards.

In the stillness afterward, we could still hear the beetle-tick of her pulse.

It might seem strange to you for Faerieland to have a rowan-tree as Queen for the next hundred years or so, but she did quite nicely, thank you. And I couldn't keep giving over baby's hearts forever. What kind of keeper would I be? We all need to find our own way and sometimes—the best times—that way is roundabout and not at all straight.

So, keep them we must, and not be frivolous in the taking or the giving. But it's *using* them that is all-important. That's what keeps them alive, what keeps that thin silver thread between the heart and its owner from breaking. It's when we add not-so-human things–a little drop of poison, a wishbone with a forgotten wish clinging inside–that they tug on that thread.

Thomasina

I wish that a missing heart just left behind an empty space, a neatly cauterised wound that no-one could ever see. But that space is filled up all too quickly with things hungrily looking for a home. And those things have voices that whisper constantly, reminding me that I will never be enough. Will never fit in, no matter quite where I go.

It was only when I realised what it was that was gone that I began to *revel* in my differences, in not fitting in. There was freedom in it. I sang down the silver thread, no matter where I was – walking along the streets, standing in a packed train – without a care for the strange looks I got. I pushed against the backs of cupboards and looked for strange creatures that might be hopping, ready to give chase. Although I had no words for it, I began to believe that there was another world, just an edge away from my own, and that if I turned the right corner or the right key, I would find it. The frost-mouth faeries breathing winter, the silver spinners weaving wishes into tiny flitting finches, the land that is forever autumn, gold and whispering and spider web fine.

Thomasina's Heart

Find an oak tree, one that hides birds' nests in its forks and knotholes. Wait until one of those tiny birds swoops in and lands in its branches. Walk around the tree widdershins, keeping your left hand on her trunk. Thrice will do it. See the bird as she takes off again, the bright blue of her wings flashing in the sun, the touch of white at her throat a patch of spilled moonlight? Those colours are for you. She's carrying your pain with her, will fly up, up, then drop it from on high so it splits into nothing more than dust and star-parts. It will not find you again.

Now you are free to remember the water-witch in green's cruel gloom, her smile a saw of pointed teeth. To remember running from

her, then carving your name into a frozen pond and watching the nix-
ies, blue and scaled with cold, swim up from the deep and lick the ice
clean from underneath, so the letters shone like diamonds. Leaving
them there like a dare, for the water-witch to find.

She gave your name to the Heart Keeper before you were even
born. We have been waiting for you ever since.

Venya

Not many people understand the language of hearts. Some can't hear
it, even when they arrive here. They don't last very long. I often wonder why their hearts call to us faeries in the first place? These aren't
the people who have forgotten their hearts. No, they are as ruthless as
the goblins that raid the Revenant Lands, taming wraiths to search for
graveyard treasures and word-souls. They are the ones who never
cared that they had ever had hopes or dreams or wishes at all.

A few of those hearts have found their way to the new Queen.

But as soon as I saw Thomasina, I knew she understood. That she
could find the door through, because she would hear the calling of
forgotten hearts in their guise of secret doorways. That night, as I
watched her sleeping through the window, I saw her singing to her
own heart in her sleep. I had never seen one like it: a shapeshifter,
light and merry and *strong*. One moment a dog gleefully snapping at
the sparks its wagging tail send into the darkness. The next, a mermaid
swimming through the invisible currents of night air. Next still, a tiny
child in the image of its owner, curled on her chest and mouthing
along the words of sleep song.

I was careful as I leant over the sleeping child, held my hand over
her chest to find just the right place to cut. My knife was a blade of

albatross bone, its handle the scaled skin of a salamander. Together, they were an instrument of fire and ferocity. Only under a faerie hand could it have been wielded as delicately as required.

Pressing the blade down near Thomasina's collarbone, I came within a cat's whisker of her flesh. If the skin is so much as scratched, let alone if blood is drawn, then the prize is lost forever. Collarbone to sternum, then back again, a perfect V-shape. The caul was silky and separated easily, almost as though it wanted to. Then my quarry, in the shape of a northern kite, slipped through. It hovered before me, burning brighter than any earthly flame. With a snip, snap, I opened the cage that sits in the middle of my own chest. It flew in and, as I snibbed the door behind it, I felt it put its head under its wing and fall fast asleep.

And if Thomasina had come with me that night, as she was meant to, she would not have spent years searching and wondering and waiting for the right door.

Thomasina

I stood atop the mountainside at sunset, barefoot on the ancient, lichen covered rocks. The breeze blew through the treetops, giving voice to the silvery eucalypt leaves. I don't understand the songs of trees, but you don't need to understand something to know its beauty. That cold evening, I felt like they were singing for me.

Their voices grew louder as the wind rushed up the gully. I stretched out my arms and it pulled them upwards; for a moment, my feet lifted from the earth and I thought I might fly away with it. But the fae do not give gifts so easily. *Especially the wind riders,* I thought.

I had been readying myself for years for this, reading everything that I could to tell how to get to Faerieland. Everything that I loved – stories of magic, faerie tales, blues music sung in a cigarette-and-whiskey voice at 3am, the way the light plays in the air at the moment between dusk and twilight – told me that something else was waiting, just beyond the shadows. After the kites, I had begun to recognise those who still had their hearts and those who didn't. We're an odd bunch, the missing ones. We *knew*, and it was the most delicious secret between us.

Some swum out in dark waters on the new moon, let the waves crash over them, waited for the mermaids to shine a light on the way from their soul-lamps made of sailors' bones and Neptune's glorious hair. Others tried to dance their way there, or walked across the oldest of countries hoping to find a doorway in a mountain, or the Erl-King stepping from an alder tree. On the rare occasion one of them disappeared, we would celebrate with mead and mulled wine. I tried to keep the jealous longing at bay, but sometimes it soured that mead in my throat.

It was only by accident that I found myself on that mountainside, having driven out there to return, of all things, a lost cat that wound up on my doorstep. When I left the owner's house, I saw the kites again, soaring and dipping in a dance that no normal updrafts could create.

Standing on the edge of the mountain, facing the gusting wind made the leaves sing and soil shake, a warm current slithered toward me. It reached out, wrapped around me, stopped my shivering. I smelled honey and pomegranates. Then, for only the second time in my life, I smelled the thunder of the storms of Faerieland. That otherworld breeze had a forgotten heart's voice.

Jump, it whispered. *I will catch you.*

As the sun slid down beneath the horizon like a pat of butter, and the clouds flamed crimson and violet and faerie-thunderous, I stepped off the edge of the mountain.

Venya

You found your doorway. And here you are.

Thomasina

"Here I am," I nodded.

I had been blown, quite literally, into the home of the Heart Keeper. It was underground, tree roots from which she had hung lamps and dried herbs wending through the room and through the floor. It was lined with shelves, upon which sat delicate glass jars, labelled with sepia ink in a spidery hand. Within each jar beat a heart and they whispered in crystal-plink voices.

Speak to her, my own had said.

"To who?" I asked. There was no-one else in the room.

You know who.

So I had told my story, and she had told hers. As if sculpted from her words, the Keeper came into view, shadowy and flickering, then finally taking her full shape as our tales converged with my arrival here.

She stood before me, whole and beautiful, reaching out her hand towards me.

"I've waited a long time," said Venya, standing by the mantelpiece over which hung a bright mirror. "But I know you have searched for much longer. You know how time works between Faerieland and your old world?"

I nodded again. Time is slippery enough in one place, let alone trying to measure it against another one entirely.

"And now you're here, what is it that you will do?"

I looked around, shrugged. I hadn't thought that far ahead. The whispering grew louder. In the mirror, a weathered man in a pork-pie hat leaned against an old fence and played a battered guitar, a cigarette hanging from his mouth. He looked out at me, smiled and lifted his head as though to say *There you are.*

"Look harder," she said. "You might find it easier if you shut your eyes."

It should have been an odd thing to say, but of course it wasn't. I closed my eyes and in the darkness, a tracery of light appeared. It was a pair of hands... my hands! I was crouched beside someone sleeping, carefully carving the air above their chest. Then I was holding a jar, dropping in tiny white starflowers to join the spinning wheel heart sitting inside it. My own sat on my shoulder, singing a song of falling in love and the voice she once gave to a man in a pork-pie hat as his fingers flew over the keys of a rickety piano.

I smiled. "What about you?" I asked Venya.

"There is much more to this than 'you' or 'me'," she smiled. "Are you ready?"

"A lifetime beyond ready," I replied.

She held out her hand to me, and we stood before the mirror together. The old musician looked back at us, tipped his hat. I had never met him, but I knew his voice sounded like gravel and honey, that his songs were vaudeville stories told under witchy moons. On the Keeper's mantel sat his heart, the size of a salt shaker, shaped like a gramophone.

"He's like you," Venya said. "He carries other worlds in the space left behind. He's waiting for you..."

He turned, slung the guitar over his back, and walked toward the dark forest behind him. My reflection and Venya's came into view, sharpened against that silhouetted forest. It was like looking into a dark pool, firelight slipping over its surface. A stone dropped into the pool, rippling its surface, and the reflections wavered. When it stilled again, there was just one. Me, with wild hair and faerie eyes, but something of the human in the chin and ears, the freckles across my skin. I couldn't imagine why I had ever thought that there were two of us there.

In the mirror's distance, the bluesman stopped, turned, beckoned to me. I was ready for him to show me the new doorways we had created with those precious, forgotten hearts. We Heart Keepers don't have mothers or fathers, but we know that human hearts belong in Faerieland. We are born with those words on our tongues and, although I didn't quite know why, I said them aloud as I walked through the mirror.

H is for Heart Keeper

Joseph Halden

Once upon a dark time, the idiot-King Donald prepared to cast the first stone from His immense trebuchet which was so powerful it could shatter the battlements in the distant land of Icanta.

His starving audience frothed suitably at the mouth. The seeds of their discontent bloomed and their little imaginations properly shaped into hate thanks to the Great Fairy.

All King Donald required now was suitable attire.

"Intrusion into His interior inhibits intelligence," I said, tucking my tail while straightening my front paws and neck. My back paw absently reached for the spot behind my ear I could never quite scratch enough.

Claudia, the King's stylist, turned to face me with a frown on her brown face. She wore a dark blue silk shirt and black trousers tied at the waist with a white string: an ensemble practical yet stylish, which was why she was the best at what she did. "Hello? Who's there?"

When intelligent speech was involved, dogs became invisible. Which was, I suppose, part of the Great Fairy's plan when she'd given me this pride-swallowing assignment. It was also important that no *real* dog ever got near the King, because real dogs exuded competing magical auras that would diminish our fairy influence over Him.

I might have turned into my true fairy-form if we weren't so dangerously close to the bloody King but just beyond a thick oak door, in a dressing room with enough mirrors to cook a dozen hens by the light of golden sun, was the idiot-King himself tied up in the rapturous glory of his own form. Transforming also drained me, requiring, as it did, so much effort to maintain my sense of self and not get lost through the conversion. In short, I couldn't flit back and forth willy-nilly. I had to face Claudia and convince her of my power while remaining in dog form.

"I interrupted yer introspection," I said when Claudia's gaze drifted sufficiently close to my French-poodle body. I resented the Great Fairy's choice of creature for this work—the King's favourite—and felt every strand of curly black hair as iron bars.

"Whiskers? W—was that you?" Claudia said, touching her fingertips delicately to her gaping mouth.

I winced. The idiot-King's name for me was probably the only thing that could have further robbed my revealing moment of its impact. And I'd thought the worst part of this assignment had been playing mother to a litter of puppies several months ago.

"Aye," I said. "I indeed."

"By the fine wool of Azaloth, that—that's incredible." She frowned, then put her hands on her hips. "How many times has the King wished you could speak? Were you giving Him the cold shoulder, you bad dog?"

"I'm a f—fairy." Saying the word *fairy* sent stabbing pain through my skull, but it was necessary for clarity. I refused to self-identify as an imp, the closest word I could speak.

Claudia looked me up and down, one eyebrow raised. "A fairy dogmother? Never heard of that before."

Now that her initial astonishment had passed, she didn't look even mildly frightened. She was even *scolding* me. This wasn't going at all how I'd planned. How was she so frustratingly accepting—even adaptive—to anything strange that happened? No one should be this calm and sane to a talking dog—no one. Yet, I'd watched her influence on His Majesty for months. Somehow, despite being philosophically opposed to everything He did, she'd maintained a calm demeanour toward Him despite His most idiotic policies. If I didn't know any better, I would have pegged her as inhuman.

I licked my lips. "Intercourse in idiot's introspection implies imminent extinction."

Claudia pursed her lips. "I'm not having sex with the King, Whiskers!"

I covered my eyes with a paw and shook my head. "S—social intercourse. Insist you s—stop. Or else." My ears rang with the words I was forbidden from speaking. Damn the Great Fairy's punishment that prevented me from saying any words that didn't start or sound with I. Couldn't she have lifted it when she'd given me this task?

"Or else what, you'll lick me to death?" She smirked and bent at the hips toward me.

"I'll invoke incredible incantations."

Claudia laughed, and reached so quickly for that spot behind my ears I didn't have time to move out of the way.

It felt good, and my back leg moved as it dreamed of scratching that hard-to-reach spot.

No! I shook my head and jumped away, standing on all fours.

"You may be able to talk, Whiskers, but you're still a sweetheart, I know it."

I'd hoped that threats of magic, and the shocking impact of a talking dog, would be enough to encourage Claudia to quit. Neither act had helped—in fact, they seemed to be endearing me to her.

Unacceptable. I needed to stop her.

The death of the King's brother had thrust Him into power without any of the preparation His older brother had. He was a turtle flailing on His back, and His early missteps met with harsh criticism that threatened His fragile ego. As a result, He'd begun wanting nothing more than to win the approval of everyone around Him. We, the Great Fairy's agents, had almost completely surrounded Him, influencing His thoughts, philosophies and policies to ensure He thought the loud minority of bigots were the majority, the people He needed most to please. The Great Fairy had ensured He would only get approval by bending to her will, and so the King was surrounded by us, her agents, who would ensure the destruction of the civilized world and a descent into total chaos. Then the Great Fairy would be perfectly positioned to save everyone, return humanity into servitude, and reclaim our status as gods.

I couldn't wait! We were so close now, and all that stood between us was Claudia, the last reasonable person who could bend the King's ear.

The fact that she was discussing philosophy with a king who never discussed philosophy in-depth with *anyone* was deeply troubling. I'd sent word to the Great Fairy weeks ago warning her about Claudia, but she hadn't believed me. The Great Fairy thought I was shirking my responsibilities like I'd done centuries before, and told me that I should handle it. There was, after all, a great deal of other preparation to do to fuel the upcoming war.

The only tools she'd left me after she'd wiped my mind of all magical knowledge was the crudest form—the karmic variety, where whatever magical influence I exerted would be reflected back on me in a chaotic manner.

I whimpered unconsciously at the thought of what I was about to bring upon myself.

"Aw, Whiskers, you're a good dog, don't worry. The King will be so happy His snuggly-uggums can talk!"

"I'll inhibit informing him."

"By being so cute? I suppose so. Come here, you." She reached again for my ear and I jumped and spun out of the way, all of my legs straight.

I needed a small demonstration of magic, something that wouldn't hurt me too much, but would show her I was capable of it. The problem was, the easiest magic for a forest fairy involved flowers, which weren't exactly the most threatening things to will into being.

She scuttled a few more times toward me. My back brushed against the red walls as I dodged and looked frantically around the gold-trimmed room for something to use. There were many oak armoires and dressers, purple tapestries, a window, a door into the King's chambers, a door into the servants' quarters, Claudia's trolley, a pile of crumpled blankets which were my bed, and a mirror.

None of it was good material with which to work forest magic. I decided on the best thing I could think of.

With my back to the wall, I jumped and stomped my paws on the wood-panelled floor, willing the red colour from the wall to transfer to the floor.

Claudia gasped and stepped back. My magic had worked—in a cloud around me the floor was now a bright red, and the wall brown.

Unfortunately, I saw in the mirror that, as a result of the magic, the colour of my fur had changed to a vibrant swirl of purple and green.

"That is a neat trick, Whiskers," she said. "Some incredible incantation, definitely." Her exaggerated nod told me how well my demonstration hadn't worked.

Growling, I darted over to one of the hanging suits on the trolley, and nuzzled it with my nose. A moment later, the suit's material was cut by invisible scissors until only the outline of a skeleton remained.

Immediately, my own fur protruded out in ragged, matted clumps that tugged at my skin.

Claudia's expression flattened.

"It's imperative ye inverse interrupt 'is 'ighness's illustrious import. Internal introspection is it. If I identify intercourse, yer identity'll impoverish."

"Are you threatening me or—"

"Aye." I bared my teeth, but worried it might look like a friendly gesture in poodle form.

"You don't want me to talk to the King?"

I nodded.

"Well, He and I are going to have a lovely chat while we get Him sorted for the big event. He's just waiting for a selection of bloomers." She gestured to a row of pants on the trolley ranging from plain black to wild-coloured patterns.

"If 'ightail it, I insist inhabit 'ere into 'ereafter."

"Threaten me all you like, Whiskers, but I have a job to do," Claudia said, taking steps toward me. "Do what you will with your magic but if you hurt me, the King will know and you'll be exposed."

"'n idiot."

She tilted her head, shrugged, then nodded. "Yes, I can't deny He's stupid. But I could tell Him what sort of devilry is behind anything that happens."

"Idiot'll insist insanity."

Claudia clutched the rack of clothes on wheels. "Perhaps. But if you kill me, He'll know."

That much was true. Forest magic that killed left unmistakable traces, so I couldn't murder her without the King becoming aware of the fairies and our designs on seizing power. I could only try and deter her with the little and dangerous magic left to me.

Claudia stuck her tongue out at me as she pushed the trolley closer to the door.

Maybe if she could no longer do her job, then the King would have to find someone else to pick his attire. But what would incapacitate a stylist?

I know. I could make her blind. It would harm my own vision permanently and unpredictably, but I could get by with other heightened senses in my dog form if need be. Then when I returned to my rightful god status, I'd have enough magic at my disposal to reverse the effects.

I bounded across the wooden-plank floor and pounced on Claudia, knocking her over. I pinned her shoulders and jammed my nose close to each eye before giving them long licks. Claudia cried out and giggled.

With each magical lick I gave, my vision exploded with lightning, and now there were starburst flickers making the room sparkle.

A moment later, I saw ghostly copies of myself in dog form, stalking around the room, after-images burning in. The room's features shifted and jolted about, their positions uncertain. The purple tapestries waved as though from a steady wind. I made my way back to my bed and tripped over my feet, no longer sure of where I or anything was anymore.

"I can't see," Claudia whispered, and I glanced over to see what I think was her outstretched hands reaching for nothing. "I—I can't see. What have you done, Whiskers? You—you really are a fairy. A wretched, evil fairy."

There. Maybe that was enough to stop her. I would have blurred vision, see ghost-copies of myself and trip over my paws, but at least I'd stopped her.

She took a few deep breaths, then slowly got to her feet. She muttered under her breath, giving herself directions to where things were. At length, her voice steadied and grew firm. "Fine. I'm fine. I can manage this."

She pushed the trolley into the side of the door, then adjusted and made her way through.

Fine? I blind her and that's all she has to say? *Fine?* From what realm does such a woman who can so quickly accept so great a theft emerge? I was too stunned, and admittedly a little frightened, to react to her departure in time.

I wanted to bite the numerous ghosts of myself roaming the room as the door shut behind Claudia and she entered the King's presence.

Unisteria's last hope, Claudia the stylist, was cursed with blindness as she returned to King Donald for His last fitting and wardrobe selection before the ceremony. They spoke and she commenced the straightening of His mind by blowing a fresh wind to cleanse the foul ones of the Great Fairy. Now cursed by the evil fairy dogmother, Claudia did not know how she would recommend matching colours and perform her other duties without the gift of sight.

Fortunately, as she ran her hands across the threads of the many pairs of bloomers, she could visualize each and every one in her mind judging only by the texture, and so she found her confidence, helping Him select an appropriate pair, and working by feel to determine where it needed hemming.

He was curious about her sudden blindness, but since Claudia knew He wouldn't believe his beloved dog Whiskers had done the work, she said that it was caused simply by many years of staring at his bright magnificence.

Being an idiot-King and easily pleased by ego-soothing words, He believed her.

As she worked on His bloomers, they spoke of things both simple and great, from what He'd had at breakfast to how to judge the calibre of a soul. She slowly wormed the thread in His mind that the Icantans, who were of a much darker complexion and therefore terri-

fying to the simple King Donald, could be judged by more elegant means that involved discourse and interaction. She slowly filled the vacancy of His imagination.

The King lamented that alas, the time for that had passed, but there was a teasing hesitation in His voice that cast a glow in Claudia's sight despite her new blindness.

Claudia returned with the trolley, stumbling her way through the door. In the meantime, I'd listened while chewing on a brown leather shoe.

"Is inacceptance innate," I said, "is injecting involvement inferior in eyes?"

Claudia's fuzzy form flickered beside a dozen ghosts of black poodles. "I accept the things I cannot change, and fight for the change that I can."

She was seriously dangerous—the marriage of two normally contradicting philosophies. How was it possible?

"Iconoclasm is inherently ixhausting," I said. "Ideally ignorance is inspiriting. Inhabiting identities in indiscriminate interdicted inlands is impossible, isn't it?"

Claudia sighed. "Your words and ways are exhausting, fairy. Do you wonder how I can accept and continue after what you've done to me? How I can fight for justice yet keep such a tolerant spirit of one such as King Donald?"

"Indeed."

How did she keep her expectations low, and maintain happiness, while simultaneously wanting for a better world? Those who were happy were ignorant of the world's progress or regress. Those who wanted better were normally angry—so angry they burnt out before they could see anything through. She was a terrifying blend of both.

"I owe you nothing, fairy, after you've robbed me of my sight. If I could see you I would kick you. But I cannot and so I continue with what's left to me."

She stormed across the floor, her footsteps knocking, and I could hardly keep her straight between the ghosts of me, the shifting red walls, the waving tapestries and the oak armoires that twisted and bent.

She'd managed to not only fit the king with bloomers, but erode some of the careful brainwashing the Great Fairy had orchestrated. All just after I'd blinded her.

I needed to do much more to her, and much worse. But what the magic would do to me in return, I had no idea.

She flicked through the armoires, her eyes squeezed shut and her lips pressed tight as she focused on the feel of each garment. It became obvious what I had to do then: take away her feeling.

I narrowed my eyes and shuddered as I stepped through ghosts of my dog self.

I'm a god, I thought. *Not a dog. A* god. *Whatever happens, I'll be a god in the end.*

Claudia paused in her search for shirt and tunic, hand in mid-air while she looked over her shoulder. "Do not come near me, wretched fairy."

I padded more gingerly, making a big circle around her before closing in. She remained still, her blind eyes darting futilely about.

I leapt in for her hand, but she snatched it out of my jaws just in time. With her other hand, which had been blurry and indistinct, she grabbed a tunic and whipped it toward me, missing by a country mile but striking me in the stomach with her elbow.

We both fell to the ground, wrestling and rolling, as I tried to get a good touch on her hands, while she wrapped the oversized tunic more and more around me.

Within a few moments, she'd somehow managed to swaddle me, and I couldn't move a fly's wingspan.

I yelped. A dozen of my poodle ghosts watched me in shame as Claudia picked me up and bumped her way to my bed in the corner. I wondered briefly if it would have been better to be blind rather than continuously seeing these mirrored illusions of myself.

"There," she said, setting me down. Her feet wobbled a bit but she was still managing infuriatingly well without sight. "May the secrets of the universe remain forever clouded to your sight, imp."

I barked. "Imprisoning His intimate intern is inimical in implied ixistence."

"If He comes in, I'll explain how much of a bad dog you've been," Claudia said. "Don't think I can't recognize the smell of chewed leather, Whiskers."

She felt for the drawers of another dresser and pulled out a selection of shirts.

As she readied to make her way back in with the trolley, I realized I had no other option. I switched into my fairy form, focusing on my identity as a god. The blanket fell loose around my neck, but caught on my wings. My body was half my previous size, with my twilight-sparkling wings making up the difference.

If the King came in now, I was done for, not only because I was a fairy, but because it would look like I'd made His snuggly-uggums vanish. Thankfully, Claudia was too blind and wrapped up in her work to notice.

My head swam as though part of my brain had been left behind during the transformation. If I rushed another shape shift without eating a big bowl of kibble, I risked losing my sense of self altogether.

I squeezed my wings through the blanket swaddle. No time to waste.

I flitted over, ran into the cloudy edge of the trolley, twirled and managed to catch one of Claudia's hands.

She sucked in a sharp breath and straightened her arm as it covered in goose flesh. I crossed the gap toward her other hand, but she backed away from me. Poodles pinwheeled in my vision as I followed her, struggling to focus on my magic.

I reached her hand just as she backed into the armoire and one of the doors pinched my wing. I yelped just as I finished my spell and fell to the floor.

The after-effect kicked in. All over my body I felt pricks like a swarm of wasps were taking turns stinging me, their buzzing wings just hairs above my skin.

I watched bleary-eyed and wincing, the stings intensifying, as Claudia pushed out of the armoire, touching it hesitantly. Her face looked pained, but evidently she could still feel. I'd wanted to rob her of the sensation in her hands altogether, but it seemed in my distraction I'd just made touch painful for her.

I fumbled, twitching toward her to finish the job, thinking how badly this would obscure my own senses, but I was too slow. Claudia shoved through the door with the trolley and I had to dart into the shadows to avoid being seen.

The idiot-King questioned Claudia again when the evil fairy cursed her with the touch of a thousand needles. Claudia answered that the magnificence of His garments on Him had overpowered her senses. As before, the King believed her, feeling His ego suitably stroked and His thirst for approval partially quenched.

Claudia asked Him to try on each of the shirts and tunics and describe them to her, for she no longer had any means to discern. In this manner, Claudia was able to pick out the rest of his attire, choosing one that matched well but also pleased His sense of authority and choice.

While they worked, Claudia spoke of the materials she'd gotten from various regions and countries, and the wonderful people behind them. Her master stroke was in selecting a garment she convinced the King was the only and perfect choice, then informing Him it was made by the enemy Icantans.

If she could have seen the King, she would have seen His lips puckered more plump than a summer peach, and she would have been glad as that was the only expression He could make when He engaged in thought.

By the chaotic winds spreading dandelion drifts to the seven seas, this was bad. I could barely fly a stone's throw without my head spinning, felt like I had an invisible nest of angry wasps biting me everywhere, and Claudia seemed on the verge of convincing the King to abandon the trebuchet and the war with the Icantans altogether, all because of some ridiculous clothing choices.

I was further away from god status than I'd ever thought possible.

The trolley rolled to a stop back in the wardrobe room. "You will burn in such a deep place that the flames will cast no light, you evil creature," Claudia said, shuddering and wrapping a shawl around herself.

"Inheriting innocence is ill-suited in ideation insofar is imps incriminated in iconoclastic interference iliminate ye."

"Why do you speak so, spell caster?" Claudia asked, her face pleated in either concentration or pain. "With the power to curse me so, do you not have the power to unhinge your tongue?"

I paused, waiting for the follow-up insults and denigrations, but they never came. Was it that obvious that I was restricted? I thought

I'd had enough practice that I could make it sound natural, but apparently not.

I tried to study the wobbling copies of Claudia's face but they gave me no further insight into her designs. From what I could see, she had genuine interest in my story, which told me my senses were not to be trusted.

"Well, do you have a story, a tale of your own? Maybe you do not, and so you spend your life ruining others? I cannot believe that such wickedness has no sad beginning."

I had to admit, I was tempted to tell her of the Great Fairy's curse. My voice had been constrained so long that creatures had stopped asking me altogether of my opinion, history or stories.

How to give voice to a story centuries old? How to explain my thirst from a young age, from a young fae mind, to regain the god status I'd had passed onto me through story? The same feeling of greatness tantalizingly close swept over me irrespective of distance or time.

Centuries ago, I'd been tasked by the Great Fairy with ensuring no animals grew close to humans. Each creature of the forest had a magical aura that influenced the world differently, and being around too many had a diluent effect on anyone's magic. The Great Fairy wanted to ensure her influence, her power, was the driving force behind humanity's development.

Back then, the rise to glory had seemed as close as it did now.

The two biggest problem creatures who could interfere with our schemes were wildcats and wolves. Rather than banish them or cast them out of sight of any humans, I reasoned that I should rule over them as was proper for my stature, in the manner of the stories I'd been told as a child.

I insisted on their obedience, and drew great pleasure from the proper feeling of godliness when they submitted to me.

In the moments when I couldn't watch them I would get the wildcats and wolves to fight each other in order to distract them from any greater schemes. The distraction of fighting worked well enough, but while trying to make them my obedient subjects, I inadvertently accelerated their domestication.

Humans grew more and more attracted to the creatures despite my best efforts. My attempts to keep things under control resulted in creations like Pomeranians, Pugs, and Afghan Hounds that threatened to expose us all, since no such creatures could be made without magic.

Before it was too late, the Great Fairy stepped in and stripped me of all but the crudest forms of magic. Furthermore, for thinking and acting so selfishly, she cursed me with the ability to only speak in words that begin or sound with I.

The long years of begging for forgiveness blurred into one another until she tasked me with this assignment. She had a terrible sense of justice and humour, the Great Fairy did, and it was probably why I'd been the one to become a dog, a creature she loathed.

I could not tell this story to Claudia even if I'd wished it. The words I had left to me would make the meaning as muddled as the swamps where fairies went to die.

I caught the change in my attitude toward Claudia, then covered my eyes and gave my head a thorough shake. She was the enemy, the one person who could stop everything from getting better again, for me to finally become the fairy I was meant to be.

She was also the only creature who'd asked of my story in what felt like eons, but perhaps that was part of the same trickery she used to sway the King away from the Great Fairy's designs.

"You offer me silence now, as another curse?" Claudia asked. "I will not complain any more about my new lot, fairy. All I ask in return is to understand where your malice was planted."

I couldn't hold back. "I've inability inform intricacies introduced in my infancy," I said. "I'm interrupted in I inquest in interminable illustriousness in imparting inconsequential interchanges inbetween individuals."

"Aye, you seek a return to greatness, as do so many," Claudia said. "And your tongue is tied until you do, so you seek to subjugate until your status is restored."

"Aye," I said.

"I thought once that happiness came with others' misery. I was teased mercilessly as a child, and I toyed with all manner of garments to try and escape the torture. Eventually, I discovered attire that would induce respect, and grant me power over others. I nearly lost myself as I lorded over them, assaulting them in the same manner I'd been. It fit with so many stories I'd had told to me, and so I had little cause to question it.

"There came a time when the clothes didn't fit, however, and my desperate search for new attire gave me enough pause to see how much I'd lost myself. In making my new garb, I discovered the means to reflect who I wanted to be, while retaining the power within myself. I no longer needed to subjugate others to maintain my identity.

"I wonder, fairy, if there is a way in which you might find what you seek without forcing others to bow at your feet?"

"Idealistic idiot," I snapped.

Claudia sighed. "That is unfortunate. I suppose you're going to do worse to me, and my ability to speak might have a ticking clock as well. I expect the worst, but aspire to the best, fairy. That does not fully answer your earlier question, but it's the best I can provide. I don't know how I cultivate this outlook within myself—if I could, I would gift it to others. Perhaps it was the marriage of conflict and ac-ceptance within my own upbringing, that created the right recipe for stamina and affirmation. I cannot explain it. I just know that I accept and understand your perspective, but will nevertheless fight for what's right until there is no strength left in me."

I wanted to keep her talking as long as possible, but she went silent for a moment, then stirred into action.

I felt dumbstruck by how she managed to throw a haphazard as-sortment of shoes into a bin, even though every touch sent gusts of pain through her. She readied to return to the King's chambers, and I scrambled for what to do.

I couldn't curse her tongue as she'd suggested. I had enough problems in that regard without bringing further pains upon myself from the realm of chaos.

Then it struck me: she defined herself through her clothing. Her creations.

I flew over to her and bit her at the edge of her cuff, tasting her blood as well as the fabric of her silk shirt. I willed my magic to make her creations invisible, and a moment later, the box of shoes appeared empty, and Claudia looked naked.

She jerked, knowing a change had occurred, but slammed the door shut behind her.

Claudia approached the idiot-King and both were now naked thanks to the effects of the evil fairy dogmother's curse. The King played at indignation, secretly flattered as He thought she meant to seduce Him.

Claudia deftly explained that wasn't the case. Instead, what she'd wanted to tell Him from the start, but had been too afraid of His reaction, was that His magnificence didn't need adornment or adulteration. She could supply Him with clothing that would provide warmth and protection that was still necessary and prudent, but that would be invisible. The greatness of His form need not be hidden from the people any longer, especially for such a momentous occasion as this.

The King frowned, disappointed that Claudia wasn't trying to seduce Him, and unsure what to make of her explanation. For at His core, He didn't think himself worthy of kingship, so flattery to such an extent as Claudia attempted went beyond His capacities.

Sensing the hesitation in His words, Claudia grew desperate, knowing this might be her last chance. She explained that such a drastic change in wardrobe was necessary to reflect and explain the change in plans for the Icantans. Instead of a boulder in the trebuchet, she suggested the King launch a bundle of seeds and flowers that would grow into a garden wherever they landed. Such a symbolic gesture would quite literally sow the seeds for renewed friendship and prosperity between the nations.

Claudia spoke at length, giving further justification and credit to the King for thoughts He had suggested and intimated in their earlier conversations. Her solution incorporated the parts of Himself He'd kept somewhat hidden from anyone's disapproval, and she encouraged Him to be brave befitting His stature and expose a grand new plan for the nation.

King Donald puckered His lips once, twice, then three times in succession, each one doubling in duration, as He put on snug but invisible shoes. It was quite fortunate that His advisors never followed Him when he was dressing, for they could have easily swayed Him in that moment.

Appearing naked before His staff, He summoned the castle's florist.

I wasn't sure at first what the side effects of my magic were until I tried to take mental account of the spells I'd cast so far. It took far longer than expected since my skin continued to prick every other moment.

I couldn't remember what actions I'd taken, and what actions I'd only dreamed of doing. My history was like a blurred reflection through stained glass. The timeline of events leading to where I now stood, along with the justifications, were torn and blended with images of what might have been. The moments created by my choices had been all but robbed from my mind.

I had an image of cursing Claudia with invisible creations, and that memory seemed more firm than the rest. I regretted having done that to her, for now my mind seemed inexorably tied to the now with only a fleeting ability to cast into the past or future. Everything I created through my existence was murky at best, if not gone altogether.

The strongest thing I could remember was that I was a god. Gods were rulers, all-seeing, all-knowing, and not afflicted by the pains of the mundane. My vague memories—or were they just dreams?—of barking, biting and fighting with Claudia left me with a hollow feeling in my stomach. If that had truly happened, none of that was me, or at least it wasn't what I wanted to be me.

I couldn't be sure if I'd done it or not. I couldn't be sure of anything I'd done, and gone also were the certainty and rationalization that had accompanied my actions.

The sense of unimportance left me staggered. If I could no longer keep a running record of what I did, how would I know if I'd made progress toward godhood? How would I know if I'd already achieved it? How could I justify my behaviour toward Claudia if I wanted to see myself as all-seeing, all-knowing, yet behaved like a wild animal?

With my leaf-dappled hair flowing over my fingertips, I pressed my hands into my temples, lowering to the wood-panelled floor as I tried to concentrate.

In the immediate future the King was going to launch a bouquet to Icanta. I was supposed to stop that in order to secure temporary chaos toward the eventual order brought about by fairy rule.

There were generals and other advisors involved in the trebuchet launch, however, who would probably sabotage the attempt at a bouquet.

Was that good, or bad? I tried to cast my gaze into the future again, but it was as though Claudia's blanket swaddle wrapped around me once more.

As my mind jerked back to the present, I imagined myself as ruler, as King Donald, and wondered fleetingly if I was a better ruler than him, if I was more fitting.

No. At least not the way I was acting. None of us fairies were. We weren't behaving as gods at all. I don't know if we ever had. I don't know if I ever had, and worse, if I could do better.

I wondered if this springing back and forth between the present and the future, as my mind seemed to be doing now, was how Claudia maintained her philosophy. Or was that her philosophy? Acceptance while simultaneously fighting for change. I wished briefly that I could return my focus to the distant future, which had provided me so much warmth and comfort in the past.

I wanted to damn her, but my darting mind reminded me that I'd cast the spell, and truly done this to myself. I'd thrown away my own sense of agency, the history paved through action, that allowed me the continuity and ability to justify the means by the end.

If the Great Fairy was willing to do everything she'd already done to secure power, what would she do once she had it?

Damn-but-not-damn Claudia. This new sight made me want to sink into the floor. I was terrified of casting any more spells.

If I helped the Great Fairy I might get my magic back. I might have a chance to be the god I may or may not already be.

Or I could help Claudia.

The notion blurred my vision more than it already was, and I teetered. Visions of us working together seemed as real to me as those of us wrestling in the blanket, and I could not push them away.

If I helped Claudia, I would be stuck with these magical impediments—yes, these that I'd brought upon myself—unable to do anything to remedy them. However, her plan sewed seeds of harmony, the same seeds I wanted to grow in a world where fairies prospered.

I wish I could remember what actions I had taken. They would have given me impetus to continue, to know what was right or wrong, but as that had been stripped from me, I was forced to gaze on the merits of everything without the continuity of time. To look upon the meaning of events in abstract, by themselves, without the obfuscating power of historic dogma and rationalization.

I had a vision of a girl finding the right set of clothing so that she didn't have to bully in order to stake her claim in the world. In my current state, it was probably the closest image I had to godliness, because it was an image of greatness that could be removed from circumstance and still hold true.

Damn Claudia.

I couldn't condemn the world and claim to be a god. If I was a god, why was it so hard to see, to feel and to think, anyway?

Maybe I could do something, regain a portion of the agency lost to me. I might not remember it, but what I did in the moment would at least be something I could call godly.

I fluttered up, blurred images of poodles, trolleys and fairy wings distorting my view, and flew through the door toward the trebuchet.

King Donald appeared naked before the masses who were stunned to silence. In long-winded, yet simple words, He explained three times over the philosophy of what He intended to do, as assistants loaded the trebuchet with the seed bunch.

Claudia had had great foresight, because the crowd would never have believed the rational response from Him if it were not accompanied by the absurdity of His invisible attire. He was, after all, an idiot, and if a portion of His idiocy hadn't remained, the crowd might not have found His new philosophy genuine. The world, it seemed, operated quite similarly to the evil fairy's balancing karmic magic.

Claudia was thrilled to hear the promise of all her sacrifice coming to bear. However, the Great Fairy's agents were woven intricately into the King's staff, and planned to sabotage the seed bunch with a boulder.

The crowd held its breath as the trebuchet readied to launch. They blocked part of their sight as the King stood beside the firing handle, his legs wide.

Claudia couldn't see that things were about to go terribly, terribly wrong, and that the war the Great Fairy wanted would come to pass.

Whiskers, the fairy dogmother, flew out into the King's entourage and barely avoided the arrows, swords and spears. She swerved until she landed on the trebuchet bundle, and wove her magic to transform the boulder into flowers. She cried out:

"I impede impudent, immoderate imprecations! I instead invoke improving imputation!"

Turning to the King, she added, "Ingage!"

The King, unable to resist the flow of the moment and the exhilaration of the crowd's attention, launched the bundle. The crowd whooped. In a short time, the Icantans would receive a care package from Unisteria.

The fairy's magic, however, had turned her wings into rocks, and she fell to the ground.

Spending all her remaining focus, she climbed up Claudia's leg and next to her heart, then willed nearly all of her magic undone. Claudia gasped as she regained sight and feel, but remained naked in her invisible clothes.

The magic's effects remained on the fairy dogmother, however, since the karmic magic had been cast by her, and was her permanent lesson to learn.

The guards pounced but right before they reached her, the fairy made a desperate, instinctive transformation into the form of a black French poodle.

None had ever seen the King act so swiftly and decisively, for He bowled His guards over and snatched up His snuggly-uggums just in time.

The fairy was saved, but the hasty transformation made her lose all memory of magic, so that she would be trapped in this form forever. Her dreams of grandeur were partly fulfilled, however, since all she could remember was wanting to be a dog.

The cruel way the guards had nearly crushed Whiskers spurred compassion from the onlooking masses, compassion that would carry forward in both Icanta and Unisteria from that day forward.

The guards, and all of the rest of the Great Fairy's agents, were exposed and extricated. However, Claudia urged compassion, and riding the tide that was already flowing, the fairies began to slowly heal the wounds between them and humanity as well, though that would take a great deal more time.

The King's fashionable new attire was mimicked throughout the kingdom for many, many years.

I is for Imputation

Alexandra Seidel

The Wirtshaus was not exactly in the middle of nowhere, but it was hidden amongst trees, at the end of a road with no other houses. It was a 20 minute walk, briskly, to the nearest house, 30 minutes until you got to what was recognizably the village.

"I wonder what they did with the horses." The noise of Jo's own voice, better than the whispering trees and chirping insects. The stables, off to the right, looked abandoned, the wood was aged and brittle. More than fifteen years since he had last seen any of this, but at any moment, he expected a ghost; the whinny of a horse, his father walking back toward the Wirtshaus from his workshop, or his mother, standing out front to greet him. Before he knew it, tears were running down Jo's cheeks.

The Wirtshaus itself was not in terrible shape, yet also not the way Jo's mother would have allowed: there were no flowers in any of the pots, just weeds, but the door and windows looked maintained somewhat, vines and smaller trees had been cut back.

From what Jo knew, the caretaker, Herr Lohengrin, came once a week and did what he could to keep this place from falling into utter disrepair.

He'd sent Jo the key that he had in his pocket. That little key seemed heavier than it should be, just like Jo's legs and luggage did.

Beware, Jo thought, but moved, forcing his feet and his mind forward. The trees whispered eerily, louder, for the wind picked up. From out of the corner of his eye, Jo thought he saw someone standing between the trees.

His blood turned ice, and his head snapped to where he'd seen the shape; there was nothing there.

Beware, Jo told himself to rein in his stamping heart. *Es ist ein Nebelschweif...* the trees, putting on a shadow play with the fading daylight.

There were three steps that led up to the door. The second was chipped on the left side where it curved and fused with the building. A heavy flower pot had done that, Jo had been so little, but he remembered the sound. He'd been playing with the horses, and the sound of chipping stone had startled them too.

Jo fished the heavy key from his pocket. He could hear himself breathe. *Don't be silly. If you cannot handle being back here, you should've just stayed where you were, should've just finished college and... settled into life on another continent, somehow.*

He turned the key. The lock clicked and opened, better oiled than Jo's German after years of disuse he'd spent living with his aunt in Canada.

Jo pulled himself and his bag inside. Lavender and Sandalwood hung in the air, a heavy blend of summer scent.

Jo's backpack thudded heavily when he put it down beneath the lintel of the once familiar hallway. His eyes washed over what had been his childhood home.

White sheets kept the dust from graying the furniture his mother had painstakingly selected, placed in the reception room just so, to make you feel at home there. Many guests had remarked on that. The dark wooden floor was as Jo remembered it, the reception desk in the same dark wood, but carved so artfully that it surprised most people when they first came to Wirtshaus Eisenberg. Jo's father had always known how to craft something extraordinary from a tree's bones.

The floorboards creaked with Jo's steps. "Hello house," Jo said in response.

The reception area had been sparsely decorated but for the paintings. Jo knew all of them but he left the white sheets on them for now. Jo's mother used to have a story for every painting, sometimes more than one, and he wasn't sure whether he could handle seeing those framed tales now.

Instead, he went up the stairs. Herr Lohengrin had said in his email that he would prepare the suite for Jo. The stairs up to the third floor seemed a much longer trip than when Jo was still young. And not orphaned.

The suite had nothing dark inside of it: there was light maple paneling and cream colored wallpaper with terra cotta filigree curving through it and it smelled more of vanilla and sandalwood than of lavender. There were even fresh flowers in a crystal vase on a little table, a table that curved almost like a living thing because Jo's father had made it so.

Jo crossed the room. It looked so familiar and yet so estranged by time. He opened the door to the balcony, looked east. Their former guests had admired sunrises from here, and Jo's mother had been happy to point out the amazing view to them when they checked in. *Von hier sehen Sie die Sonne aufgehen über den Wald,* she would tell them, *you can see the sun rise over the forest from here,* her own English accent always there to give the words that little twist.

"No way I can see the sun rise above the forest anymore." Jo stared up at a green wall that had grown so very high since he had left, almost solid, soothing green.

Beware!

Jo woke sluggishly and slowly. *Where am I?* The home that once was, of course. The moon was coming in through the window.

"Shit." Jo got up from the bed. He'd just meant to lie down for a little while, give his eyes a rest.

There had to be a lamp on the nightstand. Jo felt for it with his right hand, threw something off of it, then found the lamp. The sudden glare made him crunch his eyes shut. "Shit."

Once he got used to the brightness, Jo bent over to check on what he'd thrown off the nightstand.

"What the..." The photograph was silver framed, faded somewhat with age. It showed his parents and Jo holding a gigantic Zuckertüte almost as big as him. The three of them were standing behind a sign painted in his mother's elegant hand: *Herzlichen Glückwunsch zur Einschulung, lieber Johann!* it read. Welcome to school!

He remembered that day, when they finally got home and he got to unpack his Zuckertüte. The books and school supplies inside had seemed more of a treasure than the bits of candy.

"How did this get here?" The photograph had been in his mother's office, last he'd seen.

"Herr Lohengrin..." The caretaker was the only one that could have moved the picture upstairs. It was probably supposed to be a nice gesture.

"I should have noticed this when I came in." He put the heavy frame back on the nightstand. "Must've been jetlag."

Jo got to his feet. His stomach grumbled. The last time he'd eaten was on the plane, which now seemed ages ago.

"Shit." Feenhain wasn't a big place and nothing would be open at this hour. "I hope you put some food in the kitchen, Herr Lohengrin."

Jo turned on the lights on his way down, illuminated the place like it was meant to be.

The scent of lavender downstairs seemed even stronger now. Jo took the shortcut to the kitchen that didn't go through the reception area.

When his searching fingers found the light switch for the kitchen and the place suddenly came to live with color, a huge wave of childhood memories flooded over Jo.

The cook, Frau Heine, had kept flowers in a jar by the window, and potted herbs too. Her apron was white, and she'd had an uncanny talent for keeping it so. She'd always made a show of chasing Jo out of the kitchen, but not before he'd had a chance to grab a cookie or something similarly delightful.

"I think I forgot all about Frau Heine's cookies..." Jo wiped his suddenly moist eyes.

Herr Lohengrin had indeed taken care of the food. There were platters, laden heavily, perched on all the counters. Powdered sugar glistened like snow, ripe berries hidden under cream, roasted vegetables glazed with fine oils and sauces beckoned invitingly. Jo's mouth watered and he reached for a platter full of mini tartes arranged artfully on a beautiful periwinkle plate.

"Beware!" Jo dropped the tarte, looked around.

"Hello?" There had to be someone in the house. "Herr Lohengrin?" He couldn't have imagined that.

No answer. Jo walked to the kitchen's other exit, carefully pushed the swing door open a crack. The lights in the dining area were on and there was... music.

Maybe the village organized a party... Jo thought. He went into the dining area. "Hello?"

The reading room and the reception area beyond were also lit, and Jo could hear people singing, beautiful voices, bright as summer rain.

"Du liebes Kind, komm, geh mit mir...," they were singing, and their voices were like a tidal pull so gentle, so gentle, gently. He knew the words though, didn't he? But where–

"Johann, you must be quite hungry after your travels."

Jo spun around, forgetting for now the beckoning song. The man behind him was holding the swing door to the kitchen open, had one arm out to invite Jo back in.

"Who are you?" Jo asked.

"A friend. You know me. I set out the food for you."

"You are not Herr Lohengrin."

"No, oh no. We do not appreciate each other's company. Did you find the gift I left for you upstairs?"

"What?"

"The photograph. You looked so beautiful that day."

"What are you talking about, I don't know you!" The song was like a whirlwind at Jo's back. It made it hard to concentrate.

"Your mother was my friend, and then you. I watched you sleeping in your crib. Can you imagine the pain your *father* brought me when he kept you from me? Oh, but you have come back. I knew you would, mein feiner Knabe. Come, eat the food."

The man's face was enchanting. It kept a balance of almost androgynous proportions, and Jo, who had never looked at a woman's face that way, found himself drawn to this stranger. What had he called Jo? Mein feiner Knabe, that too seemed familiar, a memory in fog, hard to hold steady and see true.

"Look, I have no idea who you are..." The song was sweet, but also suffocatingly heavy against Jo's mind. The smell of lavender lived in the room like a grand beast.

"Sweetling, come and eat the food. Then we will dance."

Beware. There was still some solid ground in Jo's mind. "You said you knew my father. How did you know my father?"

The man's mouth curved into an enigmatic smile. "He made a bargain. I do bargain, sometimes, and I was curious to see you grown. So

I took him up on it. He came to dance with me that night, in your stead."

That dulled the song. "No, that's bullshit. He had a heart attack, he—"

"Yes. All the tales you want I will give you. Heart attacks, ill luck. A forest that never dies. Come, eat the food, Johann. My daughters are waiting."

"Beware!" Whispered, but not imagined. Jo took all the courage an orphan earns, and turned, and ran.

The reading room was empty, but women with long hair, copper and golden and raven, were still spinning their song in the reception area, dancing their roundelay. Jo didn't dare look at their faces because he feared that their beauty might be enough to stop a heart and catch a soul.

He made for the Wirtshaus's front door instead, found it unlocked. He took the front stairs in one big leap. Instead of taking the road back to the village, Jo turned left, ran around the Haus and to the back building that housed his father's workshop.

It felt like a longer sprint then Jo knew it was, but the adrenaline had him. Blood was drumming in Jo's ears, and he was afraid the man would hear too, trace him by the sound of his fear.

Jo tried the workshop door, but it was locked, and even after all these years, the wood was strong and sturdy. Shit!" Jo rammed his fists against the door.

Jo looked around. His eyes found the windows, not big windows, but big enough for him to fit through.

Grabbing a heavy stone that framed a hopelessly overgrown flower bed, Jo used it to break the window. Shards rained down, bled him where they found his skin. Jo cleared the glass away with the stone as best he could, never daring to look over his shoulder to see if the man had followed him.

Jo tried to climb in through the window, failed, had to tell his hand to drop the stone that was a useful tool and a potential weapon, tried again, managed to lift himself over the sill and into the workshop.

The workshop smelled of wood and iron and oil.

"Johann! Come with me!" The man's voice, outside, but close.

Jo looked around, but the workshop was dark. He cursed himself for having dropped that nice heavy stone outside. Desperate, he groped for anything, any tool or forgotten panel that he could use to save himself with.

There came a knocking on the door, thrice. "Johann!"

After a suspiciously long moment of quiet, the door burst inward into smithereens, the hold of hinges and lock forgotten.

"Johann, there you are!" The man's face was bright and smiling, but there was no warmth in that smile, no warmth at all.

"Beware." A whisper again, so close to his ear. Then, Jo's fingers found something, closed tight.

The man came for Jo, came at him, fast and smooth, like a snake on rippling sand, and Jo swung. He hadn't known what he'd been holding until he saw it glinting in the moonlight; a sword made of wood, polished and framed with strings of metal, but a simple wooden sword like you might give a child who wants to play knight.

The blade found the man's throat, and, amazingly, cut into it.

"Aaargh..." Gurgling babble, like an almost clogged bathroom sink.

Jo let go of the toy sword and stepped back. He was shocked about what he'd done, shocked to see the dark, dark blood, unnaturally dark blood that the man who was not a man was bleeding.

"Herr Kupfermacher!" The voice was unfamiliar. Jo watched the bleeding man, the sword still in his neck, vanish like a mirage. The sword fell to the ground; solid, real. A man was standing in the door, just a shadow with the moonlight at his back. Jo could see that he was holding a bag.

"Herr Kupfermacher, sind Sie okay?"

"Ah... ich... whoareyou?" Jo couldn't reach the words, not quite, he was just breathing too hard.

"Ach. I'm Lohengrin. I missed you. I thought I would find you at the station, but you must have been on another train. He should not have found you first." Lohengrin came into the workshop, inspected the drops of dark blood the man had bled.

"Who... was that?"

"Der Erlenkönig. It is a long story, yes, eine lange Geschichte. But iron he does not like." Lohengrin held up his little bag in front of Jo's face. There were iron filings in it, at least that's what it looked like to Jo in the almost dark. "And not either that knife."

"Oh, the sword?" Jo picked it up. It was beautifully made.

"Yes. Sword. See how it has iron worked in with the wood? Nice thing, your father must have made this."

"When you say Erlenkönig, Herr Lohengrin, do you, I mean, like in the poem? That's just a story though?" Willst, feiner Knabe, du mit mir geh'n... the Erlenkönig's words. They were from that poem, Jo remembered now.

Lohengrin shrugged. "Stories. Truth. Who knows? He has so many names though, many. Your mama told you–"

"Yes," Jo said, "she always did tell me to beware of him."

Jo looked at the sword again. *Not quite a toy,* he thought, and walked out of the workshop. Jo wondered what he would do with a sword that wasn't really a toy, a sword that lay so perfectly in his hand.

The wind made the trees whisper quietly, and there was no more singing coming from inside the Wirtshaus.

"I can take you back to the village, Herr Kupfermacher, there is a hotel where you can stay and–"

"No, thank you. Here is fine. Here is home; mein zuhause." Jo said. And just in case, he had the blade.

Lohengrin gave him a long, hard look. "He will be back. Der Erlenkönig gibt nicht so leicht auf, he doesn't give up easy, you see, Herr Kupfermacher."

Jo held the sword in one shaking hand. "He said... something about my father. A bargain." Jo shook his head, sucked in air. "What do you know about that, Herr Lohengrin?"

The older man gave another hard look. "I knew your father, Johann. He loved you. He would have told you, go, leave this place, never come back."

"I didn't ask you what my father would have told me, I asked what happened to him!" An anger, sudden and raw, not unlike pain.

Herr Lohengrin tsk-ed. "What good is that? And mind, I do not know what happened, really, I wasn't there. But your mother, she told me, Lohengrin, when he comes, protect my boy, do not let him have my boy." Lohengrin looked over his shoulder. "We best go inside. When he comes again this night, it will be from the woods. I'll tell you inside," he reassured Jo, and beckoned him to follow.

They ended up in the dining room with a bottle of Schnapps Herr Lohengrin conjured up from somewhere. He filled two glasses, brimful, and they drank. It made Jo cough, the burning trace the liquor left.

"So, tell me," Jo said, after he had recovered. Herr Lohengrin was already pouring them a second round.

"What I suspect, I'll say. Your mother came here in love, and left her family home behind, as you know, but not her... heritage, shall we say. Your aunt was luckier in that regard, but then I suspect old man Erlen never loved her the way he did your mother."

"Loved her?" Jo said. He took another sip of Schnapps, not as bad as the first.

"In his way. It is not the human way of these things. Well, but let us not linger on that. The important thing I think is, your mother knew from her family the trick to keep him away, at least for a time, for seven years, precisely.

"She told me, Lohengrin, I want to tell you, because there must be someone else that knows, for Johann. It was uncanny, almost like she could taste a bad thing come on the wind.

"There are two ways to keep him from taking something he has claimed, and he has claimed one child of each generation of your family, for a long time, your mother said."

Jo emptied the glass, and Lohengrin refilled it. "If what you say is true, then why didn't anyone tell me? My aunt?"

"I think she would not have you come. Your aunt wanted you to stay away from here, the ocean to keep him away between you. You never told her that you were coming?"

Jo shook his head. "I didn't know how."

"Well, that is that. You must know though, the two ways. The first way is the way of desperation. Your father was despaired, without your mother, and the thought of losing you. Your mother had told him as well, once she was in the hospital."

Jo swallowed. His throat had become constricted with the memories of that, how fast it all had gone, once she was in the hospital. He emptied the glass again.

"Well. He was your father. You called him that. When one is so bonded as family, one can make a deal. One life for the other. When he came for you that night, your father made that deal, and he accepted. Do you not remember?"

"I wasn't there that night I was..." Where had he been that night his father died? Where exactly?

"You were running down the road, to the village, screaming. You were so little. Maybe it is good that you forget."

Jo had no way of processing that. He had been there when his father died? How could he have forgotten running through the dark?

Why had no one ever told him that? "The other way, Herr Lohengrin," he said with eyes salty and stuck to the floor.

"A story."

"What?"

"You tell the Erlenking a story. It is what you can do, only you, because you are what he wants. It is what your mother did, come." Lohengrin, steady despite the Schnapps, rose from his chair and walked into the reception room. He pulled one white sheet off a painting. "This one. She told him about a girl who adventured. She told him the adventures, and told him of the fair lover that the girl met, between the adventures, the lover that would dance with her after every quest. And then, she told him about the final ball, the ball that would see the lover and the adventurer married by the stroke of midnight, only then, a monster came to interrupt. The bandersnatch, she called it."

"The frumious bandersnatch?"

"Eh? I do not know that. Has she told you that story?"

"I... it's a poem. Like Der Erlkönig."

"Ah. It might well be. Someone like him, he always leaves traces, such is his vanity. But the point is, the story can save you, if you tell it, and let him never interrupt, and tell it until sunrise. Because when the sun regains her sky, she banishes him, and he once more becomes a shade, a lingering fog, but nothing more. For another seven years, that is."

Jo pulled another sheet off another painting. "So these are the stories she told to keep him at bay?"

"So I understand. He appears sometimes, in between those seven years, there are always times when his realm and ours are close, but he will never be able to take you then. So long as you tell a good enough tale, and never let him stop you tell it. Your mother liked the paintings to show him, to make him look where she wanted him to look, to make him imagine the world she made with her words—oh, wait here!"

Lohengrin dashed off, to the back room of the reception area, Jo's mother's old office. Jo wished for more Schnapps, but knew that wouldn't do him any good. Only now did he notice that he had the sword his father made still in his hand.

"Here! She had this ready. But then, she couldn't use it."

Wrapped in aged paper and bound with cord, the package Herr Lohengrin put on the reception desk was clearly a paining. Jo un-wrapped it.

The noise of the tearing paper felt loud, incredibly loud. He looked at the painting, and his eyes went wide. Just then, the old grandfather clock in the hallway struck three.

Herr Lohengrin became rigid. "This is his time now. You have wounded him, but in this realm, there is no way to kill him."

"And let me guess, if he wants me, he has to take me tonight."

"Oh yes. He would not wait another seven years."

A strong wind gripped the Wirtshaus, and the back door that led from the kitchen to the garden flew open with a loud bang.

"So all I say is, I want to tell you a story, and then I just go?"

Herr Lohengrin nodded. "And you never stop, only when the sun is up, you may."

Jo nodded. He felt grateful for the Schnapps. Sword and painting in hand, he walked toward the kitchen, but the Erlenking was there al-ready, in the dining room, expecting him.

"Johann!" he said, serene as ever.

"Let me tell you a story," Johann said, and started into the tale. He knew it all, he knew it well; his mother had told him so many times.

There once was a boy, and the boy had lost his name on the wind.

It was a strong wind of course, for nothing but the strongest of winds could take a name from this boy; he was magnificent and magical and shining like the light of stars.

And because he was like the light of stars, not having a name didn't frighten the boy. He never needed one, the people that he met on his many travels called him this and that, and that was just as well; what need for a name was there?

He enchanted a dragon one time, made her turn into solid rock, and the dragon never knew his name. He stole a giant pearl from a wise oyster another time, and the oyster never knew his name. He learned the art of bird song from a dryad, and the dryad never knew his name.

The boy grew into a man, and time never knew his name, and the boy never hurt for the lack.

Eventually, the man, who had been a boy, wanted a sense of home in between his many adventures, and so he wove himself three daughters, one from hay, and she was fair as golden crop, another from a grapevine, and she had hair like fire; the third he made from the winter branches of an ancient oak, and she looked like her hair was made from raven shadows.

He gave his daughters the spell that would bind a dragon to stone so they could bind whatever else they wished, and they thanked him and called him father. He gifted them a giant pearl so they could see their own reflections in its watery surface, and they thanked him and called him father. He taught them also the song of the birds, and they sang it and wove their enchantments around the song. They thanked him, and called him father, and that was enough for the man who had once been a boy.

The man also learned to fight. He had to fight humans, with a sword–like so he struck, and like so!–and the humans were beaten, and they called him king. And he fought dwarves too with his mighty sword–like so he slashed, and like so!–and the dwarves were beaten, and they called him king, and that was enough for the king who was also a father and had once been a boy.

But then, he met a maiden. She was a human, but in her way she was mightier than a dragon, more shimmering than a pearl, and more beautiful than birdsong.

The king felt like he would lose his mind and all else that he owned, if he could not have her.

"But my love," the maiden said, "how can I give myself to you when I do not even know your name?"

"I am a king and a father and a man," he said, but the maiden shook her beautiful head. It was not enough.

"Humans travel differently to my home," the man, who was also a king, said. "It will be another seven years before we can be together.

"Then so it will be," said the maiden, and kissed him, not with lust, but with good-bye clinging salty to her lips.

The man searched for his name for the next seven years. Under the roots of an oak that was as old as he, he looked. Under the dragon mountain he scoured, but found only her abandoned hoard. In the shadow of kelp and coral he cracked every oyster, but found no trace of his name.

And when the seven years had passed, he came to his maiden, who was no longer a maiden but a woman now. "I have looked," he told her, "but I have found no more than what I am, a man and a father and a king. Will you not have me like that, my love?"

The woman shook her beautiful head and brushed the salt of farewell over his lips.

For another seven years he looked. The lard pots of the dwarves he searched, turned every coal in the forge fires of the humans, and even the nests of birds he disturbed in his search, but his name was nowhere to be found.

When he came back to his maiden who was now a woman with half a life of wisdom to her name, he said, "I have turned fire and feather and fat, but I couldn't find my name anywhere. Will you not have me as I am?"

But the wise woman shook her head and ran the red of her adieu over his lips.

So he searched once more, but this time, he asked his daughters to aid him, so eager was he to be with his beloved.

His oldest daughter understood that whole plants can sleep in crops, so she looked for her father's name in all the dreams of all the creatures, but found nothing.

His middle daughter knew that the taste of wine is not its truth, that its truth is in the minstrel's song sung after all the cups are drunk, and so she searched the strings of lyres and the melodies of flutes for her father's name, but found nothing.

The king's third daughter knew that all the secrets between the worlds are like the rings of a tree, one hidden inside of the other, and that a hard bark hides them all. She looked for her father's name under the tongue of his wise woman lover, and there, hidden behind her hard tree bark words, was her father's very name; the third girl knew it easily enough.

She rushed back to her father and told him of what she had found, and when the seven years once more had passed, the man, who was also a king and a proud father, returned to his lover.

The wise woman was older still, but it seemed like she had grown more beautiful with every wrinkle, just like a tree grows more beautiful with each one of its rings.

"I have found my name. It is right there under you tongue. I bid you say it, with the love that you have promised me, and we can be on our way to my realm."

Jo, who had not stopped, not for water or rest or too deep a breath, strode across the room, and his sword arced through the air. It cut the light of daybreak, the glitter of the sun. *Another seven years,* he thought.

"Do you remember what my ancestress said?" He looked at the man, who was also a king, and whose daughters knew the most canniest of spells.

"She called me Jabberwock," he said, and came over to Jo, and took his face in his hands. "Well played, my dearest boy, but I never loved any of them less for the play."

He kissed Jo and there was lust in that kiss, but also the salty-bitter taste of *until-we-meet-again.*

J is for Jabberwocky

Cory Cone

You are very precious to me, and always have been. Even before you were born, you were here, somewhere, and I was waiting.

You're my baby boy.

From the way you look at me, now, as you go about your work, I think you haven't any idea what they've done to you. That you were sent with him this time is a wound that should break me completely, but I have been waiting for this moment for such a long time and there isn't a thing on earth that can break me now. I knew they would send you, anyhow, because those things are cruel, and their cruelty knows no time-limit; it lasts forever, and it began immediately.

Have they ever told you when you were born? Do birthdays matter in their world? Time moves slower there, I think, or maybe it's just different.

You were born on February 22nd, 1985. You are 33 years old, but you look all of 15, standing there in the white doorway of this cramped and stinking hospital room, though still I know it is you.

It was a Friday. It had snowed all week, and then rained, and the drive to the hospital was slow and icy. The car spun out twice, but we made it. I still remember how much it hurt, the labor, I still feel it sometimes inside of me. Those last months of the pregnancy, I couldn't ever get comfortable and I was so sick of being *two* people but when the contractions began they hurt so badly I wanted to go back to the old familiar discomfort. I pressed on, of course, because the pain was a signal, an alarm ringing out, announcing that it was time—you were finally coming home.

Into the world you sprang, slick with vernix and blood, purple as a concord grape until you took that first deep lungful of air and cried. Your color returned before the midwife had even lifted you toward my waiting breasts, and you were pink and alive and good. She asked Jeffery if he'd like to cut the umbilical cord, and he said no.

(Jeffery is your dad. He's gone now. He's been gone almost as long as you have.)

I lifted trembling hands toward you, longing to touch you and to hold you, my baby boy. I was so close—that is the moment I dream of so often; how close my fingers were to that touch—when it happened. Time diluted. It swam and shook and bloated and slowed and became thick and uneven and sick. My ears rang a high tinny squeal like you get after a loud concert. Everything paused... except for *him*.

He was a squat little green monster. His fingers and toes were long with stubby acorn-like knuckles. His nose protruded from his face like a witch's finger pointing its judgment at anything he passed his eyes over. His gut hung low, sparing me a view of what might lie grotesquely between his legs. He was the most hideous thing I had ever seen in my life, and the only thing moving now within the room. His naked footsteps slapped the tile floor, a sound like a dropped wet rag as he approached me, my fingers snared in suspended animation mere millimeters from your screaming, petrified face.

My son.

When he was close enough that I could smell his oniony, garlicy breath, I saw what he cradled within those knobby fingers. Something small, something alive.

"It is an honor to do this thing."

He was looking at my body, inspecting it like I were a bloodied dead animal in a kitchen, which is how I felt at that moment, unable to move, bleeding, longing to hold onto life.

"Better life here, with you," he said, his voice thick with saliva, the sort of voice any person would run from. He wasn't speaking to me as much as at me. He didn't realize, I believe, that I could hear him. "Good life. Your brood good life, too. With us."

He nodded, and a strand of spit oozed over the precipice of his bulbus black lip and onto my naked thigh, where it merged with my blood and was gone. He lifted what was in his hands toward *you*, and had I been able to move, I'd have screamed and scratched and bitten and hurt that thing and the thing in his arms because all at once, in a wash it came over me what he was about to do.

With a free hand he extracted you from the nurse's grasp, plucked you away like a fruit from a tree, and inserted his little monster in your place. He did it mechanically, without much care at all. A thing that must be done.

I have no other experiences with which to compare my hopelessness in that moment, it was utter, unparalleled, unequivocal, complete. There I lay in pain, longing to finally touch your head for the very first time, to hold you and have you and care for you, listening to the wet splat of his feet retreat from the room with you in his arms.

And then he was gone. Time snapped back, and before I could appreciate or comprehend fully what had taken place in this room, the pain of what had come before took hold and I was crying with your replacement at my breast, drinking, soothing, and despite myself I felt better. It looked just like you, now, in the real time. Then I was asleep.

There is magic in this world and on your birthday I learned of it for the first time. It is a powerful magic, the kind that, had I not seen what

I'd seen, I'd have never been wise to. Would never have sensed what was growing in our house.

Your father, poor Jeffery, he sensed it too and his sense drove him away from all of us. He became purposelessly cruel to the child-thing. Not violent, but absent in all the ways a baby needs a father not to be. He attempted to explain it to me, the night before he left, but all he could manage was "I thought it'd be different." By sunrise the following morning, he was gone. I haven't seen him since.

From that day on I embraced the role of single mother and raised our brood parasite. He acted like any other baby boy, and then any other toddler, and I came to love him in a way, out of necessity. This doesn't mean I love you any less, because I have always and will always love you, my son, but for me to survive this long, there had to be love, or I fear I'd have gone away, too. And I couldn't go away, I wouldn't, because I always knew that this day would come.

There were periods of months, even years, where I didn't think about it too much, and tried to enjoy being a mother. It was selfish of me, I know, but I had always wanted to be one. I cried when he graduated high school, and again when he left me for college. The house grew emptier, lonelier. I would visit him when I could. I got to know his friends, his girlfriends, too. Sometimes, he'd call me when he had problems and I helped, as any good mother would.

I'm sorry, son, but I do love him.

I had to.

You don't recognize me, do you. Of course you don't. You've never really seen me before. The fat little thing standing beside you, glaring at me, who you have taken as your father all your life is called a Changeling. I didn't know this until the parasite was 15 years old. He begged and pleaded for us to get a computer, so we could log onto the Internet. Back then, the Internet was slower than it is now, but was fast enough to finally find some answers. I found others out there who had been going through this, too. We connected online, in message boards. We learned from each other and helped each other cope. Our children, it seems, were taken as servants for these things, and their own were left to be raised by us, because, and Lord knows why, they think we can provide better lives for them. Maybe we can. Maybe I did. I tried my best.

But knowing that you were being raised in a life of servitude gutted me. I rejected the idea at first, that you were answering to that hideous creature's every call, but the idea of it wouldn't leave my mind. It festered, as things like that will.

When he was 20 years old, and out for a night with his friends (who, I admit, I thought were very pleasant and a good influence on him), one of my online friends wrote to the message board that her parasite's father had *come back*. This was something new. None of us had every experienced that yet. Her parasite, a girl, had given birth, and the offspring of this pregnancy had been taken as well, and a new parasite left in its place. We wondered what it might want with a human/changeling infant, if those children were destined for slavery as well, or something greater.

When the parasite told me he was getting married, I wept.

His wife was a girl he'd met at college and become engaged to before I'd even met her. That had stung, a little, that my approval wasn't required for such a union, but I accepted her with open arms. She is taller than me, and more beautiful, and quite stern. She often corrects his manners in front of me or others, which humiliates him but makes me smile. He needed someone like her, really. She made up for what I had let go, because my love for him wasn't true; it was simply there.

Each summer, when we visited, I'd look for signs of a bump. I so desperately longed for a pregnancy, not for the baby, not for them. For you.

I believed that somewhere inside of yourself you knew that it wasn't right, that you didn't belong there. With all my being I willed upon the ether the call to come home.

And, my god, you have.

What a sight to return to. Look at the state of me now, your mother. You are horrified, I can tell, but you aren't letting on, at least not as much as your changeling father is, that squat sweaty fuck that took you from me. His fat lips are quivering with hate, and if I could move any part of my body, I'd laugh. Long and loud and in his face. Look at his horrible eyes, welling with tears! A grief I could drink for all time.

I made sure I was smiling before time stopped. I wanted him to see me smiling.

My parasite's wife didn't want me in the room for the labor, or the birth, but I had to be, or everything would fall apart. So, I tried the entire pregnancy to get the girl to love me. She wouldn't budge. I was forced to pace the bright florescent lit hallway, listening through the hospital room door to each contraction, trying to gauge how close she might be. Trying to prepare myself. Thirty long hours of this, the poor girl, before the nurse was racing down the hall with an excited yet practiced expression on her face. Time to push, she told me. You're almost a grandma. I followed her in. The girl was so distracted by pain she didn't notice me, or if she had, she didn't care. She pushed for two hours.

The longest two hours of my life.

But then a little screaming thing was gasping in air within the nurse's bloody hands, its mother collapsing backward, exhausted, delirious, excited—and the room felt cloudy, disjointed, disconnected. He was coming back. I nearly screamed; he was coming back!

I remembered that it had set on quickly the first time, before I'd even touched you, and already I could feel myself slowing like before, and I reached into my purse before it was too late and grabbed the handle of the butcher's knife I'd stashed there and lifted it out, saw it glint brightly under the hospital room lights, and it was difficult to move, a struggle, like forcing my arm through molasses. I grabbed my parasite son, your interloper, that ignorant fraud by the back of his head, gripped his hair between my fingers and turned his face toward me—he was crying, so full of joy and excitement and anticipation of this brand new time in his life—and I plunged the blade up under his chin and felt it sluice through flesh and bone and sinew and buried it deep within his monstrous brain.

And that's where I froze, my head turned toward the doorway, a triumphant grin pointed with hate at the sound of wet splattery footsteps approaching the room, coming to torment me once again.

But that won't happen today, will it? After 33 long years, today is for me.

And for you, my son. Everything I've ever done is for you.

K is for Kin

Lynn Hardaker

Gripping the miniature rose with her tweezers, Emma used a toothpick to curl down a tiny paper petal. The blossom was no larger than the tip of her smallest finger. Happy with it for now, she placed the flower on the desk. The taste of dust and disintegrating words hung on her tongue.

The bells over the door jangled to life and a man walked in. He gave her a tight smile, went to a shelf, and with his hands clasped behind his back, began reading the spines of books. Emma watched. She could tell he wasn't going to buy anything. His type never did.

She returned to the flower and to the book it lay next to. It was a discard. One of the many books from one of the many musty cardboard boxes which were frequently orphaned on the doorstep of her bookshop; sometimes with a note "free books," but usually without. She would bring them in and sift through them: throw out those which were too damaged by years of damp and slouching on basement shelves, and keep the few which she could sell. Of these, she would pick one to use to make her garden.

She took her scalpel to the discard—a volume of early twentieth century poetry—and gently cut out a page. When she first started making her garden, a couple of months earlier, she would construct a barrier of books on the counter so the customers wouldn't be disturbed by the sight of a book being maimed, but lately she hadn't bothered. It was her shop. Her book. If they didn't like it, they could leave. Sometimes they did.

The military man left, empty handed. She took her carefully cut page, folded and creased it with a bone folder then sliced it with a paper-knife. The metal passed through the slightly powdery paper with a sound like a whisper. This would be the stem.

For the next couple of hours she worked on it. First she threaded it through the head of the rose, then she cut, pinched, and twisted it, never gluing or taping, until it was perfect. Almost perfect. Thorns, it was missing thorns of course. She deftly pulled down thin strips of paper and twisted them into satisfying thorns. During this time, a few customers came and went. She sold a copy of "Tropic of Cancer" to a student with a hipster beard; an illustrated edition of "Mort D'Arthur" to a nervous woman who kept fiddling with her wedding ring; and three Agatha Christies to a woman who smelled strongly of cigarettes and gin.

There were no closing hours advertised on the door, since she liked to stay open as long as she felt like. But when it looked like there weren't going to be any more customers, she tallied her sales for the day, locked up her earnings, small as they were, in the strong box in the back room, and slid the box back under her compact, dusty sofa. Then she put the finished paper rose into an empty matchbox, locked up the shop behind her and left.

It was a short walk home, through the student ghetto to the furthest reaches of the university district where it merged with Chinatown. Home was a flat in a Victorian mansion which had been carved up and drywalled into multiple units.

She walked up the front steps past cracked recycling bins, across the porch where half a dozen bicycles were chained up, and through the original wood and glass panelled front door which had somehow snuck past the Fire Chief's inspection.

Inside, she climbed the groaning stairs to her flat on the top floor and paused on the landing. There were sounds from inside. Tom. Her stomach knotted. She unlocked the door and entered.

Tom had music playing and was sitting cross-legged on the sofa reading a book.

"Hello, stranger," he said to her. She tried to keep her smile.

"Hardly a stranger. I was at work. As you know."

She went over and gave him a kiss. He grabbed her and pulled her to him.

"Tom, I'm starved."

"Me too," he breathed into her neck.

"No, really," she pushed herself away. He smiled, but she could see it was forced.

"Dinner's ready, bit cold," he nodded in the direction of the kitchen where she could see the table set for them, bottle of wine open and "breathing" as he always liked to say.

"I'll join you in a minute," she said and went down the hall to her study, a small room with a small window overlooking the maples that lined the street. The plan was to convert it to a nursery when the time came. Not that she was in any hurry for that. She shut the door behind her. On an old table in front of the window sat her garden. She knelt in front of it and took the rose from the match box.

The entire garden was about a foot and a half by a foot. Everything had been made from the pages from old, discarded books: a moon-garden of yellowing white and ivory, speckled over with tiny markings of black ink. Minuscule words twisted into and out of the rose bushes, the foxgloves, the wall of dog-roses which surrounded and contained it.

A path of tiny paper-gravel wound throughout the garden. She reached in from above and added the new rose to one of the rose bushes near the centre. It slid in without any trouble and seemed almost to stretch out its petals when she removed her hand. Emma tried to catch the scent of rose, but it alluded her, leaving her instead with the scent of dust and old printers' ink.

She got up, gave the garden one last look, and went out to her dinner.

The garden obsession had started quite suddenly a few months earlier. One day, with no obvious explanation, she just started making tiny flowers out of one of the books she'd unpacked. This was the beginning of her miniature garden. She had the tools anyway for repairing books. And she had the time. Unknown to her, she also had the reason.

In a small dark room in the attic of her mind sat a small dark cluster of memories. At times they'd shuffle their feet, but mostly they were still and silent. Watching and waiting. There had been another garden. A forgotten garden. One which had been an occasional refuge. She'd found it by accident long ago. The garden and the figure in it.

The first time she'd found it, she was very young. A chronic sleepwalker, one night she had walked right out of the family's bungalow, her white nightgown glowing under the full-moon's light. She walked and walked until she became aware of the scent of flowers coming from the other side of a low brick wall. She stood on tip toe and could just see the heads of large white flowers. There was no obvious way of getting into the garden, but she knew in that absolutely certain way that children have, that if she placed her hand on the wall, a gate would appear. She did. And it did. And she passed through into the garden.

Every flowers was white. She was startled by their beauty and strangeness. Her stomach, which was usually knotted into a ball of anxiety, relaxed amongst the blossoms. She wandered along the white gravel path, past tall rose bushes, beds of tulips, lily-of-the-valley which dotted the ground like breadcrumbs marking her way. She followed the path and after an unguessable amount of time, arrived at a flower that was unlike any of the others in the garden.

It too was white, but not in the way of the other flowers. This huge rose glowed with an opalescent fire. Iridescent colours shimmered under its skin, and as she looked at it, it swelled open and she saw that words were written on each petal in a thin, spider-silk script. She pulled the blossom closer to her hungry eyes and began to read, and for what might have been hours or days, she stood there and read every word of every story: stories of wonder, and beauty, and magic.

When she finished, she slowly released the flower. In her state of wonderment, she wasn't startled by the appearance of the figure. He, or she—for she couldn't be certain—stood a few feet away watching her with a look she didn't quite understand. They had skin the colour of cinnamon bark and hair the colour of a full moon. It brushed their shoulders in a breeze which Emma hadn't felt.

The figure tilted its head, limpid eyes locking on hers. That part of her which would have told her to be afraid was quiet.

"Emma," the figure said, "there are others of these flowers. Stay. I'll show you. You may read them all."

She felt magnetically pulled toward the figure. It's beauty was a physical force.

"No, I... I must go back." With a gnawing reluctance, she knew this to be true.

"When you need me, you will know how to find me."

With those last words, the brightness of the figure's hair and darkness of their skin shimmered and seemed cancel one another out until Emma was alone in the garden. With quick steps, she found her way out. And with each step away from the garden, her memory of the stories, and the figure, and the garden faded until she found herself standing before her locked front door, left with only the delightful, dream-like sensation of having encountered magic.

She had no choice but to knock. The moon was low, the sky dark. Her father came to the door in his pyjamas. She told him she'd just visited a magical place, but couldn't remember where. He didn't smile.

In the days after that, nursing the welts on her backside and thighs, Emma couldn't remember what it was she had discovered, and eventually the un-pin-down-able sensation of magic was gone.

Emma and Tom lay in bed later that night with the window open to the light of the full-moon and the warm Summer air. He leaned over, kissed her forehead and whispered goodnight, settling quickly into a gentle snore. His hand lay on her belly like a stone.

She raised her arm and rested her hand on her forehead. She couldn't see the moon itself, but she could see its light, cool and viscous, on the leaves of the maple tree. As she began to float on sleep and half dreams, she found herself thinking about the day. In that wonderfully ambiguous realm between waking and sleep, she tried to remember, with a thin thread of panic, whether she'd taken her pill or not. She must have, but she wasn't sure and was still too much in the depths of sleep to get up and check in her study where she kept them hidden.

Slowly, that thought shape-shifted into another one: a girl in a white nightgown, thighs stinging with pain, standing alone on a street under the full-moon's light. Wondering, she slid back into sleep.

Her sleepwalking continued into adolescence. Though sometimes it was a ruse: an excuse not to be found in her bed. Usually, when she was truly sleepwalking, she'd wake up at the inside of the locked front door. But occasionally she'd make it out of the house; as on one warm full-moon night when she was thirteen.

She'd walked out of the house and had kept walking until she was awakened by the unexpected scent of flowers from the darkest end of an alley. Fear was assuaged as a memory danced out to her. Placing her hand on the bricks of the wall, the gate appeared and she entered the garden.

She felt giddy as she walked slowly along the path, admiring the stunning white flowers. Then she saw one which glowed with an otherworldly light. The story rose, she knew at once, and went directly to it. Pulling it gently toward her, she gazed into the folds of its petals, which opened to her allowing her to read the stories within. She read greedily. When she was done, and the moon had dipped, she let go and looked over to the figure. They looked back at her. She felt butterflies in her stomach. Had they always been this beautiful? She smiled.

"Emma, are you here to stay?"

She was confused. The idea of staying in this magical place had never crossed her mind. Or had it?

"I can't."

"Of course you could. I'd show you where to find all of the other story roses. You would be safe here."

She thought about that. About staying there, in a place where she felt at peace, reading the flowers, not worrying about her father's nocturnal visits. But she knew it was impossible.

"It's very kind, but I must go back."

With a look of regret, the figure tilted their head in acknowledgement and, as they had the first time, shimmered into nothingness.

By the time Emma reached her home and crawled through her window she fell into bed, with only a faint dream-like memory of the garden and its magical inhabitant.

The moon had moved. Tom's snoring had lulled into deep breathing. A shard of moonlight edged across Emma's face, prizing open her eyes. For an instant, she was disoriented and almost afraid. At a distant, dark place in her mind, a small group of distorted and dismembered snatches of memories rattled in the shadows.

Although she'd only been to the garden twice, and the memories had faded almost at once, there were nights when, under a watchful and capricious moon, she caught the faintest whiff of roses where roses couldn't be and imagined a person so beautiful and otherworldly that her step would falter for just an instant.

She lay in bed fully awake now. A breeze blew in, thick with the smells of summer-hot pavement and garbage. And the unexpected smell of flowers. Something came alive in her. Carefully, she slid from the bed and pulled on her clothes.

In the living room, she eeled her feet into her still-tied sneakers and crept down the stairs. Outside, the moon fell on her, full and bright. The air came in occasional bellowing gusts then stilled completely. On it, lingered the unmistakable scent of flowers.

She began to walk. No intention in mind, no deliberate choosing of a way, she just let herself wander through the slumbering streets. Through Chinatown's back alleys, past garbage bins, past empty wooden crates with the wilted remains of vegetables clinging to them. The scent of flowers grew stronger.

She came to a high wall of cinderblocks covered in competing layers of graffiti. A single white blossom peered over the top. Emma placed her hand on the surface of the wall. The gate appeared and she entered the garden.

At once, the city was forgotten. The smell of traffic and of restaurant kitchens was replaced by a dizzying tapestry of floral scents. Above her the sky was clear of cloud and smog. The full-moon hung heavy and proud while the stars took turns appearing in the black sky.

As she walked the white gravel path, a sense of familiarity and comfort engulfed her. It was a dazzling spectrum of white: a white as cold as bleached paper, a white as warm as old ivory, a yellow-white as pale as fresh butter. But, incredible as these blossoms were, she knew there was something else she was looking for, if only she could remember.

She walked past a patch of hollyhocks taller than herself, past blazing white poppies whose heads bobbed on long stems, and delicate forget-me-nots a cool, purple white. It was as she bent down to look at a cluster of these that she began to remember.

She knew this garden. It had twice been a refuge for her: once when she was a girl and once when she was a teenager; at the times when she had most needed a refuge. But refuge from what, she asked herself.

Slowly, other memories came shyly to light, as though apologetic for cowering in the shadows for so many years. Half-remembered images and feelings came back to her. Things which she had known of, but hadn't wanted to accept for anything more than bad dreams. Things she had chosen not to remember.

Then the story rose appeared before her, its opalescent fire as brilliant as ever. As she leaned in to catch its scent, its petals swelled open, but as she looked more closely, she saw that the petals had no writing on them, they were as clear as any other flower in the garden. She felt a rising panic. Where had the stories gone?

She felt a hand on her shoulder and turned to see the figure. Such beauty made her catch her breath: the dark cinnamon bark skin and the full moon hair.

"Emma, have you finally come to stay?"

She looked around her. The garden was a more perfect a sanctuary than she could imagine and she could stay here with this incredible being whose pull was irresistible. Then she thought of the paper garden she'd been making in the flat. How some part of her had remembered this; was building her own garden. She shook her head, trying not to betray how deeply this decision hurt, but how right it was.

"No," she said hoarsely. "I can't."

"This is your last chance, Emma."

She nodded, taking in the heart-breaking beauty of the being standing before her, of the story rose glowing on its stem, and knowing that this truly was the last chance she had to live in this realm of wonder, and beauty, and magic.

"If you leave now, you will never be able to return."

"I know."

"And," the figure said with an unpleasant twist of its mouth, "you will not be allowed to forget. Ever."

"Fine," she said, feeling defiant. "There are other things I must do. That I must put right."

The realisation came simultaneously with the words. There were things which she'd been hiding from, had been hiding herself from, for most of her life. And she wasn't able to do that any longer. More memory fragments came forward, memories of events and of feelings: her father's face half-lit by the moon. Fear. Shame. Her mother's sorrow. Anger. Keeping the family together. Duty. Tim. Not wanting to let him down. Duty. Not wanting to have children. Anger. Not wanting to stay.

The figure came toward her. She breathed in. They put a hand on her cheek, stared deep into her eyes with their uncanny ones. She almost couldn't find her voice.

"I can't. I am sorry, part of me would love to, but I can't stay."

"I know," they said with the first smile she'd seen on their face. "Here," they held out a hand which, impossibly, held the story rose. She looked from the glowing blossom to the uncannily beautiful face. Reaching for the blossom, she held it by the stem.

"Ouch!" For the first time, she was aware of a thorn. Taking the flower gingerly in her other hand, she sucked on the puncture. The figure looked at her.

"Good choice, Emma," they smiled at her warmly. "Can't say I'm not disappointed, but this is the best thing for you."

With a smile she would not forget to her dying day, the figure dissolved into a final and irretrievable nothingness.

The flat was quite when she returned. Emma walked silently to her study. Kneeling down in front of her paper garden, she added the story rose. She knew that now the garden was complete. She also knew that she must leave. It wasn't fair to Tim, but it also wasn't fair to her. She would talk with him, explain it to him. Another time. But for now, she would head to her shop and camp out on the sofa in the back room while she re-grouped. Decided how to take this next step in her life.

Quietly, she left the flat. With her paper garden under her arm, the uncanny glow of the story rose illuminated the way as she left for her book shop.

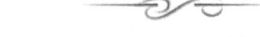

L is for Leaving

Rachel M. Thompson

When the time came for Princess Signe to marry, her mother and father despaired of finding a suitable match. Signe was fair and graceful, but also tall, with shoulders broad as her hips; proud of her strength and ever quick to settle disagreements with sword or fist. She was intelligent, and learned, but she was also young and not yet wise.

Signe saw no reason she could not rule alone. "I am strong, and I am clever, and I doubt you will ever find a man to match me."

"That may be true," said her father, grimacing down at her from the throne, "But that does not mean we won't try."

The word went out that the king and queen were hosting a singular sort of tournament, testing all who dared with trial by combat and riddles of fiendish difficulty (for they did not want a musclebound dunce for a son-in-law), all for the benefit of helping the princess choose a husband. Princes, lords, and knights gathered from all around, from nations near and far, for Signe and her kingdom were a prize too rich to ignore.

On the first day of the tournament, in the velvet dark before the first blush of dawn, Signe woke to a tapping and whistling from her window, which stood open to the warm night air. Perched there quite at ease on the broad sill was the grandest owl she had ever seen. Certainly this must be a dream! Signe slipped from her bed and padded toward the window on noiseless feet.

The owl watched her approach with solemn amber eyes. "Princess, I bring you a warning."

This startled Signe so badly that she froze, mute. Never before had a creature of the forest, let alone one so magnificent, spoken to her in the words of men. Understanding dawned. Surely this must be some fairy creature before her. The princess offered a curtsey and resolved to mind her manners more carefully than was usual.

"Lord Gheorund, who bears the device of three wolves rampant, is a prideful fool who will not accept defeat." The owl tilted his head just so, as if inquiring what she would do about it.

Signe found her voice, burning with indignation. "Great Owl, I will not pretend weakness to salve a foolish man's pride!"

"Then I shall watch from the shadows for his inevitable treachery. Listen for my signal and be ready." The owl righted himself and bobbed in a sort of bow, wings half-spread, constrained by the width of the window. Then he turned and was gone, one silent shadow among many.

The princess laid herself down again but found it impossible to sleep as she pondered which were more alarming: the warning, or the manner in which it had been delivered.

As the tournament began, Signe put the question out of her mind. She studied the combatants closely and noted the ruthlessness of the man bearing the device of three rampant wolves on his crimson shield. It came down to the two of them at last, for Signe felt it only proper that any man who wished to woo her should test his strength against hers.

The fight was brief and brutal. They were well-matched, but Signe was quicker than Gheorund the Wolf. In the end she knocked his shield away and disarmed him. Signe saluted and turned away. That was the end of the bout as far as she was concerned, for though she was strong and honorable, the princess was still young and not yet wise.

A nerve-scraping shriek split the air as a dark, winged shape dove out of the trees toward Signe's head. She dropped to the ground, and put in mind of the owl's warning, raised her shield—just in time to intercept a vicious blow from the flat of Gheorund's sword. He had recovered his weapon while her back was turned. Angry, Signe lunged to her feet and drove the astonished man back with a flurry of blows until she managed to disarm him again. This time she drove her pommel into his face and laid him out cold upon the ground.

The king and queen were confounded by this turn of events. "Clearly this man is no match for you," said the queen as she cast a doubtful eye upon the unconscious form of Lord Gheorund, "But surely you saw the strength and valor of your many suitors today. Surely someone has caught your eye?"

The entire crowd waited with bated breath for the princess' reply. Signe said not a word. She simply removed her heavy helm, still dusty from the melee, and dropped it at her mother's feet as she walked away.

That night, while all the suitors and nobles of the land feasted, Signe led a pair of servants out to the edge of the tourney green. All three bore baskets heaped with bread and sweets, all the good and wholesome foods that fairies love but make not. The servants placed their baskets reverently at the base of the trees and withdrew. But the princess faced the forest with her offering in hand. "Thank you for your warning today."

There was no reply. Very well; she expected none. Signe squared her shoulders and lifted her chin, speaking louder. "I bid you and your people welcome and invite you to join our feasting. I only hope I can prove as valuable a friend to you as you have been to me!" She gently set her basket at the base of the largest tree and left.

On the second dawn of the tournament, Signe again found herself awakened by an insistent tap and whistle. She sprang up from the bed and fair ran to the window to greet the owl. Oddly relieved, she dropped a polite curtsey to the fey creature. "Fair morn to you, my uncanny friend."

The owl bobbed with grave dignity in response. "And to you, generous princess. My people enjoyed your gifts. I come bearing another warning."

Being learned in the tales of fairies and their ways, this was no surprise to Signe. She raised a hand. "First, may I ask you a question?"

Now owls are often said to look quizzical, so she was uncertain how to gauge his response. Finally the owl ruffled his dark feathers and clacked his beak. "Ask."

"What may I do to repay your kindness?"

More ruffling and clacking as the owl considered this question. "Put an end to hunting in your royal preserve here beside the castle. It disturbs my people and puts them at risk."

That was a tall order indeed, for neither her father nor his nobles would appreciate the change, but Signe bowed her head in acceptance. She had asked, and an unnamed debt to the fairies was a heavy burden. Making this change was a bargain compared to tales of stolen children or lost years. "I will make it so."

The owl settled his ruffled feathers. "Listen, then: Lachlan, prince of the land across the southern sea, has made certain of his victory in today's challenge. Deep in the night, he crept to the Loremaster and plied him with strong drink and promises of great riches in return for the solutions to all of the riddles to be posed." The great brown owl fluffed up his ear-tufts and tilted his head, watching the princess.

Signe frowned and began to pace. "This will not be so easy to overcome," she mused aloud. "I cannot stop the challenge, for my mother and father will never allow it. To accuse the Prince of cheating I would need some proof. I don't suppose you would speak on my behalf?"

The owl slowly shook his head from side to side.

"No, I thought not." Princess Signe fretted and paced under the watchful amber gaze of the helpful owl. Suddenly, she came to a halt. "But of course! All I need do is pose him a riddle for which he has no answer."

The only reply was the owl's silent departure from her window.

One might expect the day of puzzles to be less exciting than the tourney, but Signe looked forward to the spectacle. Some of the puzzles were simply riddle questions which must be answered. Others, however, were seemingly impossible tasks in which one must detect the loophole that allowed it to be carried out successfully. Suitor after suitor came forward and attempted the riddles with varying success, some losing the battle after only one or two challenges, others succeeding at a half dozen tasks or more before falling short.

Prince Lachlan, often known as 'Lachlan the Fox', had arranged to be last at the challenges. He fair flew through them, answering each riddle and completing each task. He hardly made pretense of having to consider the answers or puzzle out the rules.

When finally he had completed all of the Loremaster's challenges, he presented himself before the king and queen and bowed deeply. "I have completed all the tasks set to me, majesties! Allow me to ask formally for the hand of your lovely daughter."

A soft hooting drifted down from the tall trees surrounding the tournament ground. It sounded like laughter.

Signe raised a hand and stood, cutting off any reply her mother or father might make to the Prince's request. "Not yet, I think. I have one last riddle for you."

The smile froze on Prince Lachlan's face, but he nodded to indicate his readiness. "Of course, my princess. What's one more riddle?"

"Riddle me this, then: What shall we call it when a man assures victory not by the strength of his arms, nor by the sharpness of his wits, but with lies and bribery in the depth of night? Is that cleverness or cowardice?" Signe folded her arms and ignored the incredulous gasps of the nobles watching the contest.

Prince Lachlan had turned pale at her question, eyes gone round with surprise, and behind him the Loremaster looked terribly ill. The Prince struggled to find an acceptable answer. Finally he asked in a low tone, "How did you know?"

At that, Signe turned to her parents with a triumphant smile. Surely, she reasoned, this must put an end to the foolish insistence on this tournament of suitors. Though she was very clever, the princess was still young and not yet wise.

"Signe, clearly this man is not your equal either," began her father the king, frowning down at the flustered Prince Lachlan, "But there were many today who showed true cleverness. Surely now you can choose—"

It was all in vain. Signe tossed her hands up in disgust and stalked away.

That evening, in the gloaming between day and night, Signe again led the way to the line where the royal wood met the tournament ground. She bade her servants lay down their baskets, piled high with bread and cakes and all manner of good things to eat. When they had departed, she placed her own offering at the base of the same large tree. "I have spoken with my father. He was most distressed at my insistence that we cease hunting here in the royal preserve. But he conceded, on one condition."

She turned her face up to the branches, searching in vain for signs of her curious friend. "Tomorrow night, at the ball celebrating the end of the tournament, I *will* choose a suitor." The only answer was the rustle of wind amongst the leaves as she withdrew.

In the warm stillness before the dawn, Signe waited restlessly in her bed for the tap and whistle of the owl. All night she had wrestled with the choice but found none of the suitors to her liking. Not one would make her happy. But she had given her word twice over and choose she must.

After what seemed an eternity of waiting, the tapping and whistle of the friendly owl released Signe from her musing. She hurried to the window. "Oh, Great Owl! I don't know what to do."

The owl ruffled his feathers and tilted his head to regard her curiously. "Have you not chosen, princess?"

"No! None of these men suit me." Signe clenched her hands into fists and began to pace, struggling to put words to her reluctance. "They want only to win a prize. They care nothing for me or my people."

Solemn amber eyes took the measure of her soul. "Does that matter?"

The question startled her to a stop. Signe turned back to the owl, eyes wide with sudden understanding. "Yes," she breathed, finally allowing her fingers to uncurl, "Yes, that is the only thing that matters."

The majestic owl gave her one of his curious bows, wings half-spread and filling the window. "Then you will know how to choose when the time comes." He turned and glided silently into the shadows.

All that day Signe was quiet and thoughtful, turning over the owl's final words. She allowed her maids to dress her in a rich gown and arrange her hair, rouge her cheeks and darken her lashes, too preoccupied with her choice to protest their fussing.

Her parents pressed her for a decision as soon as she arrived for the feast. "I am not ready," was all she said, but they left off. Her mother beamed at her, no doubt taking her proper appearance as a sign of surrender.

When the ball began, Signe found herself beset with suitors. Normally she enjoyed dancing, but she could hardly hear the music for their constant prattling about their triumphs and achievements. Each was more ridiculous than the last, attempting to sell himself to her like a hawker in the marketplace.

"May I have this next dance?"

Signe almost declined, not yet ready to listen to another listing of conquests. She paused with a polite dismissal on her lips. Something about this one was different. Though dressed in rich velvet finery and jewels of amber, he had none of the impatient arrogance of the other suitors. He held a stillness about him as he waited, hand extended and head bowed in respect, for her answer.

Curious, she placed her hand in his. "Yes, of course."

As they whirled through the figures of the dance, Signe began to relax. This prince was a fine dancer, and he kept quiet. It was positively restful. "Thank you," she murmured.

"For the dance?" His tone was light, and he kept his eyes averted, ostensibly watching the other dancers to prevent mishaps.

"For not attempting to convince me of your suitability." Signe laughed and attempted to catch his eye. "It's kinder than you could possibly know."

The prince shrugged. "You will know how to choose when the time comes."

Startled to hear the words of her friendly owl from this man, Signe faltered to a stop. "What—"

To her dismay, the king took this as a sign that the dancing was through and signaled a fanfare. Before Signe had realized what was happening, her mother was guiding her up to the dais with an iron grip on her arm. "Time to announce your choice!"

Signe looked out over the sea of expectant faces. The suitors, their retainers, and all the nobles of the land looked on. Some excited, some concerned, others with envy, but all curious and focused on the princess.

Her last dance partner gave her an odd half-bow and watched her with solemn amber eyes.

He was right. Signe did know how to choose. She lifted her chin and addressed her hopeful suitors severely. "Many of you are good men. Strong, or clever, or both. But none of you care a whit for me or my people, and I cannot in good conscience choose any one of you."

A sharp gasp from the queen was nearly drowned out by angry muttering from the crowd. This non-choice pleased no one. Not the suitors, not the nobles, and certainly not her parents. Signe could hear her father drawing breath to protest behind her.

She raised her hand. "There was only one who regarded my safety and my wishes during this contest. Only one who displayed bravery, cunning, and wisdom." She stepped to the very edge of the dais and held out her hands to the prince with the solemn amber eyes. "If you will have me, my Prince of Owls?"

The crowd remained hushed, unnaturally so. Perhaps her fairy prince would not allow them to speak. Not that Signe cared one bit for anything they had to say. Her attention was all for him.

He joined her on the dais and took her hands. The hint of a smile touched his lips, though his eyes were still somber. "I cannot leave my own people."

"I would never ask you to." Signe squeezed his hands gently. "As I am certain you would never ask me to abandon mine."

They reached an understanding in that moment. In a flash, the Prince of Owls returned to his grand feathered form. Signe, to her delight, found herself cloaked in beautiful snowy feathers to match. She flew a dizzying loop around the great hall before returning to the dais and her proper shape.

Though the suitors and the nobles were baffled by what had just occurred, and the king and queen were quite beside themselves to have an owl for a son-in-law, none could gainsay Signe's choice. For all know that nothing given to the fairies can ever be retrieved, and she had given the Prince of Owls her heart.

Signe and the Owl Prince reigned long and their kingdoms prospered. By day, Queen Signe and her consort cared for the humans of the realm. By night, the Prince and Princess of Owls governed the fairy folk, in as much as that unruly host may be governed.

Always, they ruled with courage, wit, and wisdom.

M is for Maturity

Brittany Warman

Never is a cold word. It is a word like a distant, barren shore, a beach no one visits, where there are no witnesses to the harsh ocean as she stirs in her anger. Never is a word that sleeps in the back of my mind, a word I often cannot bring myself to acknowledge. Never is my world, the vortex of pains I can tell no one.

"Never is an awfully long time."

He tells the children his world is one of magic and adventure, a place where the young have a say, where they fight pirates and fly. He tells them about fairies, about mermaids, about concepts he only vaguely understands like death and betrayal. His Neverland is one where he never has to grow old, never has to work, never has to die. His nevers blossom like beautiful flowers, shine like sunbeams on his face in the morning. And, of course, the children are delighted, are fascinated, are ready. They take his hand.

"Never say goodbye because goodbye means going away and going away means forgetting."

He has never asked why I follow him. I believe he takes it as a given, as if I am assigned to him by some divine being entrusted with his happiness. He pretends he understands me, but most of the time he does not listen well enough to understand anyone. I believe the children think we have some kind of special relationship, some kind of love between us, at least when they first arrive. The pain I feel when I think of him might be called love in some other world, but in Neverland it is nothing and means nothing.

"You can have anything in life if you will sacrifice everything else for it."

For that, of course, is the price of Neverland, the price he never mentions, that I don't think he has ever understood. Neverland is adventure, yes, is magic, yes, but there is no love here. There are no real mothers to hold their children close, no devoted sons or daughters, no lovers to kiss under moonlight. No Lost Boy will lay down their life for another, no mermaid wants anything more than a stolen kiss. No one can feel the perfect intensity of overflowing love for anything in this world, and no one realizes its absence until it is far too late.

"I taught you to fight and to fly. What more could there be?"

No one, that is, except the pirates. The pirates are all here because they have run from love in other worlds. This is why he hates them so, even if he doesn't realize it. He knows these men have experienced something beyond his imagining, beyond flying, and he resents it and belittles it. The pirates have not forgotten, as much as they probably wish they could. I have heard that the captain once lost a son to a crocodile, that that is why he came here, but I will never ask him.

"There is a saying in the Neverland that every time you breathe, a grown-up dies."

I am not sure why I, of all the native beings of this terrible place, have become aware of this truth and what it means. Perhaps it is because I have gone with him to other worlds, because I—though a creature of Neverland through and through—have gained something he has not during our night visits to windows. I would give it back if I could. To be the only fairy with an understanding of love in this world is to be lost forever. I cannot go home to my own kind; they would not recognize me. I cannot live in any world but this one for very long. And so I follow the boy who will never grow up. Watch from the shadows as he enchants the children he kidnaps. Fight with him. Take poison for him.

"Stars are beautiful, but they may not take part in anything, they must just look on forever. It is a punishment put on them for something they did so long ago that no star now knows what it was."

Someday, he will not even remember my name.

N is for Neverland

Lilah Wild

Darkness, across the metropolis. At this early hour, the city slept. The first perks of coffee, the morning edition hitting the newsstands, not yet, not for a while. Tomorrow still felt far away. From the silver skyscraper to the corner deli, everyone's hustle was hushed with night quiet, mile after mile... except for one midtown street. The twinkles of a marquee—limo headlights—flashes of heavy jewelry—West 54th stood out in the black ocean like a neon island.

Two hundred outside, wanting so badly to be one of the two hundred within. A hi-hat beat hissed from between the club's doors as Lisette and Clair circled the crowd, waiting for Larry to spot them. If you made it up to the velvet rope, you weren't getting in, a secret to all the anxious faces angling towards the door, glimmering in their charms and spells. Preening, gossiping, the masses auditioned in feathered hair and rainbows of eyeshadow, gold medallions and thigh-high boots, hoping that when the moment came, they would be judged shiny enough for entry.

Passing cars slowed down to gawk while the rejected angrily smashed whiskey bottles down the block. Female vocals moaned about ladies of the night through the haze of a hundred mingling perfumes, and Lisette lowered her eyelids, tried to camouflage her anxiety behind a jaded facade. They made a pretty pair: brunette Lisette from deep in the boroughs, dirty-blonde Clair who'd arrived from the midwest, kindred spirits new to the modeling biz. The previous three hours had been spent conjuring up allure and sophistication from within the grungy confines of their tiny East Village walkup, spritzing and powdering themselves with the latest in drugstore potions. They'd gotten inside before, but this time they weren't coming in on the arms of Halston or Capote, and their entry wasn't as assured as Lisette prayed it would someday be.

She checked her reflection in a blush compact, last mirror before their grand entrance, turned to Clair. "You bring smokes?"

"Yeah." Clair fished a pack of Virginia Slims out of her turquoise metallic clutch. "Sylvain's singing tonight," she said, thumbing a cheap plastic lighter to Lisette's cigarette.

"Oh, fabulous."

Lighting up was the fastest way to summon whatever you were waiting for: a cab, a table, Larry. Who proved the theory correct yet again. Lisette's stomach unclenched as he called their names. *Yes! He remembers us!*

"Hey, foxy ladies. Come on up. Looking good tonight," as he waved them forward, unclasped the velvet rope. A guy in a satin baseball jacket was at the front, whining at Larry. The kind who pawed and catcalled, who'd damage the night with sweaty hands and homophobia.

"Aw, come on, it's just bunch of freaks in there. What, you think you're better, man?" Rumpled hair, stubble, a guy who wasn't used to the word *no*. Must want to see the freaks pretty badly, the way he was going on. Lisette smirked, wondered if he'd resort to the desperate flash of twenties, which never worked.

"There's fifty sports bars in the area. Go to one of those," said Larry, clicking the rope back.

"Bitches," the guy spat, as the girls walked in.

Larry's voice was practiced and patient, honed from years of abuse. "Just go home. You're not getting in tonight. You're not getting in *ever*."

Lisette passed the line of security guards, turned back for just a second and sought out the loudmouth. He sounded so much like the creep who'd followed her down the sidewalk earlier today, demanding her number, heaving an assault of obscenities at her back as she tried her best to walk on and ignore him. She might not have made the cover of *Vogue*—*yet*—but she had a little prestige here, a little power. And this time, there was backup.

She smiled at him with the sweetest face in her repertoire, kissed the tip of her upraised middle finger, and walked inside.

The air was thick with the scent of Charlie and Silkience. Vodka flowed from the nimble hands of a shirtless bartender as the music simmered, bathed the crowd in disco champagne. Lisette leaned against the bar, clutching a tequila sunrise, smoldering in violet chiffon as she took in the room. Shimmering cliques encrusted the tables, the stairs, the banquettes—clusters of gossip-page baubles. Painters. Writers. Fashion designers. The socialites who hadn't had to earn their way in at all, just lucky to be born into the high life. Lisette had made it inside, but not really *inside*. Envy roared quietly, and she downed half her drink to silence it.

"Today I had a pin stuck in my hip and Rachelle kept shooting anyway," said Clair, the lights from the mirrorball picking out the sequins in her azure wrap dress.

"Oh, I've shot with her before. Total control freak." Lisette made a sour face over the edge of her glass.

"Yeah. Ridiculous, she told me not to move but I don't care how important her art is when I'm, ya know, being *punctured*." Clair licked the traces of a kamikaze from her lips, shook her head at the beckoning hand of a leisure-suited dancer.

"And you loused it all up, right?"

"Yeah. I totally ruined it for Parker's Pantyhose." Clair rolled her eyes, and they laughed through their liquor.

"God, Parker's. Yeah, I've shot for them, too. Hand lotion next week, then deodorant. *Deodorant*, can you believe it? When am I ever gonna get a decent booking? A *good* one? Screw the supermarkets, I want high fashion. I want the kind of shoots where I don't have to fucking smile." And Lisette wanted to get up to The Balcony, too, but she didn't say that out loud. The exclusive perch above the dancefloor, one of the city's brilliant dreamworlds stitched together from satin and gems and skin, sensual textures of all kinds... all that the designer ads promised, The Balcony surely delivered. If only she could get upstairs, get noticed by a famous photographer, be taken into ever more opulent atmospheres... laugh the laundry detergent boxes off as a very early part of her biography, someday.

"Patience, baby. We'll get there." Clair ran her nails up Lisette's arm. Clair, the defiantly stylish antidote to all the friends and family who thought Lisette's ambitions frivolous, shallow, *stupid*.

A leisure suit sidled up to Lisette. She suppressed a gag at an overpowering cloud of Old Spice.

"Hey baby, wanna dance?" His broomhandle whiskers tickled her cheek.

Lisette shook her head, barricaded herself behind sips of tequila. He wrapped his fingers around her arm.

"C'mon, ya shy? Don't be stuck-up, come out with me," he said, trying to drag her to the floor.

Clair slid between them and thrust her face into his. "The lady said no." She slapped his hand away from Lisette. "And didn't I already say no to you, too? Go on now. Shoo." She pushed his chest for emphasis. "Shoo, barfly. Go back to Bay Ridge." She turned back to Lisette, rolled her eyes and finished her kamikaze as he backed away, hands in surrender position, *didn't mean nothin', ladies* as he disappeared into the crowd.

They both scanned the dancefloor. Gilded eyelids drooped, pouty with narcotics, as thick mustaches swooped in for kisses.

"Wonder if JayJay's gonna show," said Clair.

"Is that good or bad, if he does?" Lisette stared at a David Cassidy knockoff dressed in tight, tight black, who was unfortunately enthralled with his pantsuited date.

"Oh, good." Clair grinned. "Reeeeeal good."

"I wouldn't mind a trip to a dark corner with him."

"What about Joey?"

"He's totally last Saturday. C'mon, share."

Clair turned to Lisette, lowered her long lashes.

"I could get into that."

Lisette paused, wondered if her friend was just kidding, when the Voice of God cut in.

"Evening, ladies."

Sweet Saint Sylvain. Six-foot-two, glitter scattered through a wavy 'fro like tiny stars, lips moistened with gloss. This evening's ensemble was a white suit trimmed with rhinestones at the belled sleeves and ankles, finished off with spike heels. A wild enigma of boy and girl, pouring out sweet, sweet soul straight from the First Book of Fierce.

"Sylvain. It's always so good to see you," Lisette purred as she wrapped her arms around him for an air kiss. "When are you on?"

"Pretty soon. You both look fabulous." Oh, that swagger, nobody could glide on stilettos like Sylvain. All her poise, all that careful, cool distance she tried so hard to maintain just melted under those all-knowing eyes. Lisette quickly sipped her drink to mask her crumbling composure.

"Got to drown the stage fright," said Sylvain, winking at Lisette as the bartender handed him a shot. He drained the glass and walked off toward the backstage door, Lisette's eyes riveted to his perfect backside.

The lights pulsed, the music pounded, and she still felt left in shadow.

"Someday, Clair."

"Dream on, baby. You are *not* on his radar."

"I'm not on anybody's radar right now."

"Was Joey that bad?"

"Abysmal." Lisette crunched an ice cube between her teeth.

"Twenty seconds?"

"And called me by another girl's name, too. Look, I'm not coming here looking for the love of my life, but Jesus Christ. They act like they're such hot shit but sometimes they're no better than the boys back home, ya know?"

"I'll hook you up with JayJay. Or, you know, we—"

Clair was interrupted by the dimming of the house lights and Sylvain took the stage. Breathtaking in flowing satin, blazing beneath the spotlight... a true Disco Angel. Lisette sighed. He stepped up to the mic, lifted his twinkling arms like a preacher about to deliver the Word.

She downed the rest of her drink, grabbed Clair's arm.

"Let's dance."

Love, I'm calling forth
Love, all I wanna be
Come and fill me with the groove

Come to me, come to me

Sweet Saint Sylvain. Starting out slow on gospel roots, hands spread across the crowd in sensuous blessing. Lisette swayed on her heels, let the alcohol stoke her libido as Sylvain climbed each octave, unleashed his sermon in a hail of acapella vibrato before the beats kicked in and the floor swam with glistening bodies.

Clair rolled her shoulders while Lisette spun around. Two lithe boys in silver body paint and roller skates gyrated beside them. Overhead, the huge mirrorball spun slowly, washing its holy light over waterfalls of crimped hair, sparkling cornrows, enraptured faces shining through sheens of sweat and drifting cosmetics.

Come to me, come to me...

Lisette raised her arms, let the midnight sun come flaming down. Opened herself to the glorious burn that seared away all pain, all sadness; this was the Sunday service that kept her feet steady on the city's cruel concrete. A path of purification by frenzied dance, chalices of euphoria, screaming orgasms that released all demons; the sacraments that allowed her to raise her head up in the mornings, get her schtick together, give her best for fluoride toothpaste and bars of soap, hide the disappointment behind grin after grin, all fake, yeah, but I'm *living*. I'm *here*.

She tilted her face up to receive the benediction, and a woman gazed down at her from the mezzanine. Blonde hair hanging in long curls, eyes ringed in kohl. A face that belonged in an ad for something expensive. Her delicate features were alight with appetite. Something about Lisette had caught her attention. All of it.

Lisette could tell she was one of those women who carried herself as if everywhere she went was The Balcony. She radiated pure grace, utter confidence that no door would ever be closed to her. That any wish was possible, kindled up with ease from her lacquered fingertips, which were presently draped over the rail. Lisette's flesh begged to be stroked by those lovely claws.

Spellbound, Lisette turned her body, danced just for the mystery blonde, for the liquid gold splash of her gaze. She swirled her hands above her head, open, Sylvain's message hot in her hips. Her dress flared out like a scrap of electric twilight, her eyes slitted, lips parted, all magnetic projection she hoped someday would sell high-end perfume, diamond bracelets, the finest evening gowns.

She closed her eyes.

You're my shooting star
My seventh-heaven lover
Come to me, my paradise
Oh baby, come take me over...

Sylvain. He spoke for her, completely. She trusted him to give her feelings voice—all she had to do was dance.

She opened her eyes. The blonde was looking away. No! Someone more beautiful had stolen her spotlight. Someone with sleeker bone structure, a fancier costume, deeper connections, better bewitchments. The shadow reared itself again, cold fear of being left out, never to rise. *Oh yes, she would.*

A redheaded seraph in a white velvet bikini gyrated on a gogo platform a few feet away. Lovely, and perfectly assured of her elevated place, even if it was just a couple feet above the crowd.

"Hey!" Lisette stepped up onto the platform. The redhead reacted with annoyance, the serenity melting right off her face with the disruption.

"What the fuck are you doing up here? You're not allowed—"

"Larry's asking for you," Lisette shouted over the music.

"What the... what's he want?"

"I don't know, some friends of yours who want to get in or something. They all look pissed, you better hurry."

The girl bounded down the steps as fast as six-inch heels would allow, and disappeared. Lisette took Clair's hand and ascended the stolen platform. Her feet confined to the small space, her movement became more inhibited, a sequence of poses more than an actual dance. She summoned up every face she'd ever imitated from the magazines, prayed that ten years' worth of bedroom-mirror practice would pay off now. She curled around Clair's back, ran her nails through her friend's golden hair, down her bare arms, projected the tease of a thousand lingerie ads.

Clair raised her arm to Lisette's neck, arched her back. The curve of her rump against Lisette's thighs, the honeysuckle scent of her hair... Lisette was momentarily distracted by the soft skin writhing against her. Clair turned around, captured Lisette with piercing blue eyes. No downcast lids veiling her desire in shyness, no smile laughing it off, but a look that shot right through Lisette as she sashayed her hips forward.

Beautiful girls flashed through Lisette's mind. Silky tresses. Smoky eyeliner. Always, always the bold display of cleavage. Not *Playboy.*

Cosmopolitan.

It always struck Lisette as strange that a women's magazine flashed that peek of skin on every cover. They were selling to the readers, not seducing them. But now, all that lipstick and eyeshadow, hairspray and perfume—all that *work*—month after month of luscious flesh that was telling her to emulate, not enjoy... she'd never realized that this erotic door was open to her too, if she wanted it.

The thought so astoundingly bright she had to look away. Lisette glanced up.

The woman was looking back at her. At them.

Gold rings flashed in the dark as she crooked her finger and summoned them upstairs.

Yes!

Lisette halted her dance, took Clair's hand.

"Come on! We just got an invite to The Balcony."

Lisette and Clair climbed the steps as lights flashed beneath their platform heels. At the top, bared breasts and lines of cocaine bordered their path like poppies in a forbidden garden. A tiny stairway led up even further into the club, the cream of the VIP area, the private rooms. The doors were close together, and one was flung halfway open to reveal a scratched-up coffee table, a sagging couch, a brick wall. Not much better than a college dorm, Lisette thought. *This* was where the uber-rich wore their biggest diamonds? These tiny rooms? Weird.

Lisette looked out over the railing, viewed the floor from royalty's point of view. Divine exaltation looked like feral rites from up here. Beneath her, solstice revelers howled ecstatic before the bonfire of the stage, the maypole's circle unwound into synchronized fingers shooting up, down, up, down. A woman in a can-can dress descended to her knees, red tulle ruffles grasped in her hands as gigantic hoop earrings swung back and forth across her face, the crowd backing away and giving her space as she got down on the floor completely and lost herself in the beat.

The blonde was all the way at the end of the mezzanine, stretched across a leather banquette. Her gown was emerald velvet and gold roses tinkled from her earlobes, ringed her fingers. Before her, a jade evening bag perched on a mirrored table, along with a champagne flute and a scrolled pillbox.

"Some call me The Lady of the Green," she said, by way of introduction.

Her perfume was something cool and earthy that made Lisette think of spring skies. She looked around—no spilled drinks, no overflowing ashtrays, not even the scent of cigarettes, here. Just the smell of rain. She breathed it in, savored the strange whiff of April within the club's smoky air.

"My husband is being an ass tonight," said The Lady. "You two look like fun. I've got some fairy dust, wanna play?"

Lisette's eyes lit up. Blow? Not like she'd need it, high as she felt, being up here, being near The Lady.

The Lady picked up her pillbox. "Sit here," she said, nodding her head toward the mirrored table.

Clair smoothed her dress beneath her as The Lady tapped a sparkling silver powder into the palm of her jewelled hand. Clair closed her eyes as The Lady lowered her plum lips, blew it gently into her face.

The dust clung to her eyelashes, her hair, snowed down onto her shoulders. She opened her eyes, the angles of her face brushed with starlight. Clair, nymph of the moon.

"Me too!" Lisette joined Clair on the mirror.

The Lady smiled, and poured out a second measure. Those lips, agents of kisses and poetry and no doubt cruelty, were aimed at her bare skin. Lisette shivered even before the dust hit her face.

A small breeze, clouds of silver shimmering down. She could practically feel it sizzling on her flesh. Now she was a nymph, too. Of forest? Of fire? Of desire.

The Lady smiled. "You two are models, no doubt."

Lisette nodded, coasting on sensation.

The Lady lifted the tie on Clair's dress, delicately tugged against the bow. "This would look incredible on your whole body."

Lisette tensed.

The club, to Lisette, had always been a place of darkened corners, discreetly raised skirts. Leaving the spectacles to the hardcore exhibitionists while she and Clair dabbled in small audacities. This was going farther than ever before.

And yet... images came flickering up from her subconscious. Ads she'd seen. Transmissions from the dreamworld: a parade of sapphires across a flat stomach, a drizzle of pink paint down a nude back. And now, *her* body, worthy, finally, of more than mouthwash and cotton balls. The Lady's pillbox housed the most luxurious couture in the world, as far as Lisette was concerned.

Tonight—tonight promised to surpass any adventure they'd had here yet.

But... Clair. Clair?

Lisette glanced over and caught Clair's lips parted in a carnal smile, a tiny nod of her head. Yes.

The Lady arched an eyebrow as Clair leaned back on the table. The bow came undone in The Lady's hand, and the dress fell away. A canvas of flesh, bare but for a tiny blue g-string. Another pinch from the scrolled box, and Clair arched her back to meet the stardust. Other clubgoers were pausing in their own bacchanals to watch.

Lisette untied the halter of her own dress, pushed it down to take disco communion full-on. Her figure had a little more weight, curviness; she got the bookings that called for a "real woman" despite her small dress size. She was down to black lace panties, a gift from a rare half-decent shoot, and The Lady's breath was a soft wind across her body, stirring up every nerve ending.

"You look so beautiful together." The Lady took a sip of champagne, ran the rim of her glass against Lisette's stomach like a scepter. The lights brought out strange tones in her face, languid and sensual, sharpening to insatiable greed, softening back into dreaminess. *What does she see in us? What made her pick us out, from everyone else?* Lisette looked over at Clair, tried to see with The Lady's eyes, Larry's eyes. Warhol's eyes.

Clair glittered, the dust blazing from every part of her body. A lust for life as grand as Lisette's, and she'd been just as fast to say yes to this. Just as fast as she was to back Lisette up when things went bad.

Clair, luminous. Everything around her seemed a little more dark. As incredible as the fairy dust was, it couldn't dislodge the aura of sleaze that swirled beneath the brightness. Nothing, Lisette mused, was *that* strong. The night could go wrong a thousand ways, and would, definitely, for some. Wads of cash going into an unintended pocket, or up the wrong nose. Sleepy spouses were promised undying fidelity while phone numbers were pressed toward suave strangers.

Tomorrow's sunshine, hot as accusation, would glare through the window at the agonizing hangover, the barren wallet, the emptiness in your bed that reminded you again and again, no matter how hard you hunted in the evenings, how truly alone you were. That was the ugly flipside to all this magnificent chaos; it wasn't often that someone got your back.

The unceasing ache to be part of something beautiful, to get inside the dreamworld... Clair had never demanded an explanation, called her superficial or stupid. She dreamed it herself.

Lisette rose up on her knees, clasped Clair in a gleaming embrace. This was the girl all the songs were written about.

Clair flung her hair to the side, exhaled. Pulled her legs up and kneeled to face Lisette, wound her arms around her back. The music shifted to a slower pace, a woman breathing heavy over a slow, slithering rhythm.

A crowd of satyrs and maidens had gathered around them. Silver-eyed vixens grinding against their sideburned dates, cocktails and heaving chests and hard-ons straining against flared slacks. She saw Joey's face in there somewhere. Dream on, sucker.

Another face stood out; not caught up in the amorous play, not caught up in the party at all. A young man stood at the edge of the circle, blond and handsome, but still and somber. Cachet enough to climb the steps and enter, but his charming features were hexed with ruin. He was staring straight at The Lady, who ignored him. Loss, anguish, some tortured backstory iced Lisette's bare shoulder, the hurt that could be dealt her at The Lady's whim. Something much more lasting and devastating than whatever the merely rich and famous could dole out when they were unhappy. Her instincts brushed against power, real power: *displease, and be broken.*

Lisette turned back toward warmth. Heat. Clair.

Night fairy, dear friend. Silky body that reflected her own, an irresistible maze of untried sensations, the one person in this city Lisette knew would never hurt her on purpose. Lisette drew back, nuzzled

Clair's chin with a brush of her nose, and her mouth was met with hunger, lips tart with liquor.

Clair's kiss exploded glass, asphalt, tore through the voices inside that told Lisette again and again that she wasn't pretty enough, distinctive enough, *yes you are, yes you are*, flooded her with neon and wildfire. How many boys they'd shared, never each other, which at the moment seemed like the most ludicrous oversight in world history. Lisette giggled, and the mirrorball caressed Clair's face with shooting stars as she leaned her forehead on Lisette's and joined in.

A flash went off beside them. They both looked over. The Lady lowered a Polaroid to her lap and plucked a white square from its mouth, waved a photo into existence. Lisette immediately thought of the guy following her on the sidewalk, trying to snatch something intimate away from her. This club was a shelter from all that, secrets safe, or so she thought. A shot like this—even just being with Clair—could be dangerous to her career. A burst of sweat dampened the fairy dust.

"Relax," said The Lady, fanning herself with the photo, gazing at it. "Really, *relax*," she said, handing it over.

Two girls, shot from the shoulders up—The Lady had left all the softcore out of the frame—*thank you*—instead zooming in on their faces. Two girls, holding each other tight, their faces spangled and sublime with shared mischief. Not a carefully orchestrated slick production, no professional equipment, no circle of makeup artists and tripods and barking commands... all the shoots were illusions, Lisette realized, contriving the moment that came so easily to her now, a moment she looked incredible in, possibly her best ever, caught only by a party toy aimed at a random point in time. Nothing more.

The joy exploding out of their features—smiling, and not selling a damn thing.

And, suddenly, a chill.

The Lady's eyes were elsewhere. Lisette looked up and there was Sylvain standing beside them, unbuttoning his shirt. The angel had entered the garden.

Tonight's the night! Yes!

The Lady stood up. "Hello, sweetness."

She picked up her evening bag, ran a hand over his bare chest as he grinned at her. Only her. Nobody else on his radar.

"C'mon, 'Tania," he said, taking her hand and leading her away.

"It was fun, girls." The Lady kissed her fingertips in a dismissive wave toward the mirrored table. "Ciao."

The crowd parted for them, The Lady of the Green and the Disco Angel, and everyone watched as they walked up the VIP stairway to a private room. Lisette would not be going any further up into the club this evening, her enchantments not strong enough, and her heart sank as the door closed.

The glamour began to leak from the faces circled around her, leaving a bunch of leering voyeurs. Cigarette smoke filled her nose, and someone's drink got bumped, splattering her skin with sticky drops of hard alcohol. The blond man shot her a look of pity, before breaking into a malicious smile and turning away. Lisette got up from the table and pulled on her dress, turned her back on the crowd. *Show's over.*

A party to which she was not invited, no, *no*. She'd just been a hors d'oeuvre for The Lady, the silly little Parker's Pantyhose girl to kill the time.

She sat on the banquette, knotted the halter behind her neck, felt tears start to well up.

"Hey."

Lisette looked up.

"Drinks?" asked Clair, as she tied her dress back together, slipped the photo inside her clutch bag.

Lisette just nodded, too crushed to speak.

Harvey Wallbangers, pina coladas, the cleansing waters of vodka. The bathroom was too public for handling encroaching nausea; they pushed through to the back of the club, threw open the door on the night air and staggered outside.

Graffiti. Urine splashes against the brick walls. A junked couch sat by the trash cans. The upholstery was filthy but they were too trashed to care. They sprawled out, mindless of the stench and stains against their dresses.

Clair hadn't said a word as Lisette tore through drinks and dances and cigarettes. Now, they sat quiet for a few minutes, listened to the honking of city traffic, two guys in the distance arguing over a slight to somebody's ego.

Lisette ran her hands through her tangled hair. The queasiness had passed. She looked down.

"The devil made me do it," said Lisette.

Clair looked into her eyes.

"The devil made me do something I was probably gonna do anyway," said Clair.

The alley rang with throaty feminine laughter. The kind of laughter that punctuates discussions of errant lovers and torrid affairs. Lisette could hear their future selves in it, wise in the world, this is what we did when we were young and *we had fun*.

Wait. *Wait* a minute. Did Clair mean stripping down in front of the whole Balcony? Or... that kiss?

"What we did... that would make an excellent shoot. In the mirrors, all those reflections..." Lisette said. Try it on, pass it off as art if that's all it was, just doing it for the camera and not the real thing, in case the real thing didn't exist. She couldn't handle any more letdowns tonight.

Clair shook her head.

Lisette sighed, dropped her head between her knees. So those weren't real sparks with Clair, either. She was done. Game over, good night.

"Lisette, you wanna live the life, or just look like it?"

Lisette looked up. Clair's eyeliner was running, her lipstick smeared almost completely off. Her face glowed with affection and lust, mixed together like a top-shelf aphrodisiac. As if she'd just read Lisette's mind, the dare all too willing to be taken.

Lisette pounced. All that glitter beneath her, Lisette's heart soared as she kissed Clair on that vile couch, drunken and dazzling beneath the stars. Brick walls, shabby furniture, not that different from the private room The Lady and Sylvain ended up in. But they didn't have *moonlight*.

"JayJay never showed up," Lisette whispered.

"That's OK," said Clair, pulling Lisette back down.

Inside this Xanadu where everyone played games with each other, Clair didn't. Clair, the shining ecstasy of the dancefloor, the safe place inside the fantasia where Lisette could be herself. There was no need to be noticed by a photographer, to go somewhere special. The hell with the career risks—with Clair, everywhere they went could be The Balcony.

Come to me, my paradise, oh baby, come take me over...

Clair broke the kiss. "Then again, it was a lovely shot, wasn't it?"

"Fucking gorgeous."

"We can get some cameras at the pawn shop, make lights out of umbrellas, hit the Garment District for whatever they're getting rid of... see what we look like without anyone bossing us around."

Paste gemstones, secondhand satin. Clair's touch could make even shag carpet wondrous. The possibilities...

Clair opened her clutch. "This guy gave me his card, discounts for... hey. The Polaroid's gone."

She pulled out a leaf.

Winter-silver, it twinkled beneath the moon. They both stared at it for a few seconds, before it crumbled into a palmful of pearly dust. The night breeze took it from Clair's hand and blew it away, down the alley, into the darkness.

Lisette breathed deeply, thinking about the blond man, the damage in his pretty face. Someone who, at the hands of 'Tania, truly knew what a bad night was.

"We'll always remember it," said Clair. "Just us. And her. It doesn't need to be shared with the whole world."

The door swung open in a cloud of weed and Aqua Velva. "Hey, it's those chicks from upstairs. Yeah, baby, put on a show!"

Lisette lifted her head. "No, sorry, you gotta be in the VIP room for that."

It was time to head to a much more exclusive studio than this one.

She pulled Clair up off the couch, and they walked down the alley to the street. Coffeepots and newspaper deliveries came to greet the imminent dawn, and the sidewalk was still full of people trying to get in. Lisette lifted her bangled arm to hail a cab as Clair dug out the Cigarettes of Summoning and lit up.

Right on cue, a taxi pulled up to the curb.

"Hi," said Clair to the driver, sweetly wasted. "We're the VIP room. And the VIP room is going to East 9th Street."

The cabbie grinned over a cigar. "Well, this is the VIP cab! Get in!"

And they cruised home, making out all the way to the soul station.

O is for Oasis

Michael B. Tager

Shortly after midnight, the cat jumped on Dale's face. "Andrew," he yelled into the darkness. "Get your damned animal." Silence greeted him. Silence and the cat, pawing at the blankets, big slitted eyes begging for food.

"God I hate you," Dale said, swinging his feet onto the cold floor.

"Miaow."

"Good answer." Now on his feet, his stomach stretched in protest. He had, he remembered, skipped dinner the night before. He had *intended* to get a gyro from the Greek diner on Aliceanna, right across from the bodega run by that hippie couple that smelled of olives, but just as he passed it, another of those damned portals opened, this time right on the median. The swarm of trolls that emerged had green skin and carried bows and wore lots of eye makeup and listened to some mystical boombox that pounded out drums and like, fiddles or something, and Dale just couldn't even.

He wished the portals would stop. They all opened the same way, with a crack of ozone and bright lights that triggered epileptics. And they always spelled trouble. He and Andrew had had that gnome a few weeks back that tried to eat them, and then that sexy dryad who'd come out of the fridge, Melody. She'd been less terrifying, but difficult to evict. They'd finally gotten her an internship with Andrew's dad and paid for the first month's rent in a shitty efficiency up the road.

He missed her sometimes, though. She'd had a tendency to lounge in booty shorts and sing in the shower in a lovely, lovely contralto. Yeah, she'd been a bit of a remote hog, but all in all, not the worst mooch.

The cat head butted Dale's legs and he blinked. "Fine, cat. I'll get you some chow." His stomach rumbled again and he patted it. "And then I'm going to get me some gyro. The good stuff, with the cucumber sauce and hot sauce and all those dope veggies. If'n you eat, I eat. You dig?"

"Miaow."

Affirmed, Dale grabbed his wallet, shrugged on a t-shirt and shorts, slipped his feet into sandals and his greasy hair into a Mets hat; he'd snag his sandals on the way out, by the door. He swept the cat into his arms, petted her between the ears and ignored the smell of ozone and the flashing lights shining from the cracks under his door. He thought about gyro, how it would taste, how he'd maybe smoke a joint on the way to the diner. He was 80% sure he had one in the glove box. Or had he already smoked it?

Dale opened the door.

Bright sunlight assaulted him. Fresh air blew the scent of wildflowers and cold streams. A wide dirt cliff beckoned, undisturbed blades of crab grass grew in between polished boulders.

"Huh."

"Miaow."

Dale inched forward, still stroking the cat. Dirt spilled between his toes. A stiff wind lifted the Budweiser logo on his chest and exposed his midriff. Soon, he was at the edge of a cliff and he looked out onto the vista. Instead of his disheveled apartment, instead of the dark streets and the promise of gyro, he gazed at his dreams.

The cat squealed and wriggled from his arms when the wind howled and snatched at the two of them, even pushing Dale off balance for a moment. He planted his feet and then looked past the cliff's edge, at the sheer rock face dropped through clouds, through scrub trees growing sideways, defying gravity like an amusement park ride.

Far beneath the birds, near the mountain's base, was a gigantic, iridescent castle, a city of marble tucked inside its massive walls. Even from high up on this cliff, the scale of the white castle beggared his imagination.

A flock of albatrosses circled hundreds of feet below him. He felt a thundering in his chest; when he put his hand over his heart he could feel it beating as fast as if he had been running a marathon.

Speaking of marathon, hunger still pecked at him.

"They probably don't have gyros, huh cat?" When there was no accompanying chirp of support, he searched for the cat, for a response. He was in a large clearing, behind him a massive cliff face loomed to the sky. Embedded in that cliff face was his cheap pine door, half open, swinging incrementally shut. Unfamiliar glyphics surrounded the door frame, etched into the stone. Dragons and monsters and fairies, dwarves and elves cavorted on the glyphs. Dale caught just a glimpse of the cat as it darted through the crack and into the safety of darkness.

He scratched his head. He'd never known the faerie portals went in *both* directions. Though, come to think of it, his cousin had mentioned something about this hole in the Everglades last week. "Dude, there was this hole in the air and I went toward it and blah blah blah womp womp womp..." Dale shrugged. His cousin said all kinds of dumb things. He couldn't be expected to remember it all.

A rumble of thunder pulled him back to the vista. Far in the distance, Dale saw black and foreboding mountains that stretched along the horizon, and beyond. The tallest peak was shrouded in clouds and a constant lightning storm. Stretching around it was an imposing black castle, all crenellations and spires. It was even bigger than the white castle. "Bigger'n Denver," Dale said. Denver was the biggest city he'd ever visited. He'd been quite impressed.

An angry welt led between the dark mountain and the one he stood upon. Perspective was impossible, but it seemed as if hundreds of miles separated the two, the land cleared as if by fire. Beyond that gash stretched heavy forest in every direction, with small breaks in cover for towns, modest castles and forts, rivers and fields.

Despite his hunger, despite his sleepiness and rising incredulity, there was wonder to be found. What dreams lay below him?

There was more to see, but Dale's mind stopped processing. He sat on the hard ground, scooting away from the cliff, and a good thing, because as he did, a shadow fell over him. A hurricane-esque gale rose from nothing. At one point his ass lifted, scrabbling at dirt. If it had continued, Dale would have been deader than fried chicken, but thankfully, the torrent of wind faded. The shadow remained, though, so he looked up. Huge wings spanned the horizon and a great belly hung low. Legs the size of airplanes; claws bigger than oaks. Scales reflected sunlight in burning magnitude.

Dale shrieked. "Dragon dragon dragon, oh crap oh crap oh crap, dragon dragon, crap crap, dragon crap."

The dragon didn't turn, just headed for the black mountain. Eventually it dwindled to a large speck orbiting the dark castle, the green sky shone empty again and Dale's fear faded.

Dale frowned. Green? He ignored the wet clinging on his thighs and focused on the twin green suns bracketing the sky. It might not have been the important detail, but he felt vexed. He stood and scratched his ass, itchy from the dirt. Two green suns? It was like bootleg sci-fi or something. Who has a green sky?

"The sky is always green. What other color could it be?"

Dale turned slowly. His capacity for surprise had dwindled. "It could be blue," he said to the woman before him. She stood a head-

and-a-half taller than him, slender to the point of emaciation. Her skin was the color of bark, her eyes a kaleidoscope, one moment green, the next a blur of reds and blues. "Blue sky."

"Blue sky. How extraordinary." Her pointed ears fluttered.

"I didn't speak out loud, did I?" he asked.

"No." Her voice was twinkling bells. "I heard your mind soul."

"Mind soul? Heard?"

She waved it away with her hand. "That's neither here nor there, is it?" Her laugh, the sound of wind chimes. "You have come."

"I have come?"

"The one who was promised. I've been waiting for a very long time."

"I don't—" Dale stammered. "Who promised?"

"There were prophecies." She seemed uninterested in explanation. "I am Lenore and you have come to liberate us from evil." She gestured vaguely at the black castle. "You are...?" He said his name and her nose wrinkled. "Dale? That's a name?"

"Yes, of course it is. It's my name."

"I think not. The ring of truth is... missing."

"Well, I guess in a way my name would more accurately not be Dale."

"In what way?" She grimaced. Her teeth were pointed.

"Well, my name's Clarence, but Clarence is kind of a bustah's name, so I go by my middle name. I didn't realize that Dale's kind of a bustah's name too, but you know what? Sometimes you have to lie in the bed you make, you know?"

"I do not know," she said. "Are you sure you are the promised one?" She moved and in an eye-blink, she was so close to Dale that he smelled berries and sweat

"You smell good," he said.

"That is true," she said. She grabbed his hand. Her grip was crushing. "You must be the promised one. After all, you came from Gaea, yes?" She pointed at the door. "We've been waiting so long—me, my sisters and above all, my mother, the Queen of the Northern Forest. We were told that one will come from the world of Gaea to our land, and he will bring the light and part the clouds."

The wind tossed her long, wild hair, matted with dirt and sticks and berries. What a picture she made, piercing the sky with her form and the stark, clean lines of her body.

She continued. "He will rid us of the giants and the dragons and the Fiend above them all." She reached into her dress and removed a bronze medallion, inscribed with a seven-sided star, covered in leaves. "I thought you'd be taller and...," she hunted for the word, "mightier?"

Dale focused on her words. "The Fiend? Above all what?"

In a ringing tone, she recited, "Above all the demons and evil in the world. The one who opposes the light. The one whose name is lost. The Omega, the Final Answer, the Ending, the Nothing, the Dark Faerie. The Endless One. The—"

"Yeah, okay." Sweat broke out on Dale's forehead. "I think I get it."

Lenore proffered the medallion. "You must be the one. I was destined to meet and guide you along. Because we are to be as one. Only we can save the world."

Dale swallowed, the dangling medallion reflecting the light of the green sun. He looked into the woman's multi-colored eyes and said; his voice a whisper. "Dude, I just want a gyro."

She cocked her head and wrinkled her glowing eyes. "Yes, of course you want to be a hero. I will guide you there." She raised her fist to the sky, her body elongating in delightful ways. Dale shook his head. No, now was not the time for attraction to a hot faerie.

"No, like a meat gyro. To eat. It's a homonym: not hero, *gyro*. It's dope Mediterranean cuisine and all I wanted tonight was to put it in my tummy." He flicked his wrist. "Not all this."

Lenore's chin waggled back and forth as if dispelling a dream. "By no, do you mean...?"

"Yeah, no. Hard. Pass." Her chin dropped and he doubled down. "No way I'm your dude."

"But my quest for a hero? I've been waiting for hundreds of years on this cliff top for my destiny. For my partner. For my throne." Her face scrunched and she thrust the medallion at him, her liquid eyes pleading with him to take it.

Was she about to cry? Dale really hoped not. "I was just going to get a bite to eat, bro. I'm no hero." He guided her wrist away and stepped back from the stunned woman.

"But the prophecies...," she grabbed his shoulder.

"Are wrong. They must be." Dale swallowed and jogged a few steps to the door to the ornate door. It was nearly closed.

"How can you say that? Only the Chosen One can help us."

He tugged on the handle but the door refused to open. Was something pulling it shut? He tugged hard. The handle burned. His temper frayed, panic rising. No way was he signing up for this. "Man, keep on chilling here. I'm sure the Chosen One or whatever will be by real soon."

With a final tug, the door groaned open another few inches. Was it enough? Before he could change his mind, Dale turned sideways and forced himself into the crack. It was a tough fit and the belly he'd been telling himself hadn't been forming? Well it resisted his efforts. He huffed and he puffed and sucked his tummy in enough to squeeze past.

Lenore looked poleaxed, green tears pouring onto the dry, greedy ground.

"Sorry lady. Like, for real." With that, Dale tucked his head and fell through.

His bedroom door slammed shut and Dale blinked at the darkness. When his eyes adjusted, he realized he was in the hallway. The door facing him was open and Andrew was in there, staring back at him. He was in front of the toilet. Peeing.

"Dude," Dale said. He turned away and crawled into the kitchen, got some cat food, fed the cat who waited patiently by the food bowl next to the pantry. "Here you go," he said.

"Miaow."

In the fridge, he found a can of Budweiser, popped the tab and drank half of it in one gulp, still sitting on the cold linoleum. Then he made his way to the living room and plopped down on the couch. He sipped and regarded the blank television.

After a moment, Drew found him. "You're drinking? It's like one in the morning."

"I've had a night."

"Oh really?" Drew sat in the easy chair and picked up a PlayStation controller. He didn't turn nothing on though. "Tell me what happened."

Dale wondered how to encapsulate it. How to explain that he might have been the Chosen One, that he might have saved a land, maybe he would have been rewarded with a kingship or, like, jewels or something? How to talk about a beautiful faerie who definitely would have taken him through carnal delights? Is there a way to encapsulate the chaos and chance that guided everyone's movements? Could anyone be anything if they were in the right place at the right time and if they wanted a gyro when the winds of fortune blew just right and opened a door to the possibility of greatness?

For some reason, he no longer wanted his gyro. He suspected it would no longer taste like delight.

Instead, Dale finished his beer and got up and went to the bathroom and peed. He left the toilet seat up. The cat found him and butted him with her head. He picked it up and pet her between the ears. The closed door of his bedroom beckoned.

When he opened it, only his unmade bed greeted him. He was asleep in moments sleeping like a baby who'd never once encountered fear.

P is for Promised One

Danielle Davis

"And don't mess with the bog fairy in the backyard."

That was the last thing Astrid's parents told Jenny before they left for their date night. So, of course, that was the first thing Jenny wanted to go see. Though this wasn't the first time she'd babysat Astrid, it *was* the first time she'd been warned about fairies living in the backyard.

"None of the other families I babysit for have fairies in their backyards," Jenny said to Astrid as she tried to wrestle the five year old into her dinosaur pajamas.

"I'm not a baby." Astrid pouted.

"'Babysit' is just a phrase. It doesn't mean you're a baby."

"I'm five." Astrid was adamant.

"So what does the fairy look like?" Jenny asked deliberately. Once Astrid got on the subject of something, she could be tenacious.

"Fairy is off limits."

"So you haven't seen it?"

"Off limits."

Jenny sighed. Astrid was nothing if not a rule-follower. She was the most biddable five year old Jenny had ever seen, which is why she was her favorite client. And the jokes. The kid was a riot for knock-knock jokes.

"Knock-knock," she said as Jenny zipped up the front of the footed pajamas.

"Who's there?" Jenny responded automatically. She was busy thinking about going to see the bog fairy after Astrid was fully down for the night.

"Boo."

"Boo who?" Astrid had tried this one out at least fifteen times already.

"Don't cry, it's only a joke!"

Jenny gave a false laugh and lay Astrid down on the bed. A cup of water and one song later, Jenny managed to edge carefully out of the bedroom and close the door. Once it was shut, she clipped the baby monitor to her belt and headed to the backyard.

Daylight savings time had lengthened the days so that the sun was only just setting, turning the horizon into a violent sunburst of color. Lavender and orange and pink swirled together like a watercolor painting above her as she made her way out into the yard.

The koi pond in the corner seemed like the best place to find something called a "bog" fairy, so she went straight to it. The pond sat in the middle of a small meditation garden that was bordered with trellises covered in creeping vine plants. It formed a semi-circle lined with bright bouquets of flowers: white-tipped amaryllis had already bloomed, as had the violet azaleas, and the apple blossoms had just begun to open their buds.

"Hello?" Jenny called. She felt foolish creeping around a garden in the last light of evening, but it didn't stop her. If there was a bog fairy hiding out here, she was going to find it.

After several long moments of silence, Jenny sat in the Adirondack chair resting amongst a pile of clover. Cicadas had already started singing in the trees and the buzz was like a summer lullaby. It was comfortable. And quiet.

Then out of nowhere a voice spoke up. "Greetings. What's your name?" Its voice sounded like a frog's croak, the words longer and drawn out as they crawled their way out of its throat.

Jenny looked around slowly, trying to move careful enough not to scare it away. It felt right that something this secretive might be skittish, as well.

Jenny tried to remember all the things she'd read about fairies, but it all turned to mush in her head now that she was faced with one. The only thing she could recall was that names were important and that a fairy should never know your true name.

"Astrid," she supplied after a moment. It was the first name that popped into her head. "And what is your name?"

The fairy ignored the question. "What do you seek, Astrid?"

Jenny finally pinpointed the fairy peeking from beneath some green lily pads. Only the face and shoulders were visible from its hiding spot, but Jenny could make out long strings of algae that covered its head like hair. It was excellent camouflage. If Jenny looked carefully, she could also see the fairy's wings, nearly translucent in the fading light, sticking out of the water behind it.

"I just came to visit you, actually." Jenny gave a sheepish laugh. What did one say when one first met a fairy?

"What do you seek?" it asked again. It rose slightly out of the water and Jenny saw it was covered with slimy algae all the way down. What skin showed through the greenery was a gray-green color. It's eyes were black, like small stones.

It cocked its head at her. "Do you not have wish of something? You've entered a sacred place."

Now Jenny felt foolish. Perhaps she'd been instructed to leave the fairy alone because this was a special area, not because the fairy was dangerous. The place did have a magical feel to it, between the gentle rippling noise of the pond fountain and all the flowers.

"I'm sorry to intrude." It seemed politic to be polite to a fairy. There was no telling what mischief might happen otherwise. "I just wanted to see if you were real. I didn't realize this was... sacred."

"Of course I am real. And is your home not sacred to you?"

"Well, of course it is. But why make your home some place where people can disturb you? Why not find some secluded lake or something away from humans?"

"The veil between our worlds is thin near water. If I do not wish to visit with humans, I simply cross over." The fairy spoke in a matter-of-fact tone. "And I find humans fascinating. You flitter about like fireflies half the time, but you are still intriguing. Plus, you have things we covet." Jenny thought she detected a greedy note to the fairy's voice.

"Such as?"

The bog fairy laughed and it sounded like a bullfrog croaking. "There are rules that govern those things. Rest assured, Astrid, I have found plenty to keep me happy. In fact, you've gifted me one tonight."

"What—"

A thin wail rose from the baby monitor, an odd, reedy cry that didn't sound like Astrid. Jenny jumped up from the chair and dashed into the house. She made her way to Astrid's room and flipped on the light. It was a risk–if Astrid was sleep-crying, the light might wake her fully–but the noise being made was too different, too frightening.

Jenny squatted next to the toddler bed and lifted the blanket back slightly.

Astrid was gone.

In her place was an odd bundle of sticks roughly shaped in the form of a body. The sticks were small and thin, like the kind used for kindling. They were bound together across the ribcage and at the joints by thin brown vines. The head was made of leaves still shining-wet and plastered on top of each other to form the face. The eyes were black pebbles.

It let out another eldritch wail, and this close the sound was like the wind racing through reeds, whistling at a higher register than any human child could match. It was a noise made for wild woods and fey hunts. It had no place in the human world, but yet, there it was, its small, squashed face scrunched up with anger.

She couldn't bring herself to pick it up.

"Quiet!" she hissed. At her voice, the changeling fell silent and gazed up at her with shiny black eyes. It was too creepy, too still. Goosebumps rose along her arms and the back of her neck prickled with apprehension. It watched her with unnatural stillness.

She raced downstairs, heart pounding in her chest, to the koi pond.

"Where is she?" Her desperate voice seemed to echo in the small garden. The surrounding flowers, so full in their bloom, seemed surreal to Jenny as she screamed her question out across the koi pond again.

But instead of answering her question, the bog fairy's voice replied, "All children need to be loved." There was no sign of the fairy, the voice a disembodied croak that sounded like it had come from all directions of the pond.

"Don't lie to me. That's no child! That's an abomination!"

"That is a child," the voice insisted. "Just not the one you expected to see."

"I want her back! I *need* her back. You can't just go stealing other people's children!"

"Oh, she'll be back. Eventually." There seemed to be a smile in the gravelly voice. "My kind cannot lie."

"Take something from me instead." An icy cold washed over her body as she made the offer. Her stomach turned over on itself with fear. "Just name it."

"You have nothing I want." The voice turned coy. "Not anymore."

"I need her back right now. Her parents will be home soon. How am I going to explain this to them?"

"I've told you she will return. I just did not say when. You cannot have her back just yet, but since you gave me the key to get to her, I will give you a favor. Do you see the lily over there?"

Jenny looked around the edge of the koi pond and saw a small swatch of water lilies near the edge. Their lavender petals stretched high around the center filaments that looked like fire. She hunkered down next to them. "Yeah. Now what?"

"Feed one to the child upstairs. It will change the appearance to the one the parents expect to see. It will appear to be their child in all aspects save one: it will be completely silent. After enough time, the human child will be returned and take its place. The parents will never know."

"Of course they will! It's their child! They will definitely notice that their talkative, human child has been replaced by a mime."

"Not even fairy magic can make a fairy child truly mimic a human. You are too complex, too rough and unpredictable." Now the fairy sounded smug, with a superior lilt that made Jenny want to find it and squeeze it into pieces.

Jenny eyed the delicate petals of the water lilies. She had nothing to bargain with and everything hinged on this fairy's goodwill. It didn't seem she had much choice. At least this would grant Astrid's parents some sense of peace. They'd just figure their daughter had an accident.

She would tell them Astrid snuck back downstairs while she was watching a scary movie. Perhaps the movie scared Astrid into silence, she would suggest to them. How could she have known Astrid was quietly watching from the stairs?

Yes. That's what she'd tell them.

She reached out and plucked one blossom. "All I have to do is feed this to the... the thing? And it'll look like Astrid? It'll act human?"

"In all save the voice," the fairy agreed.

So Jenny trudged back upstairs and fed the flower to the change-ling, who hadn't moved from its place in the bed.

The coverlet had fallen back, so Jenny lifted it up over the twiggy legs, which where plumping and becoming more like skin even as she did so. By the time the blanket was at its chin, Astrid had reappeared in the bed. A false Astrid that looked the same and felt the same, but wasn't. Boo who. It was all a joke, some horrible joke she couldn't take back.

The only difference was the eyes. They still watched Jenny with an odd stillness, a kind of flatness that spoke of a lack of emotion. Astrid's shining bright gaze apparently was not part of the bargain. If Jenny didn't pay too close attention, she could almost imagine the beady eyes holding a twinkle like Astrid's had.

"Shh shh shh," she whispered to it, though it was quiet. She shushed it until its eyes closed and it drifted off to sleep. She could only tell because of the supernatural stillness it took on. No tiny baby snores, no gentle sighs, no waving of the arms or legs. Nothing like the soft sounds and movements the real Astrid used to make.

It's close enough, she told herself firmly. It had to be.

She would tell no one about this. Who would believe her anyway? No, she'd go the rest of her life acting as if this never happened. She wouldn't say a word. Over time, maybe the memory would fade a little, and she'd be able to convince herself it never happened.

"It's close enough," she whispered to herself. But she did it quietly. So quietly.

Q is for Quiet

Megan Engelhardt

I hang birch in the eaves, birch over the door, birch in the windows. I take ribbons and beads into the forest, leave them strewn among the trees like the sad remains of a wedding. And when the moon rises, tangling in the branches like her hair among the weeds, I go down to the river to see my sister.

She comes to meet me, tall and beautiful as we always were. Long red hair drips down her back. Her green eyes are lily pads in her pale blue face. She stops with her feet still in the water and reaches out her hand.

Come with me, she says by way of greeting.

"No," I reply.

For sixty years my sister has lived in the water. Every year I have come to see her. I have grown old, white hair and wrinkles and bent back, but she is still young.

I settle on the grass, far enough from the water that she can not reach me, and I watch her. She hums, a burbling song we used to sing when we were children, alive together, alike together, one soul in two bodies.

When I first came to the water she was silent. No songs, no pleas, just a dull stare and aimlessly grasping hands. I sat further away, then, and I would talk, tell her news of our family, the village, the world outside. As the years went by, there was less to tell, until now there is no one and nothing at all. There is only me, old and tired and alive, and my sister, young and beautiful and dead.

So we sit, watching each other as the moon rises higher in the sky. My sister trails her fingers in the river, dips her toes in the shallows. This is the one night a year she can leave the water, but she does not like to go very far.

When I cannot take it any longer, the dripping of water off her hair, the never-ending river song that has no beginning or end, I stand to leave. My sister looks at me, reaches for me, asks *Come with me*.

I hesitate.

Maybe it is the moonlight, so piercing clear it reveals things long left hidden. Maybe it is that I am old, and what is the use in waiting when there's no time left? Or maybe it is because she is young, so young I can hardly believe we ever looked like that, as young as the day she died.

Maybe it is because the same power that allows her to leave her watery prison tonight compels me toward it, so that we meet on the shore, a step from safety for me and a step from her home for her.

And I tell her.

"He was going to choose you," I say. "He never said but he didn't have to, I could see it in the way his eyes followed you around Pa's tavern. Remember how we fought to serve him when he came in? How he'd laugh when we both brought him beer and say how lucky he was, being waited on by two beautiful girls, so alike who could ever choose between us? But he was going to, I knew it, and he was going to choose you."

My sister watches me silently. She was always the one with the quick tongue, but tonight it is I who cannot stop talking, finally talking, finally telling after all these years.

"It was so easy to make it seem like an accident, so easy to pretend I was trying to save you while making sure you didn't come up again. So easy to mourn..."

She reaches out her hand to my cheek and smooths away the tears that have fallen among the wrinkles. The wrinkles seem to smooth, too, as her hand passes over them.

Did he choose? she asks quietly, as though she knows the answer even though I know, I know I have never spoken of him since before the first time I came to see her in the water.

"Oh yes," I say, old bitterness like vomit in my throat. "He chose to leave. And he chose to never come back."

Even before I came staggering home, dripping wet, with the terrible news. Even before we had gone down to the river together, my sister and I. He had left for the city even before.

She takes me in her arms like she did when we were children, when our arguments were ripples in her river, quickly smoothed over and quickly forgotten.

I begin to sob. No one has held me for years. No one has touched me for years. Pitied, yes, feared, yes, but no one would touch the girl with half a soul.

Come with me, says my other half, running her damp hands over my face, through my hair. Her palms smooth over the years–her fingers leave trails of red in the white.

"I'm not sorry," I sob, petulant as a child, lying as I have spent my life lying. "I'm not sorry!"

She shushes me, the touch of her finger on my lips leaving them plump and full.

Come with me, she says, and leads me toward the water.

"Yes," I say, as the river reaches for me as eagerly as she ever did, as lustfully as he never did.

"Yes," I say as my footsteps ripple the water and I see our two faces side by side, young and beautiful and together, blurring into one.

"Yes," I say before the water fills my mouth, covers my head, welcomes me in.

I struggle despite myself, grabbing at her suddenly slippery body, reaching for her water-slick hands, but my sister makes sure I don't come up again.

And next year, when they put birch over the windows and ribbons out in the woods, we will sit on the shore together, brushing each other's long red hair, dipping our toes in the shallows, humming our river song with no beginning and no end.

R is for Rusalka

Samantha Kymmell-Harvey

"Help!" the man in the river shouted in French. "Au secours!"

The storm's deluge still raged on their forest, despite the protective mist border Tryamour and her sisters had raised.

"He is surely a spy," said Aliénor, her voice garbled through the mask.

"But he is French," said Tryamour. "Listen to his voice."

Lunete nodded. "I agree with Aliénor, sister. You know not to whom they have pledged their allegiance. He cannot come here, else we will have to flee again."

Tryamour sprinted to the shelter of the old oak trees wide canopy just beside the Meuse river and looked closer at the man. The color of his uniform was masked by the neck-high waters but it didn't matter which side he was on, they all destroyed the forests and the natural world around them.

"Don't," said Aliénor.

Tryamour shook her head. "Then we are no better than the humans, sister." She waved her hands and the curtain of mist keeping their world from view thinned. The soldier caught sight of her. They made eye contact. He opened his mouth, then hesitated, a fearful look in his eye.

Tryamour stepped into the waters and waded beyond the misty borders. The angry waves lowered until they were a mere trickle. The soldier's eyes widened.

"Who are you?" he said, still gripping his stone. "Take off your mask."

She crossed to him, feet soundless atop the river pebbles. He didn't ask her again, but shivered. His uniform shone blue-gray through the mud, brass buttons dulled. *French.* She held out her hand. "Cross the river if you want to live," she said in his language.

His touch was cold, hands pruned. His uniform stunk of sweat and humanity. She eased him to his feet. The water rushed up behind her, lapping at her heels. He clutched her shoulders, legs stumbling as if his feet were numb. His fingernails scratched her neck and she cried out. Were all humans this sharp?

The mist curtain split welcoming Tryamour back to her land. She lay the soldier down and placed a hand on his temple. Moments later, he was asleep. Aliénor and Lunete emerged from the treeline.

"You've dirtied your dress, sister," said Lunete, pointing at Tryamour's mud-soaked hem line.

"We must bring him back to the Pavilion," said Tryamour, brushing his muddy hair away from his pale face. "He is sick."

"No, sister," said Aliénor, "the cost is too precious. His very presence is a cancer to our defenses. We won't be able to stay hidden from view."

"He is not the one who destroyed our home, look at his uniform. I'll carry him myself," said Tryamour, hoisting the soldier as best she could onto her shoulder. "As soon as he is well, he will leave us."

"We don't have that kind of time, sister," said Aliénore. "His fellow soldiers will come looking for him and then our magic will be gone."

"All the more reason to hurry, then," sais Tryamour. She stumbled until Lunete took pity.

"I wish we hadn't left our carriage behind," said Lunete. "But no sense in dwelling on that. You get his shoulders, I'll get his feet."

As the sisters three strode down the forest path, the rain cleared, clouds parting. They emerged on the other side of the woods into a meadow dotted with lavender. Their Pavilion tent gleamed white against the gray skies, its chiffon curtains waving in the wind.

Tryamour and Lunete laid the soldier atop a pile of brocade pillows. Aliénor paced at the threshold, shaking her head and keeping her distance from the human. They removed their gasmasks and tossed them into the painted chest in the corner.

"Please bring me a basin of water," said Tryamour.

Lunete returned a few minutes later with a gold basin filled with clear water and a white towel draped over her arm.

Tryamour tipped the water to the man's lips. He swallowed the droplets, sighing in relief. His eyes opened. She dipped the towel into the water and wiped away the caked blood and dirt from his forehead. He grabbed her wrist, eyes wide, lips trembling. "Who are you? Which side are you on?"

"Nobody's side," Tryamour said. "But for the moment, you are safe here. They cannot see us."

"You speak French like a Belgian," he said.

"We are from Liège," Tryamour said.

His expression darkened. "I'm sorry."

Tryamour looked to her sisters. Aliénor still lingered at the tent's entrance, twisting and untwisting the chiffon curtain with her hands. Lunete sat on her cot, atop the brocade silk duvet, watching.

The soldier sat up and clutched the towel to his neck. He scanned the space around them, "What is this place?"

Aliénor's eyes narrowed. She shook her head, motioning for Tryamour to not say a word. Tryamour ignored her. "The forest outside of Verdun."

"I don't believe you," he said, eyes drinking in every rich detail of the exquisite textiles, goblets of gold on the table overflowing with fresh fruit and loaves of bread. "Am I dead?"

"No," said Tryamour, horrified. "And we are keeping you here until you are well."

The soldier pointed to the silver and moonstone pendant around Tryamour's neck. "I've seen that symbol before. It is a thing of folklore back home in Brittany."

Tryamour grasped the pendant. "Yes, we are close with our kin who live in the forests of Brocéliande. We all wear these, they protect us."

"Sister, you speak too much," said Aliénor.

The soldier smiled. "I trust I am in good hands, then."

Tryamour nodded. "What is your name, soldier?"

"Capitaine Henri Lanval. And yours?"

Aliénor intervened, nudging her sister to the side. "If you are familiar with our kind in Brocéliande, then you know you cannot know our True Names." She turned to Tryamour. "Remember that, sister."

"I understand," said Lanval. "In times of war, we must all protect our identities."

The soldier's eyes widened as if he seemed to see something in the distance over her shoulders. His hands began to shake, this body tightening. The buzzing of an aeroplane engine soared overhead. He buried his face in the pillow until the sound dissipated. His whole body trembled.

"We are protected, for as long as the Meuse accepts our mists," Tryamour said, touching his shoulder.

"I was in the field," Lanval spoke slowly, his mind venturing back. "My unit had been pushed to the river, but we were trapped. Shells rained down around us, there were screams. And the bodies..." he paused.

"Take respite," said Tryamour. She waved her hands over his eyes and he fell asleep. She watched him for a moment as he began to shake and tremble. He cried out, his tanned face contorted, immersed in the nightmare. She twisted her hands in the folds of her chiffon dress. *Something must be done.*

Tryamour joined her sisters in the meadow as they picked herbs and flowers. A gentle wind blew from the south carrying with it the stench of the soldiers encamped close by.

"I smell war," said Lunete.

Tryamour plucked lavender and added it to her straw basket. "The lavender will help mask the scent."

Aliénor crossed her arms. "Tryamour, we cannot mask the stench that has followed us here. He cannot stay. Every minute a human remains in our world, our magic weakens. He's poison."

Lunete nodded. "Every day as the soldiers get closer and closer to our forest, to the river, our border weakens. As they pollute the waters, so our mist weakens. Once our borders fall, we'll have to flee like before. Or we could be killed. All it takes is one shell to permeate the mist."

"He has been altered by this war," she said. "I cannot send him back."

Aliénor's green eyes flashed. "Taking pity on the humans is not how we are going to survive. It's not like it was before. Let the humans destroy themselves."

"There is no hope then?" said Tryamour, refusing to back down. "Dear sisters, I will not give up so easily. We have the ability to right the humans' wrongs. Do we not have a responsibility to use that power when they are in need?"

Aliénor's cheeks reddened. "They don't want us to help anymore. You live in the past, sister."

Tryamour fixed her gaze on the meadow as yet another aeroplane shadow crossed overhead. *The ghosts of war haunt us.* The buzzing was deafening, louder than it had ever been. She and her sisters covered their ears, wincing in pain. When silence once again returned to the meadow, Aliénor touched Tryamour's arm. "You see how close that was? Our defenses are weakening and it's because *he* is here, on the wrong side of the mist. Send him back. Do not delay."

When Tryamour returned to the Pavilion, Lanval had awoken. His muddied boots lay discarded beside the heap of pillows. He soaked his feet in the basin, hands gripping his ankles, white-knuckled. She'd never seen feet like that, red and gray and swollen and bloodied. He winced as he scrubbed between his toes.

"Here," she said as she brought him a towel.

He gingerly dried his feet, gritting his teeth through the pain. "It's from my boots. They are soaked through."

Her heart heavied. *This isn't fair.* "Just sit there, don't put your boots back on yet." She put some fruit and bread on a plate and brought it to him.

He smiled. "Took the gold plates when you fled? I've never seen riches such as these."

"There's so much more we left behind. We lost our people, too. Some were killed. Some scattered and went north."

He swallowed a hunk of baguette. "Thank you for your kindness."

Her eyes lowered. "You're welcome."

Lanval clasped the apple tightly in his palm. "You're sending me back, aren't you?"

The words were like darts to Tryamour. She clasped her hands together. "I'm sorry, but humans aren't' meant to stay in this world.

Your very presence is weakening our defenses. I will escort you through the mist back to your people."

Hand clasped to his forehead, his chest rose and fell rapidly. His face paled. "Please, don't send me back there. You have no idea what it's like—this war—" his voice dissipated into a whimper.

Tryamour wrapped her arms around him. The stench of battle no longer marred his clothing or hair.

"The world of men has wronged you," she whispered to him. "But I will gift you something of my world. It will protect you and summon me when you need me most."

A light switched on behind his sad, gray eyes as Tryamour removed the pendant from around her neck and slipped it over his. "It has been blessed in the waters of Avalon," she said. "When you are in danger, just grasp it and call my True Name."

Lanval tucked the pendant underneath the layers of his uniform. He held her hand in his. "Thank you," he said, voice shaking.

"But there is a price for this protection." She squeezed his hand. "You must never speak of this to anyone and never tell another soul my True Name. If you do, I am powerless to help you."

He shook his head. "I would never, for I owe you my very life. I promise."

A warmth rushed through her, filling her. The tears in the corner of his eyes brought the same to hers. "My name is Tryamour."

"I'll never forget you," he said as he ran his hands through her hair.

Tryamour breathed. His face was so handsome when cleaned. "We must go now." She strapped on her gas mask and tucked her hair back into the neck of her chiffon dress.

A day or two or five had passed since his departure. Time always worked a little differently in the fairies' world. But the wind changed direction, bringing with it an iciness to the meadow. a and Tryamour and her sisters shivered, tightening their wool shawls around their shoulders.

"Look!" Lunete pointed to the sky.

A perfectly visible aeroplane emerged from the clouds, its engine roaring. Something they had never before heard whistled through the air, high pitched, like a metallic bird. There was a thud and for a second, the meadow was silent and still. Then the ground shook, knocking Tryamour and her sisters to the ground. A reddish orange fountain of fire erupted in the near distance, raining scraps of metal down onto the meadow. Tryamour screamed, pulling her shawl over her head.

When there was silence once again, Tryamour sat up slowly. Embers floated through the air like dandelion seeds, red hot. The flowers were singed. "Sisters?" she called out.

"I'm here," said Aliénor, standing.

"Help me!"

It was Lunete. Tryamour and Aliénor found her near the Pavilion. The blast had thrown her back and she was on her side, gripping her arm. Crimson blood stained the dirt around her.

"Let me see," said Aliénor.

Tryamour hugged Lunete and stroked her hair as she cried. The metal had grazed Lunete's arm, raising great welts on her skin.

"You're going to be okay," said Aliénor. "You were lucky." Aliénor turned to Tryamour. "I'll wash it and dress with a garlic poultice. Help me move her into the Pavilion."

Once Lunete was resting, Tryamour joined Aliénor at their sister's bedside.

"How did this happen? I sent the soldier back to his own world," said Tryamour.

"Something is affecting our protection. We can't just flee, not with Lunete in ill health. It's too risky for her."

Tryamour blinked back tears. "I will go into the world of men and find what it is that affects us."

"It's too much of a risk, you could be killed," said Aliénor.

"Either way, if I stay or if I try, death is at our heels."

"I think we should go to Avalon."

Tryamour inhaled, shocked. "But if we flee to Avalon, we can never return to these lands. We must forever remain there."

Aliénor held Tryamour's hands. "It is our only choice now."

Tryamour bit her lip. "We are not leaving until I've tried."

"Remember, the path home to Avalon will not always be open," said Aliénor. "You must hurry."

Tryamour crossed the woven rug to the chest in the corner of the Pavilion. She opened the lid and removed a delicate ring of oyster shell and mother of pearl, waves engraved on its sides.

"If you are not back in time," said Aliénor, "we will leave without you."

"I understand." And she slipped on the ring.

Her purple chiffon dress tightened in strange places. The fabric twisted around her calves as it transformed into uniform pants. She was fully clad in the uniform of a French soldier, brass buttons shining, circular helmet heavy against her head. Her golden hair shortened and hands grew wider. She fastened her gas mask once more and ventured out into the meadow.

She emerged on the other side of river from the mist and entered into chaos. Projectiles screamed as they flew past her head. Cold mud saturated her trousers, seeping through to her skin—s. Shouts and screams were briefly extinguished by an explosion nearby. The flames warmed the side of her face.

"Get down! Get down!" a voice yelled.

A hand fixed on her shoulder and pulled her into a long, wide hole in the earth. Freezing water splashed around her, smearing her mask lenses. Soldiers scurried around her in the trench. Ears ringing, she rubbed the lenses, but it only smeared them worse. She pulled the gas mask off. Promptly her stomach turned. The stench of death and human waste brought tears to her eyes. A sudden acidity rose in her throat. She swallowed it back down.

Someone gripped her shoulder. His mud-encrusted mouth moved, but his words were lost in the ringing in her ears.

"Are you okay?" His words finally broke through.

She nodded.

"Look alive, soldier. You shouldn't have been out there like that. The snipers would have picked you off."

Tryamour nodded again.

"All clear!" a voice echoed throughout the trench.

A silence dampened the encampment. Every face that passed her by was pale, eyes swollen and tired, bodies racked by exhaustion and fear. The count of the dead had begun. Men hoisted bodies out of the trench, passing them onward for burial. Rats scurried along the boards lining the bottom of the trench, nimbly avoiding the puddles. Dead rats decayed, lodged between the boards and the trench wall. Her stomach turned again.

Tryamour steadied herself on the wooden braces holding up the dirt and sand-bag lined walls of the narrow trench. She continued around the bend and as she came across a small group of men encircled a small brazier warming themselves she heard laughter. It was the first laughter she'd heard in the humans' world of war. Meat crackled in the pan atop the brazier but that was not what caught her attention. The smiling face was a very familiar one. A fond one, even. *Henri Lanval.*

She must've lingered a moment too long or perhaps could not tear her eyes from them. Their eyes met, but there was no expression of recognition in his face. Her Glamour had slipped her mind in the chaos. Another soldier turned around.

"Hey you," said the soldier. "What are you staring at? These are our sausages."

Tryamour turned away, her heart pounding. She heard Lanval's voice above the rest.

"Martel, remember we're all the same down here. We've lost too many friends already," he said.

"You've changed, Lanval," Martel said. "Ever since you came back, you've changed."

Lanval cleared his throat. "Hello there, you can join us if you like. Share in our warmth."

Tryamour eyed Martel, whose folded arms and scowl did not welcome her. He took a long drag on a cigarette. She squatted beside Lanval, careful not to touch any of the metal fastenings along the wall of the trench.

"You new here?" Lanval distributed the sausages to the hungry soldiers. Martel bit into his, spraying grease into his black mustache.

She nodded.

"What's your name, soldier?"

Tryamour pressed her lips together, surprised she hadn't anticipated needing to participate in the humans' world. Maybe her sisters had been right after all.

"Yves Beaupré," she said. It had been the name of grandmother's champion knight in Liège. They still sang songs of him at faerie court.

Martel smirked. "Looks like we have a Belgian in the camp, fellas? Hear that accent."

His words stung. To her, she'd spoken with the precision of language she'd learned from listening to Lanval.

"Need I remind you that the Belgian are our allies, they paid dearly before we did," Lanval said.

"You can never be too careful," said Martel. "Spies are everywhere. Trust no one." A wicked grin spread across his ruddy face.

"What were you doing, Lanval, when you were gone? Everyone whispers about it, you know. Two weeks without word? Suspicious."

Instantly, the smiles and laughter vanished. The other soldiers leaned in. Lanval's face flushed red.

"I already explained myself to the Lieutenant Colonel. I don't need to explain myself to you." Lanval stood and strode away. Tryamour watched until his figure vanished amongst the crowd of soldiers.

Martel grinned in victory. "Watch out for that one. He claims he was lost in the forest, got separated from us. But you know who else is in the forests of Verdun, Beaupré? The Germans. Why didn't they kill him? Unless he's the enemy right?"

None of the men dared to speak in defense of Lanval. They ate their sausages, never taking their eyes off the glowing brazier. Martel chain smoked, his gray eyes wild. Tryamour twisted the ring around her finger, tempted to deliver her own form of justice against Martel's false words. *Not yet,* she told herself.

Tryamour stood. "Today, we should just be grateful to still be alive. Thank you for your advice," she said. "And thank you for your warmth." As she walked away, she heard the snickering and fake Belgian accents and laughter from the group. This time, it wasn't a laughter of joy, but of disrespect. Wetness stung her face. She wiped her hand across both cheeks. Tears. *How could they possibly think Lanval a traitor?* she thought. The words of her sisters echoed in her mind. They'd tell her of course it's unfair, it's the world of the humans.

Tryamour shrugged off the snickering. Lanval was still alive, and for that, she was grateful but her thoughts turned to her sisters. To Lunete. Every moment she spent in the trench, her home's defenses weakened.

She searched the camp, but nothing obviously bore the mark of Faerie. The only other place to search then was the forest itself. Tryamour climbed a wooden brace and peeked over the lip of the trench. The forest seemed miles away. And she'd have to cross no man's land to get back there.

"Get down!" a soldier cried, pulling Tryamour back into the filth of the trench. A bullet whizzed overhead, striking with remarkable accuracy the exposed part of the wooden brace. "You have a death wish, soldier?"

Tryamour wrung her hands. She was stuck.

A cold mist smothered the battlefield in the morning. Tryamour shivered and looked out. In the stillness of the early hours, the birds sang and if she listened closely, the gentle lapping of the Meuse river called to her. *Your sisters await you. Do not delay.* This foreign body weighed on her. Her muscles ached, her toes itched in their wet, woolen socks. The smoke irritated her eyes.

The morning call trumpet sounded, shrill. The sleeping men leaped to action.

"Stand to!"

Tryamour wove between the soldiers, searching for her Capitaine Lanval. She found him by the watch tower, his battalion lined up before him. Dark circles ringed his eyes, lines of exhaustion wrinkled his forehead. Some the soldiers bit their lips to stop them from trembling.

"Today, we have been ordered to advance our line of defense into and beyond the forest," said Lanval. He paused, as if swallowing down something bitter. "In an effort to force the Germans to retreat."

Tryamour gasped audibly. They stared at her. Fear tingled over her skin, her face numbing.

Lanval took a breath. "The forest is to stay intact only until it is no longer possible to defend our position. Today, you will need all your strength and bravery. Today, you become heroes."

"Sir, yes, sir!"

"Advance!"

The men marched up and over the lip of the trench. The stench of death still hung on the wind, lumps of bodies dotted No Man's land. Guns popped, bullets screamed overhead. Tryamour lingered at the back of the company. It might be the last time she saw him alive. He had to know. "Sir," she said. "I must tell you something."

"No time, get out there, soldier," said Lanval.

"But sir," she said, her man's voice deep and strained. "It's important. The borders–"

Lanval cut her off. "Your brothers are depending on you, go, go, go!"

She climbed the steps onto the battlefield. His footsteps were heavy on the stairs behind her. Glancing over her shoulder, she saw his face, grim and melancholy. *Hello and goodbye, dear friend.*

Bullets whistled all around them as they advanced through No Man's land. The screams of the wounded and dying were smothered by the explosions raining soot and dirt upon them.

"Advance!" Lanval's voice strained above the cacophony.

Men crumpled all around them, dead. Tryamour pivoted, panicked and distraught. Her mind racing, she bolted under a patch of thick brush. *All I need is water and I can make a mist.* The mist would at least shield all sides from being picked off by bullets. Thorns tearing at her knees, Tryamour crawled through the underbrush. Despite the constant thumping of the soldiers' footsteps around her, she still detected the faint trickle of the Meuse.

"On your feet, soldier!" The voice shouted in German.

He grabbed Tryamour and forced her up. "A Frenchman!" He started to yell for his fellow soldiers, but Tryamour grabbed a handful of thorns and blew them into his eyes. The German soldier released her, howling from the pain.

She sprinted, hearing the Germans yelling behind her. Bullets whizzed by her as they peeled bark from the trees and sprayed mud on her legs. Branches crackled beneath her boots. She tumbled, boot caught under an exposed root and landed in the shallow part of the river. The German soldiers caught up to her easily. Tryamour plunged under the surface. The rocky river bed pressed into her bony frame. She waved her hands in a circular motion, mouthing the incantation of her sisters. In moments, the currents changed. The water chilled. When she surfaced, there was a thick layer of fog upon the water.

Wheeling around in the river, she saw the Germans had made a makeshift fort on a small island, its walls still just sand bags. *It's the Germans*, she thought. *They set up camp downstream in our territory, they poisoned our defenses.*

"Gas!" The soldiers pulled on their gas masks and retreated.

Tryamour didn't move. The soldiers scurried, blinded by the billowing mist. She closed her eyes and listened. Like a steady drum underneath the Germans' voices, the Meuse sang to her. Its heartbeat pulsated in the current. The Meuse still had power in it. They hadn't poisoned her to death yet. It was time to rid the Meuse of this plague.

Tryamour opened her eyes. She waved her hands just above the water's surface murmuring words in an ancient language at barely a whisper. The water level rose sending a massive wave downstream. It rushed toward the German encampment. A horn blared and voices shouted. But there was no escape. The wooden planks cracked and split sending the soldiers downstream.

Pleased, Tryamour started toward her bank of the Meuse. Avalon awaited. As she waded into the mist, she heard a scream. *Lanval!* Heart in her throat, the ring on her finger warmed. *He's used the pendant.* She ran through mist toward Lanval. The ring glowed as she drew nearer. She emerged from the treeline into a clearing. Two men in gasmasks were fighting, their arms locked in a stalemate. *Lanval and Martel.*

Tryamour pushed through the circle of shouting soldiers, Glamour still intact. The intense scent of diesel drew her attention. That's when she noticed the metal canister of fuel in Martel's hand and his cigarette lighter in the other. Her pendant hung visible against Lanval's chest. When he saw her, Martel swung around.

"Is this your German contact, Lanval?" Martel motioned to Tryamour. "Good of you to show up only just now. Were you meeting up with the Germans in the forest?" He spat at her.

"Stop, human," said Tryamour. "This forest does not belong to you." She removed the ring. Her Glamour ceased revealing her true form. Whispers swirled around her. The soldiers backed away in fear.

Lanval's face paled. "It was you all along, wasn't it?"

Martel neared her, eyes wild. "Demon woman." He flicked his lighter open. "You scared of fire like he is? Cuz if you ask me, he's only scared to burn down this place because he's with the Germans. And you're the evil spirit who turned him."

His diesel canister swung dangerously close to her exposed skin. Sweat dripped around the outline of his gas mask.

"Stand down, Sergent Martel," Lanval's eyes flashed, gun cocked and ready. The soldiers lowered their guns, confused. They dare not speak or remove their masks.

Martel shouted. "You believe that this woman, this Tryamour, can protect us? Her weird sisters can protect us? We must burn them out of the forest along with the Germans!"

He knows my True Name, he knows everything. Trymour's heart beat in her ears, blood pulsing with anger and disappointment. "You betrayed me, Henri Lanval."

Lanval pushed his mask onto his head. His eyes were red and watering. "I'm sorry," he said, racing to her side. "I'm trying to save your home, your people."

"I'm powerless now, I can't help you," said Tryamour.

"No, please—"

Tryamour snatched the pendant from Lanval and fastened it around her own neck. "I have to go warn my sisters because of you."

Martel pushed past them. "I'm taking command, you are mentally unfit to lead this unit, Capitaine."

Lighter above his head, Martel strode to the treeline.

"No!" screamed Lanval as he launched himself at Martel, tearing his mask off, too. And as Martel tossed his lighter at the foliage, Lanval snatched it extinguishing it.

"Traitor!" cried the men. "Traitor!"

Tryamour raised the mist between them, cutting the soldiers off from their commanding officers. It thickened and blotted the soldiers from view. She heard a grunt. Martel punched Lanval. He fell. Lanval hooked his foot behind Martel's knee and pulled, bringing him to the ground as well.

"Stop!" Tryamour said, but her magic could no longer intervene in Lanval's life. They would not listen. Lanval bit his lip, stretching to reach his gun. Both shouted, blood dripping down their chins. Tryamour could watch no longer.

The river splashed nearby. It called her home. Tryamour turned her back on Lanval and started toward the Meuse. She heard the gun click into its ready position. She wheeled around. "No!"

Lanval lay flat beneath Martel, Martel's hands clasped his throat. Lanval had a pistol in his hand. The gun shot pierced the silence and Martel fell lifeless on top of Lanval. Tryamour turned he back on her Lanval and entered the river. *He made his choice.*

Aliénor was waiting at the Pavilion entrance, Lunete beside her. "You returned just in time. We must go to Avalon."

Tryamour shook her head. "But I did everything I could."

Aliénor, arms crossed, shook her head. "There is no choice now. Our time has lapsed."

"But he saved us, too," Tryamour said.

"Where is he then, dear sister?" Aliénor asked, hands planted on her hips.

Tears rolled down Tryamour's pallid cheeks. She twisted her hair in her fingers, rocking.

Aliénor huffed. "Yet another human failed your test of loyalty. Honestly, I know not why you grieve, Humans betray. It is their nature. Do not expect more of them."

"You tried which is admirable," said Lunete. She cradled her healing arm against her body. " But I agree with Aliénor."

"We must leave. Gather your things," said Aliénor.

Lanval had revealed her True Name. He had also taken a life. But he took the life to save hers. Despite his betrayal, he still acted to protect them. Tryamour sobbed. "Sister, there is one last thing I must do."

Clothed in a different Glamour, Tryamour hid amongst the soldiers in the cramped circular bend of the trench. Her sisters had granted her five minutes before they departed for Avalon. The entirety of the army in that trench was there shouting and throwing mud at Lanval. He'd been blind-folded and tied to a wooden plank. The Lieutenant-Colonel stood at a distance and a soldier with a gun stood in front of Lanval.

"Capitaine Henri Lanval, for the crimes of treason and murder, you have been sentenced to death by firing squad. Do you have any final words?"

Lanval inhaled. "I do not, sir."

Guilt overcame Tryamour. *Why won't he defend himself?* She clasped the pendant around her neck. He defended himself and her people, but he had not committed treason. His mind had already been poisoned by the war long before this moment. And so had Martel's. War made monsters of us all. She decided on the only kindness she could think of. "Stop!"

It was Tryamour's true voice. Her Glamour vanished as she marched down the center aisle. The men gasped.

"Who are you and how did you get in here?" the Lieutenant-Colonel spoke, his cheeks bright red.

"I have come for this man," she said, deliberately stepping in front of the marksman. "Capitaine Henri Lanval was washed upon our shores and I saved him. He was not with the Germans, he never was a traitor but he is guilty of taking a life. That day in the forest when Sergent Martel died, Lanval did what he thought necessary to protect me and my kin. It's not right, but nothing that I've seen here is. I'm taking Capitaine Lanval with me and you won't see him again."

She removed his blindfold. His eyes were glassy. "Why have you come for me when I betrayed you?"

"Because I forgive you."

The mist filled the trench and the soldiers scrambled to strap on their gas masks, but Lanval knew what the mist truly was.

"Where are you taking me?" he said as she led him back into the forest.

"Because you have taken life, you cannot come with us," she said. "We must be forever parted. But I can still save you from the fate they had in store for you."

He nodded. "I accept that."

Tryamour held his hand. "Then come."

Chère Maman,

This is the last you will hear from me, but you should be glad of it. I have been allowed to live in peace after surviving my nightmare. It came with a price which I have agreed to pay.
I cannot come home for then humanity's justice—death—will come upon me.

Since you will not see me again, I could not bear the thought of you wondering what happened to me. It is a strange story, but it is one you deserve to know.

I now live in isolation. It is a small island in the middle of a gleaming lake. I know not where to mark it on a map for the outside world is shrouded by mist. I've had to learn to fish and grow my own food. Sweats and screams still plague my sleep. I doubt that will ever stop. War has made me a different man. Isolation is comfort.

I dream that I may be able to reenter humanity, if I am allowed. But for now, I am safe and alive. That is all any mother could truly hope for in this our Great War.

All my love,
Henri

S is for Savior

Sara Cleto

Marrying Oberon was not, perhaps, my best idea, but it certainly was not my worst.

With his rings on my fingers, I am undisputed Queen. Of course, I was a queen before we wed. Twelve ladies attended me, washing my feet and face in dew with a trace of honey each morning and night. They dressed me in wisteria petals threaded with cobwebs and crowned me with dandelions and honeysuckle vines. My lands teemed with deer and hare, black bears and white mice, and every morning tasted like spring and the evenings, like autumn.

In this idyllic kingdom, I was proud and happy and could do as I pleased. I could walk the woods when I wanted, eat nectar at noon and roasted chestnuts at midnight. I could bed whomever I wished to have and who wished to have me. But I was beleaguered. To the east, dark-eyed sídhe, emboldened by their youth and beauty, stalked the borders of my woods, preying on my mortals with songs and screams. To the west, oceanids pushed their salty tides against my trees, urging their sea to swallow my forest whole. Sometimes, rebellions boiled up through the dirt under my feet, and I'd spend interminable days and nights searing the earth to free it of goblins. Of course, I was always the victor: my blood runs at the same speed at the rivers, the wind in the sunflowers mimics the cadence of my breath. But still, such petty exertions do become exhausting.

In this way, I met Oberon.

It is not a romantic story. When people ask him, he tells them he found me in the ruins of my own castle, that he kissed me into waking after one hundred years of ensorcelled dreams. Or he might say that he rescued me from a dragon, or a snake. Once, I heard him tell that I was the snake, and that when he cut off my head, the curse was broken and I threw myself, whole and unyielding, into his arms.

I let him tell what tales he will, for I have my own.

The truth is that he attacked my kingdom with spears and fists and men fueled with ale and stupidity. He put up the best fight, lasted the longest against my enchantments and arrows. And when, inevitably, he fell before me, bleeding and raging, I drew him to his feet. I'd spent weeks looking at him, his smooth, warm skin and his mahogany hair, the way his waist tapered just so. He was beautiful, and I was bored with my battle charms and invading spirits, and so I asked him to marry me.

After we wed, the invasions stopped, or as good as. Once a century, perhaps, we drive off unwanted fae at our borders, in our skies. When word spread that my enchantments were bolstered by Oberon's men, the prospect of easy victory dimmed. The threat of brawn and fists penetrate in a way that the promise of spellwork does not, even when the latter is stronger by far.

When the attacks on my borders—our borders now—stopped, I was delighted, for I was ready to bend my attention on more pleasant things. In the first month of freedom, I learned to dance with the sparrows in their sky-court and listened quietly to the hydrangeas and the roses outside my bedroom window until I was fluent in both languages. I admired the glint of my matrimonial rings and enjoyed nights in my silk tent with my new husband. He was flushed and eager, his hands moving clumsily but intently under the new moon.

But by the time the moon waxed full, my husband had discovered nymphs. I enchanted him to ensure he would never touch an unwilling girl, shrugged my shoulders, and returned to my flowers and my birds, my ladies and my cobweb tapestries. All was serenity, until Pan came back.

Pan, you see, was my first love. We were young together, once, at the beginning of the world. His beauty was wild and perfect and strange, marking him as human and animal, and neither. Horns rose into a natural crown over his face, and soft, dense fur covered his narrow legs, which tapered into delicate, deadly hoofs. He wove me a crown, my first, from willow fronds and violets, and placed it reverently on my brow before pouncing on top of me and burying me in the riverbank and his body. I fashioned his first pipes, cut carefully from the reeds and bound with strands of my own gleaming hair, and he played me tunes that made me dance and weep and wrap him in my wings like a precious, fragile thing. I loved him like I loved sunlight, music, and blood red wine.

Such a thing couldn't last, not between us. Even then, I had my sights on the tree-lined horizon, my fingers mixing my first potions of dust and dew and dreams. I loved him, but I wanted to know what else I could love. And Pan was hardly ready for domesticity. He could spend weeks listening to a single tree as its roots stretched in the dirt, months blowing chaotic nonsense notes into his pipes until a perfect song fell out. What need was there for sleep or sustenance, much less companionship or sex, when the shaping of the world was in our hands?

He left, or I left. It was so long ago, and I'd rather dwell on the fit of his horns into my hands than the tedium of lovers' partings. Suffice to say I left the pastures for the forests, and Pan drank and danced and became synonymous with the pipes I had made for him.

Millennia passed. I won my crown from a dryad and drew a court of sprites, anthousai, and the occasional maenad around me. I wed my Oberon, enjoyed his vigor and ignored his foibles.

And then Pan appeared in my woods.

He would not stay, nor would I want him to. He was not suited for these fairy-filled woods and political maneuverings, nor would I be content in his pastures and riverbeds. But a tryst, a time out of time in which I could feel young and foolish and in love...

And so I picked a fight with Oberon, something about a handmaiden's child, a boy he never would have wanted for his retinue had I not favored him before my husband's greedy eyes. When I refused to turn over the boy, my husband dispatched his lackey (Puck, a sweet but rather foolish sprite) to punish me: to make me fall in love with a debased animal in my woods and, in so doing, humiliate me beyond measure. My husband, I'm sorry to say, has a stunted capacity to appreciate bodies that fail to mirror his own particular shade of beauty back to him.

I let Puck drip his silly flower into my eyes (as if he could enchant me with my own blooms), and opened them when I heard my love's hoofs on the loam beside me. My husband was quite delighted by my sordid affair with the goat-man.

So was I.

When a human playwright finally heard the tale, third-hand or worse from Puck's grandson's grandson, the facts were already jumbled. I can hardly hold the story against him, even if he did write that I rutted with a donkey-headed man, an incompetent musician to boot. Now, when crowds gather each midsummer to watch his play, the giggling groundlings have no idea that Titania was in the arms of a god.

So, no, my marriage is not perfect. But I have Oberon's army warding my borders. I have my handmaiden's son back in my care; a simple spell, and Oberon forgot he had ever pressed a claim for him. I have my enchantments and hydrangeas and forest shadows deeper than the sea. I have memories of a warm midsummer night with Pan. And I have all the pleasure of knowing that, sooner or later, in days or millennia, he will come to me again, or I will go to him, and everything will be sunlight and red, red wine.

T is for Titania

Andrew Bourelle

The crate included living plants, not just seeds, of white asphodel, vetch, maquis shrubs, and various kinds of feather grasses. There were six potted dwarf olive trees and even a young cypress tree, which was turned sideways and bent practically in half to fit inside. The cypress tree looked like it needed some care to return to health, but the other plants had weathered the trip from Tuscany quite well.

Megan Sattler, the director of the Albuquerque Botanic Garden, stared at the new plants like a kid who just opened her Christmas presents and was ready to start playing.

"Let's get to work," Megan said to her master gardener, James Malcolm.

The greenhouse had two wings: the Desert Conservatory for southwestern plants, those native to New Mexico and Arizona; and the Mediterranean Conservatory, which was kept warm year-round and constantly humidified with water misters. The new Italian plants were perfect for the Mediterranean section.

"I can't believe you got all this for less than five hundred dollars," James said, straining to carry one of the olive trees.

James was still in his twenties, but he knew as much about plants as any botanist Megan had ever met. This time of year, he worked in sandals, never caring how dirty his feet got, and he always wore an Albuquerque Isotopes baseball cap.

"Yep," Megan said. "Just the shipping costs. The plants were free."

She'd found the advertisement on a gardening forum and thought it was too good to be true. A nursery in the Tuscany region of Italy was closing and wanted to unload the last of its stock if someone was willing to pay the shipping costs. Megan had emailed the nursery with skepticism and was surprised when she actually heard back from them.

Megan and James worked all afternoon to move the plants into place, mixing their native Italian dirt with New Mexico soil and organic compost. It was one of the first really hot days of summer, and both Megan and James were sticky with sweat, especially in the humid greenhouse.

When they were finished, they stood back and admired the plants.

"Beautiful," Megan said. "Just beautiful."

Megan was eating breakfast when James called.

"There's something weird here that you're going to want to see," he said.

"What?" she said, her mouth half full of multigrain cereal.

"I think we got vandalized?"

When she arrived at the main lawn, he was waiting for her. It was a large grassy courtyard full of tall trees for shade. Even though families regularly held picnics on the lawn, the space, a little bit smaller than a football field, was always lush with healthy grass.

Not anymore. There were trails of brown spots zigzagging all through the lawn. Megan examined the dead spots closely—they looked like toddler-sized footprints.

"Some kind of animal?" James said.

"But what kind of animal kills grass when it steps on it?"

Megan speculated that perhaps teenagers had come and wiped some kind of poison on their shoes. Gasoline might do the trick if there was enough of it.

"Those prints look too small to be from a teenager," James said.

"Maybe whatever they used was only on part of their shoes."

"But the gait's all wrong," James said. "Were they running around making baby steps?"

"I don't know. I'm not a detective."

"Speaking of detectives, should we call the cops?"

"I suppose so," Megan said, although she hated to think of the *Albuquerque Journal* or one of the news stations getting wind of this and doing a piece on it.

The uniformed police officer said her name was Sergeant Ellroy. She had short blond hair, wore no makeup, and looked like she was all business. After Megan and James showed her the problem, the sergeant walked around in the grass, following tracks. Megan and James stood awkwardly off to the side. The garden was opening, and the first visitors were wandering in. In the summer, the garden was busiest in the mornings while the temperature was still bearable.

After a few minutes, Ellroy motioned for them to walk over to where she was standing at the north end of the green.

"There's only one point of entry," she said, gesturing to a place where the "footprints" ran right up to the sidewalk.

It looked like multiple sets had stepped from the sidewalk to the grass.

"Where does this go?" Ellroy said, pointing to the sidewalk.

"The rest of the property," Megan said. "The Heritage Farm. The Japanese Garden. The Cottonwood Gallery. The Desert Conservatory and the Mediterranean Conservatory."

When she mentioned the greenhouses, she felt a chill creep up her back that she couldn't explain.

"Let's walk this way and see if we can spot anything," Ellroy said.

They walked the path, but saw nothing unusual on the sidewalk. Occasionally when the sidewalk led to dirt trails heading in other directions, Ellroy would kneel down and look for prints. But the paths were hard-packed, and it was impossible to make out clear tracks.

When they arrived at the greenhouses, Megan was the first to notice the broken pane of glass in the Mediterranean Conservatory. The hole was close to the ground, like someone had kicked a soccer ball through the glass. Ellroy took pictures and pointed out that the glass shards had sprayed outward from the building.

"Something broke out," she said. "Not in."

They checked all the doors and found them locked—it was James's job to unlock them each morning, but he had been distracted by the dead spots on the green. When they went inside, Megan felt a lump rise to her throat.

All the plants they'd imported from Italy were wizened and looked like they hadn't been watered in a year. The leaves were dead on the branches, and the bark was dry and brittle.

Megan spent most of her day in her office, but once word got out what had happened, there seemed to be a nonstop stream of employees "just stopping by." She was talking about the situation continually.

The Botanic Garden was part of the larger ABQ Biopark, and shared its parking lot with the aquarium, and a small narrow-gauge train took visitors back and forth to the zoo, which was a mile and a half away. By late afternoon, even her boss, the CEO who oversaw all three properties, came over from the zoo to get the scoop.

"You called the cops?" he said. "Was that really necessary?"

His name was Mark Abnett, and the only thing Megan had ever liked about him was that he usually left her alone to do her job.

"You sure it's not some kind of fungus or disease?" he said.

"Those don't kill plants overnight."

Megan left work promptly at five, feeling more exhausted than if she'd spent the day out on the grounds planting trees. She picked up Thai food on the way home and ate it on her couch, flipping through channels. She turned the TV off and tried to read the latest issue of *Horticulture Magazine* but couldn't concentrate on the words. She finally set it aside and drew a bath. She sat in the warm water and scrubbed the dirt from underneath her fingernails. Then stared at the ceiling. Baths usually relaxed her, but it wasn't working tonight.

For some reason, the day's events had cast a shadow over her mood that she couldn't shake. Megan had no social life, no close friends. She could function just fine in a social setting, chatting with visitors at the garden, doing interviews with the newspaper or local TV stations, making small talk at the annual Christmas party. But those kinds of activities exhausted her and she never sought out social interaction. She preferred working in her garden—the Botanic Garden or the small flower garden she kept at her home—to going to parties or to the movies. She was happy, usually.

But tonight, after the vandalism, she felt unfulfilled. Her life seemed empty. She wanted to tell someone about the peculiar vandalism. Not an employee or coworker. A friend.

But she had no one in her life to talk to about it.

She was wide awake before the sun rose. Rather than lie in bed, hoping to fall back asleep, she drove to work. As she walked past the aquarium to the main gate, she thought she heard laughter. It was like a child's laughter, but higher-pitched, like the cackle of the witch from the movie *The Wizard of Oz*, only more muffled. She tried to be as quiet as possible as she unlocked the gate and crept through.

The laughter, or whatever it was, ceased. But there was another noise, a mechanical whirring. She thought she knew what it was, and as she walked forward, she found she was right. Next to the Children's Fantasy Garden was a model train exhibit. Small model trains were run six days a week through bushes and plants, past miniature towns and over model bridges. The trains only ran during business hours when a volunteer from the local model train club was here to operate them. But this morning, with no volunteer in sight, all the trains were running—speeding down the tracks faster than normal.

There were also a handful of trains that could be operated by visitors. Children would press a button next to the fence and give life to smiling characters from Thomas the Tank Engine. Today, even these trains were moving, with no one there to press the buttons.

Thomas's smiling blue face came around a bend. Then, as if he'd spotted her, he slowed to a stop. All the trains ceased. In the absence of their sound, the silence was overwhelming.

Megan's heart pounded as she hurried down the sidewalk toward her office. It was all she could do to keep herself from breaking into a run.

More dead plants were discovered. Inside the Mediterranean wing of the conservatory, there were dead monkeyflowers, papyrus, oleander, jasmine, and Andean silver-leaf sage. In the outdoor grounds, there were dead daffodils, tulips, irises, and a patch of Chinese wisteria. Some of the trees—an Arizona white oak tree, a lovely Shumard oak, several cottonwoods—seemed to be losing leaves in strange patches. Some branches were healthy. On others, the leaves were drying up. There was no logical explanation. In a desert climate like Albuquerque, if trees weren't getting enough water, the branches farthest from the roots would start to wither first. It was a defense mechanism that sacrificed some limbs to save the tree. But what was happening to these trees didn't follow that pattern.

"Insect infestation?" James asked.

He and Megan were staring up at the Shumard oak.

"Could be," Megan said. "But I don't see any other signs."

"You know what it looks like?" James said, taking off his ball cap and scratching his head.

Megan knew what he was going to say before he said it.

"It looks like whatever was running around killing the grass climbed up in the trees," James said. "And wherever it went, the trees have started to die."

Megan was thinking the same thing, only instead of using the pronoun *it*, she would have said *they*.

A week later, the horse at the Heritage Farm was dead. Megan stood next to it with Sergeant Ellroy and Bob Applegate, a large-animal veterinarian who was called in to do the autopsy. Inez Trujillo, who managed the Heritage Farm, was feeding the chickens at the other barn. She couldn't stop crying, so Megan had asked her to take a few minutes so the rest of them could talk.

The horse, Starshine, had been a beautiful animal. All white fur, a majestic posture. Now he lay on his side in the dirt, his body buzzing with flies. His eyes were sunken and milky. The pink tip of his tongue stuck out, pinched between his teeth.

Ellroy took some pictures and then told Bob he could load the horse up. Megan and Ellroy walked back through the garden toward the parking lot. Ellroy's all-business demeanor seemed to be cracking. She had a look on her face of sad contemplation.

"Would you give me a tour of the whole grounds?" she asked. "I'd never been here until the other day."

They started with the Children's Fantasy Garden, which consisted of giant sculptures of plants and insects to give kids a feeling of what it would be like to be a bug in a garden. There were eight-foot-tall carrots sticking up out of the ground, a pumpkin the size of a house that kids could run around inside, and various statues of ants and mosquitoes and bees that children could climb on. They walked by the model trains and the under-construction butterfly pavilion. Megan pointed out the BUGarium but was thankful that Ellroy didn't ask to go inside.

When they were finishing up the tour, Ellroy seemed looser than she had before, more friendly. She explained that she'd moved from Las Vegas—Las Vegas, New Mexico, not Nevada—about a year ago and was still learning about the city. Megan got the sense that she probably didn't have many friends either.

"I'll tell you what," Ellroy said. "You've got a hell of a problem on your hands. Even if the malfunction with the trains is unrelated."

"I just wish I knew what the problem was," Megan said. "James has been examining all the plants that have died. He can't find any obvious cause. No fungus. No beetles. No trace of poison. Their roots are wet, so it's not a lack of water."

They were walking next to the main green, which was shadowed under the canopy of big trees. Most of the trees seemed to have dead spots now. To their right was the Dragonfly Sanctuary Pond, full of dragonflies and damselflies hovering over Lilly pads.

"Besides, what kind of disease spreads from plants to animals?" Megan said.

"To fish?" Ellroy added, pointing to the pond.

Several of the koi—two feet long and covered in white and red scales—were floating dead in the water.

That night, Bob Applegate called Megan at home. She was lying on her couch, staring at the ceiling. She'd been doing that a lot lately.

"Your horse didn't die from natural causes," he said. "He had a heart attack."

"That sounds natural," Megan said.

"Let me rephrase," Bob said. "His heart *exploded*."

"What?"

"This happens in racing sometimes," Bob said. "If a jockey pushes a horse too hard, its heart can literally burst. A horse can be run to death."

"That corral isn't big enough," Megan told him.

"I'm just telling you the autopsy results," Bob said. "This wasn't an ordinary heart attack. Someone either pushed that horse really, really hard. Or something scared it so bad it was running around in a frenzy."

When Megan hung up, she thought about calling Sergeant Ellroy. She'd given Megan her cell number, but Megan decided it could wait until tomorrow morning.

Ten minutes later, she was brushing her teeth when she received a text—the alarm at the BUGarium was going off.

Megan hurried out the door and called Ellroy from her car.

"I know you're off duty," Megan said. "And the police are on their way, but I thought you might like to know."

"What kind of bugs are in there?" Ellroy asked.

"Everything you can think of."

Megan met two uniformed officers on the sidewalk outside the BUGarium. The BUGarium had an entrance and an exit, both with double doors. A person couldn't open the second door until the first was closed—this was a precaution so no bugs could get out. It was only a failsafe since all the bugs were encased in their own terrariums anyway.

The glass of both doors had been broken. Spider-webs of cracks grew from volleyball-shaped holes at the bottom of each door.

"We haven't gone inside," one of the officers said. "We shined our lights in and the place is crawling with bugs."

Both men looked pale. She felt lucky they hadn't drawn their guns and started firing at the spiders and beetles.

"Thanks for all your help," she said sarcastically.

She'd called James and a few other employees on her way, and now they were hurrying up the path.

"A TV news van just pulled into the parking lot," James said, out of breath.

"Crap," Megan said.

She told James to go to the storage shed at the Heritage Farm and get two sheets of cardboard and some duct tape to start repairing the doors, and instructed the police officers to keep the damn TV reporters out of here—the last thing she needed was someone with a camera getting inside and recording a goliath tarantula or an emperor scorpion escaping. She told one employee, a new girl who looked as scared as the cops, to stand by the door and make sure no bugs got out.

"I don't care if leafcutter ants or honeybees come out," Megan said. "But if you see a scorpion or anything that looks like it might be venomous, catch it or kill it."

Megan turned to the last employee there, Gina Lawrence, the entomologist who oversaw the BUGarium. Megan was a plant person, not a bug person—spiders and insects gave her the heebie-jeebies. But she had to put on a strong face for the rest of the employees.

"Let's go get our bugs," she said to Gina.

The electricity was off, so they went in with flashlights. Gina unlocked the front door. Pebbles of glass rained down as she swung the door open. Fortunately, no bugs had made it into the safety corridor yet, as far as they could tell. Glass crunched underfoot.

Inside, even though there were baseball-sized holes in practically every terrarium, Megan felt relieved. She'd expected insects to be blanketing the floor like an Indiana Jones movie, but at the first swing of her flashlight, she didn't see any. Then she slowed down her inspection and saw that there were bugs all over the place, just hidden at first glance. Katydids were crawling outside of the glass on their display. An assassin bug sat on the drinking fountain. A couple centipedes were crawling through the carpet. Moths fluttered around. Something buzzed by Megan's head and she hoped it was a honeybee. What she saw the most of were crickets, which weren't part of the displays but instead were used to feed the carnivorous spiders and insects.

They needed to walk through the facility to the other side, where the storage room held collection kits and gloves and safety goggles. Gina led the way, and Megan followed, trying to control her shaking limbs.

They entered the main room, where the creepiest bugs were housed. The glass display of various African beetles had been smashed, and the insects—multicolored and each about two inches long—were crawling all over the floor. A panel of displays of various spiders were broken open, and Megan spotted a Mexican red-knee tarantula, a Brazilian white-knee tarantula, and a Honduran curly-hair tarantula. But that was it, which meant that so many others were hidden somewhere. The black widows and brown recluses might be out, and then there was...

Something brushed Megan's pant leg and she aimed the flashlight down. The goliath bird-eater tarantula was right next to her foot, its body as big as her tennis shoe, its legs spanning more than ten inches. Three of its hairy legs were resting on the toe of her shoe.

Megan opened her mouth to call for Gina, but she'd already left Megan behind. She carefully withdrew her foot, and hurried after Gina, who was now in the scorpion section. Armor-plated scorpions of various shapes and colors were scurrying along the floor. They were usually docile in their cages, but it seemed like being freed had caused them all to go into a frenzy. An Arabian fat-tailed scorpion and a deathstalker scorpion—two of the deadliest insects on the planet—raced toward her.

Megan swooned on her feet. She realized she'd been holding her breath and didn't know for how long. The floor listed like the deck of a boat.

Oh, Christ, Megan thought. *I'm going to pass out.*

A firm hand grabbed her by the arm from behind and steadied her.

"Are you okay?"

It was a familiar voice—female—but Megan couldn't quite place it. The two scorpions seemed to sense some danger from this new visitor, and they turned and went in different directions.

"It looked like you were about to go down," the voice said again.

Megan took a deep breath. Then the lights came on.

"Found the fuse box," Gina called from the storage room.

Megan looked up at the person who had come to her rescue. It was Sergeant Ellroy. She was wearing jeans and a white tee shirt. She'd come over in her street clothes—and she'd come in to help, not like the two scaredy-cat cops standing outside.

"Are you okay?" Ellroy said.

"Yes," Megan said, and she meant it.

Whether it was the lights coming on, Ellroy coming to help or just taking a few deep breaths, Megan felt much better.

The three of them put on lab coats, thick rubber gloves, and safety goggles, and spent the next six hours scooping up tarantulas, scorpions, beetles, wasps, katydids, and practically every other bug imaginable.

Her boss, Mark, showed up briefly, looking as nervous as the cops outside. He encouraged them to keep up the good work. As he was leaving, Megan told him that as soon as they were done, she would issue a news release saying that the whole Botanic Garden would be closed temporarily. Gina and her staff would need a day to make sure the bugs—at least the dangerous ones—were accounted for.

This was only part of her reason. In reality, she wanted to close the Botanic Garden to the public because she wanted to figure out what the hell was going on. This—whatever *this* was—was getting out of control.

"No," he said. "Let's just close the BUGarium. Keep the rest of the garden open. Let's not make this a bigger PR nightmare than it needs to be."

Megan wanted to argue, but he left without giving her the chance.

When they finally finished, Megan thanked Ellroy for her help. The two of them walked out of the BUGarium, and instead of walking toward the parking lot, they walked out into the main green. The hubbub from the break-in had died down—the TV reporters were gone, so were the cops—and the whole garden was eerily quiet. There should have been cicadas chirping, but they were silent. Usually there were frogs croaking from the pond. Not tonight. And there seemed to be no breeze.

"I've got something to say," Ellroy said, "but I'm not sure I should say it here."

"Why?" Megan said.

"Someone might be listening."

Suddenly the silent park seemed much more frightening. The garden was very dark, and Megan imagined someone—or some thing—spying on them from the shadows.

"Okay," Megan said. "Let's get the hell out of here."

No bars were open this late, so they went back to Megan's house. Megan couldn't remember the last time she had company, and she felt self-conscious about the dirty dishes in the sink and the pile of clothes on the dining room table that she'd taken out of the dryer but hadn't folded yet.

"I think I have a few beers in the fridge," Megan said.

"Yes, please," Ellroy said.

They sat on opposite ends of the couch, angled to face one another. Megan felt itchy all over her body and fought the urge to check and make sure insects weren't crawling on her skin.

"What I'm about to say I'm not saying as a cop," Ellroy said. "I'm saying as a friend."

"If we're friends," Megan said, "maybe you should tell me your name. I don't want to have to call you Sergeant Ellroy all night long."

"Shasta."

"Like the mountain?" Megan said.

Ellroy—or Shasta—ignored her. Her demeanor was different. She was all business, but not in the same way as when Megan first met her. She was about to say something important and wanted the situation taken seriously.

"I don't know how to say this exactly," Shasta said, "but have you considered that what's going on is supernatural?"

Megan let out a long exhalation.

"I'm relieved to hear someone else is thinking the same thing."

They talked about the timing of the events and the inexplicability of everything that had happened. Either someone was playing an elaborate joke on the Botanic Garden, or something very weird was going on.

"I don't know how," Shasta said, "but we need to put a stop to this."

Megan didn't disagree, but she had no idea what to do.

"The Botanic Garden is right next to the aquarium," Shasta said. "If the same thing that happened in the BUGarium happens there, they're going to have dead sharks and jellyfish all over the place."

Megan put her head in her hands. "I hadn't even thought of that."

"And there's a train that runs to the zoo, right?" Shasta said. "What if whatever is doing this walks down the track and gets to the zoo? What if it lets all the snakes out of the reptile house? Or frees the tigers and mountain lions and polar bears?"

Megan thought she might throw up.

"And who's to say this couldn't spread out into the city?" Shasta said. "Trees start dying along the Bosque. Dead fish pop up all along the Rio Grande."

"We don't even know what we're dealing with," Megan said.

They went online and looked at the gardening forum where Megan had initially seen the Italian plants advertised. They searched for the nursery that had sold her the plants, but she couldn't find a website for it. Megan had done all her correspondence over email, but there was a phone number.

Megan checked the time—almost 5 a.m.—and asked, "Do you think I should call now?"

"Europe's like eight hours ahead of us," Shasta said.

Megan dialed, waited for the international call to go through, and then heard a recording in an Italian voice. There was no opportunity to leave a message.

"I don't speak Italian," she said, "but I'm pretty sure that was a recording saying the number has been disconnected or is no longer in service."

As the sun was coming up, Shasta left to get a quick shower and some coffee before reporting for her shift. Megan said she would spend the day trying to track down who sent her the plants.

They had agreed on one other plan of attack: someone needed to stay overnight at the Botanic Garden to observe what was happening. So far, all the events had taken place at night, when no one was there. Maybe if someone was around, that would deter whatever was causing the problems.

Shasta had already been awake for twenty-four hours, and she was about to report for a full shift—so there was no way she'd have anything left in the tank to stay up all night again. Megan was in a similar situation. She might get a nap today, but she would have to report to work at least for a partial day. She had to deal with the press, the director, all the employees—there were decisions to be made about getting the BUGarium repaired and on track for reopening.

She decided to ask James.

"I'm finishing my breakfast," he said when she called. "I'll be in in about twenty minutes."

"Do me a favor," Megan said. "Don't come in. Take a nap this afternoon. Try to get rested up. Then come in at closing time."

"Closing time?"

Megan explained. He listened quietly and then said, "Do you really think something supernatural is happening? Like those plants were haunted?"

"Something out of the ordinary is happening. That's all I know. And it's getting worse."

Megan drove back to work, feeling more tired than she'd ever been. The morning light seemed unusually bright, as if her pupils were open too far and wouldn't constrict. She spent a few hours doing damage control: answering questions, making decisions, mostly just trying to calm down her employees. It seemed most of the bugs that had gotten out last night were now dying. Employees were beginning to panic, and they needed Megan to reassure them that they were safe.

Finally, in late morning, she locked her door and sat down at her computer. The plants had been shipped from Florence, and she tried to call nurseries in the city. The people she reached usually could speak English, at least a little bit, but still the language barrier made it difficult. Especially when Megan didn't want to come right out and say that she'd been sold plants that were possessed or haunted or cursed or whatever.

Around lunchtime, Megan was ready to give up and take a power nap when she had a thought. She searched her computer and found the number for *Orto Botanico di Firenze*—the Botanical Garden of Florence.

"Do you speak English?" Megan asked.

"Of course," the woman on the other end said. "But we are closed. I am preparing to go home."

"Wait. Please."

Megan explained that she was the director of a Botanic Garden in the United States and she had questions about some plants she recently acquired from Italy. The woman on the other end introduced herself as Greta Alfonsi, the director of the garden in Florence. She said she was willing to listen, but she seemed impatient.

Megan explained what plants she purchased and then proceeded to talk about how they died and that other plants and animals were dying in the garden. She hesitated before going further.

The woman was quiet. The silence gave Megan the impression that the woman knew what was happening.

"And other things," Megan added. "Weird things."

"I have heard of such happenings," Greta said. "Very bad."

"What is it?"

The woman cleared her throat. "This is, as you Americans say, 'Off the record.' You and I never spoke. Understand?"

"Yes," Megan said. "Please tell me."

"You have infestation."

Megan felt frustrated—no, this was more than some plant disease.

"You have infestation of *fata*. Fairies."

Megan wanted to laugh. "Fairies? Aren't fairies supposed to be good?"

"Not these. These are bad fairies. *Spauracchio*. How do you say in America? Boogeymen."

Megan met with Shasta and James at the end of the day. She insisted they talk off the premises, so they went to a brewery down the street from the garden. None of them drank. Megan and Shasta hadn't slept in thirty-some hours and James had a long night ahead of him.

"So I've heard of the boogeyman, of course," Shasta said. She looked five years older than when Megan had first met her—it was amazing what sleep-deprivation could do. "But I didn't know that it referred to *bad fairies*."

"Evidently," Megan said.

Megan explained what Greta had told her, that there were only two ways to get rid of the boogeymen. One way was to find some good fairies and they'd have an all-out battle—good versus evil on the grounds of the Botanic Garden. The other way was to use a spell that would trap them—temporarily—on a group of native plants. The plants would act as a transitory prison but once the fairies were trapped, they would have to replant the plants somewhere else. Far away.

"That's what someone did to us," James said. "I'd hate to pass this along to someone else."

"I don't see any reason why we can't take the plants out into the desert somewhere," Megan said. "Far from any other humans."

"And we don't have any way of finding any good fairies," Shasta said, then added, "I can't believe I just said those words out loud."

Megan explained that they had to do the thing—she couldn't bring herself to say "cast the spell"—at either dusk or dawn.

"Apparently that's when the layer between worlds—whatever that means—is the thinnest," she said. "We might actually be able to see these little bastards, according to the woman I talked to."

Out the window of the brewery, they could see the orange glow of sunset.

"Think we can make it?" Shasta said.

"Let's wait until dawn," James said. "You two look about half-dead. Go home, get some sleep. I'll keep an eye on the garden overnight. I'll get all the plants ready. Meet me about four o'clock."

Megan was too tired to argue. James drove back to the garden, and Shasta drove Megan home. She insisted, afraid Megan might fall asleep behind the wheel. It turned out to be a smart move because Megan passed out in the passenger seat on the ride over.

Shasta found Megan's keys and unlocked her door. Then she picked Megan up and carried her to her bed. Instead of going home, Shasta lay down on Megan's couch, set the alarm on her phone and closed her eyes. She dove into the black abyss of sleep, and it seemed like only seconds later her alarm was going off. Six hours had passed.

It was time.

Megan had worked at the garden for more than a decade and had always felt at home here. She couldn't believe how much she now feared it. The garden was like an old friend, comfortable and trustworthy, who had somehow turned unfamiliar and evil. She had to exorcise the demon inside her loved one. As they walked along the pathway past the main lawn, they could see the greenhouse up ahead, both wings lit up with fluorescent lights. The shadows around them felt alive.

"What's that?" Shasta said, pointing through the glass walls of the Mediterranean wing. It was hard to see through the foliage, but something was hanging from the ceiling. Megan ran and hurled the door open.

James dangled from the rafters from a strip of twine around his throat. His face looked swollen and yellow in the fluorescent light. His body was so still it looked made out of plastic. His toes hung only about six inches from the ground, right in front of the dead spot where they'd planted the Italian trees and grasses. He wore sandals, as he always did, and his feet were purple from where all his blood—no longer circulated by his heart—had been pulled down by gravity. His baseball cap lay in the dirt.

Megan's eyes filled with tears, and she put her hands over her mouth, as if that could help the breath racing in and out of her mouth.

Shasta studied the crime scene.

"He was hoisted up," she said. "He didn't fall from anything. Someone—or something—pulled him off the ground, then tied the rope off."

"Was it quick?" Megan asked.

"No," Shasta said.

Megan sobbed. It had been her idea for James to stay at the garden overnight, and now he was dead. She whirled around, looking in the shadows of the geraniums and lamb's ears and windmill palm trees. The glass walls of the greenhouse were all black, and she sensed the creatures on the other side watching her.

She wanted to scream at them, tell them what she and Shasta were going to do. But she didn't want to tip them off.

"Come on," she said to Shasta. "The sun will be up soon."

James had pulled one of the garden's work trucks up to the Desert Conservatory—he'd gotten that far in his work—and they began carrying plants from the building into the bed. They grabbed shrubby cinquefoil, mesquite, creosote, ocotillo, lechuguilla, yucca, and a prickly pear cactus. Megan and Shasta stayed close together, thinking—hoping—that if the things tried to do to them what they had done to James that the other could somehow stop it. As they worked, they could hear laughter from far out in the garden. It was the same cackling laughter Megan had heard before.

They drove the truck into the center of the green, which now had more dead grass than living, and cleared away the sod from a patch about six feet in diameter—they didn't want any non-native plants in the circle. Then they set out the potted plants.

Megan pulled out the piece of paper she'd taken notes on during her conversation with Greta Alfonsi.

"Why isn't this in Italian?" Shasta asked, looking at the words of the spell.

"These creatures are older than any existing language. So whatever this is." She held up the paper. "It's been translated over and over."

The wind had picked up out of nowhere, and she had to hold tight to the paper. The trees swayed around them. The cackling had stopped.

They read the words aloud. They were supposed to sing them, or chant them, over and over. But the first time through, they tripped over the words and spoke out of sync. Their voices were low and tentative.

Together alone we play together

Together alone we die forever

In the garden, in the dawn

The burning forest, the devil's spawn

Tired eyes and sleeping mothers

Restless fathers, forgotten brothers

Carve the spear, sharpen the stone

Drink the blood, eat the bone

In the mirror, a stranger's grin

In the heart, a nameless sin

Voices in the wind, phantoms in the night

A blind man with second sight

Black stars burning like the sun

I am nothing, you are no one

Together alone we play together

Together alone we live forever

On the second time through, their voices were more confident. And louder.

They heard the sounds out in the garden, not laughing anymore, but nonsensical jabber. The voices were undoubtedly distressed. The sky was blue now, and the first orange glow of dawn came through the trees. They sang the song again and again, louder and louder.

> *Together alone we play together*
>
> *Together alone we die forever*

The wind picked up, whipping their hair around their heads.

> *In the garden, in the dawn*
>
> *The burning forest, the devil's spawn*

Tree branches crashed down from the canopy. Leaves swirled in miniature tornadoes.

> *Tired eyes and sleeping mothers*
>
> *Restless fathers, forgotten brothers*

A waterspout rose up out of the pond, swirling with dead fish and frogs.

> *Carve the spear, sharpen the stone*
>
> *Drink the blood, eat the bone*

A gust tore the sheet of paper from Megan's hands, but now they knew the words by heart, and they kept going.

> *In the mirror, a stranger's grin*
>
> *In the heart, a nameless sin*

At one end of the garden, the model trains started up. At the other end, windows of the greenhouse began to crack and rain down shards of glass.

Voices in the wind, phantoms in the night

A blind man with second sight

A spark of electricity shot from the building's fuse box, and both the Desert Conservatory and Mediterranean Conservatory went dark.

Black stars burning like the sun

I am nothing, you are no one

They heard a loud, thunderous crack coming from the aquarium. Megan could only hope it wasn't the main tank exploding and unleashing a flood of sharks and stingrays and sea turtles.

Together alone we play together

Together alone we live forever

They didn't stop chanting. Megan reached for Shasta's hand, and the two sang loudly like two people in church, caught up in religious zeal. More light poured in from the dawn. The wind stopped abruptly. They saw movement in the grass, as invisible things circled around them. The grass died in the creatures' wake. Overhead, branches shook as invisible animals jumped from tree to tree. Leaves withered on the branches.

Finally, the creatures began jumping onto the native plants in front of them. Megan could see the fairies. If she looked directly at one, it wasn't there but if she looked past them and let her peripheral vision pick them up, she caught glimpses.

They were about the size of newborn babies. Their skin was black and leathery, their legs and arms long, like monkeys. Their upper bod-

ies were bulbous and malformed. Their heads, which were dispropor-
tionately large, had no eyes or ears or noses that she could see, but
they had mouths that took up almost their whole faces, filled with long
white teeth the size of fingers.

Megan had asked Greta how she would know when to stop, and
Greta had said simply that she would. She was right. Megan knew.
The garden had gone completely silent. The native plants stood still.
The creatures, which had been visible briefly, had vanished in the
bright light of dawn.

Megan and Shasta sang the last verse and stopped. They breathed
deeply, and all they could hear were their own exhalations. Then the
sounds of the world came back—traffic from Central Avenue, an airplane overhead.

"Let's get these plants out into the desert," Shasta said.

"What about James?" Megan said.

"I'm sorry. We have to leave him. Someone will discover him.
They'll rule it a suicide and probably blame everything that's happened here on him."

Megan was too exhausted to cry.

They loaded the plants into the truck and drove out of the city. They
drove south toward the Chihuahuan Desert. Both of them called in
sick to work, leaving messages for their supervisors, and then turned
their phones off. They knew their voicemails would be filled as soon
as someone discovered James's body and the wreckage at the garden,
but there was nothing they could do about it.

Shasta found a remote spot at the bottom of a canyon. The sun was
high, and the heat at this low elevation was smothering. They pulled
shovels out of the truck bed and began to work. In minutes, they were
coated in sweat.

They planted the bushes and flowers and cacti in the dry ground. Some of the plants wouldn't ordinarily grow at this particular elevation, but they didn't appear out of place. It looked like a strange oasis of natural plants had cropped up at the bottom of a dry canyon.

Megan didn't want to bring the pots back, so they smashed them and left the shards in a circle around the grove. They stood and looked down at the plants, like mourners standing over a grave.

"Do you think we're doing the right thing?" Megan asked.

She was thinking of the fairies spreading from here, killing the plants and animals in a swath that would eventually lead back to civilization. In New Mexico, they would call these things *chupacabra*. And maybe that's what they were. Maybe chupacabra and boogeymen and evil fairies were all the same thing—some ancient evil that couldn't be understood in the modern world.

"I think we're doing the only thing we can do," Shasta said.

They drove back in silence. Their clothes were dirty, their hair in tangles, their skin sticky with sweat. They kept the windows rolled down instead of using the air conditioning. The wind felt good, cleansing.

It was almost evening when they approached Albuquerque. Storm clouds were forming over the mountains, spreading out toward the bowl of civilization in the valley below. Megan didn't turn her phone back on. She wasn't ready for what was waiting for her.

She was thinking about what would happen next, as the days and years passed. She wondered if she would ever forgive herself for James's death. She wondered if, whenever something strange happened—a noise in the night, a rustling in her garden—she would be able to dismiss it as a natural phenomenon. She didn't think so. She thought that even though they were trapped in the desert, the boogeymen would follow her the rest of her life. Maybe figuratively. But maybe literally. Maybe they had started already, crawling through the desert, grinning through their big jagged mouths, their cackles echoing through empty desert canyons. Maybe someday they would find her.

"I'm very lonely," Megan said, and it felt good to say the words aloud. A relief. "I have no friends. I have no one."

"I'm your friend," Shasta said, and she reached over and squeezed Megan's hand.

Ahead of them, Megan could see sheets of rain coming down over the city. Droplets began to patter against the windshield. In the desert, rain was precious and rare. Megan imagined the water coming down on the Botanic Garden, running down the walkways in rivulets, soaking the soil, beginning to heal the plants that had survived. As the rain poured harder, Megan started to cry. Whether from sadness or exhaustion or maybe even joy for being alive, she wasn't sure. But as the water cascaded down her cheeks, she hoped it would begin to heal her too.

U is for Unseelie Court

BD Wilson

Tifa strolled through the curving hallways of Silo Abhainn to the kitchen, greeting Wren and Hale, the cooks indistinguishable in their protective suits. She selected a warm slice of bread, a wedge of cheese, and a bowl of fresh-ground milk from the selection placed out for this purpose. When she reached the garden, not long after they had reopened from the night-time seclusion, Louie and his sister were already there to make their offerings. Tifa nodded as she passed their tree, watching for acknowledgment they saw her.

The doorway and table maintained by her family was tucked in a corner, one of the most secluded areas. Tifa knelt before the flat smooth stone of the table, cleared the crumbs from the previous day's accepted offerings, and placed her trinkets in a ring around the edge. They glimmered in the rising sun, capturing the light and certainly the attention of more than one of the unseen fairies.

She placed the food in the centre, adjusting the angle of the cheese and the side of milk until something told her she had them just right. The wind blew through the garden rustling the leaves and she caught the faint strands of pipe music beneath it. She secured her gloves, en-sured they were intact, then brushed fallen leaves off the frame of the tiny wooden door her family had placed in the nook of the tree as she checked it for dents or signs of wear. It was in pristine condition, as always, as she ensured day after day, morning after morning, before making the same silent request.

Tifa closed her eyes as she drew in a long breath. Five breaths in, five breaths out, following them with a scan of her body, feeling and listening for any changes from the previous day. Her legs felt the ten-sion of the kneel, but that was as it should be. Her hands rested on her thighs, a proper weight, her shoulders set back, straight and alert. She smiled as she finished her scan, repeated the five breaths, and rose.

Every day she listened to see if there was something she had ne-glected, as she checked the door and the table. Every day she sought a sign of some guidance missed, but every day she rose in tune with her body and spirit, in tune with the sounds and life of the garden around her.

She took off her gloves, and ran her fingers up one arm along the thin lines of the Riders, visibly displayed on the back, their position no different from the day before. She closed her eyes to give thanks for her health and obedience, then pulled her gloves back on before she left the garden to join the community for the morning meal.

Here too, she was neither first nor last, as she preferred. Tifa smiled and waved as she crossed the hall, returning Thom's greeting at the food table, marking Gale and Cole who she had grown up with, and Raelyn in the corner studying a holo as always, even when she should be appreciating her meal. Tifa dodged Patrice's children, three and seven now and still rambunctious, though almost to the age where their parents would not have to worry about accidents so. Those early years were always the most fraught, next to the birth, of course.

There was no sign of June, which could be good news, could be bad, depending on how the night had gone. Tifa made a mental note to check in with the healers, to see if there was news to share, but she needn't have bothered. Almost as soon as she sat, the Council entered the hall and took their places at the front, causing all conversation to stop. Tifa's heart began to pound with excitement, and she felt the Riders on her arms tingle a warning.

Five breaths in, five breaths out, and again to calm her heart and reach balance. All the same, she'd been watching the numbers, keeping track of the children and the lost. It had to be time, it had to be.

"Good morning to all," Elder Kandra said. Her gray hair was tied above her head in a simple ponytail, her eyes smiling, causing the rare wrinkles to crinkle up in a way that never failed to lighten Tifa's spirit. Forty-six summers Kandra had lived, the eldest of them all, and even she could not remember Silo Abhainn's founding, it had been so long.

"As some of you heard, Sister June was taken to the birthing room last night." Around the meal hall, five breaths in and out as they waited. "We are pleased to announce both the successful birth of a strong baby boy and the health of our sister. Her Riders remain still and she looks forward to sharing meals with you all again."

Cheers rose around the room, Tifa's among them, her smile aching on her face as she tried to suppress her glee.

"June's son is the one hundred and fifty-first member of our community."

Here cheers wavered, but Tifa's smile did not decrease an inch.

"It is time, then, for Abhainn's first migration, to send some of our beloved members to find the location for a sibling state, and establish a new silo in harmony and good will."

One-hundred-fifty people said the Dunbar, that was the limit before they grew apart from one another, before they began to lose connection to each other, that loss the first step toward losing a connection to everything else. So, it was then that the silos split, maintaining communication, but keeping to themselves.

"The council will consider the nearest locations, from all surveillance and guidance we have available to us, but it will take a scouting party to locate the new site. It is only right, after all, for these new Elders to follow the fairies' guidance to their home."

Tifa straightened her back, though they would not announce the members of the scouting party here. There were other smiles around the room now, those who also hoped to be in the party. Too many smiles for all to be chosen, but Tifa was not worried. She had been making offerings for this moment her entire life. The fairies would whisper in the ears of the elders. Her name would be heard.

"Please have a seat, Tifa," Elder Kandra said, indicating the plush chair across from her.

Tifa sank into the soft cushions, carefully testing her position, though she knew anything in an elder's quarters would be properly made. All the same, one could never be complacent.

Elder Kandra nodded, the hint of a smile forming at her lips, before she settled herself again. "As you are aware, we are preparing for our first migration."

"Yes, Elder," Tifa said, keeping her breaths slow and measured and her expression as schooled as Kandra's.

"We have selected you as the Voice of Vision."

Tifa dropped her head to hide the grin she could no longer fight. "Thank you, Elder."

"This is a serious matter," Kandra admonished. "You must be the one to see the hints of the world beneath, to read the auspices sent to steer our course. You must be completely open to the guidance of the fae folk and free of anything that might cloud your sight."

"I understand," she said, gaining control over her expression in time to look the elder in the eyes. "I will not fail."

Elder Kandra sat back. "We have chosen well."

Tifa sat up straighter in her chair as Elder Kandra took out a soft fabric with writing.

"Your vision will guide the selection of the new silo location, but yours is not the only voice which must be heard. The team will include the Voice of Safety, the Voice of Prosperity, and the Voice of Reason."

"Reason?"

Kandra nodded. "There is always a Voice of Reason in the selection of a new silo."

"But we have no Voice of Reason here."

"Here one is not required. You must remember, Tifa, even as there are fairies who will guide us to the best location, there are those who would tempt us to the worst. In an established silo, the latter group cannot sway us so easily. Where you are going, however, you must be on your guard. Vision and Reason together confirm the location."

"I see," Tifa said in forced words. Though the entire Council decided the fate of the silo, it was well known the Voice of Vision held the final say. That was how it should be. "Who are the other voices?"

"Safety is Louie and Prosperity Thom."

These were excellent choices. Louie had been serving with the safety council since he had left the school rooms. Thom had practiced the distribution of resources even longer, being the son of Abhainn's Voice of Prosperity.

"The Voice of Reason is Raelyn."

"What?" The word escaped before she could stop it, an unforgivable lapse.

"I understand this is difficult," Kandra said, "but her drive is exactly what is required. We are so used to accepting all we are told and shown. We leave our offerings and we watch for signs and we do what they tell us."

"As it should be."

"As it should be, when you can trust those leaving the signs. The Riders were not placed on our skin by those who wished us well. The Mountain King and those who follow his vision are in the world yet and they want us to wake our Riders and be consumed. His daughter's folk guide us here, rule here, but only because our founders followed them to a place where their power held sway."

"Thanks be to the Umbrage," she said, without hesitation.

"Thanks be. But they do not hold sway everywhere and the Mountain King's people know their signs, because they were of one mind not so long ago. They will use that knowledge to trick you. They will spin all your rightful instincts and set them to cross-purposes. Someone needs to guard against that and Raelyn has the nature to do so."

"She will confuse all."

"Not if your vision is clear."

Tifa stiffened. "My vision is clear. I will find the new place of power."

"I know you will. Go now. Bear this burden well."

"I will."

Raelyn's office was cluttered with scanned holos of artifacts projected in protective casings, images of things that should have remained in the past and been forgotten. The old words were printed or scrawled upon their surfaces, though most could read them no longer. Even having learned the script, Tifa could hardly make sense of most here.

The one nearest the door talked of a hearing without saying what was being heard. She recognized Umbrage, however, poor princess. Perhaps what was heard was her warning, when she gave the ancestors a chance, and was rejected.

"We thought she'd done it," Raelyn said.

Tifa's attention snapped to her fast enough to crick her neck. Panic flared in her chest, but wasn't an injury, and there was no stirring of her Riders. All the same, she had to be careful. "What?"

Raelyn pointed to the flickering page in its globe. "That. You saw Umbrage's name."

"It's old text," Tifa said. "It doesn't signify."

"Can't read it then?" She shrugged. "We didn't just kill her as she was telling us we were in danger. That part is wrong."

"You doubt the teachings?"

"I doubt they are complete. Teachings are stories. Stories can change and often do. Our ancestors thought Umbrage was responsible for the Riders, not the Mountain King. We even got her to admit it."

"She would never do that."

"And yet, she did." Raelyn picked up a different globe and held it out to her. Umbrage's image floated in the surface, wide eyes, short hair, fae chin and ears. Sorrow set in her features, regret in her eyes. Above her head, the old text declared ADMITS GUILT. "There must have been a reason. I don't know what, but we put all the blame on her and she let us. It's strange, don't you think? That we're taught she was killed, but not why?"

"We didn't believe her."

"No. We did. We just believed her guilty, killing her for the Riders killing so many. Taking revenge, kind of like the Mountain King was, I suppose."

"You want to cast doubt on Princess Umbrage. Perhaps the only one who resembles the Mountain King is you."

Raelyn's jaw tensed. "That was unkind."

Tifa winced at the censure, though she tried to control it. "As is your disparagement."

Raelyn picked up another holo. "I have not said she released the Riders. I've only said we believed she had and she admitted to us she did."

"How is that not the same?"

Raelyn's hand rested on top of the globe and her expression turned sad. "Part of learning the past is learning what we were once capable of. If Umbrage made this admission, and she did, then it was because we forced her. If I'm right, then we treated her far worse than even the teachings say. I wonder, sometimes, if that isn't why the Mountain King's followers still hunt us."

"They hunt us because his goal is unfulfilled."

"Yes, but after all this time? I know it hasn't been much in the span of fairy lives, but we've followed the guidelines, we've learned the lessons. Why can't they just let us be?"

It was a question Tifa had never thought to ask. Even hearing it made her stomach clench, as did anything connected to the Mountain King.

"It's revenge, probably, but not just for Gaia." Raelyn lifted the orb and studied the face of Umbrage. "It's for her, as well. We made so many mistakes."

"That we did," Tifa said, though her throat tightened at the admission. Raelyn had nothing to contribute to the council. Her voice would be a distraction. But in this, she had a point.

Their belongings, only those needed for such a perilous trip, were loaded into the skiff. The curved edges made it easy to turn and it hovered above the ground with workings derived from fairy knowledge. Tifa walked beside the skiff as Thom nudged it into motion. She held her head high and her shoulders back as they left their home for the first time.

Still, Tifa frowned as she watched Raelyn, the way her eyes were so often drawn to the sides of the path, to what lay beyond the scope of their journey. It was far too close to create a silo here, too soon to be looking for a place to settle. They should be focused on what was right in front of them, and yet, Raelyn let her attention wander, roaming where it should not. All this, and she was to be a voice on the council of the new silo. It made no sense at all.

Tifa caught her attention wandering and drew in her breath, five in and five out, before she refocused her attention on the path in front of her. She followed the toadstools from the river bank, read the signs of the moss to guide them through the forest, on through dangerous tangles of roots and grasping bushes for two full days and nights before early the third morning the trees parted on a clearing and in the centre of the clearing, a fairy ring. "Here. Here is where the new silo shall be."

"Area around it is large enough," Thom agreed. "There's still light to do the survey today if we want."

"I'll set the offerings in the ring," Tifa said as the others guided the skiff to a place a safe distance away. "They will show us to what we need."

As the others prepared the camp, Tifa picked the brightest of her trinkets, the bread she had carefully saved, and a cup of fresh water. Milk would have been better, of course, but there would be none in this clearing until the new silo was established. The fairies would understand, though. They would know there would be milk enough for generations to come, after they had nuts to grind it from.

"Thank you, for seeing us safely here and for leading us to such a wondrous place." Tifa placed the offerings in the centre of the fairy ring, careful not to disturb a single mushroom, nor to let her gloved hands make contact with the grass. They had led her here, to be sure, but they would not tolerate a trespass. She had to do everything exactly right as they prepared the new silo. She had to make certain no one wavered in the slightest.

Offerings made, they each took a pack and a direction and agreed not to return to the camp until the sun began to set, to ensure they saw all they could. Tifa chose the East, walking into the still rising sun and toward where her instincts told her water would be. She followed the mushrooms and moss on the trees, certain she would discover a river or a stream, something making the location suitable. As she walked, the sun shifted from in front of her to her side, but she paid it no mind. She went where she was guided.

Instead of a stream, however, or any water at all, the fairies drew her to an overgrown field with a hulking, sharp-angled shape in the centre. Trees had made inroads on the site, as if reclaiming the space, but had not yet won. Cold built in Tifa's chest as she entered the field and circled the structure. She must have missed something, followed a trick of the Mountain King's people. Umbrage's followers would not want her in this place.

A loud screeching sound split the air and she screamed, searching for whatever hideous creature had made it.

"Tifa?" Raelyn's voice called out. "Is that you?"

"Yes." Relief flooded her as she struggled through the long grass to find the other woman coming around the side of the structure. "What was that noise?"

"Oh, the door hadn't been opened in a while. I think it was rusted. It's metal. Can you believe it? Real metal."

Her muscles tensed again at the words. "What door?"

"This one." Raelyn lead her around to where the door, the metal door, stood open in the side of the structure that was now quite clearly a building long forgotten and sealed.

It felt like ice sat in Tifa's stomach. The darkness beyond the opening was a patch of shadow deeper than she had ever seen before in her life, as if the walls eclipsed the sun. It was the darkness of a cavern, dug deep into the heart of a mountain.

"You should have left the door closed. There's nothing in there of use to us."

"It's not a question of being of use, necessarily. We need to know if it's a risk. Louie would go if he was here, but this was the direction I was given."

She didn't say, though she might have, that it was not the direction Tifa had been given either, and yet, here she was having strayed from her own.

"You said yourself, the best place for the new silo is the nearby clearing," Raelyn said. "We can't select that location without knowing what's in this one."

"We will close the doors again, cover them."

"All that will do is buy us time. Someone will open them. If this place is dangerous, we need to know that now, so we can choose somewhere else."

Tifa ground her teeth. "There is nowhere else."

"Then that's even more reason to find out what's here. If it's something we can deal with, we can do so now. If it isn't, then Louie can come up with a plan to ensure the security of the new silo."

As much as she hated to admit it, Raelyn was right. Though Tifa followed the guidance of the fairies, not everyone was as attuned as she. They might ignore the signs of danger, ignore the warnings. "Very well, but be mindful of the corners."

"I will." Raelyn agreed, and Tifa thought should looked relieved. Perhaps she wasn't as brave in the face of this entrance as she seemed. Perhaps she did feel the warnings in her body, the whispers in her ear, though they must be faint for all the attention she paid to them.

"Let's go," Tifa said, "we must be out before the sun sets."

It was as if the sun were a distant memory as they walked through the boxed-shaped corridors, not a curve or smooth edge in sight. Tifa's skin crawled, like the Riders were moving across it, but when she checked in the light of the globe they were as they ever had been. She shivered and held onto her arms as she walked by a dirty wall that glimmered beneath the grime. "Wait."

Raelyn obeyed without complaint, something that would have impressed upon Tifa the danger had she not already understood it. Tifa wrapped her hand in cloth, layers of added protection over her gloves, and then used it to wipe the dirt away from the section of wall that sparkled beneath.

"I think that's glass," Raelyn said.

Tifa jerked her hand back.

"No, it's okay, as long as we're careful." Raelyn wrapped her hand now, picking up where Tifa had left off. "It's only dangerous if it breaks."

"Everything here is a risk," Tifa whispered, but Raelyn was no longer listening.

"There are pics here."

Despite herself, Tifa's curiosity pulled her attention back to the cleared glass. Behind the fragile and dangerous surface, there were indeed images, rows and rows of people standing facing the camera. "There are so many. This could be an entire silo."

"Look at how they're dressed, all the same. I think some of them have metal on their chests. Why would they need that?"

"Offerings?" Tifa suggested. "Maybe they wanted to keep a supply close at hand. With so many, they would need more than usual."

"Except they wouldn't have been making them, not in a place like this, not then." Raelyn stepped back and looked at the dirty, angled building. "These are the people who forgot."

Slow in-drawn breath, slow out-breath. Tifa could smell disuse and complacency. "They are everything we must not be."

"Let's see what's up that hallway."

"Why?" The hallway seemed the same as all the rest, wide open, dirty, abandoned and right to be so.

"All the signs point to it," Raelyn said, pointing to the markings on the wall and the arrows that signaled a direction. There were old words there, too. Raelyn sounded them out. "Control Room. It must be important."

"Very well," Tifa said, though the words made her shiver. "But thirty minutes, no more. We do not want the others to come looking for us, only to be lost in a different part of this maze."

Raelyn frowned, but she nodded, following the arrows as Tifa marked the time. They were silent as they followed the twists and turns in the sharp angles of the ancient building. She tried to keep track of their progress, to keep the path in her mind so she could find her way out if tricksters changed the signs, but there were too many.

"Here," Raelyn said, "that door is what they're leading us to."

The door, like all the others, was rectangular, made of hard metal that promised bruising injury. The handle, at least, was a sphere, the small familiar detail like a light in the darkness. Raelyn turned it and pushed on the door. It did not open at first, and Tifa held her breath as Raelyn strained, adding more weight, forcing it. A sharp screeching filled the air when the door gave way, and then it flung open, banging into the wall.

"That was careless," Tifa snapped. "You could have been injured."

"But the door is open now," Raelyn said, just as carelessly. "Let's see what it is."

The furniture in the room was as sharp and angular as the facility itself. Metal corners glinted with promised danger and even the plastics were shaped like squares. Raelyn gasped and shuffled quickly to the right. Tifa huddled close to her as she entered the room and saw the mass in the corner to the left. There were Riders, free from their restraints, long fibrous lines reaching out to cover the surface of what seemed like a flimsy metal bed. Somewhere in the centre of them would be whatever remained of the person they had taken, but now it was impossible to see anything that had once been human.

On the surface of a desk, one of the few circular features flared briefly with a red glow before fading into darkness, repeating again and again like a beating heart, drawing their attention. Next to it sat a book, the cover illustrated, the top marked with glinting gold letters. Raelyn stepped away from her, the warmth of her presence only acknowledged as comforting once it was gone. Tifa crept back toward the door. The light from the table reflected on something beside her. This wall held another glass surface, not covered in dust this time. There were no pictures, but there was something behind it and the words IN CASE OF EMERGENCY etched at the top.

"Fairy Tales, Myths, and Legends," Raelyn said, and Tifa found her holding the book. "Why would they put the first with the last two?"

Tifa eyed the released Riders in the corner and shuddered. Five breaths in. "As you said, these are people who had forgotten."

"No, I was wrong." Raelyn peered at the cover, then turned it to show Tifa. It had a familiar image, a fairy with gossamer wings seated on a mushroom, one of the helpful kind, though in this version there was no sign of the Riders threat in the background. Instead, this had a horse with a long-spiraled horn, a man on a cloud with a lightning bolt in his hand, and a dragon. "This isn't just forgetting. These are people who no longer believe."

Tifa shivered. If that were the case, it was no wonder the Mountain King had been so desperate. She had never before felt any sympathy for his actions, but disbelief, for a fairy, was death. How could he not have been moved to make such an example?

Raelyn held the book to her chest and returned her attention to the desk. She reached for the glowing circle and pushed. A sharp humming noise rose in the background of the room. Tifa held her breath, waiting for something to come out and strike them, waiting for the Riders to take advantage of their foolishness and add them to the older growth in the corner.

Instead, a screen in the wall, the image dull and blurry, began to glow, words appearing in grey on black text.

SYSTEM SHUTDOWN TO PREVENT FAILURE. RESTORE LAST SESSION?

Y/N:

"What does it mean?" Tifa asked, before realizing the question was an encouragement.

"These squares have letters," Raelyn said. "And it's a yes or no question." She tried to press the square marked Y, but the screen filled with a mash of letters and the question repeated. Raelyn shook her head, pulled off her glove, and tried again, this time able to press the single Y.

The screen flickered, going blank for a moment before words scrolled past faster than Tifa could read. The humming in the background had not changed, nothing in the room moved, except for the text on the screen, which soon vanished. It was replaced by another image, a rectangle again, always. It appeared to be a picture of the room they were in, the door behind them closed and the lighting dim. A woman in drab green clothing was seated in a chair and in the background was an empty bed, thin fabric stretched over a metal frame. In a moment, another rectangle appeared, this time with a question.

BEGIN PLAYBACK?

Y/N

Once again, Raelyn pressed Y. The image of the room flickered and then began to move. The woman in the image was holding the book. Her hand was resting against it, almost reverently, and hope flared in Tifa's chest. It was possible Raelyn was wrong, as she was about so many things. After all, she could not see the signs, could not read the omens. Why listen to her interpretation of the past if she knew so little of the present?

"Everything we did, we did with the best intentions," the woman's tired voice filled the room as she set the book on the desk. "Yes, I know, that's not how I'm supposed to start these things, but there's no one left to review the logs, is there? Even the research jockeys are gone, the damn archiver blasting everyone with notices because no one's clicking the button and every system is a colossal fuck-up. None of it matters anymore, I guess."

Tifa's shoulders tensed and though she tried to slow her breathing, she couldn't find the calming pace anymore, five breaths becoming six in and eight out and she couldn't find where she lost count.

"We think things will start failing in less than a week. To be honest, I'm surprised communication stayed up this long. We did our best. I should leave it at that, really, but I've never been good with the lies.

Maybe I picked the wrong career." She tapped her hands on the cover of the book and sighed. "Here's the thing, people need to believe in something. It can be ourselves, it can be a god, it can be the unknowable forces of nature, but we need to believe. Things like this, the fungus spreading so damn fast, it breaks our faith, and everything we've held up, held onto, it falls."

False signs, Tifa thought. Something convinced them to ignore the truth, to stop listening, and those false beliefs doomed them.

"We can't stop it. Rumsfeld knew what he was doing, covered all the angles. He set the fungus out into the world to kill us all and if we don't stop helping it, it's going to do just that."

"They knew the name of the Mountain King," Raelyn whispered, and even she sounded unsettled by that knowledge. "They knew his name and spoke it."

"People are, you know? It shouldn't surprise me, but it does. Everything going on and they're still throwing things at each other, staging 'accidents,' or just flat out punching someone in the face. The slightest bit of damage and the fungus takes advantage. It's more aggressive than Victor described. Maybe he didn't really know what Rumsfeld had him making, but maybe Rumsfeld didn't know either. It's not like he cared. His plan was to kill us all with him."

What? The Mountain King was dead?

"Something had to stop this and it wasn't going to be people suddenly coming to their senses or rediscovering empathy. The only thing that's ever really worked is scaring the shit out of them, but how do you do that when they're already terrified?" She rested her hand on the cover of the book again. "You give them hope. We went way back, tossing out all the things that are dangerous now and relied on the ones we could use to set survival guidelines. Then, we made them believe. Honestly, I thought it was going to be harder than it was."

Turn it off, turn it off, turn it off. Tifa looked around the room, but she couldn't tell what to press. There was no message, no prompt on the screen. How did she make it stop?

"Maybe we can thank Kayla for that. I was ordered to turn her into a villain and I did. It got her killed and nothing can change that, but I could turn it around and make her the hero of the story. I'd always thought she looked fae-touched, pixie cut and all. See, my grandmother, she used to leave offerings for fairies, when she was old and losing her senses. Bread, milk with honey, beads and baubles and polished stones. It was something she'd done as a child and dementia sent her back there. Since I was a child at the time, it seemed perfectly reasonable to me. I was surprised when I learned fairies aren't real."

Raelyn gasped and Tifa's breath caught, her hands coming together to clap, though she forced them to be still.

"Funny thing is, even when I was older, if I really, really wanted something, I'd put an offering out. I know how strong that promise can be, how little it takes to reinforce it. Besides, it was an easy connection, fairy rings of mushrooms, fungus, why shouldn't it come from them? All I had to do was work in just enough reality to make it plausible, in the right light. Cast Rumsfeld as the Fairy King in his Mountain, the fungus as his curse, and Kayla the hopeful Princess who died trying to save us from ourselves." She tapped the surface of the book. "Two girls with cardboard cut-outs convinced Conan Doyle and others. We had a lot more than that at our disposal and we used it. We staged a magic show for a dying world and gave them just enough proof to get them to listen. And then we gave them the rules, which gave them hope."

"Stop these lies," Tifa said. "Whatever you did to start them, undo it."

"We need to hear this."

"We told them they would be able to avoid the Mountain King's punishment if they took care, watched what they did, where they went. We followed community building theory, used the Dunbar number and things that made it less likely for there to be people unknown to everyone in a single location. We created designs for buildings and cites, circles and spheres to eliminate the danger of corners." She shook her head. "Corners can kill, damn it. That worked well, though, because there were so many pictures of round little fairy houses, it was an easy sell. They followed our 'fae-given' rules and death rates slowed until we found a new normal, one we could survive. With that and the smoke and mirrors, it didn't take long before people either believed or saw the benefit in making others think they did. They've taken the story and run with it, now telling people they can see signs and hear whispers, guidance from the fairies after their offerings are taken, the fungus moving or changing on their arms when its dormant. From here, the story will take on a life of its own, and in doing so, give us a chance."

"Turn it off."

"We had the best intentions, but you know where that gets us. I can only hope we've done the right thing. If you're watching this, if there is anyone left alive to watch it, just know, we did it because we wanted you to survive. Sometimes lies kill. Sometimes they save. I'm not going to be around long enough to find out which this is." She held up her arm and pulled down the sleeve of her drab jumper. The Riders on her arm were red and angry, covering the surface. The woman laughed. "Fucking paper cut, if you can believe it, from the pages of the book when I needed to check something."

Raelyn dropped the book back on the table.

"The fever's already started, so I don't have much time. I'll shut the facility down to standby, but there's no one left to wake it up. We've lost so much. I can only hope we haven't lost it all. Initiate system shut down, authorization Commander Louise Schevenchko." The image froze and then disappeared, leaving the screen dark, Raelyn and Tifa's reflections gazing back at them.

"It's a trick," Tifa said. "The Mountain King's people feeding us lies."

"What if it isn't?" Raelyn said, staring down at the book, at the drawing of the pale fairy, sitting on a red mushroom with white spots, lines as loose and whimsical as the ones used to drawn the dragon behind her. "What if it's all a story, something made up to get us to do they wanted?"

"They want us to doubt," Tifa said, "to disbelieve."

"You're just saying that because you're wrong. You've been telling us this entire trip you see signs, you hear the fairies." She shook her head and then returned her attention to the squares in front of her. "I've always thought you were embellishing, but you're just lying. You hear nothing."

At that moment, Tifa could heard the pounding of her heartbeat, the blood being pushed through her system, straining at the structures that held it. The rushing noise flooded everything, almost blocking out what Raelyn said next.

"I'm going to find a way to bring this back with us, this and anything else they saved. People need to know."

"Why?" Tifa forced out.

Raelyn glared over her shoulder. "What do you mean, why? It's the truth."

"The fairies saved us from ourselves."

"There's no such thing as fairies."

Tifa's entire body went cold. This could not be happening. Raelyn had always tread close to the line, but she had never before crossed it. If this was all it took, one video with one person talking, what would happen if there were more lies on that system? If this news was returned to Abhainn, it wouldn't be long before the entire silo fell to the Riders. She had to stop it.

Raelyn wasn't paying any attention to her now. Tifa searched the room, looking for something, anything, needing a sign. She found it.

IN CASE OF EMERGENCY the setting in the wall said, and beneath that, BREAK GLASS.

Tifa's hands were in fists at her side, formed without her leave. She raised one, driving her glove-covered hand into the glass. It shattered, the unfamiliar and surprisingly melodic sound filling the quiet room. Raelyn spun, pressing back against the desk as Tifa took one of the shards in hand. The gloves, as Raelyn had said, held.

"Tifa, what are you doing?"

"You will destroy us with this," she said. "Don't you see that?"

"We can't keep living a lie."

"They saved us. If you go back, if you tell them none of it is real and they believe you, then you will put us back into the nightmare that woman described. Don't you see?"

"Tifa."

"I will protect Abhainn and our people from the threat of the Mountain King and his." She darted forward, jabbing at Raelyn face with the sharp corner of the glass. She raised her hands to protect herself, but one of her gloves still sat on the table, removed so she could hear that awful message. The corner of the shard, as they had always been told it would, pressed in, the sharp edge of the glass breaking Raelyn's skin and sending blood forth.

"What did you do?" Raelyn cradled her wounded hand against her chest and stared aghast at the blood on the broken glass.

"The Riders will take you now," Tifa said. "They will contain your danger. They're our allies, too, in a way."

"You're just like them."

"I am not." Her hand clenched around the glass shard until she thought she could feel the edge straining the protective fabric of her glove. "I am only doing what I must."

"With the best of intentions, I'm sure."

Tifa ground her teeth. "You will remain here," she said, and motioned Raelyn over toward the ancient Riders. "You wanted to hear her story so much, you will now share her fate. This is why they led me here."

"You are fooling yourself, and now you know it," Raelyn said, though she did as Tifa directed, sitting down on the ground beside the mass of fibrous threads as beads of sweat began to appear on her already flushed skin. "Someone else will learn the truth. One day, someone will tell everyone before you can kill them to quiet them. What will you do then?"

Tifa took the book from the table and tossed it into Raelyn's lap. "I believe in the fairies," she said, but even she could hear the question in her voice.

Tifa stepped through the patch of light framed by the door and out into a world of shining sunlight. The trees and bushes were no different than before she entered, and yet, they were. No matter how long she cast her gaze upon the surrounding area, she could not see the signs that led her here. There were mushrooms, of course, but they were everywhere. They dotted the forest floor in a wide-ranging swath, no discernible path to be found. She thought she could see their footsteps, two sets of indentations in the grass which split to two paths. She picked Raelyn's and followed it back to the clearing.

Their bedding, their skiff, their camp were all as they'd left them, and in the centre, the fairy ring with the offerings still in place. Neither Louie nor Thom had returned yet. Tifa knelt beside the fairy ring, studied it and then straightened her back. She would protect the silo at any cost. She stood, held her chin up, and stepped inside the ring.

Nothing. The world did not fade, the fairies did not appear. When she stepped out again to test that she could, nothing bared her way and no time except the expected had past. She stepped in and out again, but there was no change. She stepped in again, and then crumpled, wrapping her arms around her knees.

Was it her doubt? Had the fairies rejected her? Or was it worse?

She could no longer be a Voice, not if the signs were hidden from her. She would have to return to Elder Kendra and tell her to pick someone else. A rustling sound startled her into opening her eyes and she saw a trinket, knocked by her rocking, sparkling in the grass.

The offerings in Abhainn were always taken. After the night-time seclusion, they were always gone. Why close the gardens at night, Raelyn might have asked. Why close them, unless it were necessary?

Tifa watched as her hand reached out, on its own, and pocketed the trinkets. She picked up the bread, leaving crumbs on the grass as she ate, though it was stale as dirt and left her mouth dry. She cleansed it with the water, leaving nothing behind before placing the bowl back. She stood, stepping out of the fairy circle for the last time.

Louie and Thom would return. They would look at the empty offering plates, see the missing trinkets, and would be relieved. Raelyn's loss would weigh on them, especially Louie, but Tifa would tell them her curiosity got the better of her. She was lured into a tunnel of the old ways, led astray by the lies of the Mountain King's followers, and so the Riders had taken her. They would seal the doorway to the old building, they would cover its secrets for good or for ill, and use Raelyn's loss as a lesson. They would build their silo, name it after the warm and joyful sun, and Tifa would see to it the fairies came to take the offerings every morning before the sunrise.

V is for Verisimilitude

Laura VanArendonk Baugh

I took a booth instead of a stool at the Steer and Beer's counter because I figured Jimmy would want to talk, and there's a lot he might say that shouldn't be overheard by the kitchen staff. Things like, *The police have a poster up for you,* and *They fished out the bullets so they can match your gun if they find it,* and *What does the Faerie Queen think of it?*

Jimmy spotted me from the kitchen and started a Black Cow. "You're back."

"This morning."

"I figured it was recent. You still look trashed." He came over and pushed the Black Cow across my table, and I stopped pretending I wasn't craving sugar like some sort of crack addict. Ice cream and Coca-Cola disappeared at an alarming rate.

The Queen herself had opened a portal for me to return, which was an honor atop her thanks for my latest service. As I'd spent three days in bed recovering from opening my own portal to the Twilight Lands, it was pragmatic, too. But doing it herself had been a tacit indicator of just how pleased she was.

Not that anyone should ever fail to be pleased when a bunch of child traffickers get their product taken from them in exchange for some well-placed rounds, or when a serial killer loses his collection of young victims-to-be, but it's always nice to have one's work appreciated.

Still, any portal takes a certain toll on me, and I'm not equipped as well as a full Fae to make the travels. Jimmy's Black Cow was appreciated.

"So, how's that thing shaking out?" I asked obliquely. Jimmy had been with me, but none of the most relevant casings or bullets were his.

"Lots of questions, nothing bad at my end," he said. "I said you come in here a bit but I didn't know you that well, just went with you to help some kids out of a bad place—because who wouldn't answer a call like that?" He nodded righteously. "And well, you're hard to describe. Even officers at the scene disagreed about you."

I quirked one corner of my mouth. Small favors. "And you?"

"They asked me if you were a man or a woman, and I said I don't make a habit to ask my customers insulting questions."

I laughed. "Good man."

"All they have is that I offered to help look for the kids, just like you and some other good Samaritans, and I got stuck in the murder-basement and shot some A/V equipment. The most they can suspect is I'm not sharing the address of the other person who also did nothing illegal."

Which is true, because there's no law against letting a troll bulldoze a bad human through a portal into the Twilight Lands.

"What about your end?"

There was no one near enough to overhear. "The Queen called me to Court to personally thank me for my service."

Jimmy nodded. "Is that good? Big deal?"

"Very big, Jimmy. Very, very big." I sucked air through the foam of my Black Cow.

Jimmy frowned at me. "You gonna need a tenderloin with that?"

The Twilight Lands were always hard, and not purely for the environmental strain. Probably half my fatigue was psychological, but that didn't mean a fried tenderloin wouldn't help. "Jimmy," I said, "you're a good man."

"Don't let it get around." He returned to the kitchen.

The bell on the door jingled. "Dumpy little place," a male voice said. "You think the food is safe here?"

"Dumpy? You don't know what Americana looks like," retorted a woman. "This is classic drive-in."

"You know we parked outside, right?"

"Shut up and look at the menu," she told him. "No, don't bother. You're getting the fried tenderloin."

"I don't get a choice?"

"Sure, fries or onion rings. But you're getting the tenderloin."

"This is not what I imagined when I transferred here."

"This ain't Carmel, boyo. Gotta get with the culture here."

Police uniforms. I ducked my head and stared fixedly at the menu, keeping my mostly empty Black Cow in front of my face as I fished for the cherry.

There hadn't been any security cameras in the warehouse where the trafficked kids were hidden, for obvious reasons, so the police probably didn't have a face to match with the vigilante who'd shot a suspect and then vanished out of a toilet. Probably.

I sneaked a second glance as Jimmy's teenaged help set down my tenderloin and onion rings. *Bells and breadcrumbs.* The pretty black woman was Officer Sullivan. Last we'd talked, I'd hung up on her to avoid questions about a vanished suspect I had, um, helped to vanish.

"Definitely right it's not Carmel," the man—white, older than her, not looking at me—agreed. "Nobody on the north side is calling police to report their kids have itchy scalps. They'd be terrified to admit their kids might have lice. Down here, they call in like it's our problem."

"Not lice," Officer Sullivan said as if it were not the first time she'd said it.

"Itching at the back of the scalp and hairline? I've got two kids, Sandra. That's lice or dirt."

I bristled. Sure, we aren't as shiny on the east side as up north, but we've got basic hygiene.

"Parents called in because their kids went missing and couldn't remember where they'd been. The itch wasn't the primary reason. Lice is easy to check, anyway."

"And you think something happened to the kids, and the itchy scalp is the clue." He shook his head. "Do you have any idea how paranoid that sounds?"

"I do. But we had a copycat serial killer abducting kids last week, and my paranoia switch is stuck on overdrive."

I understood. My own paranoia switch had only two positions, suspicious and overdrive.

The indicator was wiggling between the two right now. Kids gone missing? But they'd been found or had come back pretty quickly, because the police hadn't been called until after they were home complaining. While it was curious that they couldn't remember (or weren't saying) where they'd been, an itchy head wasn't the worst that could befall a kid, and Officer Sullivan recognizing me was a bigger risk.

They placed orders as I crammed onion rings into my mouth, anxious to escape before Officer Sullivan tired of the argument and started looking around. I grabbed a to-go box from the nearby stash for the remains of my tenderloin and headed for the back door.

There was a man at the last table, reclining in the booth seat like Jeff Goldblum in a centerfold for PlayDino. I automatically avoided his eyes and then instinct jerked my attention back to him. I stopped mid-stride and stared, without any shred of his cool collection.

"Hello, Robin," he drawled, smiling like a cat with three fish at the bottom of a very shallow barrel.

He would eat my discomfort like candy, so I shut my mouth, took a breath, and tried to articulate a coherent sentence. "Puck."

His smile flickered—that wasn't his preferred name these days—and he straightened in the booth. "I've been waiting for you."

"Back in a minute," I said, and I started forward again as if I'd been heading for the restrooms.

He snorted. "Which one do you use?"

It could have been a simple question, but from him it wasn't, and from him it stung more. I didn't answer and kept going, eyes on the first door, hitting it hard. It was locked, and my palms thumped hollowly. A male voice inside growled, "In a minute!"

I went on to the next and pushed the unlocked door open. I went immediately in, but not fast enough to escape his, "Well, I guess that's an advantage, anyway."

I locked the door and leaned against it, ignoring the aged toilet.

Bells and breadcrumbs.

What was he even doing here? No, that didn't matter, not first. First was checking escape routes. But there was just one door to the toilet, and opening a portal would only leave me exhausted in the Twilight Lands, where he could just step across and find me helpless.

Using the back door would take me right past him, and then he could follow me into the back lot where we would be mostly unobserved. Better to face him in the human Steer and Beer, where he had to play it low key.

I flushed the toilet, ran water a moment, and then gritted my teeth and pulled the door open.

I breezed past him, sitting on the edge of his table, and reclaimed my previous seat in front of my dirty dishes. I knew he would follow.

He took the bench seat across from me. His black hair was oiled back, showing off enviable cheekbones, and he wore a black leather biker's jacket over a russet t-shirt. Black jeans and boots completed the biker-Goth ensemble. He tends to over-compensate.

I've mentioned before that Shakespeare did no favors to the Queen or her Court, and poor Goodfellow suffered almost as badly as the Queen herself. Humans who know only the last century's stage interpretations probably think of a smiling boy-child in a flower crown, or maybe a comely young man in shaggy pants and a few complimentary leaves.

Thing is, *puck* is essentially the same word as *pwca* or *bog*, once accents are accounted for, which means the figure now generally depicted as a chubby-cheeked cherub of rustic mischief could also be fairly called a boggart.

Goodfellow (a name conferred in hopes of good behavior, rather than due to it) is sensitive to the fact that today he's thought of as a jester and errand boy, if he's thought of at all. It means if I get really desperate to temporarily quiet him, I can choose the right moment in front of the right audience to take advantage of, say, the word's similarity to "pug," or how it can fit into a limerick in much the same role as *Nantucket*.

The right moment is definitely not when I'm alone in the human world with no sympathetic and higher-ranking Fae protector.

I wished I'd left some rings on my plate so I would have something to occupy my hands. I almost wished for the police to turn and notice us. "Okay, let's get it started. Why are you here?"

He was enjoying this. "I was slumming for a bit, thought I'd stop by and see where you hang out. Oh, and I hear you owe Odile a favor."

"Lady Odile," I said.

I was gratified to see him hesitate almost imperceptibly. "Indeed, that is how you should refer to her," he recovered, but I'd already seen his reaction. It stung to be corrected by me.

"Who's your friend?" Jimmy shoved a chair to the end of our booth and sat down, facing us both and visually blocking

Goodfellow's exit. I felt a simultaneous rush of gratitude and concern. Jimmy doesn't know much about the Court or the Twilight Lands.

I gestured across the table. "Jimmy, this is Robin Goodfellow." I wasn't sure if Jimmy would recognize the name, not being real big on either Shakespeare or English fairy lore, so I tossed him an easy catch. "He's from back home."

Goodfellow snorted. "Home? To you?"

I set my jaw and kept my eyes on Jimmy. Goodfellow's jibes weren't anything new, but I hated hearing them in front of Jimmy for the first time.

Jimmy only looked at him appraisingly. "Another Robin?"

Goodfellow's mouth turned down. "The Robin," he answered. "This Robin may be my namesake." His eyes slid to me. "If your mother had enough schooling to know that much."

My stomach clenched, and I hated myself. Why did I let him get to me? Yet words could be powerful, and no one knew that better than the Fae, bound to their word and never lying.

Jimmy pulled a rectangular pillbox from his pocket and began to toy with it to occupy his hands, as I longed for something to do with mine. Maybe I should have picked up one of those fidget spinners when they were briefly a thing, if I could have found one without any steel in it.

"So what brings you to my place?" Jimmy asked.

"Not your place in particular," Goodfellow said. "I came for Robin Archer."

My tenderloin-stuffed stomach sank. That had been my assumption of course, but it was disheartening to hear it so plainly.

"I mean, everyone was talking about it, so there has to be some A-class entertainment going on here, right? Circus in town?"

My mouth operated without my permission. "Kids in danger is not entertainment, Puck."

"I wasn't talking about the kids," he said quickly. "I was talking about you, screwing around and doing whatever it is you do." Goodfellow reached out and cuffed my head. "Silly thing."

Humiliation scorched through me. A hot retort rose but I bit it back. Goodfellow was a powerful being, both inherently and politically, while I can barely open a portal and have almost no political currency. I could endure his bullying a little more.

"Got a bit warm in here all of a sudden." Jimmy's pillbox rattled as he turned it over and over. "Now, I don't know much about your people," he said, his gaze on the box, "but isn't there some tradition about hospitality and manners?"

Goodfellow smiled a patronizing smile. "I am not this person's guest," he said with an eye roll toward me, "and he—she—this is not my guest, either."

Look, I've been around a lot longer than the they-ze-hir-whatever conversation and I tend to pass for what's most useful at a given moment, so I generally don't care a whit about pronouns. But I don't particularly care for "this" in the tone for describing something found on the bottom of a shoe.

Not that I could do a thing about it.

Jimmy frowned uncertainly. "It's my place, you know."

Goodfellow sighed with the effort of tolerating an ignorant human. "You did not invite me here, sir, nor have you served me bread or salt. So we are not bound by hospitality, either."

"Heh," said Jimmy. "Good to know." He extended his arm and smoothly dumped the contents of the pillbox down the back of Goodfellow's collar.

Goodfellow shrieked and leapt vertically out of the booth as if it had caught fire. Ball bearings scattered in all directions as he thrashed and shook out his jacket and shirt, slapping at his torso as if they were bees. A few bounced in my direction and stung as they struck my jeans and upraised arms, but the contact was brief and the burn faded quickly.

Not like having them inside one's shirt or, apparently, one's boxers.

Goodfellow was swearing fast and hard, but most of it was in one of the older languages, so the police officers had to make their guesses based on his hopping and slapping and shaking out of clothing. Officer Sullivan turned in her seat, eying the balls rolling across the floor and then looking back toward us. "Everything okay over there?"

I ducked my face toward the table. "We're good," Jimmy called back. "I just spilled some pellets, startled him. He's sensitive about bugs and stuff."

Goodfellow bared his teeth in a poor attempt at a soothing smile. Sullivan wasn't convinced, but she saw she wasn't going to be invited into the situation and turned back to her food with her new partner.

Goodfellow settled into his seat, his eyes blazing. "You—"

"If you're in my place, I expect you to be polite," Jimmy said evenly. "Might keep that in mind."

The look Goodfellow gave Jimmy should have needed a license.

"I appreciate you coming by," Jimmy said, "but next time consider buying something like a proper customer. By the way, you happen to know Lady Odile? Queen's maiden or someone?"

Goodfellow's eyes bulged and his jaw dropped in an apoplectic indignation.

Jimmy carried on. "Oh, don't be like that, she's really nice. If you know her, please give her my regards and tell her I'm looking forward to Friday, and seven's fine. I don't have a phone number for her."

I was staring at Jimmy just as hard as Goodfellow was, but the puck didn't notice, caught in his own outraged horror. He struggled out of the booth, limbs not quite working correctly. "I'll be back later," he snarled, somewhat disconnectedly, and he stomped toward the door. He slipped on a scattering of metal spheres and almost went down, catching himself with an arm flail and supernatural agility. He flounced outside with an admirable attempt at dignity and contempt.

"I gotta get a broom before someone gets hurt," Jimmy said.

"What?" I managed, and it wasn't about the broom.

"Slingshot ammunition," Jimmy said. "Cheap, easy to pack. I got to figuring that carrying some iron would be a good idea, just in case."

"Later," I said. "First—Lady Odile? Friday?"

Jimmy grinned. "Right? And you said I didn't have a chance."

Okay, look, I get it. The whole half-breed freak-of-nature thing, it's awkward. I know it's pretty weird to take dating advice from someone who is definitely not in that scene. But still, when it comes to the Fae, I am the local expert. So it hit me kind of hard to hear that Jimmy had ignored my warnings. *"What?"*

"I asked her out."

I boggled. "She is a Fae of the Court. More, she is one of the Queen's Maidens. *The Queen's. Maidens.* What about 'out of your league' was unclear to you?"

"The part where she was smoking hot?" Jimmy shrugged. "I just... it seemed like a good idea at the time."

In Jimmy's defense, Odile is one of the high Fae and as such tends to make human brains lose efficiency when they're around her. I have no doubt that Jimmy remembered my warning right up until he got within eyesight of her again—which must have been when she pulled us out of the death-trap cellar.

"So right there, almost literally over my dead body, you asked her out."

"Oh, come on. You were only mostly dead. You'd stopped twitching by then."

I sighed. "Jimmy. She is major league, trading card, Hall of Famer. You are playing T-ball."

"Gotta start with a dream."

I snickered despite myself. "Still, it's kind of worth it, just to hear you name-drop to Goodfellow. Oh, man."

"Yeah, I noticed he was uncomfortable with that. I guess he didn't expect me to know any other Fae, right?"

I laughed harder, tears breaking free. "Oh, no, Jimmy, it's so much better than that." I choked. "He's Odile's ex."

I was so delighted with the slingshot ammo comeuppance and Jimmy's blundering into the most sensitive point of Goodfellow's ego—and yeah, some relief in there, too, now he was gone—that I simply slumped in the booth and laughed. I laughed and laughed right up until Officer Sandra Sullivan took a seat beside me, effectively trapping me between her and the wall.

I stopped laughing.

"Robin, I think," she said with a cool smile. Her new partner was on his feet a little distance away, his hands folded and his eyes on us.

I straightened on the bench. "Officer Sullivan."

"I've had an eye out for you," she said. "Though I admit I was surprised to see you hung around after we got here."

"Wasn't exactly my choice," I muttered.

Jimmy cleared his throat. "Look, officer, I've cooperated—"

"Mr. Sanderson, you've answered every question we've asked you, which I appreciate. Except you didn't tell us where we could find... I'm sorry, how do you prefer to be addressed?"

"Just Robin is fine," I said wearily.

"How am I supposed to know what day people walk into my place?" Jimmy asked. "I didn't know you were coming in, either."

"Look, officer," I said, "could you please leave Jimmy out of this? He didn't do anything except serve me a tenderloin. I bet he checked out on everything."

Officer Sullivan pursed her lips. "Well, the suspect is still missing, but yeah, Mr. Sanderson looks okay."

"So it's just me. And everything I told you on the phone is true, and me saying it again at a station desk won't make it more true."

"Robin—if I can call you that—we have procedures to keep the law. And I have paperwork. I'm going to have to ask you to come in with me."

I was ready for this. "Am I being detained, officer?"

She gave me a disappointed look. "No, you are not being detained. But if you are really concerned about those kids, you will help to find the man who tried to kill them, and you."

That man wasn't going to be a future problem, but I couldn't exactly explain that. "The kids are safe now, officer. That's what I care about."

"Can I sweep up these metal balls before someone gets hurt?" Jimmy asked.

Officer Sullivan waved her hand. "What was up with all that, anyway? Those things electrified or something?"

Jimmy shook his head. "No, of course not. Just a weird guy."

She looked at me. "Looked like you two had a history."

I didn't answer.

Jimmy stood and retrieved a push broom. They paid no attention; they weren't interested in him.

"So, Robin, are you going to come in and answer our questions about Mr. Jackson?"

"I can answer whatever you want right here." Well, sort of. "And you can tell me about the kids who went missing and came back itchy."

That got her attention. "What do you know about that?"

"Nothing more than you said at your table," I admitted. "But you've got a weird feeling about it, and that makes me curious. And whatever you don't know about me, you know I'll help those kids if they need it."

She frowned. "That is officially crazy, you know that?"

"Tell me about the kids."

"Nobody's asking you about those kids." Her partner didn't have any idea who I was, but he was backing Officer Sullivan to the max.

I ignored him. "Were they missing?"

She considered and then answered me. "For a while, yeah. Reports were they were gone for a few hours or so, it varied, and then came home. No red flags, no Amber Alerts, just a bit weird."

I don't actually think I inherited any of the useful magic of suggestion, but every once in a while I feel maybe there's a tiny shard of it there. Officer Sullivan's willingness to talk about the found kids instead of the missing suspect was such an example. "And they came home on their own?"

"Yes, or were found close to home. No bruising, no signs of trauma. No complaints, really, just tired, a couple mildly ill. They say they don't remember much of what they did while they were gone, just hung out with friends or played or whatever."

"Tired? A little ill? Blurred memory?"

Officer Sullivan's eyes locked onto mine. "You think...? But there's no typical tells of assault or abuse."

"What are you talking about?" asked Jimmy, funneling steel balls back into his pillbox.

I could see she didn't want to articulate it. Saying things aloud makes them real in a way that thinking does not. So I said it. "Date rape drugs can do that."

Jimmy used some of the special words he saves for people who would give kids date rape drugs. "Can you test the kids?"

"Maybe," she said. "Got to have a reason, though, and we don't want to terrify parents if nothing's going on. Kids being tired or losing track of time isn't that unusual, after all."

She was right. If this were an isolated incident, one kid who couldn't articulate how he'd spent his time while sick and tired, it wouldn't raise an eyebrow. It needed a cluster of repetition to become noticeable, and then two highly paranoid people to become suspicious.

I shook my head. "Kids metabolize the stuff faster than adults; it'll be difficult to get a positive if it's been a few days."

She looked at me. "You think somebody's hurting those kids? Because if we've missed that—"

"I don't know any more than you do, I promise."

"You just hang around and keep an eye out for kids in danger." She gave me a skeptical look.

"Something like that."

"I don't mean to interrupt," drawled her partner with exaggerated apology, "but weren't we talking about something from last week? Something about a missing suspect and this person of interest dodging questions?"

Well, so much for any shred of suggestion. "There is nothing further I want to contribute. Best of luck to you finding him. Officer Sullivan, if you need to reach me, tell Jimmy."

She gave me a dissatisfied look. "You wouldn't hold back on me, would you, Robin?"

I answered honestly. "I was as much a victim as any of the kids. I have no reason to want to protect him."

"And you don't know where he is?"

It had been a week; he'd probably been excreted in a dozen different places by now. "I really don't."

She blew out her breath. "I might want to talk to you again. Here's my card."

"Thank you, Officer Sullivan."

I stayed in the booth as the light faded. Somewhere out there, Goodfellow the Puck was nursing a grudge. Somewhere out there, someone was preying on innocent children.

Jimmy rattled the front door to check the lock. "You planning to stay the night?" He sat at my booth. "Hey, now everyone's gone, can we talk about the psychopath who came to see you?"

"Goodfellow." I blew out my breath. "Yeah."

"I take it you're not anxious to run into him after dark."

"Nah. He won't hurt me. Probably. At least not without an audience."

"Run-of-the-mill bully?" Jimmy shook his head. "You think if you lived a thousand years or whatever, you'd get past middle school."

I snorted. "You live a thousand years, you get bored, I guess, start to fixate on things like whose blood is purer. Racism isn't new."

Jimmy shook his head. "That's not it."

I looked at him. "What, you've known the guy ten minutes, and you've got a better fix on this?"

"Oh, he makes out it's about him being a pureblood and you being a halfbreed, sure. But that's not what's getting at him. No, I think he's jealous of you."

I stared at Jimmy like he'd sprouted onion rings for ears. "Goodfellow is a lot of things, but jealous of me isn't one of them."

"Did you even listen to the guy?" Jimmy gestured. "Tell me if I've got this order right. He's feeling a bit chafed after Lady Odile lets him off. You get a big public sendoff by the Queen. He shows up here to knock you down and make himself feel bigger, but he really needs an audience for it to count, and probably the right audience he wants to impress."

I stifled my first laughter and tried to think about it. "Well, you're not entirely wrong. But I don't know..."

"Oh, all this doesn't make him not a racist, of course," Jimmy added. "It just means it's rooted in fear of what he hasn't done, what you're doing that he can't."

I blinked at Jimmy. "Huh?"

He shrugged. "Racism isn't being proud of what you've done, or you'd just be proud of yourself. You've got to lay claim to someone else's accomplishments if you don't have your own, but draw a line that says not everyone can do the same thing. It's all compensating."

"Jimmy," I said, "that is dangerously philosophical."

"You can't stare at a deep fryer all day and only think about frying."

"You're a middle-aged, white, gun-toting redneck in the American Midwest. You know a lot of people wouldn't believe this of you."

He shrugged. "I can't help other people's prejudices."

I laughed. "Okay, so let's say your theory is correct and Goodfellow is jealous. Does that change anything?"

Jimmy shook his head. "Nope."

"Well, you're a big help."

"I thought the slingshot ammo did the job."

"There is that." I turned to look at him and admitted, "I'm not sure how I feel about that. I mean, that stuff will hurt me, too."

"The handgun you're carrying would hurt me, but I know you wouldn't use it on me."

I jerked a shoulder in a shrug of agreement. "Fair. You ready to throw me out?"

We went out the back door. As Jimmy locked it behind us, I spotted movement in the shadow outside the street light. My first thought was that Goodfellow was waiting, but I realized the truth a heartbeat later. "Jimmy!"

I ran and knelt beside the kid, gathering him into my arms. His pulse raced against my skin, but he lolled over my forearm, grinning hazily at nothing. "Power up," he said, tripping on the consonants.

Jimmy called 911 and we got him inside. Jimmy made another call, and Officer Sullivan arrived in civvies almost as quickly as the ambulance.

I met her eyes as she turned away from her initial consult with the EMTs. She came to where I stood. "Okay, what is it?"

"Look at the back of his scalp."

She looked at me, and then she turned and went back to the EMTs. They handed her a pair of gloves. The boy was on his side, so he wouldn't choke if he vomited, and she was able to part his thick, black hair to examine the back of his head.

She found them, too—little red pinpricks scattered across the back of his scalp from ear to ear, not far above the hairline. They were already fading; in another half-hour they might be gone entirely. She pulled out her phone and took a few photos, and then she spoke again to an EMT, who nodded.

She came back to me. "So let's jump ahead and say he tests positive for a drug. What do you think those scalp marks are?"

"Not a clue. But I'm going to guess that's what he was drugged for. This kid just took the dose harder or something."

She nodded. "So who gave it to him?"

I had no answer for that.

"We've got to ID this kid and get his parents or guardians," she said. "And we've got to figure out where he got this stuff and what happened to him. You found him in the parking lot?"

"I'll show you."

Officer Sullivan was searching the area for evidence. I stood near the back door of the Steer and Beer, watching her. I wasn't paying enough attention to notice Goodfellow's approach behind me.

I did *not* jump when he spoke. It was more of a sharp twitch.

"Waiting for me?" he asked.

I shook my head. "Not now, please. Kids are in trouble."

He was visibly checked. Children mean too much; none of the Court would be unmoved by that. "What? How so?"

"I don't know yet."

Puck had always been a lonely sort, craving attention and friendship, even before Shakespeare. He'd done small services for households which welcomed him and mischief to those who didn't. If Jimmy were right, if this might be about jealousy...

No, this was stupid.

But I didn't have a lead this time, and...

I took a breath and a chance. "I need your help."

Goodfellow stared. "What?" He gave me his most skeptical face. "What are you up to?"

I sighed. "You know I can't lie to you. Don't make me repeat it. Kids are in danger, and I need your help to take out the bad guy."

He liked the Hollywood language. Anything to get away from the chubby cherub image. "You need me to be the muscle?"

"Eventually," I said, not untruthfully. "Once we find the guy."

"You don't know where he is?"

"We don't even know who he is." I went for direct. "We need bait."

Goodfellow's nascent enthusiasm quelled. "You want me..."

"...To go out as a kid and try to get caught. Yes."

I expected him to kick harder against the idea of posing as the childish image he hated, but Goodfellow actually considered it. "And then, when we have him, we stop him."

"That's the idea."

He jerked his chin down once. "I'm in."

"What?" demanded Officer Sullivan, more than a bit of indignation in her voice.

I jerked around to face her. "Er—"

"What are you talking about? You can't just—and you can't use someone as bait for—and he doesn't look anything like a kid, no one is going to believe.... And you cannot go vigilante on my streets!" She was confused, but not enough to not also be angry.

Goodfellow smiled. "Officer, but a moment, and it will be simple." He raised his hand and blew across his palm, and dark green dust floated into her startled eyes. She started, and her eyes did not track him when he stepped back.

So many things I did not inherit. "How long will that last?"

"A minute or two," he said. "Shall we meet here tomorrow? Two hours before twilight?"

"See you then."

We split in opposite directions before Officer Sullivan recovered.

"What's the bait of choice?" Goodfellow asked as we walked down the sidewalk.

I mentally reviewed my researched list of children who had disappeared. "Say about eight years old—a girl, as the last two were boys and it had been pretty even before that. Good hair."

Goodfellow nodded, and a moment later I was walking beside a young girl with perfectly distributed freckles to match her thick, red-gold hair. She giggled and twirled, tipping her head to catch my eye.

"Very nice," I admitted.

Pucks are particularly good at glamour. Even Shakespeare's contrived little speech pays homage to the puck's shape-shifting skill. So when I tell you Goodfellow was a cute little girl, I mean she could have taken the pageant prize, sold lemonade in a paper cup to the officer come to shut down her unlicensed stand, or won the trip to Europe for shilling enough Girl Scout cookies—to diabetics. I wasn't merely impressed, I was seething with jealousy, but I'd been there before and there was nothing to do about it.

"Off to hook a bad guy!" the adorable little girl said cheerfully, and she skipped ahead. I almost cautioned Goodfellow not to overdo it, but even the skipping looked natural on that picture book-perfect character.

I followed along at a discreet distance, keenly aware of the Walther against my waist.

The late autumn light was golden and glorious. Goodfellow did a perfect impression of a distracted child, pausing to examine a twig or picking up particularly colorful leaves to make a bouquet. The slanting light gleamed in her red-gold hair.

"Hello there," said a smiling man on the opposite sidewalk. In an earlier era he would have been called "distinguished-looking," with his glasses and touches of grey at the temples. Today, someone might say he looked like one of the incarnations of the Waynes' butler Alfred. He checked for traffic and crossed the street.

This was our guy. You do this job for a hundred years or so, you still can't always recognize who's capable of it, but you get to know what it looks like in action. I faded to one side of the sidewalk and busied myself tying a shoe behind a bush.

"Hello," said the little girl, with perfect innocence and charm. I almost wanted to buy her a lollipop myself.

His hand moved around the shape of her head at a distance, as if stroking her aura. "Such lovely hair. What's your name?"

She pursed her lips and swung her arms in nervous displacement. "I'm not supposed to tell strangers."

"Oh, then, I'll tell you mine," he said. "I'm Jason. Now that means we're not strangers, right?"

The little cherub—I snorted to myself—considered this. "That's right," she concluded with a pleased smile. "So you should call me Katie."

"Hello, Katie," the man calling himself Jason said. "I'm just going to visit my kittens. Do you like kittens?"

I rolled my eyes. A hundred years and they're still using the same handful of hooks.

Katie's eyes popped wide. "Can I see them?"

"Of course! It's not far. Do you want a cookie while we walk?"

Bells and breadcrumbs, I'd forgotten the drugs.

Goodfellow wasn't stupid, but he hadn't spent as much time in the human world lately, what with the steel and exhaust fumes and strip mining and everything spoiling the neighborhood. He knew our villain wasn't a poisoner, because the kids were found mostly healthy. He'd know doping was a possibility, but his knowledge was woefully out of date. He wouldn't be looking for anything like Special K or its competitors.

The angelic little Katie accepted the cookie with delight.

Jason led Katie to a spacious house on one of the twisty back streets and guided her into a back door heavily screened by evergreen bushes.

I prowled about the outside of the house, eying the usual points of entry. But like any good villain, he had his secret lair properly secured.

I stepped back and thought. It was one of the classic old houses of the neighborhood, so there might be a coal chute. But the door I found had been locked decades before, with a thick layer of rust which promised impossible resistance. I walked back a few steps and looked at the second story.

Many of these houses still had early heating systems, or updated systems in early floor plans. It wasn't unusual for the heat to be uneven, resulting in chilly rooms to reinforce the local history of hauntings and over-warm rooms which even in fall and winter were often balanced with—

Bingo. I spotted an upper window open a few inches.

I skimmed up a nearby sycamore and jumped for the window, hoping it hadn't had burglar locks added. It hadn't; it was a safe neighborhood, so long as you weren't a kid catching the eye of the local malefactor.

I wriggled through the window and eased myself to the hardwood floor. Original, and undoubtedly creaky. I summoned all the Fae grace I had inherited, crept to the open door, and listened.

Just one voice, Jason talking to Katie. The rest of the house was silent. I slipped out the door into the unlit hall, found the stairs by the gradient of light spreading upward, and made my way toward the source of the voice.

"Aren't you sleepy? Just lie down right there and you can wait for the kittens. You don't have to take a nap, not if you don't want to, just wait there."

The man was practiced with sweet-talking kids. I didn't hear Katie arguing, either, so apparently that cookie was doing its work.

I reached the base of the stairs and crept through a short hall opening onto several rooms. It was easy to determine where Jason and Katie were, with an open door streaming light and sound. I eased forward, face to the wall, and slid to where I could just see into the room.

Katie lay face-down on a padded table. She was not restrained physically, only chemically. Jason was pulling tools from a sterilizer and arranging them on a tray. "Your hair is so beautiful. You're going to make someone very happy."

My chest filled with hot outrage before I remembered this wasn't a trafficking gig. And he wasn't a photographer, not with the instruments. So what about the hair, then? And what was he doing to the kids that didn't leave a surgical mark?

Jason left the room by a far door, humming to himself. I glanced behind me and rushed to Katie's table. "Goodfellow," I whispered. "Can you hear me?"

The adorable little girl lay still, mouth open against the protective paper.

I looked at the instruments. There was a kind of scalpel, and something like a zit extractor, but everything seemed unfamiliar.

I glanced at the far door, where Jason had exited. No sign of him yet. I looked back at the table. "Goodfellow, you need to—"

Jason hit me across the base of the skull with something heavy. Oh, yeah, open door behind me.

I didn't black out, not entirely, but I got real helpless for a moment. Jason zip-tied me to something like a dentist's chair, and as soon as I recovered enough for the adrenaline to kick in, I got a fresh jolt of blended pain and panic.

Jason was standing over me, mouth set but eyes wide. "How did you get in here?" he demanded. "Who are you?"

"Is this how you treat me?" I demanded, covering fear with outrage. The chair arm was padded but the steel frame was uncomfortably close. "I came to see how it's working, and this is how I'm treated?"

Jason hesitated. "You're not the patient." He made a gesture as if ruffling his hair.

I started to reach for my own hair in unconscious mimicry and was stopped by the zip tie. "What? No. Obviously."

"Then what are you doing here?"

If there was a patient... "Reconnaissance," I said. "To check out your facility and process."

He stiffened with an air of affronted indignation. "I feel I've more than adequately represented myself. Everything is done properly here, from hygiene to aftercare."

I wondered what kind of euphemism that was.

He took a handful of Katie's hair, not roughly. "Look at the quality of this hair. This is gorgeous material."

I swallowed—it was Goodfellow, not a kid, no need to get upset yet—and kept my voice level. "What about the donor?"

"Oh, she'll be fine. Minor irritation to the collection site, no real aftereffects. Nothing to worry over, nothing to feel bad about."

"Unharmed?"

"Well, obviously I can't say not a hair of her head." He laughed and looked faintly annoyed when I didn't join him. "But she won't miss a little, and someone else gets a social life, and everyone is happy except some FDA bean-counter who doesn't get to push paper for eight to twelve years."

I blinked. This was about hair? This was—hair transplants?

"So you find a kid with nice hair, you bring them in for... collection, you put the hair in clients, that's it?"

"That's it," he said proudly. "The world's only successful transplants from another donor, minimal risk of rejection. And it will all be FDA-approved eventually, I can assure you. This is just the fundraising phase, so I can present both finished research and the millions they want to stamp approval."

Hair. He was stealing hair.

Okay, really, after my usual fare of sex traffickers and mass murderers and various kinds of horror, this was almost nice to hear. Just hair. If he'd been doing this with consenting adults and legal approval, all of it would have been absolutely fine.

But it was illegal, and it was kids who couldn't and hadn't given consent.

"Now that I've explained myself," he said, "maybe you'll tell me who sent you? Are you really with a patient, or are you trying to steal my technique?"

Before I could respond, someone knocked at the door, in what had to be a coded knock. Three quick, a pause, two, a pause, four more quick knocks. Jason checked his watch, muttered a profanity, and— "I'll be right back"—left the room.

I twisted in the padded chair. "Goodfellow! Can you hear me?"

No response.

"Hey!"

No response.

I took a breath. "You stupid little cherub, the human pal of a halfbreed is dating your ex. Doesn't that mean anything to you?"

No response. He was really out.

I could hear Jason and the newcomer speaking in the entry. "I hope you don't mind I'm early," the guest was saying. "I thought it would take longer at the airport, and then there was less traffic than I expected..."

Jason wouldn't want his client to see his donor/victim and a security compromise, so I probably had a few minutes while he settled the early arrival in another room with a drink and a magazine, or whatever underground medical labs did for their shady clientele. If I had Goodfellow's magic to work with... but I didn't.

But Jason had left the long ends of the cable ties extending past the chair arms, and while I lack most of the more striking Fae characteristics, I do have lithe fingers. I twisted my wrist and managed to catch the loose end of the tie.

"Let's just settle you in while I finish with the previous patient. If you need anything just knock, the same knock you used at the door."

It was almost cute, like we were in a secret tree-house instead of an illegal hair transplant lab. I nearly snorted. Okay, an illegal hair transplant lab was kinda cute, too.

But seriously, abducted and drugged kids. Not cute. I could tip off the police, but they couldn't get a warrant based on hearsay. I needed something to get them inside. Also, I needed to get out of these zip ties.

I wriggled the free end of the tie toward the head. The tie cut into my wrist, and the tie's tongue slipped on the face of the head. I spent a few minutes willing it into the slim gap.

Jason came back into the room. "What are you—stop there!"

I didn't stop, but the stress of a hostile audience made the task more difficult.

Jason came across the room, reaching for a medical tool from a tray. I was about to get scalpeled. "Wait!" I shouted. "You don't know what you're up against!"

What he was up against was an unmagical clod zip-tied to a chair, but sometimes you have to lead with a bold statement.

He didn't wait, which I guess was only fair since I'd kept on trying to free myself. He jabbed the scalpel against my throat and I stopped fiddling with the cable tie. "Now, who are you?"

I looked from him to Katie, slumped face-down over the table. Her hair was still a brilliant red-gold, but she seemed taller and heavier than she had been outside. Jason had dosed the adorable Katie with enough to put a child down for a couple of hours. But it was Goodfellow who had eaten the cookie, with a Fae metabolism engineered to make him near immortal. This was about to get really awkward.

"Listen," I said, "you really don't want to do this."

"You say you're here for a client, but you didn't present any bona fides or even make an appointment."

"There's no point to an appointment if the whole point is to see what's going on when you don't think someone's looking," I said reasonably. "And while I can indeed report how seriously you take security, the point has been made, and you can put the scalpel away now, thank you."

"First, you tell me who you work for."

"Whom," I delayed.

Katie groaned.

"Who do you work for?" Jason demanded.

I gritted my teeth. "Her Majesty," I said.

It figures, right? I inherit none of the useful Fae traits like shifting shape or charming a threat or making money of leaves, but I sure get the sensitivity to iron and the inability to lie. Hybrid vigor, my pale genderless *derrière*.

Jason found the truth harder to believe than a decent lie would have been. "Her Majesty? I'm pretty sure the Queen of England doesn't need an underground hair transplant."

"I have to agree with you there," I said, distracted from thinking of anything more clever by the fact that little Katie was moving on her table behind Jason and she wasn't shaped quite right. "Look, Doctor, I can explain to your complete satisfaction, but first I would really like for you to get me out of—"

Something lurched up from the table behind Jason. Katie screwed her face in childish petulance, her red-gold hair streaked with darker tones, her face blocky and harsh. "I don't want to!"

Jason whirled around and took a step back. Katie shouldn't have been talking under the drug's influence, and she certainly shouldn't have been standing up from the table. She also shouldn't have been six feet tall and showing fangs.

I leaned in the chair, but I couldn't get away. There was no telling if Katie!Goodfellow would be lucid or wildly out of his drugged head.

Jason rallied; he had a lab to protect and a client to keep, and he needed to control the situation even if he didn't understand it. "Hey, Katie," he said breathlessly, his hands raised in a calming gesture. "Can we talk? You want another cookie?"

Katie's eyebrows, now a thick black, drew down over her eyes. "Don't like your cookies."

With Jason distracted, I started again on my zip tie. My wrist bled, but I didn't like the look in Katie!Goodfellow's glazed eyes, and I wanted some distance.

Jason lunged for a nearby rack of drawers and retrieved a hypodermic needle. He turned back to Katie, looking like Gene Wilder facing Peter Boyle in *Young Frankenstein*.

The plastic tongue slipped into the head and levered the ratchet mechanism away from the teeth. I jerked my hand free.

"Katie," Jason warned, "you need to sit down, or I'm going to be angry." He raised the hypodermic and seemed to waver between a traditional or overhand grip.

Before he could summon the courage to rush Katie, I drew my gun. "I wouldn't, Doc. It might just make her angry."

He wheeled on me and checked himself when he saw the gun. "What? You can't do anything if you're here without a warrant, none of this is admissible—"

I shook my head. "I'm not police. I came with Katie."

I saw him try to process this. "Who is Katie?"

I grinned. I didn't usually have this kind of leverage to negotiate, and it was a pleasant experience. "She's not a little girl, as you might have guessed. She's not even a she. Tell you what. You can call the police and turn yourself in, or we can do it for you. Your choice."

"I want out," Jason said. "You can't hold me."

"I can't," I agreed. "Nor do I want to. I'm not police, like I said." I jerked my head. "But I'm not your immediate problem."

Katie!Goodfellow, it seemed, was a surly drunk. He made a face at Jason and his hypodermic, and then he twisted and punched a computer monitor to the floor.

"Hey!" shouted Jason, and Goodfellow lurched toward him. Jason made a valiant stab with the needle, which Goodfellow batted away like a martial artist deflecting a bad punch.

I transferred my gun to my bound hand and set to work on the remaining restraint. Jason ran through the lab, dodging desks and tables and rolling carts, and Goodfellow came hard after him, making up for the lack of his usual agile grace with a special antipathy for furniture and equipment.

The ratchet popped free on the zip tie. I worked around to the door and opened it just in time to see a chubby balding man in a tight polo shirt bolting down the hall, smart enough to know the sounds from the lab did not indicate successful customer service. I let him go; who knew if he knew the source of the hair, and I had bigger concerns in the lab. I didn't know if I could safely extract Goodfellow, who was looking less cherubic and more boggart with each pass around the room.

"Goodfellow! If you can hear me, stand down and let me take care of this."

Goodfellow didn't abandon his chase. "Get the bad guy."

"We've got him!" I snapped. "We're done here."

Goodfellow overturned a rolling storage cart, scattering gauze and rolls of tape and other supplies. "Get the bad guy!"

I sighed and spoke to Jason. "I'm afraid you're going to have to tell him you surrender."

Jason, already in a disbelieving panic, gaped at me. "What?"

"Get on the ground and surrender. He's traditional, he'll honor that."

Jason dove through a gap between a refrigerator and a desk. "What?" he repeated.

I pointed the gun. "Get on the ground!" I shouted.

Jason made a little sound and flopped to the floor, rolling his eyes back to look at Goodfellow shoving aside the desk. "I'm sorry!" he yelped. "I give up! I'm sorry! Please don't hurt me!"

Goodfellow lumbered to an uncoordinated halt. "Surrender?" he asked, sounding disappointed.

I kept my gun on Jason with one hand and drew my phone with the other. I snapped a pic for ID—not gonna lie, smart phones are nifty—and then pocketed it. I pulled Jason's phone from his pocket and dialed 911. They picked up on the fifth ring. "What's your emergency?"

I rattled off the address and hung up, triggering immediate dispatch. "Okay," I said to Goodfellow, "we're done here."

His face fell. "That's it?"

"That's it," I confirmed. "Police will take it from here. Our job is done."

He scowled. "I want to do something else."

I looked around the wrecked lab. "Haven't you done enough?"

He shook his head petulantly. "I need to do what you do. What's left to do?"

Had Jimmy been right? Was Robin Goodfellow jealous of poor Robin Archer?

I turned toward the hall. "No time, Goodfellow, we've got to go. Come on."

He made a sullen face like an angry Hulk refusing to Banner. I cast about for something to draw his attention.

There was a calendar on the corridor wall, I saw suddenly, with a nice big, glossy print of Sir Joshua Reynolds' rococo depiction of *Puck*, the one of a pot-bellied toddler sitting on a mushroom and wearing an actual diaper. I pointed it out with a certain glee. "Oh, look, you have a fan. See your picture on the wall?"

With a roar of fury, Goodfellow attacked the calendar, tearing out the picture and pieces of wall plaster. I let him make confetti, and then I suggested we move on up the corridor and out the door before the police arrived.

Jason, smart enough not to move while his intended victim was ripping chunks out of the wall, did not emerge while we were watching from nearby plantings. We saw two police cars pull into the drive, lights flashing, and the officers spread around the house as one went to the front door.

"That'll do," I observed, and I placed a hand on Goodfellow's upper arm. "Are you coming to, yet?"

He shook his head like clearing flies. "Sort of?"

"C'mon, let's get out of here." I guided him away from the house and down the dark street.

Goodfellow's pulse raced and he would usually answer my questions, if obliquely, but occasionally swept his hand as if to push something away. We'd paused twice along the walk for him to vomit into a convenient bush, but that seemed to have passed, and I propped him in a park bench and waited.

I'd broken into my stash of protein bars when Goodfellow crossed his arms over his abdomen and groaned. "Bells and breadcrumbs," he muttered.

"You in there?" I asked. "How do you feel?"

"Wretched."

"How about, wretched and victorious?"

Goodfellow closed his eyes. "You set me up, Archer."

"I didn't," I answered. "I never expected you to eat the cookie. Who actually takes candy from strangers?"

He opened his eyes. "We got the bad guy."

"We did."

"Is that what you do? All the time?"

"Well, not exactly like that. Usually there's more shooting and trying not to be killed. And usually it's over something more serious than stolen hair."

Goodfellow closed his eyes again. "I wanted to be a hero."

The words stopped the bar halfway to my mouth. "You did?"

We are Fae, or near enough in my case, and we can't lie. We are very, very good at half-truths and deflection and misdirection, but the lingering influence of the ketamine was as good as truth serum for sluggish Goodfellow. I sat forward. "Why? Why me?"

Goodfellow didn't look at me. "The Queen praises you before the whole court. I used to be famous, now I'm a joke. I want what you have."

I stared. This really was about middle school politics. That's a Fae for you, live a thousand years and never grow an adult perspective.

Of course, I was getting a new perspective, too.

"No worries then, Goodfellow," I said easily. "We got the bad guy. Even if he doesn't confess, there's enough evidence and kid DNA in there to keep him. You and I are heroes. Together."

Goodfellow gave me a hesitant, sleepy grin. "Really?"

"Really." I sat back. "And if you play your cards right, I won't even tell anyone how you smashed up a lab in a botched glamour after eating a drugged cookie."

The sleepy grin disappeared. "Botched glamour?"

I cleared my throat.

"There once was a Fae who quite sucked,

His glamorous hair almost plucked.
He ate cookies, got smashed,
So a med lab he trashed.
But in the end, the bad guy got pucked."

Goodfellow snorted. "That's terrible."

"Sorry." I took a breath; I had to play this card while Goodfellow was still doped enough to give me a straight answer. "Truce? In case we should work together again, for the protection of the children?"

Goodfellow gave me a skeptical look. He was coherent enough to know that any "truce" benefited only one of us. But then he nodded. "You couldn't have done it without me."

I merely smiled. I couldn't have agreed without a lie.

W is for Wear Wigs

Michael M. Jones

Ever since I discovered Club Xanadu, it's like I've become two different people. In my normal life, I'm just Simone Rinaldi, the quiet girl in the hoodie and baggy pants who sits in the back of class and never, ever raises her hand or draws attention to herself. The one who looks away, who stammers, who skulks from one place to the next. Easily overlooked, easily forgotten. No friends to speak of, no social presence, certainly no love life. I'm counting down the days until graduation, until I can go somewhere new and reinvent myself properly. I'm just a name on the attendance sheets, a lingering question for the yearbook and class reunions to come. Who was Simone, they'll ask. Then they'll shrug and move on to who got married, who got fat, who got famous.

But several times a week, I venture through the night-shrouded streets of Puxhill, making my way down Caravan Street and into the Gaslight District, where it feels just a little darker, a little wilder, like an entirely separate world. Two lefts and a right down its cobblestone streets, and there's Club Xanadu, a riot of light and sound against the darkness. Here, they know me at the door, they let me right in no matter what sort of line there is outside. I've heard grumbles before: Why would they let *her* in without a wait? Who is she? Is she famous?

Inside, I'm transformed by the music, the lights, the very atmosphere. Somehow, Xanadu turns awkwardness into grace, plainness into beauty, shyness into confidence. Somehow, it invigorates me, lures me onto the dancefloor where I shed everything I hate about myself. I'm lost in the sensations.

Lost...

...and found.

Because whenever I go to Xanadu, *she* shows up not long after.

Chiara. Tall, lithe and ethereal, she is grace and style personified. So close to my own age, but infinitely more confident and worldly by comparison. Her outfits are always perfect, showcasing her pale skin, thick blonde hair, vivid blue eyes, long legs and lean curves. Silver bracelets loaded with charms dangle from her wrists, giving her the sensation of constant light in motion. I met her my first night at Xanadu, back when I was still a nervous wreck lured into the club by rumors and curiosity. She picked me out of the crowd, took me by the hands and drew me onto the floor. That dance fanned the flames of passions I never even knew I possessed. She danced with me for hours, bought me fizzy fruity drinks to restore my energy, kissed me at the end of the night and called me Stella, her Star.

I came back the next night, yearning for more, and she gave it to me; I accepted everything she had to offer like a starving person at a banquet.

Ever since then, Xanadu has felt increasingly like my real life, school like a faded shadow, a routine to be endured only until I can leave it all behind. And so long as I follow the rules, go to class, do my homework, no one, not even my parents, notices the distance in my eyes or the longing in my heart.

I've suggested that Chiara and I meet in the daytime but she always refuses. She prefers this fantasy to real life... and I can't blame her. After all, that's why I'm here, right?

Tonight, as always, I arrive and promptly give myself up to the dance floor where the driving beat of the music catches me, invigorates me, encourages me to leave behind my worries and just *be*.

And then... there she is mirroring my moves like we've been doing this all our lives, like she's my opposite self. It's glorious. The lights are bright and it's loud and I'm sweaty and it's fucking *perfect*. All is right with the world. Her eyes meet mine, her lips curve in this wicked smile, and my heart about explodes with joy.

That's why, when the song ends and we wordlessly agree to take a quick break to grab some bottled water from the bar, I manage to ruin everything.

"Hello, Stella," says Chiara, as she presses the ice-cold bottle to her forehead, drops of condensation falling to roll down perfect alabaster skin and oh my god, it's distracting and I have to tear my eyes away from one particularly bold drop heading straight down her low-cut silver top.

"I love you," I blurt out.

The entire club seems to skip a beat, the lights flickering, the music dragging on a single note for a second longer than it should, and something in Chiara's eyes flashes and is gone again, though her smile never wavers.

Everything I am and hate comes rushing back, and I'm no longer the radiant, confident star of the dance floor, but a painfully awkward girl who's never, ever told *anyone* in the real world how she feels like this. I can feel a thousand eyes on me, and I just want to melt into the floor and vanish forever.

I've been wanting to say this for so long, but I've always known that what we have is built on fantasy and if I voiced the words, I'd break the spell.

And here we are.

"Oh Stella," Chiara says. Her hand is on my cheek and then she's kissing me with a softness that melts my fears away, and I cling to her out of relief that she didn't vanish like a dream. She kisses away my attempts to apologize, to walk back the sentiment, and slowly, so slowly, my breathing returns to normal even as life in Club Xanadu goes on around us without pause.

Soon though, she releases me, and gazes at me with wide eyes the color of evening storms. "Do you mean it?" she asks.

This is my chance to deny it, I understand. We could laugh it off, pretend it never happened, and nothing would change. One word to maintain the status quo.

"Yes," I whisper. I clutch my water bottle in both hands, as if drawing its coolness into me to temper the fires within.

"Ah," Chiara says. Her smile is weaker than before. "I—"

Oh god. She doesn't need to say any more. My hands open, the bottle falling to hit the ground in an echo of my plummeting heart. "I should go," I say.

She catches me as I turn away, her fingers almost blazing hot against the bare skin of my arm. "No, please. We need to talk. I—I really like you, Stella. More than I should. There are complications. Please, can we talk about this?"

"Outside?" I ask. It's so loud in here, and there are so many people, and I feel exposed like never before, now that so much of my normal self has returned. She shakes her head. "Not outside. One of the private rooms."

I blink, a faint blush coming to my cheeks. Xanadu has a whole bunch of rooms in the back, supposedly for private parties or when people get overheated and need somewhere to recover. But we all know what really goes on in them and what it means to go back there with someone.

"It's not like that," she says. "Just to talk somewhere away from the crowd."

She takes me by the hand and we weave our way through the dancers and into the hallway which leads to restrooms and more. The private rooms are, of course, watched over by security, but Chiara just says something I can't quite make out to a giant bald guy, and he lets us pass with a quick nod. His eyes linger on me in a way I don't like. It's not sexual, but for some reason, I shiver.

The private room is small and surprisingly comfortable—not at all the sordid den of iniquity I was expecting... padded couches along the walls, a small cooler in one corner, a table in the middle with a basket of fruit, a box of tissues, a couple of old magazines—it feels bizarrely normal.

We settle onto a couch, Chiara tucking her legs under her, while I sit on the very edge and look anywhere but at her. "I—" I begin.

"Hold on," she says softly. She pulls a small silver charm from the bracelet on her left wrist, speaks a single sharp syllable, and tosses it towards the door, where it flickers and vanishes. I can feel a subtle pulsing in the air, like a heartbeat, slow and ponderous.

"What was—?"

"A privacy charm," she tells me. "It won't last long, unfortunately. Not in a place like this. And I only had the one—they're expensive. So pay attention."

I open my mouth to ask more anyway, but she silences me with a finger to the lips. "I know. But we don't have time for questions. Stella, you're in danger. Xanadu is a trap. I'm the bait, and you're the fish on the hook." Her eyes are wide and pleading as she captures my attention. "Please understand, I didn't mean—I never expected—Look, you can still escape, but only if you publicly, loudly, repudiate me. Reject me, leave, and never return to Xanadu no matter how great the temptation. Forget me, forget all of this."

"Why would I want to do that?" I ask. "What's going on? Why are you acting so weird? I—" tears come to my eyes. "If you don't like me, just *say* so. Don't play games, please!" My fingers dig into my thighs as I try to stop my hands from shaking.

She shakes her head. "I wish it was that easy." She glances towards the door. The heartbeat is faster now. "My name wasn't always Chiara. I used to be normal. Like you. Then I came here, where I met a guy who charmed me, made me feel special, made me feel perfect. And when I finally proclaimed my love, he laughed, and promised me the world... and then abandoned me. This place, it's a trap created by the Unseelie Court of the Sidhe." She scowls. "The Fair Folk."

I'd read enough fairy tales to know what that meant. "You mean—"

"Yes," she says quickly. "But trust me, they don't like what you were about to call them. This particular bunch, they feed off our energy, and our passion, and our hopes and dreams. This club exists to build you up before they suck you dry and spit you out as an empty shell of the person you once were." Her smile is full of bitterness and remorse. "Like fattening the calf. And someone like you—or me before that—is a rare prize indeed. The higher you rise, the further you fall."

And I'd risen so very high, thanks to Chiara. "This sounds so ridiculous," I say, still trying to deny it. "I don't know what sort of game you're playing, or why..."

"Think, Stella! That air of magic. The way everything's always seemed too good to be true. The way they never check your ID or ask for money. The way you can dance all night and still feel great in the morning. Have you never wondered why so many of the people here seem *too* beautiful? Like they just don't quite get the hang of being human?" Chiara clutches my arm again, with both hands, her tone frantic. Her words come as fast as the increasing heartbeat of her charm, and I know, deep in my soul where I don't want to, that it all makes sense.

"So you and I were never real?" I ask.

Her eyes shimmer with tears to match my own unshed ones. "Not at first, no. In you at first, I saw my replacement. They need people like us to act as... anchors. Or touchstones. I'm not sure what, exactly. We're what makes it possible for them to draw the spirit from their guests. But because of that, there's also an escape clause. Find someone to cultivate, to prepare, and when they take your place, you're free to go." She pauses before adding, "Get them to love you, and betray them. Oh, they *love* that last bit. Heartbreak is like catnip to them."

I shove away from her, stumbling to my feet. "So *this* was all an act? A way for you to escape? You were, what, going to hand me over to these... these *monsters* in exchange for your own freedom? Everything was a lie?"

She pauses, and then nods in a way which causes my heart to shatter like a rock through a window. "Yes. That's why you *have* to reject me, before it's too late. Go, before we don't have a choice."

The heartbeat is almost a constant thrum; our time is drawing short. "Why are you telling me this, then? You have your chance, take it!" I spit at her angrily. I should hate her; she's betrayed me. Or... has she?

It's all there in her eyes, the tears she sheds freely, in her posture. She's practically crumpled onto the couch, unable to face me. How does she seem so small now, when on the dance floor, she's a goddess in motion? She flickers before me, and for a split second I catch the glimpse of someone else... someone very much like the nobody I am in the real world.

"Because I—I can't do it. I can't destroy you to save myself," she whimpers. "Go, Stella. Please."

I could. I'm furious with Chiara for the deception, the lies, the way she made me feel good about myself. There's a white-hot anger within me as I think about the dances, the kisses, the sweet words and how all this time she was just playing a part.

And yet... she never truly lied to me. I'd been so caught up in the fantasy, I never dug beneath the surface. We never talked about our real lives because I'd wanted to leave it all outside. And...

My hand is on the doorknob. Her charm is no longer beating, just humming, and I turn back to look at her. Maybe it's the anger which gives me confidence, or maybe I was always capable of this and never believed it until Chiara made me feel like I could do anything in her presence. I see her now, a broken girl giving up her opportunity at freedom and—"Do you love me?" I ask.

She blinks, lifts her head to meet my gaze. "I..."

"Yes or no."

"Yes," she whispers.

And I release my grip on the doorknob, cross back to her in three swift steps and pull her to her feet. I kiss Chiara with all the fierce passion she fostered in me. The feel of her charm winks out, and in its absence, I can detect... a gaze upon us. It had always been there, in the periphery of my senses, in the background all along. I break the kiss. "Then we figure this out together," I tell her. "Surely there has to be something we can do to win both our freedoms."

Chiara blinks at me, startled, and then draws in a deep breath. She wipes away her tears and gives me a shaky nod. "Yes. They... they love contests. Games. Riddles. Anything which has the possibility of entertaining them for even a few minutes."

I smile at her. I take her hand, our fingers interlaced. "We can do this."

She opens the door, and we exit into the hallway. The bald guy from before is still there. He looks at us, at our clasped hands, and arches an eyebrow. "Huh," he says. "Gotta be honest, kid, some of us didn't think you had it in you. Guess I lose the bet."

Chiara gives him a confident smile. "Sorry, Bruno."

Bruno shrugs. "Eh, ain't like I care. I just work here. Guess you'll be wanting the Lady, yeah?"

"If she's not busy..." Chiara all but purrs at him. Once again she's the fearless girl who drew me onto the dancefloor and unlocked my hidden self. For a second, I almost panic, thinking that everything before was just an act and what have I gotten myself into it, but she squeezes my hand and I know, I just know, we're in this together.

Bruno tilts his head as if listening to something, though I don't see any indication of a radio or earpiece. After a moment, he speaks. "She's in her private booth. Go on up, kids. And... good luck."

Chiara blows him a kiss. "Much appreciated." She leads me across the club again, though this time I feel many more eyes upon us. The music no longer tugs at my soul like a seduction; instead, it possesses an older, more primal beat. The lights flicker with their usual multitude of colors, but as they flash and strobe, I catch sight of inhuman shapes among the crowd. Wings, tails, horns—here and gone again. People with catlike eyes, ears that rise to a sharp point, too many joints in their fingers. In between them are the regular people dancing obliviously without a care in the world.

They're pulling back the curtain for me, allowing me a glimpse at what lies underneath the fantasy. I don't know what's more disturbing: that I was blind to this for so long or that it doesn't frighten or unnerve me as much as it should.

Chiara brings us to a corner of the room I've never even considered before, where a short flight of stairs brings us to a platform which has a perfect view of the entire dancefloor. More of those comfortable couches ring a low-set table, while a single plush chair is set, thronelike, between them. The couches are occupied by an array of people, male and female and neither, all so painfully beautiful it hurts to look directly at them. A woman sits regally on her throne, regarding us with cold eyes and a dazzling smile.

I fear her.

I love her.

I want to be her.

I want to die because I will never be worthy of her.

Chiara squeezes my hand before releasing it... but not before slipping something into my palm. One of her charms, judging by the feel. It has sharp edges, which bite against my skin, and the sensation breaks through the fog of emotions inspired by the lady on the throne.

No... the Lady. I don't need to be told to know this is her domain, her territory, her subjects surrounding us.

Chiara fluidly falls into a kneeling position, and I instinctively mimic her.

"Is it done, then?" the Lady asks. Her voice is rich and musical, like liquid silver, and it strikes me to the core with its sheer presence. "Have you enchanted her, my child? Have you stolen her heart?"

"I have," Chiara murmurs, eyes cast to the ground. Neither of us can bear to look on the Lady in all her glory

"And is she ready to take your place? To become my new siren, while you walk free?"

This is the moment when, if Chiara truly planned to betray me, to seize her freedom at my expense, she'd do so. Inside, I tense up—with apprehension, with anticipation—and wait for her answer. "No, my Lady," she replies after a moment which lasts an eternity.

Is it possible for a heart to leap and sink at the same time? Until this second, I hadn't realized how much part of me had wanted this. The fantasy, with everything it had to offer.

"No?" That single syllable trembles in the air, like the moment before an avalanche.

Together, we force our gazes upwards, to look at the Lady, who has leaned forward on her throne to examine us. Through the blinding beauty, I can make out... curiosity? Annoyance?

"No, my Lady," Chiara repeats "She is not ready to take my place."

"Ah. And yet you claim to have her heart. So what is this, then? A sacrifice for me? An offering?"

Chiara pauses, and I hold my breath, willing all my strength to her. "She is not a sacrifice either, my Lady," she says.

And the Lady, our great and terrible hostess, slowly stands to loom over us. The music and lights of the club wrap around her in a storm of displeasure. "You have denied me three times, mortal, and have yet to explain yourself. Why do you waste my time?"

Chiara trembles but her voice is strong as she replies, "We wish to bargain for our freedom, my Lady. Both of us."

"You wish..." The Lady turns her attention to me, the force of her will pressing down upon my very soul, and it's all I can do not to break and beg for mercy. I feel a hundred eyes on me as her courtiers all witness this spectacle with an excited murmur. We've disrupted their revelries, and they find this... interesting. The Lady seizes my chin in long fingers, forces me to look directly into her eyes, which are ancient pits of starlight and shadow. I writhe against the touch, which burns without heat, but to no avail. "Tell me, child, is this *your* wish as well? To bargain for freedom? For the cold uncertainty of the mortal world? For the dying flesh and hateful stares, the chill winds and rotting inevitability of your fragile human existence?"

In her eyes, I see what she has to offer.

Beauty. Popularity. Confidence. An unending celebration in which I'm the star. A fantasy life where I can be exactly who I've always dreamed of being.

It's tempting, of course. Haven't I been trying all along to shed my old self? The Lady would give it all to me. Chiara could go free while I took her place.

One word would give me everything.

The charm pulses in my hand, reminding me of everything I could lose, as well.

"Yes," I say with all the boldness I can muster. "Yes! I—*we* wish for freedom!"

"Hmm." A sound like thunder, as the Lady considers this. She releases me with a little shove, so I go sprawling to the floor. Chiara is by my side in an instant, helping me up. We will no longer kneel before the Lady. Win or lose, it'll be on our feet. "I could strike you down for your insolence, children. Here in my own territory, I could destroy you and none would say a word. I could feed you to my pets, or transform you into something useful. You must realize that, yes?"

We nod. "Yes, my Lady," says Chiara. "We realize that. But... would that be as much fun as a bargain? A challenge?"

The Lady's laugh is a beautiful thing with darkness at its core. "Oh, child, you *are* playing with fire. But you're not wrong. It would be entertaining. Very well. For breaking the monotony and giving us a moment of amusement—for making me laugh—I'll grant you this request. An opportunity to win your freedom. Succeed, and I release you both from any and all obligations and service to me. Fail and..." Here, she grins with too many teeth. "You're both mine for eternity... and rest assured I'll find ways to make you regret it. Do you accept?"

Chiara and I both nod.

"Splendid. Now then. What shall it be..." The Lady taps her cheek with a thoughtful finger as she contemplates our fates. "Riddles? An impossible task or three? Oh, I've got it! Something I haven't done in centuries. A shapeshifting challenge."

Before I can protest, since I know I can't shapeshift—oh, wouldn't that have been convenient?—The Lady snaps her fingers, and we're transported in the blink of an eye to the center of the dancefloor. Once our place of joy, now the site of our potential damnation. The people formerly on it, Fae and mortal alike, have been shoved aside, now ringing it as our audience. Bright spotlights stab down to create a clear circle around us.

The Lady appears at the edge of the circle. "Since you two seem to desire each other so much, your challenge is easy: hold on, no matter what. Let go for any reason, and you fail."

That's all the warning we get, the only chance we have to grab hands and lace fingers and prepare ourselves before the Lady steps back and the ring closes around us. The lights dim in the rest of the club so that truly, all focus is on us.

Chiara's skin is warm and sweaty against mine, and I wonder if she can feel my heart racing through our connection. The charm she gave me rests in our clasped hands like an anchor. She meets my eyes, and in them I see fear and love and trust and—

She's a snake, lunging for me, but somehow I have her by the neck so she can't bite me

I'm a weasel biting her fiercely as her coils wrap around me

She's a bird of prey, talons digging into my skin

I'm a wolf snapping and tearing

She's a panther with sharp claws

I'm a lightning storm

She's the wind

I'm the sun

Suddenly we're ourselves again, as human as we ever get, still clinging by the hand for dear life, still somehow connected despite all that. The charm bites into our palms, which have become slick with blood, but we don't let go. Chiara's eyes are wide but focused on me and she mouths "I love you," at me right before we change—

I hate her. Evil, conniving, treacherous girl, she was going to betray me to the Lady just to save herself. She used me, seduced me, toyed with my emotions and even now I'm just a pawn in her desperate games. With my free hand I lunge for her, furious beyond belief.

She's terrified of me, that much is clear. She tries to pull away, to run, to flee, to escape my retribution. Her breath comes quick and shallow, and she pushes but I won't let her go, I can't release her hand and I don't remember why anymore. I want to ruin her but it's vital we stay connected—

Despair washes through me. It's all meaningless. Pointless. Cold reality settles in and I wonder why we're even bothering when all we'll win is the ability to grow old and die miserably in the mortal world where our love won't survive and flourish. Tears come to my eyes as the whispers inside my head remind me of how awful I am, how pathetic, how I only belong here in Xanadu. I should give up. Is it worth the struggle?

Chiara's hand remains entangled with mine, but when I muster the strength to look at her, I see disgust and revulsion in her features. I can feel it: I'm dogshit on the bottom of her shoe. I'm that secret shame, that horrible mistake, that thing you push down into the pit of your stomach and try to forget and deny and—

No. No. No.

I redouble my efforts to stay connected to her, letting the bloody charm in our palms connect us, and it cuts through the miasma of despair and disgust and the fog clears and—

We change again. Our minds are ours but everything that makes me Stella, which makes me beautiful and confident and loved, has been stripped away like a coat of illusions. My old self, for everyone to see and pity and mock. Not even Simone, just... me. The original me. The one I was looking forward to leaving behind.

I can't even look at Chiara, afraid of what I'll see in her eyes now that she knows the buried truth. And yet I must. I can't live in ignorance if we're to succeed.

I'm not surprised when I turn my head and find myself connected to a stranger as well. Oh, there's shadows of my Chiara, wrapped around a skinny, drab girl who I'd never even have noticed under normal circumstances. Someone just like me, drifting through life while waiting to see what she'd become. But her eyes are the same... and her smile.

It's the smile which convinces me. She knows. She's always known. She accepted me all along.

"Hello, Stella," she whispers.

"I love you," I reply. And because we never let go throughout all our transformations, it's easy to come together for a kiss.

"Enough!" interrupts the Lady, sounding bored. "Congratulations, children. You've beaten my challenge and won your freedom. Enjoy being... mundane."

We break the kiss and look to her. The magic in Xanadu has shattered; it's just another nightclub, one that seems dreary and sleazy as the lights come up and the music fades. The Lady's courtiers have faded back into the remaining shadows, their beauty a cheap lie. Even the Lady has lost much of her grandeur.

Together, Chiara and I bow our heads and walk towards the door.

We leave Club Xanadu behind us as we return to the real world. No sooner have the doors shut behind us, when there's a sound like a sigh and a groan, and air rushing to fill a vacuum. I look back and am entirely unsurprised to see that where the club once stood, there's now just a vacant lot. The Lady, out of spite or boredom or whatever, has moved on, taking her revels with her. There will be no returning to Club Xanadu for either of us...

And that's probably a good thing.

At last, we finally break our handhold, our fingers cramped and sore and still streaked with blood. The charm falls to the ground with a clink and a clatter. I bend down to pick it up.

It's a heart. Of course. I tuck it into a pocket, and give Chiara a soft, uncertain smile. "So. Reality."

"Afraid so," she agrees. "Think we can handle it?"

I laugh. "We just won our freedom from a Faerie Queen. I think we can handle *anything* after this."

Arm in arm, we begin to walk off into the welcoming morning.

"One question... I was in Xanadu for a while. Um... what year is it, anyway?"

I tell her.

"Oh my god. This *is* going to be complicated..."

I've no doubt we'll work it out.

X is for Xanadu

Michael Fosburg

A gentle snow was falling when I found you, washed against driftwood the waves had worn smooth as a child's palm. Crabs were tangled in your yellow hair, and gulls had made meals of your eyes. You were beautiful, even then. Your empty eyes stared into mine and seemed to ask for an end beyond this indignity, so I took you in my arms and carried you away from that seaside crypt. But before I did I looked long into the distance, following the pale scar of the shore until it became forest, and thence to far gray cliffs, to Castle Binnorie.

My cottage was small for an Ogre's needs. Its thatched roof leaked and the doorway barely accommodated our bodies as I brought you across the threshold, apologizing as your limp hair brushed the unclean rushes.

Ogrekind are not repulsed by the dead, which, perhaps, is why men hate us. We do not eat the dead; that dark libel was levied against us by the ancient chieftains of men, who warred against us and reduced us to the scattered few we are today. We do *repurpose* the dead, however, because we believe that a piece of us lingers when we die, asleep in our cold flesh like an ember on a bed of ashes, and can be coaxed, even in death, to sing.

I saw a shape in you, there on the beach, heard the beginnings of your song on the salty wind. You were not your end, would be more than offal delivered to the shore by an indifferent sea. Reverently I removed your sea-damp dress. I brushed aside your hair. With precise and bloodless cuts I removed the breastbone from your pale chest; sinews I stripped from your graying muscle and bone. I unraveled the bruised rope of your innards and snipped long strands of your fair hair.

What remained of you I buried in the garden, and come the spring your empty eyes would see the renewed earth through lavender, thistles and bluebells. And as the golden light of evening filtered through the bare trees, I found your harp.

Before men came to rule these lands Ogrekind were more than the solitary creatures we are today. We had kings of our own; we had artisans and thieves, scholars and drunkards, holy men and soldiers. Few who remain retain that culture in any meaningful way, for when Ogres go too long without civilization they regress, body overgrowing spirit, the fires of our intellect sputtering to embers. But not I, for all the memories of my people live and breathe in me. You could call me a minstrel, though in Ogrish the word for my trade sounds more like a cry of pain, which is fitting, because we wear the memories of our fallen people like a yolk. And we sing. Our voices are deep and unlovely, more suited to warcries and dirges than songs.

I learned the minstrel way from my father, who passed on the knowledge and stories of our people to me, and when the knights of Castle Binnorie filled him with arrows for their drunken sport I rescued his body from their camp while they lay deadened with drink. I found a song in him as I found a song in you, and the skin of his broad back became the face of a bodhran, so that when I beat time upon him I remembered our old glories, the forgotten fire of our people. But my father had died fighting men, so the voice of his bodhran was timbered with rage, its face marred with the scars of his death. Every song was a cry for vengeance, an argument for war.

But not your song. When I ran my fingers across your golden strings the notes I heard were sonorous and sad. Your voice was lovely yet tremulous, as though you had forgotten how to *truly* sing, but were remembering. And so I lost myself in the discovery of your voice, and the short winter days passed in a fugue, without fire or food, as I composed the song of your life.

But truly, it would be a lay of death.

For on a crisp winter morning your song carried high on the wind off the sea, through the sleeping forest, and came to the ears of a huntsman on the trail of an arrowshot stag. He followed the song, beguiled and curious, and came upon my old cottage.

He saw me, a hateful Ogre, when I emerged to fill my lungs with the snow-touched air. We stood spelled by each other until he broke our trance and ran back into the forest.

They came that night. The air glowed with the fires of their torches, and their rough voices bruised the winter silence. I lay you gently aside and looked to the axe that hung on the far wall, used only to hew wood these long and lonely years. I remembered Father shoving me away in the last moments of his life, a wild fear in his eyes as the knights of Binnorie had at last crested the hill. There hadn't been words in that farewell, and no words could have truly sealed that final moment. Lumbering away from me and howling the death cry of Yog-Saru, Father stood tall against the knights of Castle Binnorie.

The shame of running—of living—has never left.

That shame stayed me when the men kicked in my door. I stood tall. I fought like a brute, like Yog-Saru himself, for Ogres are larger than the largest men, and stronger than three besides. I struck down three with my axe like they were saplings, and when the axe was knocked from my hand my fists were as iron cudgels, and men fell like winter wheat before me, rattled in their armor, dazed or dead. But their numbers overwhelmed me, and as the armored horde pinned me down the butt of a spear cracked me across the head. The world exploded with light. I still heard your song through the ringing in my ears.

"We need it alive!" someone shouted, far away.

The second blow sent me spiraling into darkness.

I came to my senses briefly, trussed in iron, drawn away in a bear cage. My cottage burned. I thought of Father, and the song of his bodhran—burning now, the last piece of him gone—seemed to pound in time with the pain in my skull. But *you* were still beside me, thrown into my cage upon my senseless form. The harmonic curve that had been your breastbone rested on my own. I laid my hand on your cool strings and thought I heard your voice, *truly* heard it, but it was only the whisper of flames gnawing the bones of my cottage.

Days might have passed, or hours; time had no weight in the dungeons below Castle Binnorie. As my cell had been made to hold much smaller creatures, I was forced to sleep slumped over, neck stiff and sore, painful lumps throbbing on my skull.

I no longer heard your song. Where were you, I wondered, as hours joined days, as my beard grew ragged, as the filth in the corner of my cramped cell grew putrid. I seemed to dream with open eyes, and dreams grew into memories like ivy climbing the walls of my mind, dreams of Father leaping into the air as the arrows fell around him, dreams of your strings beneath my fingers, the gold of your hair flashing in the brittle winter sun.

I sang to remember I was still alive. I sang the *Lay of Lugh Ten Oxen*, strongest Ogre to have ever walked the world. I sang of *Dag the Selfless*, a wandering minstrel who braved the arrows of Binnorie so that his coward son may live. And I sang of the fair sea maiden who floated to my shore, whose eyes were the thistle, whose hair was soft heather, whose body was the broken cliffs over the sea.

I slept and I woke, dreamed of voices stabbing me like knives, and sometimes dark eyes watched me, eyes glittering with torchlight—eyes that might have looked like yours. A woman's low voice just outside my cell.

"*...makes no sense for her to have wandered so far...*"

I tried to focus my mind, to will away the swarm of feverish dreams that obscured understanding.

"*...they've been known to steal women, my Lady...*" A man's dulcet baritone, dripping with disgust.

I passed beneath the world again.

"*Ogre*," someone said, perhaps much later, or not long after. He uttered the word like an oath.

I rose through fever dreams to resurface, sweat-soaked and palsied, into the dank dim. My eyes fought to focus through a crust of pus. A man stood just outside my cell, hands gripping the bars, looking down at me. I struggled to rise, pain like red rivers flowing all throughout my body. The man stepped back, struck by my size.

"You found her. *Took* her," he said.

I opened my mouth, but my throat was raw, and what came out was a sound like rock scraping rock. A wet wracking cough tore through my body, doubling me over. He looked on in disgust. He was tall for a man, with a beak of a nose and coal-black eyes. Woad spirals adorned his cheeks—the mark of a knight.

I hated him instantly.

He stepped to the bars. A spear had appeared in his hand. Fear and fury warred in his eyes. "You will tell me where she is, *creature*." He struck the bars with the spear. I flinched. *"Tell me where you've hidden her."*

Navigating my fevered mind was like walking through thick, sucking mud. In my sorry state I did not realize he was speaking of you, and so I shook my head, seized by another coughing fit.

"Water," I croaked.

"Answer me."

"I know nothing," I managed, and this seemed to incite the knight further.

"Then water you shall have," he said, and his eyes were as cold as the sea that delivered you to me.

He left, and soon the dungeon filled with armored men. I was dragged from my cell with spears digging into my back and put in heavy chains and marched through cramped stone halls, up stone stairways, and those I passed spat on me and screamed epithets or shrank away.

Up and up and up I went, my body sagging but propped up by the sharp pricks of spears, my knees screaming with each new step. I was led down a long hall, and I smelled salt, and felt the brisk fingers of the sea wind, and was at last led out into the blinding sunlight. I staggered, and felt spears needle my back. I swayed on my feet, and when my eyes finally adjusted I beheld a great stone courtyard that overlooked the sea, and more humans than I had ever seen gathered in one place.

The Court of Castle Binnorie had come to see me judged.

They were a somber lot, clad in furs and dark robes. Grim were their faces, and the eyes that followed me to the center of the courtyard brimmed with loathing and accusation. Bowmen stood with arrows nocked, regarded me like some venomous snake. In truth, I felt weaker than a worm, and less dangerous besides. Two men dragged me by my chains to the center of the gathered people, shackled me to a stone post, and forced me to my knees.

A tall woman stood to address me, and all eyes turned to her. With a start, I recognized your face in hers, aged gently and lined with fresh sorrow. Here stood your mother. Beside her was a dark-haired girl—your sister, perhaps—and the hateful woad-marked knight. Your sister grasped the knight's hand, but the knight did not return her grip with any enthusiasm, but rather stared daggers at me, desperate need in his eyes.

"Ogre," she began, "I am Lady Gwen of Clan Binnorie. All authority flows from me, so consider your next words wisely. You stand accused of abducting my youngest daughter, Finna, and of murdering men who were sent to free her. On pain of death, how do you answer these charges?" She regarded me levelly. There was no passion in her eyes—only resignation and sorrow.

I mustered my strength, cleared my throat.

"And how shall I die, should I not answer to your satisfaction?" I asked. Shocked murmurs from the gathered Court. I suspect most weren't expecting an Ogre capable of coherent human speech.

"You will be thrown from these cliffs into the sea," the Lady Binnorie said.

And I thought of how I found you—*your name was Finna*, I thought—lifeless upon the shore, and wondered. I gathered my wits, drew deeply of the brisk salt air, and rose unsteadily to my feet. Bowstrings tensed; spears trembled. The crowd shrank away. They were suddenly a ridiculous sight, and I grew bolder, found courage in their cowardice.

"I am Druga son of Dag, he who was hunted, murdered, and *desecrated* for sport by the so-called *knights* of this castle. I am innocent of wrongdoing against your daughter, and I am justified in the killing of your men, for they set upon me in my own home like *brigands*." My voice, coarsened by thirst and illness, carried clear on the wind. I was a minstrel, and I knew how to stir a crowd with words alone.

The woad-marked knight stepped forward, red-faced and sputtering.

"This beast insults us! Insults our knights! Let me—"

"*Tristan*," the Lady Binnorie said, in tones of command and rebuke, and the knight visibly restrained himself. To me, the Lady said: "I was not aware that any men of my Clan killed an Ogre in such a shameful way." She sighed, rubbed her temples. "My late lord husband was not... shall we say, *circumspect* with his authority. You have my sorrow, and my apologies, for what befell your father. It is not the way of this Clan any longer." She raised her hand, and someone began moving through the crowd. "But your capture was not unjustified." A man stepped forward, and I recognized the huntsman who had followed your song to my woods. "A witness of sound mind claims to have heard a fair voice—a *young woman's* voice—coming from your cottage." Her stare became hard. "Do not waste my time with frippery, Ogre. I will have the truth of this from you."

I stood ringed by hostile faces, spears and arrows at my back, weakened, bound in iron, and ten short steps from a long plummet into the winter sea. I felt my end draw near, and with it came a feeling of overpowering *relief.* No more wandering, or shame, or isolation in the deep woods for fear of men. Let them fill my body with iron! Let them throw me bloodied into the sea! I would find Father on the endless grassy expanse of the *Maigha* and no longer feel ashamed.

I would bring an end to it.

"I will speak truly," I said. "But for that, Lady, I will need my harp."

A spasm of grief darkened the Lady's face.

"Bring the harp," she said.

After heated protest from Tristan and the other assembled knights, the Lady Binnorie ordered me unchained. Bracelets of raw flesh circled my wrists from where the irons had eaten away skin, and my body ached with the memory of chains.

When they finally brought you to me, the crowd grew silent. They beheld and admired your pale frame, engraved with fluid Ogrish runes; they saw how your golden strings caught the light, and heard the clear peal of your voice as my trembling fingers brushed your golden strings. Your beauty left them baffled, for how could an Ogre have created such a thing? Your mother, too, looked upon you in wonder, but I saw the pain in her eyes increase.

"Proceed," she said, as though drawing an arrow from her breast.

My hands remembered your body; my ungainly fingers, made dumb with hunger and thirst, still plucked your clear notes, brushed resonant chords from your bright strings.

And thus it came to pass that I sang your song for the Court of Castle Binnorie. My fingers flew across your strings as I sang of finding you. I plucked discordant notes as I took your from the restless shore, soaring sharps as I found in you a magnificent harp. Your resonant voice danced with the wind off the sea, echoed off the stone cliffs—

Pain exploded in my ear. You tumbled from my nerveless hands. Tristan stood over me, eyes wild, face so red with fury that the woad on his cheeks appeared purple.

"*Defiler!*" he roared, lifting his spear to thrust it home.

"*Stay your spear,*" called the Lady of Binnorie, her voice like a thunderclap. Tristan drew up short, looking wildly over his shoulder at her. He was trembling.

"You heard it from his own foul mouth, my lady," he said. "He *defiled* her. He doesn't deserve your *mercy!*"

Lady Gwen was weeping now, but her eyes were hard. Through the ringing in my head, I heard your sister crying.

"Is this the truth of it?" the Lady asked me. "You merely found her thus?" I opened my mouth to say *by the two hearts of Yog-Saru, I swear it is the truth*.

But then your voice rang out across the stone courtyard.

You rose from where you had fallen, the air around you shimmering like the horizon on a summer day. Your strings moved, caressed and plucked by some unseen force, and everyone in attendance heard your voice, fair and soft, as though you spoke through the susurrus of breeze-tangled trees.

And you played for us a bitter song.

It began with a handsome knight come to this land from across the sea, who sought an alliance with Clan Binnorie. Tall he was, woad-marked and fierce, and he wielded the spear like a legend of some by-gone age. He was charming and chivalrous, and soon he had won permission to court the daughters of the late Lord Binnorie.

To the older sister, dark of hair and eye, he gave sapphire rings and silver bands—for such baubles were plentiful in his homeland, and they meant nothing to him. The darker sister found herself falling in love with the handsome knight.

(The darker sister grew tense, looked to Tristan questioningly.)

But to the younger sister, fair of hair and eye, the knight gave his all. He lay awake at night, tantalized and tortured by the smell of her golden hair, and her slender body was all he could see painted on the dark walls of his closed eyes. He promised to slay for her twelve wild boars, so that their marriage table would be as overflowing with boun-ty as his heart was for her. He plucked for her wildflowers from the mountain, and hired minstrels to sing for her songs of devotion.

But the fair sister denied him, once and finally, for she did not share his love.

Her rejection grew in the knight like a cancer. He began to shadow her steps, sullen with strong drink, and beseeched her with growing anger until one evening he followed her to the cliffs over the sea, where she had gone to watch the ships set sail beyond Castle Binnorie.

Your song rose to a discordant crescendo when the knight laid hands on the fair sister, to steal what she had refused to give, and how in his fury at how she screamed and fought seized her by the throat and squeezed until the light left her eyes.

And with a minor fall, the handsome knight pushed her lifeless body over the edge, into the darkling sea.

A funereal silence fell upon the Court of Castle Binnorie.

A sharp crack, loud as thunder, rent the air. You had fractured along some invisible fault; you fell back to the ground and shattered into a dozen ivory shards.

Your golden strings were scooped up by the wind and lain at the handsome knight's feet. Tristan's face was drained of color, and the knuckles that gripped his spear were white.

The Lady Binnorie turned to face him. Her lips were a bloodless gray line in a face that had aged ten years in a moment. Her hand was on her breast, as though to keep her own heart from shattering. "Did you kill my Finna, Tristan from Across-the-Sea?"

"My *lady*, surely you don't think me capable of such barbarity!" he said, licking his lips, eyes darting about, searching for friendly faces. There were none. "This bloody *Ogre* has spelled you all! This wizardry is *guuurkk*—"

Blood filled his mouth. Tristan staggered, turned, eyes wide; the hilt of a dirk protruded from his back. The darker sister pulled it out, and with a banshee shriek of rage and grief that haunts me still, she plunged it home to his heart.

The handsome knight was left where he had fallen. The courtyard emptied until only a handful of knights, the darker sister, and the Lady remained. The young woman wept still, face buried in her mother's shoulder.

"Toss him over," the Lady said, breaking her silence. Three knights advanced on me, and I closed my eyes and began the death chant of Yog-Saru, but the knights drew up short, instead stopping at the corpse of Tristan and hauling him to the edge, where he was unceremoniously thrown over. My eyes followed the smeared blood to where stone met sky, and still I could muster no satisfaction, hateful as the knight had been. You were gone from the world now, truly gone.

Your mother and sister approached. The younger woman's eyes were haunted. The Lady extended a hand. I flinched, wary, but her eyes stayed me.

I took it.

"We do not take such *liberties*, with our dead," she said, watching as the knights began collecting the fragments of Finna's harp. "So I cannot truly accept what you did to my daughter, Druga son of Dag— our gods forbid it." She looked away. "But you returned her to us— gave us the truth of her death. Allowed us *vengeance*."

My tongue was thick and clumsy in my mouth. I was beginning to realize that I would live to see the sunset. I cleared my throat, overcome.

"I wish I'd known her in life, Lady."

She nodded, thought in silence for a long moment.

"Our people have caused yours great suffering. I am ending that in lands held by Clan Binnorie. You and your kin will find sanctuary here, and safe passage through our borders."

I was struck dumb for the briefest moment.

"There aren't many of us left—and fewer still who would be willing to trust in the promises of men."

"Then it begins with you," she said, and took her daughter in her arms.

Winter mellowed to spring, and I finished rebuilding my cottage in the woods. It was a good cottage, as Ogre dwellings go—built to Ogre dimensions and to Ogre tastes. Built to endure, and for another generation to inherit. I laid fresh rushes upon the dirt and new thatch upon the roof, and soon songs drifted on the air from the strings of a new, though inferior, harp.

When the first thistles and bluebells bloomed in my garden your mother and sister arrived on dappled white horses, and we three stood before your grave as the day drew down to dusk and the wind carried your song from my lips over the budding trees and across the sea.

And after they departed, I removed a fresh set of bagpipes from their hiding place. I blew a long, lonely dirge, and I heard in its skirling the torment of a man reduced to the air of an evil memory. I looked beyond my garden into the flowering woods, to where I'd buried the second corpse that had washed up on my shore, and patted the woad-marked bag as I pulled from it one last pleading wail.

Y is for Your Song

Beth Cato

Lord Zipperdell's invitation to his estate came as a delightful surprise. As he undoubtedly surmised, the news from the human realm had left me in a state of grey dismay for some time. Whereas he had for years collected the ephemera of humanity, with a specialization in modes of transportation, I had directed my studies to humans themselves. I had prided myself on my understanding of their ways, and their idiotic self-annihilation left me much aggrieved.

I arrived at his domicile forthwith, wherein I was escorted to the large outbuilding he dubbed "the garage." He met me at the door.

"I would never have expected the Queen to approve an importation so quickly!" I said, exchanging formal kisses to his cheeks.

"Nor would I, Lady Madia!" His eyes shone with happiness, as mine surely did. He was a handsome man by any standards, some centuries older than me, his ice-blond hair in bold contrast to his almond-toned skin. "Apparently, Her Majesty believed that humanity's condition lent more urgency to my petition. I hope that more good news will follow for you, as well." Several of my own petitions idled with Her Majesty's secretary. "Shall we?" He motioned me along.

The garage was a sight to behold, even for one such as I, accustomed to the ways of magic. Lord Zipperdell had established two long hallways, with cordoned-off sections along each where he showcased his pieces within their native environments. Had I stepped closer to the yacht, which by all appearances sat on mere wooden floor, I would find myself transported aboard an enchanted re-creation of the boat in action in the Mediterranean. It was a favorite among Zipperdell's guests; most human indulgences were trivial compared our own creations, but the Champagne he kept chilled aboard was surprisingly good. Less enticing, the nearby exhibit of a Model T would render the world into a living street scene from early 20th century America. For each display, I had been the primary consultant for his contractors on matters of context and accuracy.

"My curator is trying to acquire new pieces for me, but circumstances on Earth are making that increasingly more difficult," Lord Zipperdell said. "Many machines are dead, you know—"

"Yes, an Electromagnetic Pulse was part of the initial assaults."

Several humans lurked about the premises, attending vehicles. A man polished a red race car to a mirror-like finish. A bit further down, a woman worked on the wing of a 1930s airplane, an Electra. She granted me a small nod, which I returned. I'd spent many hours interviewing her. Quite fascinating, even by fae standards.

"Yes, well, this machine was found in a tunnel beneath a collapsed facility. We were unsure what it was, and that made it even more difficult for us to find an attendant for it." He traced a sigil in the air; the human would be transported to us from his holding pen. "I haven't spoken with the person yet. I thought it best to wait for you."

I pressed a fist to my heart in acknowledgement of his favor and respect. "I will be happy to help," I said, and privately thanked the trees and stars that he hadn't repeated his past foolishness by interviewing his new acquisition by himself. He couldn't grasp how being kidnapped from one's native realm, away from family and all familiar, might make a human upset.

With a slight popping sound, the human appeared before us. He was pale-skinned and fairly tall for his kind. Shabby clothes hung from his emaciated body. His hands curled into fists.

"I'm sorry," I said, my arms extended outward in an attempt to lend comfort. "I know this must all be alarming and strange to you."

"What are you things? Where am I?"

"Things!" scoffed Lord Zipperdell, and I was quick to continue, lest he speak more. "We are what you would call fairies. Yes, some of us are small and sparkly, but others are more humanoid in size and appearance."

"Fairies! Like in stories? You exist?"

I gestured to us as evidence. "Lord Zipperdell has brought you here to act as an attendant in his garage. He collects human vehicles–"

"Attendant?" He looked around. As he was out in the hallway and away from any illusions, he could see the cars, planes, trains, agricultural implements, etcetera, some with humans nearby. He spun around to view the nearest contraption, and gasped. "I'll be damned. That's a Zamboni."

The vehicle was large and quite box-like with a black seat inset at the back. Bright imagery of fruits and vegetables and a large breadstick covered the majority of the chassis, along with simply stated words on why a local grocery establishment was the best around.

"Oh good, he does know what the machine is!" Lord Zipperdell clapped in delight.

"But I don't–" the human began.

I froze the moment. It was a risk–Lord Zipperdell's power came more from family prestige than magical prowess, but if he were paying attention, he might have detected my spell in the making and stopped me. Fortunately, he had not.

"Don't say what you're about to say, not in front of Lord Zipperdell."

The man took in the presence of Zipperdell and the other people, stiff as statues. "You froze time around everyone but us?" His voice shook. The shock of our world was clearly getting to him.

"Yes. To prevent you from committing a terrible error. You were about to say you don't know this machine?"

"Oh, I know it, but I'm a hockey player. I haven't even ridden on a Zamboni since I was a kid."

Hockey. I knew the sport. Played on ice and other smooth surfaces. I had read of machines that smoothed the ice between periods and knew that Zamboni was a popular brand name for the vehicles, but I had never seen one before. I had done little scholarship on sports, nor had my compatriots.

The court liked shiny new activities, especially ones given to violence.

This might be quite an opportunity for me.

"How are circumstances on Earth right now?" I asked.

He shuddered. "Bad. After the power went out, people went all *Lord of the Flies* within days." I recognized the literary reference. "There's no food. Lots of fighting. It's... the end of the world, really. Lotta people already dead."

"Do you have family?"

"My parents, they..." He pressed a hand to his face. "And my friends, I don't know. Things have been crazy."

Good. He wouldn't try to negotiate for them to be brought here as well, which would be to no avail. I recalled that hockey players often had cosmetic issues as consequence of their battles. The Queen typically only approved of the importation of younger humans—we do like things to be *pretty* here. Fortunately for him, this fellow seemed pleasantly intact despite his recent travails.

"I see. Well, be aware that if Lord Zipperdell thinks you're useless to his collection, he'll drop you back into that mayhem."

Horror made his face even more pale and gaunt. "But if I stay, what's meant by being an 'attendant'?"

My stamina was wearing thin. I had to make this fast. "I won't lie. You would be rather like a cosseted pet. You would maintain this machine and conduct exhibitions when guests come." I shrugged. I didn't know what else the people did in their time here, and this man certainly didn't need to know about other complications like the extension of his lifespan.

"It sounds kinda like slavery."

"Something I imagine has come back in fashion on Earth as well," I snapped. "I cannot hold time much longer. Can you do the job?"

"Why do you care?" he asked. Aha! Despite his desperation, he had some wits about him.

"I'm a colleague of Lord Zipperdell. He specializes in human artifacts, especially vehicles, whereas I study humans. I want to talk to you, to understand hockey. No one else here knows of it–"

I saw the shift in the face then, the realization of a deeper horror than starvation and degradation. "Hockey is my life. No one here even knows about it?"

Time's grasp became more slippery, but still I held on. "No. But perhaps we can change that. Can you operate the Zamboni?"

Fear, dread, despair flickered over his face. "I think so. Yeah."

I didn't give him time to deliberate further. Time resumed its progress. I gave the man a pointed look.

His face was blank for a moment as he retraced what was said before my spell work. "Yeah, I know Zambonis. Sure."

Lord Zipperdell grinned. "We'll get you set up in the mansion with the others. You'll need to tell us more about this machine and what we need to maintain it. I imagine such supplies will be getting harder to find on your world, so we must know right away!"

"Mansion?" asked the man. He couldn't absorb many more shocks today, that was clear to me.

"Lord Zipperdell, the man is half-starved and quite overwhelmed by the delights of our world. Let's grant him some time to recuperate, hmm?"

"Oh, yes. I suppose so." He looked with longing at the Zamboni.

"Lord Zipperdell!" called a servant. "I have a message from court, sir–"

Trees and stars, that was some fine timing. Lord Zipperdell stepped away to read the missive, and I moved closer to the human. He stank, which was something of a novelty.

"I don't know what's happening anymore," he muttered.

"I will call the chamberlain to get you situated. I imagine you'll need a physician soon to attend to your nutritional imbalances." He needed to be well for my thorough interrogations. If this hockey thing caught on at court, maybe my increased status would encourage the Queen to approve my petitions before my select humans succumbed to extinction.

"Hello, Lady Madia." The woman's voice caused me to turn. It was the aviatrix. "How's he taking the news?"

"As well as I can be expected." I shrugged.

"Holy... is that Amelia Earhart?" the hockey player asked, sputtering.

A weary smile lit Amelia's face. "I'm still recognizable, huh?" She moved past me to take the man's hand, as if he were a child. That was about the level of his mental state at the moment. "What's your name, mister?"

"Joey. Joey Cartright."

"Well, Joey. Life's been treating you rough, but come along with me. I'll get you taken care of." Amelia gave me a nod, accepting the man into her care. Which was just as well, because I was all too eager to return home and to my books. I needed to refresh my knowledge on the sport of hockey and see what materials I could find on ice-smoothing machines. The man needed to perform his job well enough to avoid exile, at least until my interviews were done.

I looked around but to my dismay, Lord Zipperdell had departed the garage to attend his other business. I would need to find him soon and thank him most heartily. This new angle of study was just what I needed to distract me from humankind's imminent demise.

Z is for Zamboni

Thank you for reading

F is for Fairy

We would appreciate it a great deal if you would leave an honest review on Goodreads and wherever you purchased this book.

Your stars and a couple sentences mean the world to us!

Truly.

The importance of reviews cannot be overstated—they often make the difference between a book's success or its utter failure.

Always Be The First To Know!

Whether it's a new release, a call for submissions, cover reveal, super sale or I just want to share a new story I've written, you will always be among the first to know if you sign up for my newsletter.

I promise to respect your privacy and your inbox. I will only email you when I have something exciting to share, probably about twice a month.

Subscribe now and you'll receive a free download of my award-winning post-apocalyptic short story, "Starry Night" as a welcome-to-the-newsletter present!

Subscribe to Rhonda's Mailing List!

http://bit.ly/StarryStory